LITTLE
OWL

LAURI SCHOENFELD

Paperback Edition 2021
Published by Twisted Whisperings

Original copyright © 2021
by Lauri Schoenfeld
All rights reserved.

Publishing Partnership with Candace Thomas
Shadesilk Press

Compilation Edited by Talysa Sainz

Cover Design by Monika MacFarland
Ampersand Book Covers

Formatting by Christine Nielson
Nielson Editing Co.

Published in the United States of America
BISAC
Psychological; Thriller; Murder; Suspense; Mystery
ISBN
978-1-7352331-1-6
Library of Congress
2021910292

I dedicate this book to my husband and three kids, who've been my biggest supporters throughout this eleven-year writing journey. They're the reason why I constantly fight to be the best version of myself. Also, to my thirteen-year-old self with a dream to write and publish a book . . . WE DID IT!!!

ONE

Owling, Utah
Monday, October 18th
8:15 a.m.

ADALINE POURED herself a cup of coffee and rubbed her eyes. Continual nights of sleeplessness wouldn't be sustainable. She knew that. She wanted to crawl back in bed and not get up for a while. If it weren't for the girls, she'd be there now.

For days.

Weeks.

Who knew—it all blended together.

Her daughter, Leora, had been having reoccurring night terrors and claimed someone was watching their house. Adaline pretended not to show her discomfort, or to mention she felt this all the time. Her insomnia came from the fear that childhood monsters had never left. They weren't the kind of monsters with snarling teeth or claws that pull out your eyes, but people. They wore a skin and looked pleasant, but evil lurked inside, underneath their sinister and perfect smiles. The ones that brought her back to her childhood home. When they had hovered over her, she'd wished to be taken away or put out of her misery.

No one came back then.

They were dead. Adaline knew they were, but fear of their arrival sat on her chest in the form of anxiety.

Adaline took a deep breath and placed two heart-shaped plates on the wooden table. She glanced out the window. The newly carved pumpkins sitting on the porch were invaded by specks of white.

Dammit.

The snow was not in the plans for her daughter's Halloween-themed eighth-birthday bash, happening in only a few days. She didn't want to come up with another new idea.

"Good morning, beautiful."

Adaline jumped, spilling some of her coffee on the freshly painted yellow counter—a side perk of last week's insomnia binge created while the world slept. Yellow should invigorate joy. She hoped the joy would rub off. "Morning." She turned around and smiled at her husband, Cache.

Cache had this smirk he'd give her that was a perfect blend of mischievous and playful. She adored it. Adaline also loved his short, curly, brown hair. Running her fingers through it gave her a sense of calm and joy. The curly strands bounced back like a slinky.

He leaned in to hug her. She embraced him, fighting the urge to play with his now smooth and groomed hair. Cache didn't like his hair messed up before work. Stepping back, he peered at her. "You didn't sleep again last night. Are you taking your pills?"

She hated those damn pills. They made her feel worse than she felt without them. That's saying something. In the past, Adaline only took them occasionally to stop being asked if she took her pills, until a few months ago when she got worse and her depression escalated. They didn't work. "Nope." She turned to drink her coffee.

"Why? They're supposed to be helping you."

Adaline stood in silence, staring at her coffee and watching it spiral from her sip. "They don't work." She glanced back at him.

He scratched his head. "You haven't tried it long enough, honey. You need to stick with it."

The handle on the mug in her hand grounded her. She clung to it, placing all her emotions inside. Adaline was so tired of being told by other people how to feel. That she somehow didn't know her own body, heart, and mind.

How the hell would they know?

Cache wrapped his arms around her waist and hugged her from behind. "I just want the best for you."

Adaline didn't say anything. Nothing nice would come out of it. She continued to grip her mug and stared out the window. Whimpering and tugging on her robe drew her attention. She peered down at two brown eyes and a pouty nose. "Hi, puppy." Her five-year-old daughter, Eliza, loved pretending to be a dog. Adaline diverted out of Cache's hold and placed her coffee on the counter. "What's the matter?"

Eliza whimpered again. "I can get you my step stool, Mama."

She wobbled around the kitchen, half-human and half-dog, and lugged the stool toward Adaline. "Here you go. This will help you reach daddy."

Adaline bent down. "Thank you, my star. That will be helpful, indeed."

Eliza smiled, then paused.

"What is it?"

"I don't think the bad dream spray is working for sissy," she said. "Moving is scary."

Adaline didn't blame her for being resistant to change. When they went down to Salt Lake City a few months ago, everything came together so quickly. Cache got a new job opportunity at a business firm, and they found a nearby cottage home with a big backyard with lots of room for all their needs and more. Their neighbor, Ms. Dunbar, owned an antique store in Salt Lake City called Lost Treasures. The previous manager left, and she asked if Adaline would like to be the new manager. Adaline loved the idea of being surrounded by beautiful items needing a home. She understood and related to it. Now, with all the change coming in a few weeks, uncertainty and fear begged her not to leave. To take it all back. Nothing happy happened without a price. She learned that long ago and worried safety and happiness was too good to be true.

Adaline brushed Eliza's forehead, and a brown ringlet bounced in place. "I will talk to your sister, and we'll figure it out. Pinky promise." She put her finger out, and Eliza latched on to it with her own little one.

Eliza seemed satisfied as she bobbed into her chair. "You kissed my sandwich, mama. I love it." She began eating her peanut butter and jelly sandwich, complete with one bite already taken. She liked to call it a "kiss." One only her mom could give.

"What time is it?" Leora came around the corner of the hall, rubbing her eyes. She yawned. Her long blonde hair was tangled in a circular web across her scalp.

Cache trotted toward her and picked her up in his arms. "It's time to get up, sleeping beauty, and help your mom go party shopping. Someone's having a birthday."

"Daddy, put me down."

"Not until you tell me who's birthday it could be," Cache said.

Leora wiggled around. "Okay. Okay. It's my birthday."

Adaline gazed at Leora's swollen eyes and pale skin. Sleeplessness was taking a toll on her too. So many nights, Leora would make her way out of bed, screaming and crying, and stare out the bedroom window.

Adaline caressed Leora's cheek with her fingertip. "Do you want to talk?"

She tilted her head. "Someone's watching you, mom."

One of the only techniques that calmed her racing heart, even for a moment, was counting, so she closed her eyes and counted in her head.

One . . . two . . . three . . . four . . . five.

She knelt and brought Leora inward, hugging her. "No one gets to take me away from my sunshine. I'll stay with you and keep an eye out tonight."

She smiled. "Okay. You'll stay with me?"

"Yes. You, my sunshine, have me forever and ever. And you have that amazing dad of yours too."

Cache pointed to himself, making a statement of agreement. "No one is watching you or your mom. Your imagination is just going wild and telling you things that aren't happening."

Adaline picked up the turquoise pillow on the couch and choked it a few times. "It's real to her, Cache."

"Of course it is. But there's nothing to be afraid of."

How many times had she heard that growing up? How many times had people told her she was lying about the abuse happening in her house? Her imagination has gone wild, they'd say. Her parents were well-known and good people. To fuck, they were. Let's keep pretending there aren't horrible people in the world or fear isn't something everyone goes through.

Adaline tapped on Leora's nose. "Why don't you hurry and eat, and then you girls can go outside and play for a bit while I get dressed."

Eliza grinned. "There's snow. Daddy, can you stay and play with us?"

"I would love to, but I have a meeting," he said. "Raincheck?"

She pouted. "Okay, next time."

He kissed the girls on the head. "I love you. Enjoy the snow and spending time with your mama. Lucky ducks."

"Bye, Daddy," they sang in unison.

Adaline fluffed the pillow before putting it back on the couch. "Don't forget to pick up that 'thing' this morning."

"Will do. Take your meds. They'll help." He brought Adaline in for another kiss before he opened the garage and stepped out.

Adaline pulled out her phone and glanced at the long list of errands and chores for the day.

Ugh.

She often wished a magical fairy would make the long list of things disappear with a wave of her wand, and she could spend the day playing with the girls. Party shopping was a priority—if Leora still wanted a birthday bash. Adaline peered up from her phone to see the girls no longer at the table but getting their boots on.

"Where do you both think you're going?"

"Mama, you said if we ate, we could go see the snow," Eliza said.

Adaline looked at the time on her phone and cleared her throat. "I did, didn't I?"

They both smiled and rushed to hug her.

"Get your coats and gloves on and stay in the front yard," she said. "Love you."

"Love you back," Eliza said it like a wind chime dancing in the air.

Adaline planted her hand on Leora and rubbed her back. "I believe you. It's okay to be afraid."

"I'm okay, Mama," she said. "Just tired."

"If you see anything strange, scream. I'll come right out," Adaline said.

Leora looked up and nodded.

"Make sure to stay—"

"In the yard." Eliza threw her hands in the air. "We know it. You tell us a thousand times."

"Well, now a thousand and one times," Adaline said, holding up her phone. "Wait a moment. I want to take a picture."

Eliza smiled on command and Leora rolled her eyes. They both leaned into each other and Adaline snapped the picture. "Beautiful."

Nodding, they both waltzed out the door to grab the snowflakes.

Adaline smiled and paused, taking in their laughter. There was nothing better than giggling and hearing their joy over the small yet beautiful things, like snow—a reminder of why she didn't stay in bed.

She walked to her bedroom and put her phone on the nightstand to charge. The battery was low. Adaline let her robe fall to the floor, took out a long-sleeved t-shirt and black leggings from her top drawer, and got dressed. Opening the bottom drawer, all nine pairs of her forest green fuzzy socks welcomed her. She grabbed a pair, put them on, and went to the closet to find a hat.

Errand day equaled hat day.

Sitting on the bed, Adaline thought about how to support herself and Leora in sleeping better. So many sleepless nights. Nothing seemed to help either one of them.

What am I doing wrong?

Adaline stood from the bed and went into the kitchen, peering out the window. She couldn't hear the girls' high-pitched squeals or giggles of delight that she always heard when they played outside. Lifting the blinds, she glanced left and right.

Nothing.

I'm sure they're all right.

No sound.

Her heart picked up pace, and her feet moved under her before she knew she had left the kitchen. The fast motion made her shaky knees feel as if they were in control. She took a deep breath, but her chest clenched harder. Adaline yanked her coat off the hanger in the hall closet and slammed the door.

"Leora. Eliza? Are you okay?"

She yelled louder as she stepped down the front porch. The snow fell quickly, and the tire swing rocked back and forth, but there was no sign of wind.

Left. Right. Left.

"Girls, I don't want to play games right now. Come out."

No movement or sound answered her.

Adaline ran to the shed as her body shook. The girls loved to play doctor in there where they'd take care of all their pretend farm animals.

Keep it together. Don't freeze. Keep it together.

The air in her lungs grew shallower and she tightened her grip on her coat pocket.

One . . . two . . . three . . . breathe.

She opened the shed. It smelled like old, wet wood, mold, and leather. There wasn't a place in there the girls could hide and not be seen. She gasped.

No. Please, God. No. Don't do this to me.

Tears poured down her cheeks.

Her pulse thrashed, and her legs moved, but her body felt slower. It was taking too long. Was she running or not moving at all? Her head spun, and she focused on only one thing, the front door.

She gripped the doorknob, threw the door open, and rushed inside. She bent down to look under the couch and leaped back up, after only seeing dust bunnies mock her. Adaline pushed the couch, and the lamp on the side table crashed to the ground. Gripping her hair, she counted.

She kept counting as she moved to the girls' bedroom. Her heart skipped, seeing their door wide open.

They're just sitting on their bed—nothing to worry about.

Butterflies and rainbows flew across the ceiling, saying hello in place of her girls. The room held scattered toys and remnants of playtime, and their beds nurtured stuffed animals, but not them. She covered her mouth.

"No. This can't be happening. NO." Adaline clung to her stomach and tried to stop herself from hurling up the coffee she just had.

Her arms shook, and her legs wobbled. Every nerve in her body felt like needles pushing through her skin over and over. She reached for her heart and patted it to remind it to beat.

Adaline raced from their room and opened the front door.

They must be out here somewhere. Don't freeze. Focus.

She ran down the steps. She slipped on the sidewalk and watched the sky move above her right before she heard a crack in her eardrums. Her eyes begin to shut without her consent.

NO.

Leora. Eliza. Mommy's coming.

TWO

Adaline Rushner
Monday, October 18th
9:30 a.m.

CHILLS RADIATED throughout Adeline's spine, and numbness gravitated down her arms, leading into her fingers. Pressure in her head felt like a boulder, weighing her down. She tried to force her eyelids open, but the intensity of the sun overwhelmed her. The wind howled wildly, and snow clung to her face and hair like a leech, taunting her to get up or she'd be buried alive from the downpour.

The girls.

Adaline covered her eyes from the sunlight grazing the ground where she sat and got onto her knees, wheeling herself to stand up.

There weren't any homes for miles, and the closest one was Ms. Dunbar, a mile down the street. No noise. No one outside, only the whistling of the wind that screamed with her panic. Adaline glanced left, then right.

Nothing.

Please, God. Don't be real.

She hobbled inside, forcing her legs to move as her limbs felt like putty attempting to gain circulation and grounding for the next step. Turning the corner into the great room, Adaline's mental awareness that her girls disappeared pushed her toward their room, and she opened the door. The bright pink walls showed off a dramatic flair, just like most days, but today it choked her as the room stayed the same but held silence. Too much silence.

No girls.

Pinkerton, Eliza's bear, and her other stuffed animals still sat on the bed, as they always did, smiling at her. She wanted to punch them in the face for not being the thing missing instead of her girls.

No.

She held her head and paused to process. Her head pounded with intensity, and she could feel the thumping in sync with her pulse, thrashing pain, and alarm throughout her body. Adaline pressed her hands to the doorframe, holding it tight as she escaped from their room.

Move. Go.

Adaline planted her hand on the wall with every step she took to grab her phone from her unmade bed. Leora's birthday list lay next to it, beckoning her to pick it up first. Adaline grabbed the paper and read it. All her daughter wanted was a camera and a king-size bag of butterfingers.

She clung to the list and screamed, tears leaving her eyes, as Leora's dainty handwriting was an imprint that she had just been there. She grabbed her cell phone and dialed 911, pressing it to her ear.

"911. What's your emergency?"

"My daughters are missing. Please hurry."

"Absolutely, ma'am. We'll get there as soon as we can," said the operator. "What's your location?"

Adaline scratched her head, forgetting her address. "One moment." She moved into the front room where the basket of unpaid bills sat, and she turned one over to view the address. "It's 863 Creston Drive."

"City?"

"Owling. 863 Creston Drive in Owling." She said the address with force.

"Okay. I'm dispatching an officer right now. What's your name?"

"Adaline. Adaline Rushner."

"Adaline, are you hurt?"

"No. I'm fine. I need to find my girls."

There was a pause for a moment. "An officer's on their way. I need you to stay on the phone with me, okay?"

"I have to call my husband." Adaline removed the cell from her ear and heard echoes of sound coming from the speaker.

"Mrs. Rushner?"

She ended the call and pressed Cache's number at the top of her favorite list. Adaline moved to the front door, still holding the phone to her ear. It rang a few times.

Pick up the damn phone.

The call went straight to voicemail. Adaline choked her cell phone as she waited to send a voice message, one she didn't want to leave. Her hands shook as the beep rang for her to speak. "Cache. The girls are missing. I need you to come home. Please." She hung up the phone.

Maybe they're at Ms. Dunbar's.

Adaline peered at the time on her phone. 9:30 am. Would she be home from her back appointment by now?

Ms. Dunbar, her elderly neighbor, called now and then to check on the girls or tell her how she forgot to do one thing or another. Usually, it was about remembering to take out the trash. It was garbage day. Adaline always wondered if she scooped their home with a high-tech telescope. She opened the door, then stepped back inside again.

Ms. Dunbar's house isn't too far.

She took a deep breath and walked gently down the porch steps, careful not to slip again. Adaline turned in a circle to check every angle from the front yard.

If the girls come back, you'll be able to see them from the house.

Her phone rang and she jumped, taking her from her train of thought. Adaline didn't recognize the number, and she wanted to keep the line open if Cache called back. She rejected the call and placed her phone in her coat pocket.

The wind lashed at her hair, and the extra tug sent pain through her head again. She cringed and speed walked to Ms. Dunbar's, looking back every five steps. Adaline normally loved the silence and the significant gaps between houses. The beautiful seclusive safe house. At least, that's how she always saw it. Cache didn't mind being hidden in the countryside either, and he'd drive an hour to and from work each day to his city job without complaint. She wished he didn't have a city job and never left at all this morning. Their home had been safe, secure, and private until today. The snow pushed the growing corn stalks down, holding them captive, and the bitter cold felt like a slap at her heart.

Why would they come down here?

"Because it's familiar."

Without telling you?

"You, shut up." She shook her head and ignored the questions slashing in her mind.

The time pinged in her head, and she gazed at the clock on her phone again. She swallowed hard and gasped. One hour. She had been unconscious for an hour after the girls disappeared.

They're gone. How are you going to find them now?

Adaline stopped and gazed behind her to see if she could see her girls running back inside the house, huddling together for warmth. The road held vacancy, just her and the bitter snow, reminding her that every second was too long for them to be gone.

Turning the corner on Ringwood Street, Ms. Dunbar's house appeared the same as the last time she went over a month ago to help collect apples from her tree. Her arthritis had gotten worse, and she called Adaline to see if she and the girls could help. In return, they each could take a basket of apples home. The girls loved the idea of picking their very own apples. They insisted on making tarts or pie that day, and because none of them could decide on which one, they made both. The smell of cinnamon, apple, and honey invigorated their kitchen for a few days as they baked with laughter and joy. Adaline frowned. Ms. Dunbar's red car wasn't in the driveway, and she picked up the pace, moving to the front door. She pounded on it a few times.

"Ms. Dunbar? Are you there?" she called. "My girls. Are they with you?

Silence.

"Ms. Dunbar? Answer your damn door. My girls need to come home now."

No one came to the door. Adaline moved toward the back of the house and knocked at some of the windows. "Ms. Dunbar? Ms. Dunbar? I need your help. Please."

Leaning against the side of the house, she slid to the ground and held her legs to her chest. The phone slid off her hands like butter.

Her head pounded harder, and the snow spiraled around her. A loud siren blared in the background; it sounded muffled but sharp at the same time. Adaline covered her ears and tried to stand as the sky spun like she was in the eye of a tornado, clouding her vision. She clutched her chest and began to breathe fast, and her legs shook as she tried to steady herself. Clinging to her stomach, she closed her eyes for a moment, taking a few steps in the direction of her home before opening her eyes again. Every movement in the snow sounded like someone crunching chips right at her earlobe. She kept moving and switched from opening her eyes to closing them to stop herself from vomiting. Two police cars pulled up right in front of their Creston Drive home, and Adaline began to run as she got near. A tall man, Officer Brandstrom, stepped out of the vehicle and stared in her general direction, while his partner, Officer Mills, got out of the second car. Everyone knew each other in this small town. The spinning took over, and gravity tilted sideways. Someone lifted her arm to pull her up, and she clung back to save her fall.

"Are you feeling sick?"

Adaline focused on the voice and her surroundings as she fought to open her eyes.

She hunched down further and shook her head in reply

to his question. A red object lying underneath the fallen snow caught her eye.

Eliza's glove.

Adaline picked it up off the ground and pressed it to her cheek. Staring up at the officer, she showed him the glove. "Brandstrom, they're gone. The girls are gone."

He gazed at her with empathy, the same look he gave her when she first went into the police station three years ago to report Eliza's doll had gone missing. Eliza wouldn't back down until her friend had resurfaced. They rescued the doll from their barn, and Officer Brandstrom stayed for dinner with their family that night. The girls quickly invited him to be an official part of family dinners on weekends.

"Are you hurt?" he asked.

"No. I'm just afraid." Adaline held her hands together.

"Did you see who took the girls or where they went?"

She paused to catch her breath and cleared her throat. "They went outside. I stayed in for only ten minutes." Her voice trailed off and she wiped a tear from her face. "It just started snowing. You know how the girls are. They had to be out there that moment. I didn't hear them, so I went to look out the kitchen window, and they were gone."

He cleared his throat. "You didn't see or hear anything?"

Adaline shook her head.

He brushed back his hair and gazed at Officer Mills. "We need to check inside and see if we can find anything. We called Cache. He's on his way."

"Understood." She walked behind them, stepping inside her home, and sat on the couch. The mosaic pillow lying in the corner taunted her as the colors begged to be traced, just like what Leora would do on her days of high anxiety. Tracing calmed her down, or maybe it was the entrancement that came with it. Adaline gripped the pillow and put it under her chin while both officers marched through the house, doing checks and speaking on their radios.

Why wouldn't Cache pick up the phone for me? Did they speak directly to him?

She lost the girls. They were right there at the table, eating the peanut butter and jelly sandwiches she kissed. They had party shopping to do for Leora's birthday. All the party shopping. With lots of giggling and another night of staying awake. She'd watched enough shows to know that every minute with a missing kid was time you couldn't get back in saving them. One fucking hour. Where were they? Who had them? Why didn't she listen to Leora more? Why didn't she keep them inside?

Adaline's heartbeat picked up pace. Closing her eyes, she took deep breaths and inhaled the air. Her lungs burned.

Stomping came from around the corner of the couch, and Adaline gazed up from the pillow nestled in her chin. Brandstrom cracked his neck and peered at every piece in the living room with wide eyes. He usually walked with confidence and held his head high, but his muscular toned shoulders showed tension as he stopped scanning the room and stared directly at her. Abbott opened a water bottle, handed it to her, then pulled a fleece blanket from the sofa chair and spread it on her legs. "Addi, how long ago did the girls go missing?"

She put the water bottle on the table as her hands shook. "One hour ago."

He cleared his throat. "Why didn't you call it in before this point?"

"Because I passed out, and the moment I came to, I called 911," she said. "You can't find anything, can you?"

"You passed out and woke up an hour later?" Brandstrom clung to his chin. "How did you pass out?"

Adaline peered at him, hoping he could be hypnotized to stop asking questions and find out where Eliza and Leora were. "I tripped. You know how clumsy I can be," she said. "Please, we're wasting time. I'm really fine."

"I care about your girls. If you give me vague answers, the more we lose time to find them. You tripped and passed out?" he asked. "Walk me through this?"

She glared at him, then turned to stare out the window before regaining eye contact. "I ran down the porch stairs to find the girls and I slipped on the sidewalk, smacking my head. I guess it was pretty hard because here we are an hour later and I lost all that time, Brandstrom. I did. I know."

He held her gaze and placed his hand on her shoulder. "Could they be at a friend's house? Relative? Anyone they'd be familiar with?"

Adaline swallowed hard. "I already went over to Ms. Dunbar's house, and no one answered. That's the only place they'd go. Everything else is too far for them to walk by themselves. It's cold. They can't be out in the cold like this."

"Anyone else you can think of?"

She pinched her ear. "My Aunt Arlene, but she's nowhere near here and wouldn't have any reason to come down our way."

Brandstrom took out a notebook and a pen from his pocket. "Do you happen to have her number handy?"

"I'll get it for you."

He waved at Officer Mills to come in his direction. "We

need to call this in and get an AMBER Alert out for Leora and Eliza Rushner."

Officer Mills smiled gently at Adaline and confirmed his understanding with a nod to Brandstrom before walking outside.

"Stay put. I need to get you checked out and make sure you're okay."

Adaline rocked back and forth, trying to calm her mind, but all she could think about was how the most precious things in the world to her could disappear. How could she lose their girls? Why hadn't she heard anything?

THREE

Adaline Rushner
Monday, October 18th
10:00 a.m.

THE ROAR of a car engine speeding down the street took Adaline from her internal demons that chanted shame and guilt on a never-ending record in her mind. Replay after replay.

I lost the girls. What will he think of me? They were right. I am no good.

She shook her head and paused to catch her breath. Adaline perked up from the couch, throwing the mosaic pillow on the floor, and cleared her throat.

Cache. Please be home.

How can you want to see your husband and run from him at the same time?

"Be quiet." She rocked back and forth, biting her nail as her gut told her Cache would question her, yet a yearning for comfort held stronger.

The engine turned off abruptly in front of their home, and a door slamming shut had her racing outside before she could think any further. Adaline hobbled down the stairs, flinging herself into Cache's arms. He dropped his briefcase on the ground and hugged her tight. Cache looked into her eyes, and for a split second, she felt safe.

Cache released Adeline from his embrace and picked up his briefcase. The warmth of his hand leading her lessened the discomfort and fear she had raging inside her. A burst of heat rushed through her as she stopped at the open front door and gazed inside. Sweat dripped off her forehead.

No, I won't go in.

She didn't want to walk in and see it all again. The lamp shattered from peering underneath the couch. The half-eaten sandwiches the girls didn't come back to eat. The house filled with silence instead of laughter and singing. They were walking into foreign territory. A life that wasn't theirs. A nightmare and a fear no mother ever would wish on another was now their reality.

"Addi, who did this?" Cache asked, putting his briefcase down by the front door. "Did you see who took the girls?" He held Adeline's face into his palms, caressing it gently. "Addi, think. You were the last person with the girls, and we need to know what happened."

"I don't know. I didn't hear anything."

He stared at her, and his hand left her chin as judgment took the place of concern. Cache smirked at her, but he seemed distant in a way that made her wonder what he was hiding. She'd seen this look for weeks. He'd smile, but he was someplace else where she couldn't reach him.

Officer Brandstrom shuffled into the great room and put his hand out to shake Cache's hand.

"Cache."

"Brandstrom."

They both held their shoulders back and had almost identical worry creases extending on their foreheads.

"What have you done to find our girls?" Cache asked.

Brandstrom placed his hands in his pocket and licked his lips. "We'll do everything we can until we find them."

"What progress have you made?"

Adaline held his arm. "Cache. Take a moment."

Cache flung his arm away from Adaline and glared at her. "Well, you sure did, didn't you? A whole hour of it."

"That's not fair. You know I love our girls." Adaline clung to her hand, digging her nails into her skin.

Cache paced and gripped his head. "That's not the point. You didn't take your medicine, did you?"

Brandstrom stared back and forth between them holding concern for his friends but examining them as if observing possible suspects. He cleared his throat. "Cache and Adaline, I know there's tension here. I'm going to need you to start at the beginning of today and go over the events that have taken place so we can gain some time."

Cache stopped pacing and turned around to stare at him, and Adaline nodded. Abbott proceeded with his questions. "Okay. What time did you wake up?"

"I got up at 7:00 am to get ready for work," Cache said.

Adaline gazed at them both and bounced her knees. "I was up all night."

Brandstrom took out his pad of paper and jotted down a few things, peered up for a minute, and stared at Adaline. His nose scrunched and he arched his eyebrows in a way that made her think he was questioning her.

He's not your friend. You're in trouble.

"You didn't sleep at all?" Brandstrom brushed his mustache.

"Leora couldn't sleep. She believes someone has been watching us and has night terrors all the time about it."

Cache stepped forward. "There's no nightmares or anyone watching us. She's got an overactive imagination."

Officer Brandstrom crossed his arms and glanced down at his watch. "You daughter felt someone was watching your house, and you never reported this. Kids see more than we give them credit for. How long has she been saying someone's been watching your house?"

"A week, Brandstrom. She's been convinced something's going on, and I've tried to comfort her, but it didn't help." Adaline moved her hands back and forth to calm her racing nerves moving up and down her arms and legs.

Brandstrom walked around the great room and wrote as he moved. He gazed up from his notebook and glanced down at the sandwiches on the table. "Is this what they last had to eat?"

Adaline nodded. She looked at where he was and held her stomach. Leora didn't eat much of anything for breakfast. She'd be cold, hungry, afraid, and have no way to reach them. No phone. Telling the girls they needed to have their coats, boots, and gloves on was one of the only things that told her they might be okay.

"Any other questions you have?" Cache asked. "We want to find the girls."

The kitchen table screeched as Brandstrom turned quickly from where he stood to move back into the living room. He faced Cache with a firm stance and clenched his jaw. "When did you leave for work today?"

Cache stared back at him without flinching. "8:15."

"You went straight to work, no stops?"

He swallowed hard. "A bought a camera for Leora for her birthday."

Brandstrom unbuttoned his top collar and stretched his neck, then scratched his throat. He kept his glance on Cache as he did so. "Adaline?"

She intertwined her fingers together, waiting for him to respond to where she was. "Yes."

"Walk me through your morning?" He continued to stare in Cache's general direction. Her head continued to play ping pong with her sinuses. The urge to grab her head and hold it to relieve some of the pressure was strong, but she didn't want to draw more attention to the two men questioning her every move at the moment. She growled silently but could feel the sound waiting to unleash at the base of her throat.

Burning.

Raging heat and fury.

She gulped a few times, trying to force it down, but the bite sprung out as she opened her mouth. "If you're going to ask me a question, look at me when you're talking." Adaline covered her mouth and peered down, not waiting to see the reactions and judgment she felt she'd see.

"All right. I can do that," Brandstrom said. "What's the last thing you remember?"

Slowly, she glanced up to make eye contact and not try to look away, especially after what she just said. "I made peanut butter and jelly sandwiches for the girls. The girls never eat unless I take a bite of their sandwich."

Office Brandstrom frowned. "You were playing Kiss a Roo?"

Adaline's hands began to shake. Every peanut butter and jelly sandwich needed first to have a bite taken by her, a kiss-a-roo, a love bite, before the girls would eat. It had been their game since they were both three and could handle eating solid meals without choking or gagging. They wouldn't be able to eat without her.

"Adaline?"

The room spun again, and she hoped this time it could take her back in time to undo all the things she didn't do and try to make it right—starting with listening to her daughter about her nightmares more. Maybe then she could've stopped this from happening. They'd be shopping for balloons, cake, and packaged games right now instead of vanishing into thin air. She gazed at Officer Brandstrom and nodded lightly.

"What do you remember next?" he asked.

"It started to snow, and the girls wanted to go play. I told them it was fine as long as they got their gloves and boots on and stayed in the yard."

"Where did you go?" Brandstrom jotted a few more notes in his notebook.

Adaline stared at the ground. "I went to get dressed for only a few minutes. I told the girls I would be right there."

"I see. And, when did you notice your girls were gone?"

She lifted her head and pointed her finger toward the kitchen window. "It grew silent. It's not normal for those two. I ran to the kitchen window to make sure they were right where I told them to be, but they weren't there. So, I ran outside to look for them."

Cache punched the side of the couch and began pacing again around the great room. "I should've stayed home." He opened the fridge and placed the milk on the counter.

Adaline sneered at his comment and bunched her fists together. It didn't matter if she took the pills or not. Being numb seemed to be right there, at the surface, but at least without drugs, she knew something wasn't controlling her. Adaline was tired of feeling influenced by situations that continued to haunt her, that no one but her seemed to understand.

"What happened next?" Brandstrom asked.

"I looked all over the yard, and in even in the shed. They weren't there, so I went back inside to see if they went to their room."

"Do you have a recent picture of them?"

Adaline grabbed her phone and tapped in her PIN. "Here. I took this a few minutes before they disappeared."

"That will help. I need you both to fill out a missing person's form." Officer Brandstrom held up his finger to her and seemed to be listening to someone in his ear. He turned around to face the opposite direction.

Adaline stood waiting to hear what was going on and moved a few steps toward the fireplace. Her foot stepped on a hard texture, and she glanced down at the floor to see what it was. A golden locket lying on top of glass pieces from the broken vase she ran into earlier caught her attention. An engraving of an owl peered up at her as the chain lay on the ground. She knew this locket, but from where? Adaline bent down and picked it up, and her body reacted with intense muscle aches. Pain. Discomfort.

Cache placed his glass in the sink and began moving back into the living room. "What's going on?"

Adaline quickly put the locket in her coat pocket and shook her head. "I don't know."

Officer Mills appeared around the corner, and his stance held defeat. He didn't say anything but seemed to be waiting for Officer Brandstrom, who still had his back turned to them. Cache gazed at her, and waves of alarm and panic filled her body. He reached for her hand, and she took it. Stepping closer to him, she stared at each one of them, waiting for who would move first, and watched Cache react in the same way. The room became dead silent. The last twenty-four hours held nothing but quiet, and it made her stomach churn. She began to hum to create some noise.

Officer Brandstrom placed his hand on his head. "Understood. Thank you." He continued to stand in the opposite direction for a moment. It seemed he was avoiding looking at them.

She stopped humming and squeezed Cache's hand tight. "Brandstrom. Did you hear anything?"

He turned around and gave Officer Mills a head gesture, one they both understood. "My partner will stay here with you and finish taking your statements. The paramedics are right outside. They're going to get you checked out, Adaline."

"No. I'm just fine." Adaline let go of Cache's hand and stepped toward him. "You said we're losing time. This doesn't help."

Officer Brandstrom lowered his eyebrows and gazed at her. "It does if you want to be cleared as a suspect. Stay here and get checked out. Don't make this harder on yourself."

"Where are you going?" Cache asked. "What did you just hear?"

"I'm sorry, but you both need to stay here in case someone calls," Brandstrom said. "Mills will be here with you and you'll be the first to hear anything at all." He said that last statement by holding eye contact in the corner of the room, rather than at anyone.

Adaline watched him disappear out into the snow, and she glanced up at the corner he had just spent time looking at before he left. Origami butterflies danced on the wall, full of life, free and joyful, just like her girls. She held her heart and clenched the locket in her pocket. "My girls."

FOUR

Adaline Rushner
Monday, October 18th
10:30 a.m.

RIGHT AFTER OFFICER ABBOTT LEFT, a few paramedics came into the house and hastily moved around Adaline. Each one of them carried a blue duffle bag over their shoulders. A tall woman smiled at her and placed a bag lightly on the couch, then unzipped it. She began pulling out some supplies while another gentleman knelt in front of her and looked into her eyes. "I'm Zack. The guy behind you is Collin, and beside me is Kat," he said. "I'm going to ask you some questions and get some vitals from you."

"Sure. Do what you need to do." She cleared her throat and bounced her leg up and down."

"What's your name?" he asked.

She held her hands together in her lap. "Adaline. Adaline Rushner."

"Adaline, what day of the week is it?"

"Monday."

Zac smiled. "Good. What's the date today?"

Adaline shook her head, annoyed at the dumb questions. "October 18th."

He paused for a moment and stood to grab what appeared to be a stethoscope with a wristband from Kat. "What's your pain level at—from 0 being no pain at all, to 10 being intolerable?"

"A three, maybe." She shrugged.

Zac made a few sounds in understanding and then gazed in the direction of someone behind her. "We believe you have a small concussion. I'm going to check for tenderness on your face, neck, and head."

She nodded and sat very still as he moved his fingers together to warm them before touching her face. Every winter, Adaline did the same thing with the girl's hands, and their fingers would always linger in hers even after they were nice and toasty. Their fingers would be so cold now, and she wasn't there to keep them snug. Adaline closed her eyes.

Please be out of the snow. Mommy's coming very soon.

The paramedic gently felt her cheekbones, and then he moved to her neck. She cringed.

"There's some tenderness there around the base of her skull." Zac said it out loud, and Kat nodded in response. He stood, walked around the couch, and directed his fingers to her head, moving in a careful and rhythmic motion.

Adaline could feel him parting her hair. The pain was manageable until he got back down to pressing at the base of her skull again. Adaline jumped and moved forward. Kat gazed at her with a kindness in her face, a quiet apology.

"I'm sorry. There's swelling there," Zac said, coming around the couch to face her. "You took quite the hit." He mentioned a few numbers to Kat, and she wrote them down. They had their secret code of names and numbers, which made no sense to Adaline, but it didn't matter as long as they went through this quick. He grabbed the mosaic pillow from the floor and planted it underneath her elbow, and then took the stethoscope around his neck and brought it forward. "I'm going to take your blood pressure. I need you to turn your arm outward to me."

Zac slid the cuff up her arm, just an inch or two above the inner bend of her arm. He started to inflate the cuff, and the tighter it got, she could feel her throat, heart, and stomach tighten as well. It felt as if her stomach was being wrung out like a dirty dishcloth. Tighter and tighter. Adaline took a deep breath and counted. After counting to fifteen, the cuff loosened and began to deflate slowly.

"110/69. That's good," he said, unstrapping the cuff from her arm.

Kat handed him a little flashlight and he gave her the cuff. Collin, the other paramedic, seemed to be the observer. "I'm going to check and see if your eyes are dilated. I need you to look directly at the light and hold for a moment. Right eye first."

She did what he asked, hoping it would be like it was in her childhood. If she obeyed and followed directions, it would all be over soon. Adaline trembled.

"Collin, can you get a blanket for Mrs. Rushner?" The paramedic followed his directions promptly, and he continued to shine the light at her eye. "Good. Let's do the left eye now."

The blinding intensity hit her eye, taking her back to

when she awoke in the snow, and the sun blurred her vision. She flinched.

The paramedic put the flashlight down, then peered at Kat. She wrote something down on a piece of paper, and he gazed back at Adaline. "Are you feeling sick?"

"No. It's just cold in here." She rubbed her arms.

He stood and grabbed an object right above her. A blue fleece blanket draped in his hands, and he gave it to Adaline while he looked back down at her. "You've been through a lot. We're just going to check your pulse and then your breathing."

"Am I done after that?" she asked, bracing the blanket to her shoulders.

"If these check out, then we'll have you fill out a form saying you're all clear and we'll be on our way." Zac scratched his cheek.

After the last two tests, Adaline jumped up quickly before another random question could come in. The paramedics began packing up the equipment and talking amongst themselves about what they would pick up for dinner and whose meal would taste better. Philly Cheese Steak won. Her stomach gurgled at the thought of eating, and nausea hit again. Adaline stood tall instead of holding her stomach to not give herself away.

Don't show you're sick. I'm doing these stupid-ass tests for Brandstrom because he asked. The girls need me, and I can't afford to have the paramedic rush me to the hospital.

Zac placed his hand on her shoulder. "You have a small concussion and are going to need some rest for the next few days. Put an ice pack on your head by the base of your neck. It will reduce the swelling," he said. "If you're vomiting, losing consciousness, or having a difficult time waking up, you need to go to the hospital immediately and seek medical attention."

Right? That's going to happen.

Adaline nodded her head to appease him.

"The tenderness should be gone in about 7-10 days." He pulled out some paperwork and a pen. "This copy is yours, going over what I just mentioned. This other one states that I went over this information with you. Sign right here on the line."

She took the pen and signed the piece of paper in his hand and grabbed the copy of the instructions for herself.

"Take it easy." They walked out through the front door, and she followed, standing in the doorway. Cache sat on the porch staring at his shoelaces. He had a thing with paying attention to the knots in his shoelace when he didn't want to talk. Perhaps that's how he felt. A knot, stuck together and bound to something he couldn't undo. He wanted to but didn't know how. She worried many times that he hoped to release her.

The moment the paramedics were out of sight, she cradled her aching belly and stepped back inside. Adaline wanted to lock the door and have no one else come in. Their home was their safe space, or at least it had been until it became a missing person facility. A call came in on Officer Mill's radio, and he quickly left the kitchen, marching down the hallway and into the second bedroom on the right.

Cache stepped from the porch and moved in the house toward her. "They cleared you?"

"Just a little bump, nothing to fuss over." Adaline rubbed her arms to comfort herself as she peered down the hallway after the officer. "He got a call. The officer. It's probably the girls, right?"

He turned in her direction and touched her chin. "We'll find them." Cache held out his hand, and she wrapped herself in his arms.

"I'm sorry I lost that time, Cache," she said. "I'd give anything to have that back. One hour is a long time."

Cache released her and nodded. "I should've stayed for breakfast with you and the girls instead of rushing off to work so quick." He scratched his chin. "They'll be okay. They have to be, right?"

"Right." Adaline released her hold on Cache. "I'm going to go see if I can find something in the girl's room."

"What do you think you're going to find?" he asked.

She clung to her elbows and peered into his eyes. "I don't know, but I can't just stand here doing nothing while our babies are out there." Adaline brushed past him and walked down the hallway to the girls' room. Her hands shook a few steps before getting into their room, and her throat constricted as she stood in the doorway, holding down a rushing river of feelings trying to escape. The room held the candy-coated scent of strawberries and cream from Eliza's favorite dog, Pinkerton. She had gotten into the perfume cupboard one day to give her dog a makeover starting with a real bath, complete with bubbles and a container of perfume. The smell never went away, even after several spins in the washer.

Adaline grazed her finger across the multiple stickers on the headboard.

I know you love stickers. Mommy will get you more when I go to the store.

She breathed in slowly and exhaled. Sitting around and waiting for her girls to come home wouldn't work for her. She needed to figure out who took them and why. There had to be a clue. Adaline opened the closet and sorted through their clothes. She searched through each of the pockets, unsure of what to look for but determined to find something. The last dress in the closet had a vibrant blue color that reminded her of the ocean. Adaline hugged it tightly, then hung it with care back on the hanger. She went to their sock drawer, the nightstand, and bookshelves, going through every page of each book.

Nothing.

There has to be something.

A bookmark with a unicorn saved Leora's spot in *The Secret Garden*. She read it every night for weeks and could almost recite the story line for line. Their bulletin board showcased all their masterpieces—pictures of flowers, a smiling sun—blue like her favorite color—and clouds that rained sprinkles. A family of four little stick figures held hands in one of them, and hearts cascaded above their heads with the words "my happy ending" printed in multiple colors.

Adaline threw the book at the door and sunk to the ground. Her heart immediately ached for Leora's favorite story that she just chucked across the room. She crawled to get it and noticed a fuzzy pink journal tucked between the closet and the girls' dresser. Leora always kept her diary in a safe and clean area. It seemed odd that the journal was left in a place where it could get ruined. She picked it up and placed her hand on the cover. It had a big heart on the front, and the words "my eyes only" were embroidered in the middle of the heart. They'd all been informed many times that no one could touch this special book. Moving to Leora's bed, without hesitation, Adaline flipped to the last entry in the journal.

October 11th,
I need a camera to catch the bad guy. Last nite I saw him outside
my window. I went to sleep and he was there too, in my dreem
with the owl. My mommy was there but she could not see me. I
dont like the owls. I don't think Mommy can see them anymore,
but she needs to remember the little owls so the bad guy will go
away. I need to help her. Leora V. R.

Adaline shuddered, and the muscles in her body
stiffened as the shiver crept through her veins. She pulled
the owl necklace out of her pocket, laying it in her hands.
The emerald green eyes of the owl stared back.

I should've looked at this journal before. I could've prevented
this from happening.

Why did Leora have these dreams? And who watched
her outside the window?

Picking up the journal, she re-read the entry again.

Remember the little owls, so the bad guy will go away.

Adaline stood and moved to Eliza's bed. She grabbed
Pinkerton and nuzzled her nose in its soft fur, inhaling the
sweet aroma. She moved to Leora's side of the room,
picked up her star blanket, and pressed it to her face. It
held a freshly washed scent, just the way Leora liked it.
Adaline lay on the floor between both of their beds. Staring
up at the ceiling, she wished on the plastic glow in the
dark stars that guarded all the girl's dreams and happy
thoughts. Or maybe it brought their nightmares instead.

Please come back home. Come back home to me.

FIVE

Adaline Rushner
Monday, October 18th
3:30 p.m.

A LOUD BANGING awoke Adaline from the sleep she didn't know she took, but the drool on the side of her cheek said otherwise.

What time is it? How long was I asleep?

Light escaped through the semi-closed blinds. She wiped her face and sat up. "Girls. Is that you?"

Pinkerton fell from her lap, and she placed the star blanket next to the stuffed bear to tuck it back to sleep in her place. Adaline stood and ran toward the sound. She turned the corner into the living area, where snoring became an undertone of volume just barely beneath the banging.

The snoring belonged to Cache, who slept on the couch in a position that resembled Gumby. His arms outstretched in a fashion that one could only think had to be cutting off some circulation.

She walked toward the front door and opened it. The outside screen whipped back and forth, making the unpleasant sound she heard. A blizzard thrashed urgently, and the ground now held inches of snow she hadn't seen a few hours ago. Adaline held her shoulders.

It's too cold. The girls can't be out in this white hell.

A police car sat out front with an officer sitting in place. He appeared to be focused on something she couldn't see and he wasn't moving much.

Was he still here because her concussion wasn't a good enough alibi? Did he get the job to watch over the house and alert Officer Brandstrom when the girls come back? Were they in danger from someone? Who would even take the girls? None of this made any sense.

She marched back into the house and stared at the clock on her microwave.

3:30 pm.

Adaline rubbed her eyes and gazed at the bright red numbers again. The paramedics left around 11:15 am. Four hours. Had she been out for four hours instead of finding something more about her girls?

"Cache? Wake up." She moved to the couch and tugged at his knee. "You need to get up. We can't sleep. We have to stay awake."

He jumped from the couch, smacking his arm against the coffee table. "Shit."

"There's more snow now. We've lost four hours, and they're still gone." Adaline rubbed her arms again. "Why aren't they home?"

Cache sat and held the bridge of his nose. "I know how you feel."

"If you do, then get up. Let's leave."

"Stop. You're still a suspect, Addi. We can't just leave," he said.

She glared at him. "Are you kidding me? Have you even looked outside? Have you?" Adaline opened the blinds and waved her hand at the window. "I have an alibi. If the girls are outside, they'll die in this. Don't do this to me."

He continued to hold the bridge of his nose and stare at the ground. "You're not cleared just because you have a concussion."

Adaline let go of the blinds and gripped her coat, squeezing it between her fingers. "So, that's it? You're going to sit there and do nothing?"

Cache tapped his foot in an annoying pattern. Maybe it was morse code? She might be able to understand that faster than whatever communication this was with him, not even looking at her and barely speaking. There was no fire or drive in him as he just sat there, tapping.

"I don't understand. Do you know something I don't know?" Adaline asked.

The tapping stopped, and he raised his head to stare at her. It was the way she peered at the pills she kept being told to take but didn't want to. Adaline recognized the anger and distaste in his eyes. "What the hell do you want me to do? I can't fix this. They're gone, and if they've been outside, they're dead already." He looked away and smashed his fist into the coffee table. It crumbled to the ground, piece by piece, some glass holding on to what used to be.

Adaline covered her mouth and watched Cache as his bleeding hand shook. "Honey." She moved into the kitchen and pulled out a clean cloth from the top drawer.

She soaked it under running water and wrung it out before walking back to Cache. Adaline reached for his hand to clean the blood from his knuckles, but he pulled his hand away.

"I'm fine." He turned his body away from her.

She shook her head and threw the washcloth at him. "Suit yourself."

The doorbell rang a few times, and Adaline's heart thudded as she opened the door. Officer Mills stood outside. "Can I come in?"

Adaline moved aside, letting him trudge past her. He walked way too slow, like gravity had changed and become thicker. Each step was sinking into quicksand. She waited for him to say something, but he didn't. Cache gazed up at Officer Mills, and they both nodded to each other. Before Adaline could say anything, her cell phone rang. She gasped and leaped to grab it from the couch. "Hello."

"It's Brandstrom." He paused for a moment. "Have you taken your girls to the dentist lately?"

Adaline clung tighter to the phone. "A few weeks ago. Leora grinds her teeth with her night terrors. We got her a mouthguard and had Eliza checked at the same time. Why?"

"Did you have them examined by Mr. Yardley?"

"Yes. What's this about?"

Brandstrom cleared his throat. "We found something and need to get your girls' dental records faxed over to verify the information. I'm going to call Mr. Yardley, and I'll let you know what we find out."

The room spiraled like static around her, unable to process what he just had said. "Verify what information exactly?"

"It may not be anything at all."

Cache stood next to her, his hand on her arm. Adaline took a deep breath before asking the question her mind wanted to ignore. "What did you find?"

"That's all I can say right now, but I'll let you and Cache know once I hear anything," he said.

Adaline dropped the phone on the ground and held her chest. She tried to brace herself from the spinning by gripping Cache's arm. Her body grew cold and switched off. Numbness took over.

Cache rubbed her hand, picked up the phone, and paced back and forth. She reached to him, but nothing happened with her arms as her body fell toward the couch. She lay motionless. Numb.

This is not real. Wake up, Adaline.

She shook her head, and the nerves in her neck stretched like taffy, further and further away from consciousness.

Officer Mills bent down near her face to look at her and extended his hand to offer support. She peered back and quickly glanced away as his blue eyes held no promise, no hope, and no fight. Isn't blue the color of hope? Isn't his job not to give up? To not look at people in a way that says all is lost? Instead, it resembled drowning in the sea.

Adaline gazed at the butterflies in the corner of the ceiling. The same ones Officer Brandstrom stared at before he left and made a false promise that he'd be back. Calling on the phone is always easier to deliver messages that you'd rather not convey in person. She put her hands in her coat pocket and clung to the owl necklace, rubbing it like it would grant her a wish. Her eyes focused on the yellow counter that she painted on one of her insomnia binges. A week ago, Adaline watched a home decorating show that talked about ways to make your home more joyful and lively. The idea of painting the color you wished you felt intrigued her at the time, and even brought hope it could work to pep up her mood. Yellow mocked Adaline now, reminding her that joy was not meant for everyone.

Fucking counter. I hate you.

SIX

Adaline Rushner
Monday, October 25th

A WHOLE WEEK had gone by since the girls left to play in the snow and vanished only moments later. One week ago, Adaline planned to have a birthday celebration for Leora with a Halloween-themed party, a pinata, and a five-layered cake with all the toppings. Her birthday was two days ago, and they didn't celebrate. There was no cake, no party, no laugher or music, no guests, and her girls hadn't come home.

She'd cleaned up more glass, tears, blood, and throw up the past few days than she ever remembered with the girls. Not the kind of party anyone should have. Adaline sat on the girl's bedroom floor, waiting for them to come back and have a tea party with her. She wasn't the only one who anticipated their arrival. Multiple stuffed friends circled a picnic blanket, ready for their special feast that Eliza put together every Monday.

Today was Monday, and they'd never missed a picnic until now. Adaline held the camera Cache picked up for Leora's birthday present. The item they thought she wanted to capture the beauty in the world, but she wanted it to catch the bad guy that lurked and watched their home at night—the one who probably took them.

Adaline could've stopped the kidnapper if she had listened more closely to her daughter.

I haven't given up. I'll find you, my sunshine and star.

Ms. Dunbar stopped by yesterday to bring a basket of apples so that once the family got together, an apple pie baking day could happen. She gave Adaline the same faces everyone else continued to give her. The "all hope is lost" and "sorry for your loss" looks, even though hope would never be lost when it came to finding the girls. Not for Adaline.

The last they heard from Officer Brandstrom, he had talked to their dentist, Mr. Yardley, to get the girls' dental x-rays faxed over for examination. Adaline had never been one to know or care much about forensic science or lab results, but it sounded like they found a body. It felt awful to wish it was someone else's kids they found instead of hers, but she clung to hope and continued to pour tea into the little ceramic cups sitting in front of Pinkerton and his other stuffed friends.

Cache hadn't said much since that call. He mostly lingered in their bedroom or went out to the shed, staying there for hours on end, like a ghost that haunted himself.

Adaline's cell phone rang from the living area.

She jumped, knocking over the teacup next to her, and continued to sit, frozen in place. Her shoulders tensed, and her throat tightened. The phone had become a 50/50 game that played with her heartstrings every time the alarming blare sounded from that stupid box of communication.

Did they find your girls? Or will they still be missing?

Adaline stood, and her knees shook under her. She took small steps and tried to focus on breathing as her mind told her not to pick it up—the phone lay on the kitchen counter and continued to ring. The number on her cellphone belonged to Officer Brandstrom She reached her hand out and pressed the answer button, bringing the phone slowly to her ear.

"Brandstrom," she said in a whisper.

"Addi. Is Cache home?"

She nodded even though he couldn't see that. "Yes. Why?"

He cleared his throat. "He didn't answer his phone."

"Cache isn't speaking much to anyone, but I can deliver a message to him." She gripped the phone tighter.

"I need to talk to both of you together. I'm on my way to your house."

Adaline's mouth felt dry. She opened a cupboard in the kitchen and grabbed a glass. "Why?"

He paused. "I'll see you both soon."

The phone slid from her hands, and the glass dropped onto the floor. She should've never answered and continued with the tea party instead.

———

Officer Brandstrom pulled up to their house ten minutes after he called. Adaline and Cache were already at the door, waiting to let him in and watching his every move.

He got out of his police car with no urgency or

confidence in his step, staring at the ground. She wanted him to come back to the house previously, but now maybe he could hear her telepathically telling him to get back into his car. Adaline swallowed hard and placed her hand on Cache's shoulder. He opened the door and gazed back at her, his hurt mirroring what she felt inside.

The open door carried a breeze that whipped at Adaline's cheeks, and she shivered. Officer Brandstrom stepped in, holding his hands together and nodding to them both. "Cache. Adaline. Can you take a seat?"

Cache shut the door and stood in place, not moving from the entryway.

"I'm fine right where I am," Adaline said. "What's going on? Did you find the girls?"

Brandstrom glanced down again and wiped his face. "There's been confirmation that the bodies we found a week ago are Leora and Eliza." He shuffled his feet. "I'm so sorry. I have the number for the funeral director to help you walk through the next steps."

Adaline ground her teeth. "No. You're lying. Why would you lie to us?"

"I'm not lying to you." He handed the paper with the phone number out toward her.

"I'm not calling a funeral director. They're not dead."

Cache's eyes raged like a bull as he looked up and moved deliberately, ready to charge. "What happened?"

"You should take a seat."

Adaline shook her head and watched as Cache took a few more steps toward Brandstrom, hoping that his face wouldn't end up like their coffee table.

Brandstrom rubbed his chin. "Their bodies were found a few miles down the dirt road."

"I want to see their bodies. It might not be them," Adaline said. "You have to be sure. I'd know."

"It's not possible for you to see them."

Cache stepped in front of Adaline and peered at him. "What the hell do you mean it's not possible? We want to see our daughters."

"They were burned alive." He gulped, and a rogue tear slid from his eye. "There's nothing to see. That's why we ran the dental records, Cache."

Adaline stepped backward and held her stomach. "NO. We have a tea party, dammit. You have the wrong girls. Mine are coming home." She braced herself against the wall, and Cache walked toward her.

"Do you know who did this?" Cache asked.

"Does Braxton Wheeler mean anything to you?" Brandstrom put his hands in his pocket.

Cache squatted and bunched his fists. "He did this?"

The name sent chills through Adaline's body, remembering how the man called her a slut at Cache's old job and followed her to her car, promising a good time, right before he pressed himself up against her while she tried to fight him off. He was stronger. Much stronger.

"That piece of shit sexually assaulted my wife, and I got him fired for it." He stood. "Where is he? I'm going to kill him?"

"He's dead," Brandstrom said. "We identified his body with your girls."

Adaline slid down the wall and sat in a puddle of numbness, holding her knees. Tears slid down her face. She couldn't think or move. She pretended that instead of hugging her knees, she was hugging the girls. Warm bodies with laughter, noise, whining, complaining, messes, asking a million questions about the world, sleepless nights, and endless days of worry about being a good mother. She didn't cherish those moments enough.

Please don't leave me. Come back.

SEVEN

Two Weeks Later
Owling, Utah
Sunday, November 7th

ADALINE DIDN'T WANT to leave her home.

Multiple boxes sat on the porch taunted her as moving day had arrived, whether she wanted it or not. She sat on her daughter's tire swing, arms outstretched, the wind tugging at her hair. The screen door to her home slammed, and the sky turned black. Her hope clouded but still lay dormant. Cache walked toward her, worry lines creased as he stared in her direction. She could pick out that face a mile away and know what he was thinking. Adaline clung to the owl necklace wrapped around her neck and rubbed the green pendant on its belly like she'd be granted a wish.

Cache stopped in front of the tire swing and squatted to be eye level with her. "I noticed some stuffed animals packed in a box." He paused. "It's been a few weeks since the girls' death."

Adaline stared at him. "They're alive. Leora and Eliza will be back."

"No, they're gone." Cache looked at her, wide-eyed, and stood.

"Why don't you believe me?" She'd tried to talk to him about what she felt time and time again, to have him understand that everything would be okay. The girls *would* come back home. He never listened. Sadness dwelled in his hazel eyes, and hope no longer lingered in his limbs.

"We need to move on. I miss them too, but we can't live like this anymore," he said.

Adaline held the rope of the tire swing between her fingers. "Like what? Like how you think a move is going to make me better. I'm not crazy."

"I didn't say you were," he said, holding out his hand. "You wanted the house with the picket fence."

"That's when our girls were with us. We can't go. They won't know where to find us. They'll come here."

Cache brushed his hand through his hair and peered around the yard. "We're locked in a contract." His knee bounced and his eyes didn't greet hers. "I need my wife."

Adaline glanced at the snow on the grass and gripped the rope tighter.

He thinks I'm losing it.

She let go of the swing. "I'll pack the last boxes so we can go."

"Thank you for trying." Cache squeezed her hand and walked to the house.

She shook her head at his comment, her boots crunching in the snow as she followed him. The footprints left behind would be gone by the next snowstorm. Adaline would be forgotten by this place she called home. She paused, taking a deep breath. The porch stairs creaked and the front door moaned as she entered her vacant house.

"We don't need to take all this stuff. Let's get rid of some of it," Cache said.

She winced, trudged into the living room, and closed the oversized box of stuffed animals with packing tape. "We do need it, okay? I'm packing for all of…"

"All of who?"

"For me. I want these for memories," Adaline said.

Cache caressed her face and kissed her forehead. "Of course. I understand that. We have about a three-hour drive into Salt Lake City and should leave before it gets dark. I'm going to make another round to see if we got everything."

Adaline nodded and turned the corner toward a room with bright pink walls.

She halted.

The playful color burned her eyes. She closed them tight. Familiar voices spiraled around her. Shocked, her eyelids flew open and she gasped. Her girls' faces stared from the wall—pleading for help. Adaline gripped the door frame for support as her head spun.

We can't leave. This is the girls' home.

She fled from the room and out the front door, holding her stomach. The November breeze made her shiver.

Cache came up behind her and rubbed her back. "Do you want to talk about it?"

She didn't know. What would that accomplish? It wouldn't fix the longing she felt or the fact that the color pink now nauseated her. "Remember when we painted that wall after we found out we were having a girl?"

He smiled. "Pepto-Bismol pink, how could I forget?

You were determined to get that specific color. I think we went to four stores in one day to find the right paint."

"Eight stores total. Four stores for paint, and the other four included bathroom trips and snack breaks."

"That's right. You craved peanut butter both pregnancies." He laughed. "That was eight years ago. Hard to believe, isn't it?"

Adaline nodded her head. She wiped tears from her face and glanced up at him.

Touching her chin, he gave her the same distressed look as before. "We're going to be okay."

Pulling away from him, Adaline gazed at the yard. "I was so nauseated, but so happy to be sick. We were going to be parents, you know." She smacked her boot on the porch. "We were on the same team eight years ago. Now... it's different."

Cache paced the porch and grunted. "We're going to our new home. You're going to love it, just like when you first saw it."

"Sure," she muttered.

He shook his head. "Why are you being so difficult? We need to try to move on."

"You keep saying that. I don't feel the same way you do." Adaline pushed past him and walked down the steps. She got into the front seat of the car and waited for him to follow.

Cache sat in the driver's seat. "I'm sorry," he said, reaching for her hand. "I'm trying to help, even if you don't see it."

She paused for a minute and took his hand. "How are you okay? You act as if nothing has happened." He didn't respond, but he never did. She wished Cache would talk to her about what he was thinking, feeling. Anything.

Cache started the SUV and backed out of the driveway. As they pulled away, Adaline looked out the side mirror to catch a glimpse of the tire swing that hung from their famous monster tree. It used to bring joy, peace, and continual laughter. Now it only held remorse, a haunting reminder of what happiness used to feel like. Most of the time, Adaline felt as empty as the house now stood. Nothing would change that.

EIGHT

Adaline Rushner
Salt Lake City, Utah
Sunday, November 7th

THE SUV STOPPED, and Adaline's head bounced with the jerking motion. She opened her eyes, immediately regretting her decision. The stores were gathered so close together in Salt Lake compared to her hometown of Owling, where there was only one grocery store and one gas station, a mile apart. A small town fit for a small-town girl.

"Are you okay? Why did we stop?" she asked.

"Black ice. We started sliding, but we're good now," Cache said.

Adaline gazed up at multiple tall buildings and billboard advertisements. Snowflakes fell on the ice-covered streets, and cars slowed down as if disaster was about to strike. People gathered around trucks handing out food on the street corners, and a little girl with fuzzy pink boots waved to someone passing by. Adaline held her own hand and looked away.

Look at the towers, Mommy. They touch the sky.

She shook her head and closed her eyes.

Find me.

Adaline gripped her hand tighter and peered at the back seat. "Not right now."

"Honey, look at me," Cache said, shaking her shoulder.

Adaline stared at him. "What's wrong?"

His forehead wrinkled. "There's no one in the backseat. It's just us. You and me."

She looked back to see a seat full of packed boxes. Adaline turned around and stared at the floor. Placing her hand on her heart, she ached to understand the hope and despair that wrenched her.

"It's okay," Cache said.

Adaline shook her head and peered up at him. Dizziness fogged her mind, and her fingers twitched as she gripped his arm. "It's hard not to . . . talk to them. It's a habit, and I like it."

"Like what?"

"Having conversations with them." She paused. "I think it's fairly common for other people, too. You should try it. Maybe you'll be able to express your feelings that way."

"By talking to something that's not there, Addi? That's not helpful. It makes it harder to move on," he said.

"Maybe this is my only way of understanding."

Cache clenched his jaw. "I'm trying to understand. I really am. How exactly is this helping you?"

"I can't tell you. It just . . . does." Adaline squeezed the door handle and stomped the floor.

"It's been a long day. I think we're both tired." The

traffic light turned green and he continued to drive. "We're almost there. Why don't you close your eyes and relax for a minute?"

Adaline dug her fingers into the palm of her hand. "I'm okay. I don't need to relax."

"Please? For me?" he pleaded. "Close your eyes."

For him? What about me?

She peered in his direction and admired his hazel eyes and curly dark hair. Her heart belonged to a man that looked like him, but not the one that had lost all faith in her. They were different now and going in opposite directions, but she loved him still. "You're not the surprise type, and I'm not in that kind of mood."

"I think you'll enjoy it. This is me . . . making an effort."

Adaline hesitated, biting the inside of her cheek. "Okay," she said, closing her eyes. Everything in her screamed to go back to Owling, that all this was a terrible misunderstanding. She held her hands together and rubbed her fingers in a circular motion.

The SUV swerved to the right and then continued straight until she could hear the sound of Cache tapping the brake, putting the car into park. Her stomach ached.

"Okay. You can open," he said.

Adaline stared at the small yellow home in front of her and diverted her vision to the moving van parked in the driveway. She bit her fingernails and bounced her leg up and down. Clearing her throat, she focused on the object that Cache wanted her to see. Everything looked exactly as she remembered it—but with a new addition. A white picket fence wrapped around the large yard. It was the same one she had shown him from a home magazine that she said she'd have one day.

"Is that the right fence?" Cache asked.

She nodded and scratched her head. "How—"

"A few weeks ago, I hired some guys to put it together. I wanted you to have something special."

"It's exactly what I wanted," Adaline said, looking away from him.

They even house shopped together with the girls and fell in love with the house she now looked at. The girls had twirled around in the backyard with the sun hitting their faces. Leora's long blonde hair glowed, and Eliza's brown ringlets bounced in every direction. It was to be their home, the four of them.

But that was before. She couldn't step into this house without her girls. It wasn't right.

Adaline tilted her head. The house looked like a cottage but reminded her of a dollhouse. With the white picket fence and the multiple trees arching over the place, it had a rustic and elegant charm. The snow falling from the branches had originally been magical and cozy; now the twigs resembled fingers reaching toward her, beckoning to hold her captive.

She turned to Cache. Adaline knew he was waiting for some sort of reaction out of her. "It's still lovely…the fence is perfect."

"But…?"

"But, I told you I didn't want to leave."

"We had a contract. We couldn't back out of that." He glanced away. "You said you loved this home. I believe the wraparound porch sealed the deal. Why don't we go inside so you can see it again?"

Adaline rubbed her arms. "We could've backed out of the contract, and I'm tired of you ignoring me."

Cache gripped the steering wheel and clenched his jaw.

"Can we go inside now, or are we going to sit in the car and argue?"

A part of her wanted to stand her ground, but she was too fatigued to fight. Adaline got out of the car and walked to the front door. She paused as a flood of emotions froze her.

The oak front door had gold handles, which made her feel like she was jumping into a storybook—a story she would've read to the girls before bed, and they would imagine they were the dolls prancing around the yard. Cache opened the door and held it for her. Adaline brushed past him. Piles of boxes spread all over the floor.

"You let the movers come in without us being here?" Adaline asked.

"I gave them an extra key so if they arrived here before us, they could start unloading."

"How could you let complete strangers around our most precious things? They should've waited for us," she said. "Where are they?"

Cache gazed at the ground. "I'm going outside for a minute."

He left, slamming the door on his way out.

Adaline frowned.

Strolling into the kitchen, she let her fingers glide across the stainless-steel appliances showcasing a setup made for a master cook.

Too bad that wasn't her.

Polished wood floors covered the dining room and kitchen, and a large fireplace summoned her into the common area. The inside of the house looked smaller than she remembered, more confined, like a prison. She walked upstairs to examine each of the four bedrooms, moving past the one Leora and Eliza picked months ago. They claimed it by kissing their hand and touching the door.

The same room. They loved being close to one another.

Adaline needed to run away from this place that held her hostage, that told her she should move on and create a new chapter in her life.

She was suffocating.

Owling held the last moments of her girls, and she'd walked away from them by moving to Salt Lake.

What kind of mother would do that?

Her instincts had told her to stay in Owling, and she didn't listen, but Cache needed her as well. She couldn't be in both places at once, which made her feel raw, torn up inside. Adaline would always fail one way or another, choosing between the two.

Cache came back into the house and walked upstairs. "I'm sorry I didn't ask if the movers could come in. I know you have trust issues, especially after what happened."

She leaned into him and he wrapped his arms around her waist.

"You look sad. Don't you like it?"

He really thinks a house is going to make me feel better.

Adaline nodded. "No, this is beautiful. I just think I'm a..." She halted and let go of Cache.

"Are you okay?"

Her eyes shifted around the room. "I'm fine. Why?"

"You're scoping the room like you've seen a ghost."

"Just lots of dust and..." She bent down toward the ground.

We like it, mommy. Please, let us stay.

Her hands shook, and sweat dripped from her forehead. She couldn't breathe. Adaline gasped and clung to Cache's shirt.

One . . . two . . . three . . . breathe.

Inhaling, she tried to focus on the rhythm of her heartbeat. Her fingers steadied, and a surge of air filled her lungs. Adaline braced herself on the railing. "I'm okay. I'm going to start unpacking a few boxes."

"Nope. You have other plans," he said. "It's been a long day, and the movers just came back. I'll go get some extra hands to bring in the mattress. You need to take it easy."

He left and Adaline slowly walked downstairs, holding the railing. She looked in the front room for the big box marked *sheets*. It wasn't hard to miss, being the biggest one she had packed. Adaline took a box cutter out of her coat pocket and sliced the tape. She reached in to pull out the contents. Her arms cradled pink butterfly sheets, and she sniffed the fabric. It still held a distinct, lingering scent of strawberry from Eliza's stuffed bear, Pinkerton.

Reality stared Adaline in the face, a version that wasn't her *real* life. Leora and Eliza were supposed to have the childhood she never had, free from terror, abuse, and pain. She held the sheet to her cheek and sang lullabies to the soft fabric.

"Mommy will find you, my girls. I know you're out there."

The door clicked open. Adaline turned away to plaster a fake smile before looking at Cache.

"Here it is." Three men with black shirts, matching black hats, and a logo that read Mendon Moving Brothers came through the door behind Cache and waited for his instructions about where to put the mattress. "The room is upstairs, first door on your right."

"Keep it down," Adaline said in a hushed voice, putting her finger to her lips. She rocked the sheets back and forth in her arms.

Cache knelt next to her. "Let me take those sheets for you?"

"No." She leaned backward and pressed the fabric to her cheek.

"Okay. I'll be right back. Cache grabbed their king-sized sheets from the opened box and headed upstairs.

Once he was out of range, Adaline turned to the butterfly sheets and sang a lullaby.

The sound of pounding feet filled the house as all four men came down the stairs. She glared at them but continued rocking.

Left. Right. Left.

"Anything else, boss?" said the tallest Mendon Brother, with long blond hair and uneven sideburns.

"We can take it from here. Thank you for your help, and drive carefully on those icy roads," Cache said, giving the man a tip.

The man shook his hand, and Cache closed the door behind them. He picked Adaline up and carried her upstairs to their bed. "This is where you'll be spending the rest of your night," he said, lying next to her.

She didn't resist and closed her eyes, waiting for him to fall asleep. Leora and Eliza would have a room ready for them when they came back home.

NINE

Cache Rushner
Monday, November 8th
7:00 a.m.

CACHE TURNED over in bed to find pillows wedged against his back and the covers ripped off the mattress. He knew all too well Adaline must've been sleepwalking again. She started doing it every night after the girls died.

He staggered out of bed, rubbing his eyes before he entered the hallway. The first two rooms were vacant. Turning the corner, Cache stumbled into a pile of empty boxes flung across the floor. He kicked one and moved the others out of his way.

What the hell?

He watched as purple stars reflected off the bedroom wall out into the hall. He hunched over, holding his aching chest.

Not again.

Entering the bedroom, a star lamp on the floor glowed

next to Adaline's sleeping body. She clenched a large stuffed teddy bear that nuzzled underneath her chin, and she half-smiled—he would take that at this point. The room meticulously resembled the way it had last been left at the Owling home before the girls' deaths.

He leaned down and caressed her face. "I need to leave for work soon."

She wiped her mouth, stretched her arms, and gazed up at him. "Where am I?"

"You put together a room in your sleep last night. Don't you remember?" he asked.

She raised her eyebrows, peered around the room, and giggled as a small child would when seeing snow for the first time. For an instant, her blue eyes lit up in a way that seemed like a new discovery to him. It had been a long time since he saw her eyes dance.

"I remember. The girls want us to stay…or they would want us to be happy," she said.

Cache wished he could be just as amused about this whole situation, but it wasn't funny. Why couldn't Adaline move on? It's not like he wanted to, but holding false hope was destroying him—couldn't she see that?

"They would've loved it," he said, looking at the ground. Cache placed his hand on her shoulder. "Maybe it's too soon for you to go back to work. Taking another day to relax might be good?"

She shoved his hand off her shoulder and tightened her grip around the bear's neck. "I'm fine."

"Okay. Ease up on the bear," he said, smirking. "You got that thing in a chokehold."

Adaline glared at him.

"Bad timing on the jokes. Got it." Cache hesitated. He never knew what he would get from day to day. She was fragile and unstable. Sometimes she'd take the same statement seriously, other times she'd laugh and move on, but chancing it wasn't a good idea. He learned the hard way, many times recently. Cache stood and glanced at his watch. "I guess I'll go get ready then."

She looked up at him and her lips turned upright. "Thank you for getting me up."

"No problem. Can I help you find anything before I jump in the shower?" he asked.

Her face twisted back into the Adaline he didn't know anymore. Anger possessed her body, taking form. "You know exactly what I need to find. Daughters."

"Okay." He scratched his chin. Cache wished he knew what was going on in her head. She seemed distant and odd since the tragedy. He wanted Adaline to let him in; he wanted to tell her how hard this was on him, too. She lived in her own land, and he played along in hopes she'd come out of it, at some point, but when would that be?

"That's it? Okay?" she asked.

"We've been over this."

Adaline stared at him for a minute. "You don't want to be late on your first day."

Taking a deep breath, he bent down and kissed Adaline on the forehead. "Have a good day," he said before leaving the bedroom.

After showering and putting on a suit, he rushed downstairs and grabbed his briefcase on the counter.

Please let her stop searching through the past.

Cache worried that his hidden secrets wouldn't stay buried for much longer. He shut the front door to the unknown—not sure what he would come home to this time.

TEN

Adaline Rushner
Lost Treasures Antique Store
8:30 a.m.

Parking her silver Chevy on Ivy Lane, she glanced across the street and pried the newspaper open. She flipped through the pages until she found page five, the business section, and scrolled down to view Lost Treasures, boldly saying hello to the readers. Ms. Dunbar wanted a grand opening with the new manager in town.

Adaline laid the newspaper on the dashboard and grunted. She opened her wallet and pulled out a picture of her girls. She kissed her fingers and touched the photo gently, taking in their beautiful faces.

"Once you come home, I'll show you all the treasures I find."

Placing the picture back in her wallet, Adaline got out of the car and strolled toward the store. The windows needed some show-stopping displays, and the shelves had to be stocked before the store could open.

Peering at the items in the window, an old record player and a grandfather clock stood on one side, while an array of handheld mirrors and jewelry boxes beamed on the other. Adaline glanced at the keys dangling in her hand. She clicked the key in place, turned the knob, and opened the door to her store. It still smelled like a blend of old wood and mildew even after all the cleanup she'd done months ago, when family and possibility had been her reality.

Candles. Where did I put them?

Shutting the door, Adaline turned on the lights and placed her purse and winter coat on the front counter. She went to the closet, looking for the vanilla candles she had seen laying around.

Damn special hiding spots. What good are you, if I can't find you?

She huffed, brushed dust off her pants, and went to the back room to retrieve display stands to put in her windows. She tugged on a closet door positioned at the back of the room. It was a very inconvenient place for a door, and it put up a good fight every time she tried to open the thing.

The bell at the front of the store rang, and the clomping of boots sounded.

Adaline hesitated and patted her pocket for the keys. Empty.

I didn't lock the door?

"We're not opened yet. But, in an hour you're more than welcome to check out the store." Adaline tilted her body to peek through the aisle. She couldn't see anyone, and the pounding from the boots had stopped.

"Hello?"

Halting, she peered around her store as uneasiness set in. Her skin prickled and she swallowed hard.

"Is anyone there?"

The store bell rang again.

Get a grip. They just left.

Underneath the display case lay her keyring. She bent down and moved her fingers under the case, retrieving the keys as they dangled on her thumb like a Christmas ornament.

Adaline shook her head and chuckled while locking her store. She walked back to the closet door and paused.

Boots. I didn't hear the boots.

Clomping returned, inching toward her, and jangling sprung from her shaking hand. The attacker clung to her shoulders and sniffed her hair. "Little Owl. It's been so long," a man said in a whisper.

She froze.

Little Owl. I know that term. From where?

"I haven't seen your face. If you leave now, I won't report this," Adaline said.

Laughter erupted, and the man's strong arms shoved her into the closet. The door creaked loudly as it slammed shut.

"*No.* Let me out now."

"If you continue to scream, the people outside waiting to see your filthy store will die . . . or will they? Kind of like your girls," said the voice, softly. "Bye-bye. I'll be watching you."

Adaline gripped her chest, breathing heavily.

My girls. He mentioned them.

"Where are they? Tell me right now." She pounded on the door. "Don't . . . leave me in here."

Adaline fumbled for the light switch, but the darkness made it impossible to see what was right in front of her. She ran her shaking fingers up and down the walls until a sharp object hooked into her skin. Pain shot through her hand. Grabbing at her arm, she steadied it and felt a splinter of plywood hanging from the center of her palm. Adaline let out a whimper, yanked it out, and threw it in front of her. A clanking sound rang out in the tiny confinement she was trapped in.

The doorknob.

She moved in the direction where the sound came from and put her hand out to grab the doorknob. Cold metal grazed her palm. Adaline winced and gripped it, turning the knob with force, pulling as hard as she could. Her hand slipped off the knob, flinging her backward. She landed on her tailbone with a grimace.

Memories of when she was eight and her mother stuck her in a closet came rushing back. The closet she sat in was no bigger than the one she lived in as a kid.

How did you get so stupid?

I wish you were never born.

You make me miserable.

I never wanted to be your mom, pigeon.

I hate the person you are.

Why couldn't you be different?

I wish you would leave and never come back.

I don't love you and never will; deal with that.

Every syllable her mother yelled out stung Adaline's heart. The bitterness and hatred were like poison pulsing off her tongue. Adaline told herself that they were just words her mother didn't mean, but over time she started believing what was said.

She held herself in a fetal position, peering through a black abyss that turned her into that scared child again.

"Are you still there?"

There was no answer.

He's gone.

"Anyone, please help me? Is there anyone there?" she said, banging on the walls and floor that surrounded her. "I need help."

Her voice wavered, sounding unfamiliar, yet she remembered it like an old friend. Holding her hands together, she sat in silence.

This isn't happening. Not again.

She pulled at her hair and kicked the door multiple times, but it wouldn't budge.

Go to your happy place. You're not the same person anymore.

Adaline hummed a song and swayed back and forth, rocking herself to stop her trembling body. Her heart raced and she felt dizzy. She repeated the tune a second time, until her nerves subsided some. Adaline planted her shaking hands on the concrete and let the cold ground her.

Think.

A noise came from inside her store. Adaline got up quickly and pressed her ear on the wood door. "Hello, anyone?"

Welcoming light streamed in, and she fell backward as the door smacked open. Adaline lay on her back and held her knees up to her chest. "Don't come any closer."

A tall man stepped forward. "I just got you out of here. Calm down."

Adaline raised a leg, ready to kick him in the gems if he kept moving. "Got me out? You're the bastard that put me in here." Her arms shook with fear and anger. "Where are my girls? I know you have them."

He put his hands up to surrender. "No, ma'am. I swear, I didn't do this to you and I don't know anything about your girls." Adaline stared at him. He appeared to be in his fifties, and his shoulder-length, wavy brown hair held an *I need a shower* look. He was tall and lanky, but in his hazel eyes, she saw kindness and intensity.

"Are you hurt?" he asked.

She lowered her leg and planted her hands on the ground. "You didn't put me in here?"

"I'm looking for a job. There's a hiring sign on the door. I'm Seth," he said with a smile "Can I help you up?"

Adaline looked down at the man's feet. No boots, only sneakers with holes. She glanced around. No one else was inside the store. "Thank you for getting me out of the closet."

"You're welcome. You should really call the cops about this."

She stood up and hustled to the front door. "I really need to get back to it."

Seth grinned. Adaline watched as he moved to the door. He had a distinct walk, almost like he was counting his steps. "I can take a hint. Nice to meet you."

Adaline locked the door behind him and peered through the window, at the line outside on the street corner of Ivy Lane for the Grand Opening.

She grasped her neck and gazed at the opened closet she'd just escaped from. Her nose scrunched and tears slid down her face. Sinking to the ground, Adaline gave into the raw emotion eating its way through her soul.

Through her tear-filled vision, a piece of paper with bold lettering mocked her on the ground. She wiped her eyes and crawled toward it.

You can never escape me. I will make your life hell, like

you did to mine. Your girls were only the beginning of your pain.

Bunching her fist, Adaline crumbled the paper in her hand and marched to the front of her store. She stood outside staring at the crowd, taking a moment to memorize every face one by one. "If any of you think you can scare me away, you're dead wrong. Do you hear me?" she yelled. No one said a word. Adaline turned to lock the door and then ran to her car.

ELEVEN

Seth Duncan
Monday, November 8th
9:30 a.m.

HE ARRIVED at his apartment suite—or that's what he called it to make it sound more appealing than the dump it was. The Grand Capital Motel. That name was deceiving. It didn't have the feel of Grand, but it was better than where he had come from. Seth didn't have a job yet, and money was low, but not for long. He planned on making something of himself and changing his life around.

"Excuse me, sir. How long do you plan on staying here?" a pretty lady asked as he passed the front desk.

He grabbed his wallet and pulled out a credit card. "A week."

She took the card and rang it through. "Your card was declined. Do you have any other form of payment?"

Seth took out a fifty-dollar bill and handed it to her.

"There must be a misunderstanding. I'll pay you tomorrow for a weeks' stay," he said.

"This will get you a night's stay, maybe two," she said, winking at him. "Mister...?"

"Duncan."

"Mr. Duncan, sir."

"I'll see you tomorrow then," he said.

The lady smiled. "Looking forward to it, Mr. Duncan."

The morning sure had gotten interesting quickly. He had heard of the grand opening on Ivy Lane and thought he'd check it out to see if they carried an old watch compass. That poor lady sure seemed upset, but being locked in a closet at work couldn't be a walk in the park.

Seth stopped in front of his room, number 203, and opened the door. He had a bad habit of locking the door. After what he'd been through, locking the door was the least of his problems. The bedroom smelled of wet dog and stale perfume.

That's what you get for a cheap room.

The bed had stains on the covers, and the mattress caved in the middle, creating a pit.

No way am I getting stuck in that hole of filth.

He took off his coat, laid it on the bed, and sat on it. Seth placed his hands on his lap, careful not to touch the bed. He proceeded to take off his sneakers, but the yellow carpet looked like it was Big Bird's fur infested with germs and dirt. He put his shoes back on.

Seth scanned the room for the remote to find it in the bathroom, which only made the place that much more disgusting. His backpack lay on the bed as he tried to jiggle the zipper to come undone. He reached his arm through a small opening to grab a sanitizer wipe. Grocery stores were the stock place for them; the containers were right by the shopping carts in the front entrance—easy access. Technically he wasn't stealing, because he didn't need to pay for them. Seth cleaned the remote control with the wipe, debating if he wanted to watch the news, but decided against it. His stomach agreed, growling noisily. He looked down at his watch. It was noon. Time to get lunch.

Tomorrow will be a new day.

He wanted to find purpose, for someone to need his help—and Mrs. Rushner appeared to be that someone.

TWELVE

Cache Rushner
Rushner Home
6:00 p.m.

CACHE PULLED into his driveway after a long day at work. He sat in the car, not sure what he'd see once he got inside. He hoped Adaline had stayed home and taken care of herself a bit. Years of waiting were finally paying off. New opportunities at work had been given to him today. Ones he wanted to share with his wife, but being excited didn't help her feel better. Anything that would make her happy was good enough for him, especially since it seemed he couldn't give her what she needed. Cache felt clueless to know what that could be. They had been moving in different directions for months, even before the girls' deaths. He could feel the tension and frustration building up inside him.

The outside lights weren't turned on. Getting out of his car, he noticed the mail hadn't been gathered either.

Not looking good.

Stepping inside, the house was quiet.

"Addi, are you home?" Movement jostled from the front room. He glanced toward the lump on the couch and moved quickly over to the area. "Are you okay?" She had a blanket on and was curled up with it covering her body and face.

"I'm fine. Just another headache," she said in a whisper. "Can you please turn off the light?"

"Sure." He dimmed the lights. "Let me get you something to take off the edge."

Cache went to the cupboard, retrieved a large bottle of pills, and filled a cold glass of water.

"Here you go," he said, placing two pills in her hand. "I'll start a fire, and you'll warm up more quickly." He grabbed the box of matches on top of the fireplace. The match crackled as it hit against the rough patch of the box. A flame lit in his hand.

Adaline shuddered. "Cache, no. Blow it out. I don't want a fire, please." Her voice pleaded with him. He arched his eyebrows upward and blew out the candle.

Her reaction to the fire wasn't new, but they had made progress in the past.

Another setback.

He blew it out and sat next to Adaline on the couch, placing his hand over her leg. "How was your day?"

She swallowed the pills. "People waited outside to come into the store." Adaline looked at the ground.

"You went to work today?"

Adaline paused, then nodded, changing the subject.

"What about you? What happened in your day?" She sat up, attentive.

He hadn't seen this kind of interest in his needs for months.

This is good. Should I tell her my news?

He paused and scratched his chin.

"Cache. I'd love to know," Adaline said, reaching for his hand.

"I was assigned to be in charge of a board meeting today."

"A board meeting, already? You weren't prepared for that, were you?"

"No, but the adrenaline kicked in, and I pulled it off," he said.

Adaline leaned in, hugging him. "That's wonderful."

He gripped her, holding tight. They hadn't had this closeness in a while, and he longed for it. Her perfume drowned him in desire as he leaned in and smelled the base of her neck. She glanced up at him, and he tilted his head, bringing her lips to his. Cache caressed her face as a soft kiss turned to sparks of passion that had been dormant until now. Adaline gently clung to his hair, and his hands glided down her sides, still tangled in a tight embrace. She stopped kissing him and leaned away.

"What is it?" he asked, reaching for her hand.

"I was attacked today in my store."

He got up from the couch. "What? Did you call the police? Adaline glanced away. "No."

"Why the hell not?" He paced the floor, gripping the base of his neck. "Why didn't you call me?"

"I'm fine, thank you," she said.

Cache leaned down and looked at her. "I'm worried about you. Are you okay?"

"I'm fine now, but I have something I need to show you

that's proof I'm not crazy." Adaline scoured the room. "Do you see my coat?"

Cache stood and grabbed her coat hanging over the loveseat. "It's right here."

"Okay, in the pocket. There's a crumbled piece of paper."

Looking in both pockets of her coat, Cache's fingers went right through the fabric. "Nothing's in it. There's a hole, though."

Adaline bunched her fingers together. "That's just not possible. Give me the coat."

He brought it to her and watched her eyes grow wild as she opened her pockets, scratching through like a rampant dog. "Where is it?"

"What are you looking for?"

She glared up at him. "I got a threatening note, and it was my proof that I'm being followed, which you don't seem to believe."

Cache put his arm on her shoulder. "You said you were attacked. Let me see."

Throwing the blanket on the couch, Adaline stood and crossed her arms. "Why, so you can make sure I'm being honest? I'm going upstairs for a while."

"Babe, that's not what I'm saying. Tonight's date night. Why don't we go out and get some fresh air?" He grabbed his keys out of his pocket. "I saw this great Italian restaurant down the street from my work. It smelled divine."

Her eyes sank. "Can we stay in tonight an order takeout? I don't feel like going anywhere right now."

Cache hesitated. "Sure. We can go out some other time," he said, loosening his tie.

Adaline's face relaxed, and the tension in her eyes eased. "I'm going upstairs."

"Okay. I need to order the takeout. I'll be up shortly."

She nodded and went upstairs, moving in slow, lethargic movements.

Cache called the Italian place by his work, but they didn't do deliveries. He looked through his phone to find a pizza place nearby that delivered and called to place his order. Fifteen minutes until it was ready. He set his phone on the kitchen counter and walked into the living room.

He grabbed the remote off the coffee table and turned on the TV to see a shot of Lost Treasures filling the screen. Cache watched a clear shot of Adaline yelling at people outside the antique shop. He sat and watched for fifteen minutes, rewinding and fast-forwarding to get a visual on her face.

"It's unclear why the store didn't open today. The death of the Rushner girls has us all on edge these days," said a brown-haired reporter.

Great. It's only been a few days, and the media's following us.

Someone knocked at the door. Cache paused the TV and dropped his gaze. He cracked his knuckles and stood in place, trying to make sense of why Adaline left that part out about her day.

Was she attacked?

Is this another story of hers?

He didn't want to think she'd make up being attacked, but they'd been through all this before. She claimed everything she said was true, but she never had any proof to back her stories up.

The doorbell rang and Cache opened the door to a

young man, who handed him his food without saying a word.

"Thank you," Cache said, giving him a generous twenty-dollar bill. The kid nodded and ran to his car.

Cache shut the door and went upstairs. He paused, wondering if he should bring up the store incident with Adaline or wait and see if she told him herself.

Not tonight.

He didn't realize how hungry he was until he smelled marinara and garlic. His stomach growled to the rhythm of his heartbeat.

"The food's here, and it smells almost as good as the Italian place I passed today."

When he turned the corner into his bedroom, Adaline was fast asleep on their bed.

He sat on the floor, leaning against the base of the bed, and raised his slice of pizza in the air as a toast.

Cheers. Congratulations, Cachie boy. Eat up.

His first few bites turned into angry mouthfuls. At least he had something to take his frustration out on.

THIRTEEN

Rushner Home
Tuesday, November 9th
8:30 a.m.

OFFICER ABBOTT STOOD above Mrs. Rushner, waiting for her to reply. He was grateful he got ahold of her husband, because for the past fifteen minutes, she hadn't said a word. The lady's chin trembled, and her eyes held fear. He bent down and tried to speak to her again with a strict tone.

"Miss, I'm here to help you. Are you okay?"

She tilted her head upward at him and squinted her blue eyes as the sun hit her face.

"I...don't...know."

"I'm Officer Abbott, and this is my partner, Officer Keaton. Your neighbor called to report the accident over here. Can you tell me what happened?"

"Why are you outside, ma'am?"

She clutched her chest and breathed heavy and fast. It

seemed she was trying to stand up from her porch bench but wasn't strong enough to steady herself.

A gust of wind blew in a repulsive odor, stinging his nose. He still couldn't get used to the Great Salt Lake stench. She didn't seem to appreciate it either, as she cringed and held on to her stomach. She hunched down further and nodded her head in reply to his question. Her hands shook as she held the bench tightly. "My—my husband, you have to call him. Our girls are…alive."

"You have children?"

"Yes, two girls. Please, I need…to call him now."

"He's already on his way," he said.

Mrs. Rushner paused to catch her breath and cleared her throat. "I lost our girls. What is he going to think of me now? They were right. I am no good." She rocked back and forth, biting on her nail.

Abbott couldn't wrap his head around what was going on here. Mrs. Rushner said her girls were alive and then claimed she lost them. She seemed borderline delusional. Something about her was very familiar to him, but he couldn't place it. "I need to ask you some questions to understand what happened."

She sniffled and grabbed at her head again. "I'll answer your questions."

"Where are your girls?" he asked.

"They were in the kitchen, and someone took them, again."

Officer Abbott peered at her. "Again?"

Clenching her fingers together, she looked at him from the bench and nodded.

A car door slammed, and a man with well-trimmed brown hair and sideburns walked toward them. He appeared to be around thirty years old, 6'1", in good shape; he held no sign of being panicked, but more concerned.

Abbott stepped toward him. "Mr. Rushner, I assume."

"Yes."

"I'm Officer Abbott, the one who called you. Let me just make sure everything is all clear before we enter into your home."

Officer Keaton gave him a thumbs up from the front door. "Okay, we're a go. I need you and your wife to fill out a missing person's form and walk me through this morning."

"I understand. Can we speak in private in a moment?" Mr. Rushner asked.

Abbott stared at him and nodded. "All right." He began walking to the front door and paused.

Mrs. Rushner stood. Sweat dripped down her forehead and her lip quivered.

"I'm right here," Mr. Rushner said. He held her hand, and she followed behind him.

They made their way inside the house to furniture in shambles and broken shards of glass covering the wood floor where lamps and vases had fallen. The room looked like an intruder had come into their home and ransacked it. He waved Officer Keaton over and leaned in. "The other rooms?"

"Clean. No sign of tampering."

"They were right here and then they were gone," she said.

"Who?" Mr. Rushner asked.

"Leora and Eliza. They were eating and then they went outside, so I ran after them. I'm not sure what happened after that. Maybe I tripped or got hit in the head. I don't know."

"Ad." Mr. Rushner kept rubbing his wrists, and the tone of his voice echoed stress directed toward her.

"Are Leora and Eliza your children?" Abbott asked.

"Our girls. Officer, they're alive still. We need your help." Mrs. Rushner held an object in her hand that dangled between her fingers—a gold chain with a green pendant. He stepped closer, trying to get a peek. On the face of the pendant was an owl. It was the same one left at the crime scene of his daughter, Aspen, when she disappeared a year ago. Abbott held his face and paced the floor.

Did the necklace mean something to her?

What was she hiding?

Mrs. Rushner stared at the kitchen table with horror. "How could I lose them again?" She gripped her throat, sunk to the ground, and screamed.

FOURTEEN

Adaline Rushner
Tuesday, November 9th
9:15 a.m.

ADALINE COULD BREATHE EASIER NOW, but inside she was still screaming in ways that made her body crawl. The girls had been so close to her, confirming everything she believed for the past few weeks. They were alive.

"Take some deep breaths, honey. I'm right here." Cache had concern in his brown eyes as he caressed her face. He gave her a paper bag and rubbed her forehead.

Officer Abbott positioned himself right next to the kitchen table. His eyes narrowed on her for a split second before he spoke to a short man with black-rimmed glasses.

"How do you feel?" Cache asked, handing her a glass of water.

She gripped the glass with shaking hands, trying to bring it to her mouth. The water spilled and rushed between the cracks in the wood floor. Setting the cup down, Adaline stumbled toward the front door. She felt winded, like there was no air in her lungs to supply her every breath. She studied the two men with Officer Abbott. Her neck stiffened. A lanky man with pale skin brushed past her, and the hairs on her arm stood upward. "Who is he?" Adaline pointed in the man's direction.

Cache stepped close to the door and kissed her on the head. His tough arms wrapped tightly around her shoulder blade. "He's here to assist." He paused and opened her hand. "Why are you still holding on to that necklace? It's caused us enough pain."

"We believe different things." She held the middle of the owl pendant and closed her eyes. "What if they aren't who they say they are?"

He intertwined his fingers into hers and turned to face her. "Did you see the girls like you did before, in the car?"

Adaline opened her eyes. "I didn't imagine it. I saw them like I'm seeing you now."

Officer Abbott shuffled into the living room and raised his eyebrows. He placed his hands in his pocket and licked his lips. "Mrs. Rushner, did you do this to your furniture, or was it someone else?"

"What? No. Someone was in my house with the girls," she said.

Officer Abbott raised his voice and gestured to the jumbled mess in their living room. "Your neighbor said she heard screaming and came to check on you. When she passed your front room window, she said you were tearing your house apart."

What's he talking about? She had the urge to jump up and run away. Nothing made any sense to her. *I would remember if I lost it, wouldn't I?* "

Cache stepped toward her and squeezed her hand. "My wife's been through a lot."

Officer Abbott took out a ballpoint pen and a small notebook from his pocket. Scrunching his nose, he examined the room like he was taking inventory and jotted down some notes. "The thing is, Mr. and Mrs. Rushner, my partner was informed by your neighbor that she's never seen you with kids since you moved in a few days ago."

Adaline cupped her mouth with her hand. She peered at him like a fly she wanted to swat. Cache paced the floor, the blood vessels in his forehead bunched together.

"I've never met our neighbor, but she sure knows a lot about us. Maybe she's in on this attack." Her voice raised an octave.

Officer Abbott frowned and stared at her necklace. "Mrs. Rushner, could you indulge me for a minute? That necklace is unique. Quite rare, I'd say. Do you mind me asking where you got that from?"

"Officer, what is this about?" Cache asked.

"Just making conversation. It really is one of a kind, wouldn't you say?"

Adaline held it tightly. "Yes, I would agree. A friend gave it to me when I was a child."

He wrote something in his notebook and gazed up at her. "Is this friend still around?"

"Not that I know of. Why?" she asked.

"No reason." He tilted his head and stepped backward.

She grabbed her phone and scrolled through her pictures. "Please, I'm begging you to look at this picture for one minute."

Abbott hesitated before taking the phone from her. He stared at the picture and gasped.

Why did he gasp?

Adaline watched his hard exterior turn soft for a minute while he gripped her phone in his hand.

"This here is your oldest?" he asked, pointing to Leora's face.

"Yes," she said.

He crossed his arms, tilted his shoulders back, and looked away from the picture. His solid build grew stiff and his expression turned heavy.

"Addi, why don't you go get a few of their favorite items to show Officer Abbott," Cache said.

"That's a good idea." She squeezed his hand and walked slowly around the corner.

Cache believes in me. Don't get angry with Officer Abbott. It will only make things worse.

She grabbed Pinkerton and Leora's journal and halted before turning the corner.

"Our girls are dead, Officer. This is a misunderstanding," Cache said. "We moved to get away from the media and to get a fresh start. Can we settle this and have you go on your way?"

"She must be dealing with quite a bit of trauma to believe she saw her girls. You need to get her checked."

"Thank you for your concern, but my wife's been this way before today," he said. "She's struggled with PTSD and hallucinations for a long time."

"You said she was attacked though, is that correct?" Officer Abbott asked.

Neither one of them is on my side.

Adaline cleared her throat as she walked out of the bedroom. "Yes, I was attacked yesterday at my store, and my girls were taken by an intruder. Here are my girls' items. I need to fill out a missing person's report."

Cache and Officer Abbott exchanged looks and glanced back at her.

"What are you both waiting for? We're wasting time." Adaline placed her hand on her heart and smiled. "Cache, could you get me a drink of water, please?"

He nodded and walked to the kitchen.

Adaline leaned into Officer Abbott and held his arm. "You gasped when you saw the picture of my daughter. Why?"

"No reason."

"And my necklace?"

"I told you. It's one of a kind. My wife likes antiques," Abbott said.

"I don't believe you. I'm not lying, and deep down you know something's off here."

Officer Abbott rubbed his hands together and turned away. "Thank you, Mrs. Rushner. I think I got all I need. I'll be in touch." He walked to the front door and glanced back at her one last time before he left.

FIFTEEN

Dr. Lynchester
Tuesday, November 9th
12:00 p.m.

DR. LYNCHESTER GOT into her office after an early lunch and shielded her eyes from the blinding light coming through her windows. The week seemed to drag on forever, and it was only Tuesday. She dropped her daily planner on the desk and unlatched it to see what appointments were on the agenda. Having only a handful of sessions a day was all she could handle. Distancing herself from her client's problems didn't work well. She took home every case in her mind, stewing over how their lives could be better or how she could possibly help them.

Opening her cabinet, Dr. Lynchester pulled out some files and put them in order according to appointments. She had half an hour before her next session began.

"You can't go in there. You don't have an appointment today," the receptionist yelled down the hall.

Dr. Lynchester glanced down the hallway, took a deep breath, and walked toward the front desk. She held a finger up to her client. Taking the phone out of the receptionist's hand, she put the receiver to her ear.

"Yes. I'm sorry for the noise." She paused. "How can I help make it better for you? I agree, and I understand why you're frustrated. Your next session will be free of charge." Placing the phone in the cradle, Dr. Lynchester glared at the receptionist and directed her attention to her client. "Make yourself comfortable in my office. I have some time. I'll be there in a second."

"I'm sorry," the receptionist said.

Dr. Lynchester turned back toward her. "Tayla, please don't do that again. We'll discuss it more later."

She nodded.

Strolling down the hall, Dr. Lynchester shook her arms out before entering her office. She turned the corner and smiled. "We don't have an appointment until next week. Are you okay?" she asked, taking a seat in her lounge chair.

The client looked sleep-deprived and unwell. Her eyes drooped, and her skin held an unhealthy yellow tint. Normally she dressed nicely, but today she wore an oversized T-shirt and jeans with multiple holes in them. Sections of her hair were matted and hadn't been combed.

"No. I'm not well. I'm not sure I can do this anymore."

"Do what? Talk to me about it," Dr. Lynchester said.

"Follow through with the plan." The client fidgeted, and her hands shook.

"What plan? The action plan we talked about three weeks ago?"

She snorted. "You think I care about your plan? There's a bigger plan at play here."

"How about you enlighten me on this bigger plan?" Dr. Lynchester sat at the edge of her seat and hunched over just enough to show her interest.

The client bounced her foot up and down. "I can't. That's the problem. I want to, but I can't. They know too much. If I make a wrong move, they'll know I failed."

"Sometimes you have to show people you're in charge. Tell them you won't follow the plan."

Loud laughter echoed across the room. "You shrinks are funny. You always think talking is the solution for everything. See, I'm in too deep now, Doc. There's no getting out of this one unless I want to die."

Chills ran across Dr. Lynchester's back and she pulled her sweater on. "What are you into? I can help you." She reached for her hand. "Is it drugs? Money? Is someone harassing you? I can get you protection."

"Drugs . . . not this time. Money?" The client paused. "Money's always a problem, isn't it? You get in bed with the wrong person, and before you know it, they control you."

"So, you're being harassed? Is someone harming you?"

"I've been harassed by this person for a long time and—"

"And what?"

The woman held her finger over her mouth and stood up, retrieving something from her pocket. She continued to gaze around the room and began throwing books onto the floor. The client brushed past, stuffing an object in Dr. Lynchester's jacket. She moved close to Dr. Lynchester's face.

"There's no saving me, Doc," she whispered in her ear. Stepping back, she kicked the chair next to her foot. Her voice raised as she walked out of the room. "Thanks for the enlightening conversation." The door slammed shut, knocking Dr. Lynchester's lamp off the side table, shattering it into pieces.

She gazed around her office, taking in the mess her client just made. Oddly, there was no anger as she tore the office apart; it was more like a distraction of some sort. Dr. Lynchester bent down to pick up the pieces of the lamp. Something caught her eye in the mix of glass, and she leaned closer to retrieve a black object.

A bug.

The room had been bugged. She remembered the item her client left her and placed her cold hand into her jacket pocket. Something crinkled in her hand as she gripped it and brought it to her face. An old piece of crumbled newspaper gnawed at her curiosity as she opened it. Big bold letters written in Sharpie said "Protect Adaline" across the header.

SIXTEEN

Adaline Rushner
Tuesday, November 9th
12:30 p.m.

ADALINE AWOKE to the house being empty and quiet. Her mind still felt foggy, but a new sense of being vigilant awakened after Officer Abbott's curious reactions to both her necklace and Leora's picture. The eagerness to find out the truth activated, giving Adaline energy and purpose.

She moved to Leora's bed, replacing Pinkerton gently in its place, and without hesitation flipped to the last entry in her journal.

October 11,
I need a camera to catch the bad guy. Last nite I saw him outside my window. I went to sleep and he was there too, in my dreem with the owl. My mommy was there but she could not see me. I dont like the owls. I don't think Mommy can see them anymore,

but she needs to remember the little owls so the bad guy will go away. I need to help her. Leora V. R.

Adaline shivered.

Little Owl.

The man at her store called her that. She dropped her head into her hands.

Remember the little owls so the bad guy will go away.

She lay down on the floor, resting the journal on her chest. It moved up and down in sync with her breathing. Adaline closed her eyes to focus on the day's events and mouthed the words "remember the little owls" a few times.

A fire blazing, her parents screaming, and an unknown face staring at her, as a memory flashed in her mind.

She jolted as she gasped for breath, and the pages in Leora's journal scattered across the floor. Adaline scrambled to pick them up and choked on what tasted like smoke.

"Addi, what are you doing in here?" Cache frowned.

She looked up at him. "Fire."

Cache came to her, gripping her hand. "What fire?"

"I saw them burning…screaming."

"Who?"

"My parents," she said. "I felt the intensity of the heat on my arms."

"You're going through a lot of trauma," he said. "Let me go get your pills."

"But I saw a face in the flames."

"Whose face?"

She picked at her nail. "I'm not sure. It's blurry. Why can't I see the face?"

"The fire your parents died in was an accident. Let it go," he said. "You need some sleep."

Adaline shook her head. "You're not listening to me. I don't think my parents' death was an accident, and I don't think our girls missing is a coincidence. I know something. Why can't I remember?"

"Come here." He pulled Adaline into his arms. "I can't go through this. Not again. I'm not going to sit in this room with all their toys and pretend like this isn't killing me."

Adaline held his hand. "What do you mean, again? We have to have faith."

"I don't believe in faith."

She peered away. "Then believe in me."

Cache's cell phone rang and he let go of her hand. "I need to take this call. I'll be right back."

Adaline nodded and dug her fingernails into Leora's journal.

Who was the person with the blurred face? Who would take the girls? How did my parents die?

Too many unsolved questions.

"I'll take care of it," Cache said from the hall.

What's he up to?

Too many secrets, even within the walls of this prison she lived in. Whoever had been targeting her and watching her girls in the weeks before they were taken had no idea what she was capable of. Now there would be no mercy.

SEVENTEEN

Officer Abbott
Salt Lake Police Station
12:30 p.m.

EASTON ABBOTT HAD SPENT most of the morning at the Rushner's place. Both the husband and wife had a different story about what happened to their girls, but he couldn't think of anything other than the owl necklace he'd just seen. It teased him all morning and pulled at his heartstrings.

He bunched his fists.

Aspen.

Abbott rubbed his bald head and went to the coffeemaker, placing a Styrofoam cup under the spout. Walking back to his desk, he positioned the cup next to a picture of his daughter and tugged on the beaded bracelet around his wrist that said "Daddy." He wished many times that she'd miraculously be found, but after a year, hope had vanished. The picture Mrs. Rushner gave him of their daughter, Leora, looked exactly like his daughter, Aspen. That brought some mistaken belief back that there could be a chance.

He took a sip of his coffee and opened his laptop. In the search engine, he typed "Rushner" and paused.

Don't do this.

It's over.

Move on.

Abbott tapped his fingers on the desk and stared at the picture of Aspen. The remorse taunted him, and his craving intensified. Opening his cabinet, he looked at the bottle of Vodka enticing him to forget the pain.

"How are you holding up, Champ?" Chief Stalk asked.

He slammed the cabinet and turned around in his chair. "What?"

"I heard you were the first patrol officer at the Rushners' place today. I knew their case would hit home," he said. "I'd hoped you weren't the one to respond to it."

"Why would it hit home?" Abbott asked.

Chief Stalk peered at the laptop and pointed. "Looks like you were about to do some research."

He grimaced and nodded.

"That case is never one you want to witness or hear about. Just awful." The chief shook his head. "We all know about that, don't we?"

Abbott cracked his knuckles. "I'm not following."

"The Rushners' just moved here. Their girls are the headliners right now and all the media has been talking about," he said. "The Brutal Owling Murder. No need to send a missing person's report."

Holding the desk, Abbott realized the comment the chief mentioned earlier was directed at him.

Aspen's disappearance.

He looked away. His job had enough for him to see firsthand that the news hadn't been something he paid much attention to. That explained why the Rushers' appeared to be at war with each other. Grief takes you down roads you don't plan, until it happens, and coping with it becomes a whole different beast. Abbott understood that well.

"Champ?"

"Yes, Chief?" Abbott asked, staring at him.

Tapping his foot, Stalk stared back for a minute. "Do we have a problem?"

"No. I can handle it."

"That's not what I'm talking about." He took off his glasses and peered down at him. "Is this case too close to home?"

Abbott sank his head and took another sip of his coffee. "We're good. I'm clean *now*."

"Good man." Chief Stalk patted him on the shoulder. "What did Mrs. Rushner say happened?"

"She believes someone was in their house this morning, with her girls, which clearly is not possible," he said.

"I see. Mr. Rushner?"

"He mentioned they had . . . died."

The chief nodded. "Okay. I need you to file a report. Also, can you call and tell the Rushners' to come into the station?"

Abbott scratched his head. "Sir?"

"She's off her rocker claiming she saw her daughters, but maybe whoever hurt their girls is after her. Or, there's always a chance she collaborated to harm her own children and is staging this whole thing." He combed his mustache. "They just moved to our city. We need to figure out what we're dealing with here."

"Is the murderer still at large?"

"They believe the man who captured them is dead as well," Stalk said. "It doesn't hurt to keep an eye on this situation though."

Memories flooded in of the night his partner knocked on the door, telling him the news about his own daughter. After she vanished, he became the worst version of himself. There wasn't a reason to keep the world safe if he couldn't even protect his own child. Abbott closed his eyes.

The owl necklace.

What if Mrs. Rushner harmed his daughter or knew information about what happened to her? And if she was in on hurting those girls of hers, he wanted justice to be served.

His hand trembled. "I absolutely agree. We should investigate them more."

Chief Stalk patted him on the shoulder. "Thanks, Champ."

He squeezed his phone and dialed the number written on his report. Abbott shook his head, the desire for a shot of whiskey nearly overwhelming. He *hoped* this wasn't too close to home.

EIGHTEEN

Adaline Rushner
Tuesday, November 9th
1:00 p.m.

THE POLICE STATION held an aroma of coffee, and Adaline couldn't see any sign of their girls. Her hands shook as she gripped her purse.

"Where are they?" she asked.

"Officer Abbott just said they need more information, honey." Cache held her hand, and she could feel that his shook too. Their nerves seemed to be flowing an anxious and excited dance together through their fingers. She could taste the energy flowing through her. Adaline stood on her tiptoes and scanned every area of the room. Her eyes grazed over a dead tree in the corner, and her heart sank. A water fountain and some cups were on her right side. She let go of Cache's hand to fill a cup with water, then moved through the desks to sit next to the tree. She slowly let the water soak the soil to feed the already dead tree, waiting for it to come back to life and stand tall on its own. For its essence to come forth. It didn't move, and dread grabbed her. It was gone. This beautiful creation had no more strength in its limbs. She held her stomach and walked back to Cache.

"Love you. Don't forget that, okay?" Cache said.

"I love you too. We're going to find them."

He kissed and squeezed her hand, and she squeezed back.

A big office toward the back had glass doors that read "Lieutenant Stalk." Adaline knew he had seen them come in, but he still sat at his desk without acknowledging their presence. The man's head was as shiny as a marble, and his dark brown mustache looked overly groomed, like he combed it multiple times a day. She tapped her foot and cleared her throat.

"They'll be with us in a minute," Cache said.

"They can't just call and leave us here to wait. He's just sitting there."

"We're not the only ones who have problems."

Adaline growled at him and let go of his hand. She stomped to the lieutenant's door and knocked with force.

The man glanced up, shook his head, and opened the door. "Can I help you?"

"Excuse me. I'm looking for Officer Abbott. We're supposed to meet him here. He's expecting us."

"Mr. and Mrs. Rushner, I presume. Thank you for coming in so quickly. I'm Lieutenant Stalk, and I asked Officer Abbott to call you."

"Do you know where our girls are?" Adaline asked.

"Can you both come in and take a seat?"

Cache exchanged a glance with her, and they made their way to the hard chairs across from his desk. He placed his hand on her leg, and she could tell he was bracing himself. Adaline put her hand on top of his, the warmth comforting her. Sitting at the edge of her chair, she held still almost forgetting to breathe.

Lieutenant Stalk moved his mug of coffee to the side. He tapped his fingers on his desk with perfect tempo to the ticking of the clock and glanced at Adaline. Holding her gaze for a moment, he shifted his sight on Cache.

Why was he acting so weird? My girls are fine, I can feel it.

"All right, folks. Listen, I'm aware you just moved in and want to make sure there won't be any more disturbances."

"I don't quite understand your question," she said. "We just moved here, less than a week ago, from Owling. Honestly, we don't know any of our neighbors yet. I've been so busy unpacking, I haven't been able to do anything else. We've kept to ourselves."

Cache didn't move. Adaline squeezed his hand in hopes it would jolt him out of his trance. Nothing.

Lieutenant Stalk shook his head. "I'm aware of your story. Most people are, so carrying on that your girls are alive is drawing attention and creating chaos."

The sound of her heartbeat thrashed in her ears, and tingling ran up her arms. Adaline could see Cache talking to her, but the volume muffled.

She had to make a move. No one was on her side. She had to leave and never come back. Adaline ran for the door and held the doorknob, but it wouldn't budge. Arms grabbed her waist and pulled her backward as she kicked at the ground. She couldn't hear herself scream, but she raged her protest, and the room got heavier until the spinning stopped and she let go.

NINETEEN

Cache Rushner
Police Station with Officer Abbott
1:30 p.m.

ADALINE'S FACE was swollen and blotchy, adding years to her fair complexion. She'd finally settled down. Cache held out his hand, waiting for her to take it, but she kept her fingers clenched together. It still stung thinking about his little girls' bodies, lifeless and charred, and imaging the pain that they endured. He'd thought he would have all the time in the world with his princesses. Many more daddy/daughter dates, plays, tickle contests, and backyard games of hide-and-seek. Cache had held hope they would find the girls in time. He'd had faith then, and it failed him . . . and Adaline. She, however, never stopped believing. The only way he slept at night was knowing the bastard who took his girls had died too.

Cache gripped his neck.

"Talk to me," he said.

Adaline sat in silence. She stared at the spot in front of her on the floor.

Cache put one hand on her knee and lifted her head with the other. Her eyes held emptiness and something else he hadn't seen before. Not fear or sadness. They didn't dance to life but were cold and dark. He used to be able to look right into her eyes and know exactly what she was thinking or feeling. She was always so easy to read, until now. He had no idea what went on in her head. That unsettled him. He covered his mouth with his hand, unaware of what to say or do.

"Mr. Rushner, can I have a minute?" Officer Abbott asked, peering at Adaline. "Mrs. Rushner? Can I get you a drink?"

She shook her head at him. "A drink? How strong of a drink will you get me?"

Officer Abbott winced at the comment.

"She'd like a Coke," Cache said.

"I can speak for myself. Haven't they done enough? Now they're asking me if I could use a drink. What I could use is some support." She leaned in toward Cache and whispered in his ear. "The girls are *not* dead."

Cache tilted his head and whispered back. "Leave this alone. They're gone, my love." He went to embrace her, but she shoved past him and ran out of the police station.

"You can take her home, and we can talk later," Officer Abbott said.

"What the hell is this? I told you, our girls are dead." He bunched his fists. "Why bring us back in? Do you think this is funny, messing with our emotions like this?"

Abbott put his finger to his lips. "Mr. Rushner, lower your voice. I didn't do this." He gestured for Cache to follow him. "The lieutenant will be with us shortly."

"Give me a minute to make sure she's okay."

"Of course."

Cache went out the front doors of the station to spot Adaline sitting in the car, her head leaning back against the seat, her eyes closed. He went back in and approached Abbott. "We do need to talk, and we need to talk *now*."

Abbott opened his arm, leading him into what appeared to be the holding room, a small enough space to fit a card table and two chairs. There was barely any room for much else.

"I have some questions, and you need to get some things off your chest about this case. So why don't you start by telling me what's wrong with your wife."

"Why are you being so secretive and bringing me in this room?"

Clearing his throat, Abbott sat down in a chair. "When you lose someone you care for, everything changes. We change." He gulped. "I gave up on wanting to save people. Just trying to be a lifeline for them."

Cache dug his fist into his pant leg. "She's decorated a room in our new house for the girls. She puts plates on the table for all of us, and she wants things to be ready for when they come back to us." Cache paused and wiped his eye. "You saw it when you were at our house."

"She's in shock. With what you've been through, that makes sense," he said. "What happened that morning?"

Cache moved his chair backward. "I'd left early to get my oldest daughter, Leora, a present. It was her birthday that week, and she kept asking for a camera. She seemed obsessed with needing one at that very moment, but you know how impatient kids are." He paused. "My youngest asked if I could play in the snow with her. First snow of the year. I asked for a raincheck and left to get Leora's gift on the way to work.

I missed my last moment with Eliza.

"Then what happened?"

"An officer called me an hour after I left saying there had been an accident."

"What did you see when you got home?"

"Adaline didn't know where the girls were. Once the police took our statements, they hoped she could provide some information that would lead to finding the girls," Cache said.

"Did she provide any information about who took them?"

"No. Not a thing."

"Were you angry with her?" Officer Abbott raised his eyebrows.

"To be honest, a little bit. I just wanted to know something, anything, that happened from the time I left until the time I got back."

"Do you think what she said was true?" Officer Abbott asked, folding his arms over his chest.

"I believe she believes it's true. Other than that, I don't know."

"Why don't you believe your wife?"

"I just don't think she's with it. She's confused. Like I mentioned before, she has massive PTSD. I'm afraid she's going backward with all the recent trauma."

"Mr. Rushner, I need to ask this. Do you think your wife would hurt your children . . . or other children?"

Cache stood from his chair and ground his teeth. "Officer, my wife grew up with abusive parents who treated her like shit, but if there's one thing I'm positive about, Adaline would never harm our children. She loved those girls."

"I'm sorry. I had to ask."

Cache's shoulder's lowered and his jaw loosened. "I understand. I'm just tired of reliving this."

"You believe your girls are dead?"

"Yes. They did an autopsy report, and it was verified that the bodies were our daughters. Believe me, I wish I wasn't such a realist sometimes, but I am. If the cops say that they're dead, then they must be. Why would they tell me otherwise?" he asked, out of breath.

"How has your wife been acting lately?"

"She's changed," Cache said. "I expected that. She's struggling in her own way, but she seems like a whole different person—withdrawn, tired, depressed, and she gets angry or upset over everything. She's impulsive and neurotic all the time.

"She could probably use some counseling."

"I don't know if counseling will be enough. It would be a struggle, but well worth the try."

"I can help you with that. Here's a psychologist I wanted to refer you to. Here's her number." Abbott handed him a piece of paper.

"Thank you. Should I wait for your lieutenant, or can I go?"

"I'll give him the information. You can leave, and here's my card too." He cleared his throat. "I know how tragedies can make you turn into your own worst nightmare. Get her some help before it's too late."

"Will do." Cache thanked him again and headed to the car to find the door wide open, and Adaline was long gone.

TWENTY

Officer Abbott
Salt Lake Police Station
2:00 p.m.

ABBOTT SAT at his desk with his hand under his chin, staring at a page full of scribbled notes he took while talking to Mr. Rushner.

Something's not right. He seemed too calm.

Mrs. Rushner was a different story, but she at least showed emotion to what was going on. His eyes felt heavy and his head ached.

"Abbott, what were you doing with Mr. Rushner?" Lieutenant Stalk asked.

"Gave him the number for his wife that you requested, sir."

"Why don't you head out and take the rest of the shift off? This is a hard case after everything with your daughter."

He clenched his jaw and rubbed his bald head. "Not

yet. I've got to get this file finished before I have you look over it." Abbott cleared his throat. "Do you think the Rushner case could be connected to other cases?"

"Why? There's no evidence showing a connection to other cases."

The necklaces, ages, resemblance of the girls.

Abbott looked down at the floor. The kidnapper could be targeting certain young girls. His Aspen, Leora, maybe others.

Lieutenant Stalk scratched his mustache. "What's going on here?"

"Nothing."

He peered at Abbott and raised his eyebrows. "If you say nothing's going on here, I believe you." He walked toward his office and shut the door behind him.

Holding his wrist, Abbott felt for his bracelet, only to feel smoothness. The bracelet wasn't there. Looking over his desk, he frantically moved picture frames and papers to find only dust. Abbott traced his steps back to his car, holding on to his wrist.

I can't lose it.

Looking in the window of his car, he saw the colorful bracelet on his seat, summoning him. Smiling, he unlocked the door and grabbed it, putting it back where it belonged. He paused to take a deep breath and went back into the station.

His headache made it hard to focus. Abbott went to the restroom and turned the faucet on. Leaning his head down, he took a handful of water into his hands and splashed it on his face. The water helped him to wake up a little more.

Focus.

He grabbed a paper towel and dried his face and

hands, removing the excess water from his fingers. Opening the door, Abbott fumbled in his pocket to pull out some aspirin. Since he stopped drinking, headaches occurred regularly from withdrawals. He craved a sip of vodka at least a couple of times a week, but his AA meetings and his regular AA buddy calls helped him to repress the urge. Abbott put the aspirin in his mouth, tilted his head back, and felt them go down his throat. He flicked his bracelet and opened the bathroom door, bumping into the lieutenant.

"Got another headache?" the chief asked.

Abbott nodded. "I'm going to head out."

"All right. See you tomorrow."

He put his coat on, then walked out to his car. Starting the engine, he drove down the street to an abandoned gas station and pulled over. Taking a deep breath, he took out his phone.

He scrolled through the photos he took the day his daughter went missing. The details of the object were already etched into his mind, from the gold chain to the silver owl centered in the middle. But the green eyes of the winged bird haunted and teased him. Just like the first time he held it when it was left in his daughter's place.

Mocking him.

He was a cop, yet he couldn't protect his own child, and the bastard thought he'd leave a token showing he now possessed his most precious gift.

Abbott growled and covered his face. An owl necklace at another crime scene. He held his chest.

No. How is this possible?

Could the person who kidnapped Aspen be back to start again with other families?

TWENTY-ONE

Cache Rushner
Tuesday, November 9th
2:00 p.m.

HE GLANCED DOWN THE STREET. This wasn't the first time Adaline took off because she was upset. She avoided her problems like the plague. He took out his cell phone and dialed her number, only to hear her ringtone nearby.

Great, just great.

Cache peered into the car to find her phone on the passenger seat right next to her purse.

Why would she leave her purse?

When Adaline got upset, she would leave her phone at home. She had a hard time staying mad at him for long and would give in if he called, so she never took it with her. But her purse? Glancing down the street again, he squinted against the blare of the sun. A post office and laundromat sat across the street and, right next door, a hamburger joint. The Adaline he knew four months ago

123

never ate when she felt upset, but so much had changed, maybe she would now. Further down the street, a large patch of ice invited skaters to take a spin.

The girls loved to ice skate. The snow always made them happy.

A car horn honked, pulling him from his thought. He jogged across the street and down to the skating rink that had enough power to light up the whole city. A family of four held hands, all covered from head to toe in winter gear. One little girl with blonde curly hair had a pink princess snow hat with matching gloves and boots. Her little sister had the same outfit except in purple. They laughed and giggled as their dad twirled them in the air while he skated. Their mom watched from the cold ground where she had fallen for the third time since Cache watched, but she was in good spirits. The little girl would pull her mom up only to have her mother pull her back down and hug her tight. They played this game a few times.

This was supposed to be their family. It *was* their family, a few months ago.

Someone sniffled from behind him. Cache turned and spotted Adaline sitting on a bench, dabbing at her raw nose.

"Addi? Why did you leave? I was worried," he said, sitting down next to her.

"I got tired of waiting in the car. I know you were talking about me. For once, I'd like to not be treated like a lunatic," she whispered underneath her breath. "I'm not crazy, Cache."

"Ad, I don't think you're crazy."

"You don't? Because I'm pretty sure you do. You walk on eggshells around me," she said, looking at the ground.

"I don't. I promise."

"That's it. Stop lying to me. You don't believe that the girls are alive, do you?"

"They're not alive. They died." He paused before he continued. "I need my wife. Please. Stop this nonsense."

"Nonsense?" she said, raising her voice.

"Please, lower your voice. There're families here." He grabbed her hand. "Why don't we talk at home?"

Adaline looked at the family skating on the ice rink. "We were happy like that once. Remember?"

"We can still be happy like that. We have each other."

"How can we have each other when you don't trust me? I don't like the way you look at me—like you think I'm going to explode and lose it any moment," she said. "I need you, too. Do you know that I left the grand opening of my store?"

Cache's face fell. "I saw the news last night when you fell asleep. I was hoping you'd tell me yourself. Why did you lie to me? Trust goes both ways."

"I told you it went great because I didn't want to disappoint or upset you…again."

"You don't disappoint me."

"Stop." Adaline sneered at him. "For once, tell *me* how you're feeling rather than talking to a complete stranger about it."

Cache held the base of his neck.

"You go first. You haven't told me anything since the day the girls died. I have no idea what happened, and I need some answers. Ones only you can give me."

"You think I have the answers? You really think I wouldn't tell you what happened to our girls if I knew?" She wiped her eye. "Who do you think I am?"

"You believe so much that they're alive, yet you have

no information as to what happened. Look from my perspective; I left my three girls for a short time. You were all safe, happy, and enjoying the snow. I come back to all three of you gone—vanished. All I have left are pictures of burnt bodies and a wife who I don't recognize anymore." Cache swallowed hard and glanced back at the family on the skating rink. He wanted that life. The one he couldn't have anymore.

"I did vanish, and I'm not the same. But neither are you."

Cache peered back at Adaline. "How can you blindly believe something with no proof? You've given me none, yet you're mad that I'm not following you."

Adaline clenched her hands together. "I know how I sound. It's not rational, and I don't have proof. Things come back to me in spurts, and I don't understand why. But when you love someone, you never give up on them. When they change, you find a way to see who they are and start to mold back together again."

"It goes both ways."

"I agree. We both have to work at this. We've both changed, which means I need to see you as you are now, and you need to see me."

"I can do that, but you have to let go of the girls. They're gone. We can't move forward when we're looking back."

Adaline laughed. "I guess that's that. You'll never believe me, but I'm not giving up on myself and our girls."

He placed his arm around her shoulder. "I'm not asking for you to give up on yourself."

Adaline moved his arm from her shoulder and looked away. "I can't be with someone who doesn't support me," she said, getting up from the bench. "Please take me home."

Cache grabbed at her arm as she twisted out of his grip and walked away, not looking back. She used to always glance back when they got in fights, but not this time. This fight was different, and he knew it. He slammed his fists against the bench, making a cracking sound. Pain surged through his fingers. Cache looked up to see people staring at him—just not the right person.

TWENTY-TWO

Officer Abbott
Tuesday, November 9th
3:30 p.m.

Sitting down at Sally's diner on Main Street, Abbott took a menu from the shelf. He glanced at the specials and debated which one sounded good. Having a drink was much more appealing than food at the moment. He shook his knee and fidgeted with his fingers.

Come on.

He glanced down at his watch, only to realize the second hand had frozen in place. Abbott tapped a few times, hoping to give it a jolt.

"Excuse me, miss," he said to a waitress.

"Yes, are you ready to order?" she asked, with the biggest smile he'd ever seen.

Wow. Her cheeks have got to hurt.

He tried not to show his amusement at her extreme

enthusiasm. "Not quite, but I would like to know the time."

"Sure thing," she replied in a southern accent.

Weird. She just changed voices.

She laughed. "I get that look a lot. I'm trying out for a part as Patsy in the Broadway play *Oklahoma*. Have you heard of it?"

"I can't say I have," he said. "I'm not much for musicals."

"That's too bad, sugar. They're good for you," she said, smirking. "Gives you more culture. Everyone needs that in their life, you know." She paused. "Oh heavens, here I am talking, and I can't remember what you asked for. Guess I'm not getting a tip tonight." She snorted and patted her leg. He couldn't figure out if she was laughing or choking. It seemed to be an odd combination of both.

"Um, the time would be great," he said.

"That's right. Let me go check."

The waitress had his nerves tangled in a knot with her energy, and waiting while she barked jokes wasn't settling his urge to leave.

"Abbott?"

He turned toward the sound of his name.

"Hey. Thanks for coming," he said.

Sam Wendell hugged him and sat down at the table. "It's good to see you, man."

"You, too. Why are you down this way, anyway? And don't tell me it's because I called," he said, punching Sam in the arm.

Sam smirked. "It really was though."

"Shit, dude. No, really, why are you down here?"

"I just got into town an hour ago for business. Besides,

what's an AA buddy if you can't call them when you need help?"

"Noted," he said. Sam still had the same spiky brown hair with red tints on the edges which he had made fun of the last time he saw him months ago. "Still going through your punk rocker stage? You're thirty now. A tad old for that, don't you think?" Abbott said, raising his eyebrows at him.

"Yeah, yeah. What about you, tough guy?"

"You're the same size as I am now. Can't dog the muscles," he said, kissing his arm.

Sam leaned in toward the table. "So, what's going on?"

Abbott shook his head. "I'm having withdrawals."

"What's bringing those on?"

"I came across a case, and there are new leads that have unfolded."

"Why kind of new leads?"

"They have to do with my daughter." Abbott held his fists together. "Evidence from my daughter's disappearance has developed in this other case I'm looking into."

"How did you stumble upon this information?" Sam asked.

"A lady needed some help, and she reminded me of myself when I first lost Aspen. She's angry, confused, and holding on to some false hope that somehow her daughters are still alive." He looked away. "She's drowning in self-pity, just as I did. The only difference is I drowned my worries in shots of vodka and whiskey."

"Do you feel the need to save her?"

"Oddly, yes. I couldn't save my marriage, you know. I lost everything all at the same time. Everything I worked so hard to make stable and great just fell apart."

"Are you looking back into this case because you want answers for yourself, or do you want to help this woman?" Sam asked.

"I need closure."

"You still feel responsible for your daughter's disappearance? Why?"

"I'm a cop. Isn't that what we do this for—to protect our families from all the shit we see and hear about? Taking down one dangerous criminal after another to make the world a better place."

"You've got to stop, man," Sam said. "We can't save the world. Bad things happen." He paused, deciding what to say.

"Everyone keeps saying that. Even Peyton was mad at me. The way she looked at me before she left, full of disappointment." Abbott held his head.

"I can't tell you if she blames you for that day or not, but your wife had plenty of reason to be mad. Your drinking almost ruined your marriage. That's why we're here, talking to each other," he said. "Take it a day at a time. Being separated doesn't mean it's a done deal. Keep working at it."

Abbott sighed and sat in silence for a minute. "You're right." He picked up the menu, pretending to decide what he wanted to eat. "What kind of business brings you down here, really? You're a county officer in my city. Don't you think you should tell me? I'll find out soon enough, anyway."

"You're not going to let this go, are you?

He shook his head.

"Let's just say there's a girl that's in a bad way who needs my help, too."

"Oh, you've been seeing someone, finally?"

"Nothing like that," Sam said, fidgeting with his phone.

"It has to do with her, doesn't it? The girl from your past, the reason you became an alcoholic in the first place." Abbott peered at him. "She's bad news, and you know it. Nothing good will come from this."

"I don't expect anything from her, but she needs help."

"That's what you've said before, and then she left you. You can't save her if she doesn't want to be saved."

Abbott could take his own advice. His wife seemed to be okay with the separation much more than he was, and it took everything in him to not constantly try to fix it the way he wanted it to be.

TWENTY-THREE

Cache Rushner
Wednesday, November 10th
7:00 a.m.

CACHE AWOKE to a fire truck screeching down the street. He sat up and scratched his head while cracking his neck. He'd never slept in a car overnight before and hoped to never do it again. It was the worst sleep he'd had in years. Coming home yesterday, he attempted to resolve the fight he had with Adaline at the skating rink. It blew up in his face. She wouldn't let him in, and she'd gotten angrier from the time they talked in the park to the ride home. Usually, she just needed a moment to blow off some steam. Cache presumed that an all-paid, amazing sleep suite in his car was the ticket to her calming down.

He fumbled to open the car door, still feeling groggy. Cache shuffled out of his car, making his way to the front door of his home. He pressed on the latch, expecting to hear a click and an invite inside, but it was locked. They hadn't had a chance yet to make a copy of the house keys. Not working in his favor.

"Addi. Honey, can you let me in?" he said, trying to be discreet. No more visits or attention drawn to them or their home if he could help it.

The sound of flip-flops hitting the floor came closer to the door.

Good sign. She's letting me in.

The door opened a crack, and Cache could see Adaline's nose and one of her blue eyes peeping through the space. "What do you want? I thought I made it perfectly clear I don't want to be around you right now."

Don't get mad.

He bunched his hands together and hid them behind his back. He smiled at her through the crack in the door.

"I understand where you're coming from. I said something stupid, and I take it back."

"What do you take back? The part where you don't believe me, or the part where you don't believe me?" She scrunched her nose and looked away.

"I don't want to see you sad. I know things have been hard on you. Please let me help you."

"Please. I need some time, okay? I can't handle any more of this right now."

"Any more of what?" he said, confused.

"Of this," she said, drawing a circle between the two of them with her finger.

Cache pressed his hand up against the door and looked down at the ground. "Okay. If that's what you want." He bit his lip, trying to control the tone of his voice. He didn't feel calm, but if he lost it right now, he would lose his shot altogether—if he even had one. "Can I get some of my stuff for work?"

She considered, then opened the door, moving away. He stopped in front of her and grabbed at her hand. Their fingers touched briefly until she moved them to her side. He wanted to hold and shake her at the same time. How could he make Adaline understand that he believed and loved her, but this was in her head—without making her feel like he didn't care?

Walking upstairs, he went to the closet and pulled out some suits and his leather work shoes. He grabbed a duffle bag from the top shelf and went to the bathroom to retrieve his toothbrush and shaving kit.

She just needs more time. He scoffed. *Now who's in denial?*

He picked up his things and began to walk downstairs. Adaline's eyes held his the whole way down, begging him to stay, but her body language said otherwise.

Cache clenched his jaw and bunched his fist.

"Please don't come back until I'm ready, okay?"

"When will that be?"

She shrugged her shoulders. "I don't know."

"Okay." Cache opened the door and walked outside. He was beginning to hate his car just for being the only place he was able to go in the past sixteen hours. He kicked it, crushing a hole in his headlight.

Damn it.

Loud scrambling came from behind him, and an annoying voice saying, "Turn the camera on," made him flinch. He didn't have to turn around to know who it was. That nosy reporter, Sienna Rhoades from Channel 5 News, who reported Adaline's disappearing act from her grand opening, stood in their driveway.

Cache bolted, got into his car, and swerved out of the driveway. He drove until he spotted the first motel he could find and pulled in. Grand Capital Motel. He needed to be near Adaline, even if she didn't want him to.

I'm still her husband, and I'm not leaving.

His wedding ring swirled around his finger. He watched the ring's motion for a minute and thought about how their marriage looked kind of the same. Always moving in a circle, full of confusion, chaos. A whirlwind of emotions tied them together. He had to make this work.

His phone buzzed as a text came through.

"You're not taking care of it. Must I remind you we'll handle it ourselves if you can't."

He grabbed the steering wheel and strangled it with no mercy.

Cache got out of his car and looked at the big, bold neon sign on the rundown building that said "Motel." It had the feel of an old Hitchcock movie where a serial killer was staying in the room next door. No one sat at the front desk, and he had no desire to be late for work, especially after missing yesterday. He smacked the bell on the counter multiple times.

"Take it easy on the bell. What did it do to you?" a young woman with a nose ring asked as she came from the back room. "How long will you be staying?"

"A night. Maybe two," he said.

She looked at his hand and raised her eyes. "You're married?"

He didn't like the way she asked that question, like she was his therapist trying to get him to admit some kind of guilt.

"Yes," he said with hostility.

"I'm sorry, we just don't get many married men here, if you know what I mean. It's not really the best place to stay." She looked at the security camera with a lifted brow.

"Is everything all right?" Cache asked.

She nodded her head and bit her bottom lip. "Yep. Will you be staying one or two nights?" she asked again.

"I'll pay for two."

"Of course." She entered his information into the computer and gave him the total before accepting his credit card. "You're in room 204." Her hand shook as she gave him his card and room key.

Cache snatched it from her hand, and she pulled her arm away, fast. He gazed around the grungy room and nodded at the girl before he left. "Thanks."

He got his things out of the car and headed toward his room. Cache threw his suits over his shoulder, not paying attention to where he was going, and ran into a man about 6'7" with greasy hair and a thin build.

"Oh, I'm sorry. Let me help you get those." The man leaned over to get a suit coat and tie from off the ground and placed them back over Cache's shoulder.

"Thanks. See you around," Cache said, walking back toward his room. He spotted 204 and opened the door. Once inside, he flung his stuff on the bed and smacked the wall.

Now what do I do?

TWENTY-FOUR

Seth Duncan
Grand Capital Motel
9:30 a.m.

THE GUY that just moved into the room next to his had bags under his eyes that resembled a lunar eclipse.

Poor guy.

How bad could it be? By the looks of it, he had a nice job or had inherited a chunk of change. He carried tailored clothes over his arm, yet he was staying at this dump. The man fascinated him, and he couldn't help but let curiosity get the best of him. A loud bang crashed into his wall.

Great, he's got anger issues.

Seth huffed and went to get ready for his day. He would look for a job, starting with the Lost Treasures Antique Store. He brushed his teeth and put extra soap under his armpits. The evergreen scent came close to wearing cologne, just a tad cakier. He grabbed a sanitizer wipe and cleaned the phone in his room before he brought it to his ear.

"Yes, hello," he said to the operator. "Could I please get some extra shampoo sent to the room?"

"Sir, we're short-handed this morning. You'll need to drop by the front desk to pick it up."

"Okay. Thanks, I guess. On second thought, I'll just get it later." He hung up the phone and gazed at the clock.

Broken.

Cracking his knuckles, he counted to twenty. Being punctual was the only option for him. No clock would make things trickier to accomplish that goal. He shut the door and began walking. Ivy Lane was only a block away. If he hurried, he could make it on time and make a good impression.

Drawing near the store, a camera crew parked in a spot across from the antique store.

Oh, man. She's going to need all the help she can get today.

He picked up pace and got to the front of the store where the sign said, "Open." He let himself in and locked the door.

"Hello. Is anyone here?"

"I'll be right there," a voice yelled from the back of the store.

He moved up and down the aisles, peering at all the items on display. A footstep shuffled behind him. "I'm sorry. Can I help you?"

Turning around, Seth glanced at her matted hair and swollen cheeks. The tears welling up in her blue eyes made them sparkle like the sun gliding across a waterfall, ripples of deep blue mixed in with turquoise. "You need to get away from the window."

She froze and grabbed a candlestick holder made of glass off the shelf and held it over her head. "Don't you come near me. Get the hell out of my store before I call the cops." The distress of using a beautiful piece of work as a weapon showed all over her face.

Adaline moved forward toward him, still holding tight to the object. "Get out."

Walking toward the door, he stopped. "Just so you know, ma'am, the news crew is right outside. If you open the door, you'll be front and center."

"Why should I believe anything you say?"

"I can tell by the way you're looking at me. You're afraid, but not afraid that I'm going to hurt you."

She lowered the candle holder. "Are you some sort of psychic?"

"The eyes tell you all you need to know. I don't need to read minds to understand that."

"I agree with you on that." Adaline went to a side window and peered out.

Seth stood near her, watching the Channel 5 news crew sit on the curb in front of her store, preying like vultures, waiting for her next move. She braced herself against the wall.

"I told you it wasn't a good idea," Seth said.

Her breathing was out of sync, and she hunched over, staring at the ground. "What did you say your name was?"

"Seth."

"Okay, Seth. What are you doing here?"

"I need a job. I thought we could help each other," he said. "It looks like you could use some assistance around your store."

She crossed her arms and gazed at him like she was

trying to peer into his soul. "What's your story? I need to know something about you before I let a stranger help me run my store."

"I just got out of a prison." He stopped and placed his hand over his mouth. *Did that just come out? Yes, it did.*

Adaline laughed nervously. "You're serious?"

He gulped. "Yes. This was a bad idea coming here, thinking I could move on with my life. Sorry to bother you."

"No. Wait a minute. What were you in for?"

"Protecting someone I care about that couldn't protect themselves." He flinched.

Being locked up, even if it wasn't his fault, was what he deserved. He had sins to pay for. Taking the blame for someone else so they could have a better life than he did was his saving grace.

"What happened?"

"There was a fire." He scratched the side of his face repeatedly.

Adaline's face whitened.

"Are you okay? You should sit down," he said.

"No, no. I'm good. I just didn't sleep well last night," she said, not looking directly at him. "For some odd reason, I feel like I know you. Have we met before the other day?"

He grinned. "I would remember you."

"You just seem oddly familiar." She brushed her short, blonde hair back. It tucked perfectly around her ear. "You can start today. Now, actually. I could use help stocking a few things on the shelves and in the display cases."

Seth patted his pants and grabbed a box in front of him. "Where do you want this?"

"In the back would be fine," she said, pointing toward a large closet.

Now he could start over and make a new life for himself, starting with Adaline.

TWENTY-FIVE

Adaline Rushner
Lost Treasures
10:00 a.m.

SETH MENTIONING a fire sparked something in her. Not an enlightening fuel, but a darkness that made her feel as though she were choking or being strangled. Adaline hated fires from the day her parents were killed in one. They had never treated her well, but she still felt a sense of remorse for their death. This was something else, and she couldn't figure it out.

What really happened the day my parents died?

After reading Leora's journal yesterday, she couldn't shake the feeling that what she thought she knew to be true wasn't true at all.

Why was she even asking this question when she knew what happened that day?

You're losing it, Adaline.

She grabbed at her head.

How did I get home that night, and where was Aunt Arlene?

Adaline tugged her hair and pressed her thumb on the owl locket around her neck.

Stop it.

Banging sounded outside her store. She was quickly reminded about the Channel 5 news, stalking her for a comment about her girls being murdered.

Maybe I should just tell them what happened?

Who would believe her, though, when her own husband didn't?

"Are there more boxes I could move to the back?" Seth asked.

"Um, yes. Over on the side there, by the restroom." Adaline shook her head and twirled a loose piece of hair, dangling in her face.

She felt like a wasp's nest came and sat on her brain, clouding up her thoughts. Her body was struggling to move at its normal pace.

Adaline huffed.

She grabbed a box by the bathroom and unloaded the contents of the new creations and finds. A gold and turquoise watch with butterflies centered on the face had been one of her favorite pieces. Adaline debated even putting that one on display or keeping it for herself. She put it on the display shelf, with the other jewelry pieces, nicely surrounding the watch as the centerpiece.

"Ma'am?" Seth asked.

"You don't need to call me ma'am. Adaline is just fine."

"Okay. A man is staring in your window. Would you like me to ask him to leave?" he asked.

Adaline glanced toward the window and squinted against the sunlight reflecting off the glass pane. She shielded her eyes and looked toward the man again. Her pulse raced, and her mouth felt dry.

No. It can't be. What is he doing here?

She hurried into the bathroom, fixed her hair and makeup, and dusted her hands off before pulling some lip gloss out of her pocket. The red tint helped to make her flushed cheeks look more natural. Adaline hadn't seen him in twelve years, and the last time she saw him wasn't on good terms. He still had the same boyish charms that intrigued her when she was younger. Blond hair, blue eyes, a grin to melt her heart, and more muscles than she remembered ever seeing on him.

Why now? Couldn't he just let me live my life?

"Are you okay, Miss Adaline?" Seth asked, walking toward her.

"Um…I mean, yes. Yes. Yes."

"You already said yes." He grinned.

She smirked at him. "I guess I did. I know him from a long time ago. He's…an old friend."

The sound of tapping glass echoed through her store. She fidgeted with her fingers and hurried to the door.

Slow down. You don't want to look excited.

What am I going to say?

Adaline opened the door to let him in. The news crew ran like a herd of elephants to enter.

She froze.

"That's enough. You're not getting any comments out of her today," the man at the door said. "Move along."

Adaline let out a breath that she'd been holding since she saw the news crew stationed in front of her store.

"Hi," he said, closing the door and moving closer to her.

"Hi back, Sam." Adaline wiped her sweaty palms on her shirt and reached to shake his hand.

He chuckled. "A handshake. Surely, I get more than that. We've been through way too much to only give each other handshakes."

"I know, it's silly. I don't know what to say after leaving things the way we left them." She looked at the ground. "Sam, I'm sorry I left you. I was afraid. Afraid to let you get closer to me."

"Addi, I know you, and I knew you back then. I knew what I was getting into when I asked you to marry me."

Sam took her hand and brought it to his face, clearly seeing the wedding ring. Adaline slumped.

"You were able to let someone else in," Sam said. "I hope he treats you well."

"His name is Cache. I would introduce you, but we're not exactly talking right now." She twirled her wedding ring around her finger and looked down at her watch. "Can we catch up another time? I need to start pulling some customers in."

Sam's face dropped. "Sure. I'll be in town for a few days. Here's my number."

"Thank you." She moved to embrace him. "It's good to see you again."

"You too. We do need to talk, okay?"

She nodded. "Right after work, I'll give you a ring."

Sam smiled and left the store. Adaline glanced at Seth and noticed him hiding behind boxes but clearly glaring at Sam.

Why is he so protective?

Adaline raised her eyebrows and took a better look at Seth. He appeared to be in his late fifties. His shoulders rose while he watched Sam leave in the way she'd imagined an older brother would react. Being an only child with abusive parents, her reoccurring dream as a kid was to have a big brother who could protect her from all the evils she'd witnessed. Maybe he had a younger sister, and that's who he protected that put him in prison. She caught one last glance of Sam before he disappeared around the street corner. Seeing him brought back memories she wanted to leave alone, but they immersed her anyway.

TWENTY-SIX

Sam Wendell
Wednesday, November 10th
10:30 a.m.

STROLLING down Ivy Lane after leaving Adaline's store, he didn't know what to think. She seemed happy to see him, which was a great sign. He had missed her, but it was painful to see her married to someone else. He spat on the sidewalk to get the distaste out of his mouth that had been sitting on his tongue since he saw her wedding ring. He'd kept tabs on her through the years, so he knew about her marriage, but it hadn't hit him until just then.

They'd been best friends in Owling, since the age of seven. That was, until he proposed and she ran. They had shared everything. She'd confided in him, and he'd kept her secrets. Whenever her mother beat her, they would meet in the cornfields, and he would hold Adaline until it turned dark. He wanted to protect her from the one person that should be taking care of her, but her mother didn't have a soul.

He stared down at a barking dog that was rubbing a little too much on his leg. "Shoo, go find someone else to rub on," he said, gruffly.

Laughter arose behind him. "Wow, you sure told that dog, brother. Don't you have a heart? You can't even pet a tiny dog?" Officer Abbot asked.

"Sure. It just didn't come with me today," he said with sarcasm.

"You saw her, didn't you? Cause you're in that mood."

"What mood?" Sam asked.

"You know, the mood that only a woman can create. You're happy-go-lucky one minute, you feel like a complete screw-up the next."

They both laughed.

"Wanna grab a doughnut or a cup of coffee at this bakery? They're pretty good. You have to try the jelly-filled one," Abbott said.

"Jelly-filled doughnuts?"

Abbott glared at him. "What?"

"Jelly-filled doughnuts?" Sam wiped at his eye.

"Aren't you funny? Only little girls wipe tears from their eyes."

Sam punched Abbott in the arm and walked into the bakery. "Why don't you go get a seat and I'll get the doughnuts. They're on me," Abbott said.

"What next? Do I need to hold your hand and walk you to the bathroom, too?"

"Possibly. I'll consider that." He winked at Sam and turned around to give his order.

Sam sat down, weighing the options in his head. Adaline seemed fine, but he had heard otherwise from his sources. Staying a few more days just to make sure seemed like the route to go. Seeing her was harder than he'd imagined, and he hated that she had that effect on him.

"Earth to the princess," Abbott said, placing a jelly-filled doughnut in front of his face.

"Are you kidding? You really got me one?"

"Would you shut up and take a bite already? This girl really has you all uptight. Who is she?"

Sam took a bite of his doughnut and moaned. "Okay. Good call. They're better than I thought they'd be. I'm not taking back my comment, though."

"Wouldn't expect any less." Abbott laughed. "Stop diverting the conversation. Who is she?"

Sam grinned. "Her name is Adaline."

"Adaline." Abbott paused. "As in Rushner? Adaline Rushner?"

"Yeah, why? You know her?" Sam asked, raising his eyebrows.

"That's the case I was talking about, man. The case where I might have found new information about my daughter's disappearance."

"Back up. Start from the beginning. I need to know everything, do you understand?"

"Whoa, Sammie. Take it easy. Why do you need to know?" Abbott asked.

"She could be in trouble, that's why." Sam moved his doughnut to the side as hunger left him. He could only concentrate on how much Abbott knew.

What am I going to do if he knows too much?

He nervously looked around the restaurant and moved his chair closer to the table. "What do you know?" Sam asked, in a whisper.

"Why are you whispering? What are you involved in?" Abbott leaned in, pressing his elbows on the table.

"Nothing. Please answer my question. How did you stumble onto her case?"

"Yesterday we got a call from her neighbor about an incident at the Rushner home. I was the patrol officer who took the dispatcher's call. I went to check it out and see what the disturbance was all about," Abbott said.

"And?"

"You know I can't share this information with you."

Sam peered at him and moved in closer. "I know. We've helped each other out through a lot of shit. I need your help, man."

"Will you tell me what's going on?" Abbott asked.

"I can't right now. Just trust me."

Abbott ground his teeth before speaking. "Brother, I'll be forced to stop you if this becomes a problem."

"I know," Sam said, looking down at the table.

"She claims her dead daughters were in her house. I related to her with the feelings I had after my daughter was taken from me."

"Did you find any proof someone had been there?"

Abbott stared at Sam. "None. Look, I talked to her husband, and he doesn't even know what to do. She thinks they're still alive and is acting out."

Sam shook his head. "What did you find that relates your daughter's case to the Rushners'?"

"Honestly, it's nothing. I was upset and sleep-deprived."

"Abbott, tell me. I can decide for myself," Sam said.

"Pictures were taken of the crime scene. In one of the pictures, a necklace was dangling from one of the girls' fingers."

"What kind of necklace?"

"A gold locket with an owl engraved on the front," Abbott said.

Sam gasped. "You need to call your Lieutenant Stalk, now." He looked at Abbott and studied his face. "This was the exact necklace at the crime scene for your daughter, correct?"

"Yes, it was, and Mrs. Rushner wears one around her neck." Abbott leaned in. "You tell me what you know."

"She got it as a kid. That's it." He closed his eyes remembering the owl necklace clinging to Adaline's neck the night her parents burned alive in their house.

The Owl Keeper was back in town.

TWENTY-SEVEN

Owl Keeper
Wednesday, November 10th
3:00 p.m.

ADALINE'S SMILE SEEMED GENUINE, real in a way he hadn't seen before. He didn't like this new side of her, trying to do everything herself.

Full of independence.

Strength.

Stubbornness.

She needed him to save her, even if she didn't remember, and he was the only person fit to protect her. That was his job.

Vulnerability equaled her beauty. The damaged, broken soul with fire and anger, but such innocence, made her Adaline. His Adaline.

Seeing her vulnerable pleased him. It was an unspoken invitation to be near and present. A teasing reminder she still had a hold on him and he had one on her. He liked that he could see her and she couldn't see him. Even though he longed to remind her of the bond they shared, watching would do for now—until the urge came again. She needed to be broken again, and he knew what had to be done.

Not for long. Just a little more time.

He rocked himself back and forth singing a tune in his head.

There was a little owl,
High in a tree.
She tried to fly away,
But couldn't get free.

TWENTY-EIGHT

Adaline Rushner
Wednesday, November 10th
6:00 p.m.

CLOSING the store with an extra pair of hands made stocking shelves and putting things out for display much quicker. Seth turned out to be a huge help.

She said goodbye to him and put her jacket on. Whipping it around her to get it on, a breeze of Sam's cologne intoxicated her nose. Adaline closed her eyes and breathed it in. Ferns, rain, and earth lingered in the scent that she knew so well. He wore the same thing twelve years ago. Comfort embraced her for a minute until she opened her eyes and let her mind wander. The way she felt toward Sam confused her. Their chemistry resurfaced today, but she loved her husband and wanted things to work out. With Cache, she never had to look at her past. She wasn't the disturbed little girl from the headlines.

All she had to be was herself.

Be Cache and Adaline. A certain freedom came with that.

She stared at a picture of them in her wallet and smiled. The faces looking back at her looked happy. At least, until now.

Sam showing up complicated her already heightened emotions and brought the past trudging along with him.

Dammit, Sam. Why did you have to come back into my life?

As Adaline got into the car, music blared through the radio. She didn't feel like listening to it. There was already too much chaos in her head. Turning it off, she pulled up to her street to spot news crews lurking outside her house.

Leave me alone already.

She had to face them sometime, whether she wanted to or not. Adaline pulled into the driveway and stopped the car as a face crowded her window with a microphone.

"Mrs. Rushner, we have a few questions."

She didn't respond and stepped out of her car, trying to move past the overly persistent reporter. Fumbling with her keychain, Adaline tried to find her house key with no luck.

What do I do now?

Multiple reporters gathered on the porch behind her shouting questions at the same time. She braced her hands against the door as sweat dripped off her back. She turned her head toward her neighbor's house, and a lady waved in a frantic motion.

Is she waving for me?

Adaline breathed deeply and closed her eyes. Counting to three, she ran through the reporters toward her neighbor's home. The lady who lived there opened the door, ready to give her a safe place to hide. Stepping inside, she fell on the floor, and the woman bolt-locked the door behind her.

"Thank you,…"

"Maggie," the girl said with a small smile.

"Thank you, Maggie," Adaline said, brushing her hair away from her face. She glanced around the lady's house. Her home was full of antiques that made Adaline's mouth water with excitement. "Your home is beautiful. I can see you love antiques."

Maggie smiled. "They're my grandma's old trinkets I could never get rid of."

The lady seemed to be around her age with red, curly hair and freckles. She had a warm presence about her.

"Thank you for calling the police the other day. I'm fine, but I appreciate your concern," Adaline said.

Maggie nodded.

Odd silence filled the room. "So, what's your story?" Maggie asked.

Adaline flinched. Maggie's boldness took her aback. She wished she was more of an open book, but sharing personal things with people, especially strangers, wasn't going to happen. "I'm not sure what you mean."

"Well, since we're neighbors now, and I did save your ass back there, I want to know who you are. The only thing I know about you is that you claim to have daughters, and the news doesn't really paint a pretty picture of you," she said. "Everyone deserves to be seen in a good light. Frankly, you could use a friend."

Having someone care about her that knew only the bad things was quite refreshing. "Why do you care?"

"I just do. I don't know," she said. "Never mind. Don't worry about it. You don't need to tell me anything." She walked away looking hurt. "Can I get you a hot chocolate?"

"That'd be wonderful."

Adaline sat down on the couch and twisted her purple scarf in her hands.

Maggie came into the front room and gave her a snowman mug filled with hot chocolate and little white marshmallows.

"Marshmallows?"

"Haven't you had a hot chocolate with marshmallows?"

"It's been a while. I used to with my girls, but—" Adaline stopped, realizing she didn't want to share anymore.

Maggie stared at her sympathetically.

Adaline didn't want to be viewed as a sob story to someone she knew nothing about. It made her feel weak. She placed her hot chocolate on a coffee table close to the couch and held her hands together.

"Is the hot chocolate too hot? I can add whip cream. That always cools it down, and who doesn't like more cream?" Maggie fidgeted in her chair.

"No, really, this is perfect." She picked up her mug and brought it to her lips, sipping slowly. Adaline paused, savoring the rich chocolate taste in her mouth. The marshmallows had melted, giving it a small hint of cream. She closed her eyes. "Yum."

Maggie laughed.

Adaline opened her eyes, not realizing how vocal she'd been about her hot chocolate. She thought she had silently enjoyed her sip. Wiping her mouth with her hand, she smirked feeling embarrassed. It's delicious and really hits the spot."

"That it does. I drink at least three cups of hot chocolate a day. Pretty sure that the calories I'm trying to burn while working out is from all the hot chocolate I consume throughout the winter months." She paused. "You can take off your coat."

Adaline sat further back on the couch. "I'm okay. I'll keep it on." Something pinched her leg and she moved to grasp the object from underneath her. A small picture frame of a little girl no older than eight stared back at her. "Is this your daughter?"

Maggie stared at the picture with sadness and snatched it out of Adaline's hand. "No. I don't have kids." Her eyes seemed to dart around the house with discomfort.

The coziness Adaline felt in this home earlier turned to a sour pit in her stomach.

What is she hiding?

Maggie peered at the clock hanging on her wall and looked out her window. "The reporters still there. I need to make dinner for my hubby. Would you like something to eat?"

Adaline didn't even realize anyone else was in the house. "No, I'm good. Thank you." She cleared her throat. "What does your husband do for work?"

"Oh, he's an artist. He's actually in his office working on a project right now."

Adaline stood up. "Do you have a restroom I could use?"

"First door down the hall on the right, but don't go down any further. My husband doesn't care for interruptions or…visitors."

"Sure." Walking down the hall, she wondered what was going on with Maggie's husband. She acted a tad scared of him. Turning the light on in the bathroom, a bright pink reflection caught her attention in the mirror.

Mommy, come play with us.

Adaline whipped around, but there was nothing there. "Girls, I'm here," she whispered to herself in the mirror. The pink tone called to her. Something was in the room across the hall that kept reflecting onto the mirror. Quietly, she looked back to where Maggie stood prior. No one was there. Adaline tiptoed on the carpet toward the other room at the end of the hallway. Pepto Bismol pink erupted on the bedroom walls, and butterflies embellished the space. Two tiny beds sat opposite each other, and a princess table with teacups stood in the corner. She gripped her fingers together and gasped.

The room moved like she was thrown overboard into cascading waters. It hurt, and she couldn't breathe.

"The food's about ready."

Adaline stared wide-eyed in the direction of Maggie's voice, her heart racing.

She's coming.

Leaving the bedroom, she moved quickly back to the bathroom and closed the door. She sat on the toilet, feeling queasy, and held her stomach. Why does she have beds for little girls if she has no kids?

She flushed the toilet and turned on the faucet, pretending to wash her hands. A man and woman were speaking in the hall with raised voices. Adaline peeked through a crack in the door. Maggie handed the man a plate with multiple sandwiches stacked on top of each other. He put his hand out to grab it. She couldn't see his face. Maggie tilted the plate toward him before he took it, and a mark of some sort was made in each one.

No, it can't be.

They were bite marks, like how she would kiss the girls' peanut butter and jelly sandwiches before they had a taste. Their little game of Kiss-a-Roo.

It's nothing. Breathe. Let it go.

Stress was taking over, making her paranoid. Adaline smiled a few times in the mirror to see which version seemed closest to a genuine one. She pulled up her lips to create her own. Turning off the faucet, she opened the door and switched off the light. Walking toward the kitchen, Maggie frantically wiped the empty counter with a dishcloth.

"Can I help?" Adaline asked, giving her a rehearsed smile.

"I'm about done. Why don't you sit back down? I'll be right there." Her voice wavered when she talked.

The smell of peanut butter got stronger the more Maggie wiped the counter. "Peanut butter and jelly?" Adaline asked, raising her eyebrows.

Maggie glanced up, and her cheeks reddened. "I know. Not really the meal of champions, but we like them."

"You said you don't have children?"

"Not yet. One day, maybe."

Adaline noticed Maggie's hands shook. "My hubby gets hungry when he works."

She kissed the sandwich. That's my thing.

Her heart thrashed and her legs turned to putty. "You don't have kids?" Adaline asked again, her voice rising to a new pitch.

Maggie turned around, placing her hand on her hip. "No. You just asked that. Remember I told you that twice already, silly. You don't look good. Are you feeling sick?"

"No...I'm fine."

Maggie came toward her, and she moved a few steps backward.

"Where are they? You have my girls."

A tall man stepped out of a room into the hallway, and Maggie covered her mouth.

"What's all this noise? I told you to keep it down," the man said.

Adaline pointed at them. "You have my girls. Give them to me now before I call the police."

The tall man had a sly look on his face. "You brought over the crazy neighbor. You sure know how to pick them. We don't have your kids, lady. Get out of my house. Now."

Maggie looked like a deer caught in headlights. "Please leave, Adaline."

"I'm not leaving until I get my girls." She sneered at them.

The man walked toward her. Adaline lunged, but he caught her before she got to the next room. He threw her over his bulky shoulder, a tight grip around her legs. Adaline hit him in the face and kicked him once in the gut, but it didn't even faze him. "Put me down. I'm going to find my girls, and don't you think for one second that you're getting away with this. Do you hear me?"

The man opened the front door and placed her on the porch. "Get off my property, now."

Adaline turned around to flashes of cameras and reporters staring at her. She was put out in the sea with the sharks, and they were going to swallow her whole.

TWENTY-NINE

Sam Wendell
6:45 p.m.

SURFING the channels at his hotel, waiting for something good to catch his interest, was pointless. The box of static couldn't hold his focus while Adaline filled his thoughts. Hell, he missed her, and now she crept right back into the shattered, locked part of his heart she'd created.

Sam stood and paced the floor. She told him she'd call him after work, but he hadn't received any calls yet. He checked the clock for the fourth time.

She should be home by now.

With the Owl Keeper back in town, Adaline would be his target. He grabbed the phone and dialed her number. It rang twice before he heard a whimper. Sam stopped pacing. "Are you there?"

"I need your help."

"Where are you?" he asked.

"I'm at my house—256 Dreary Oak Drive. Please come quick."

"Adaline?"

She didn't reply.

He glanced at his phone to see it disconnected. His pulse elevated. He tugged his ear and ran out the door.

He better not be there. I'll kill him.

Sam hit the steering wheel when he got into the car. He grabbed his phone to punch in her street address on the GPS. Once it highlighted his route, he yanked his phone out to call her again. It went straight to voicemail this time. Sam stepped on the gas.

"Next street turn right," the phone instructed.

The streets in the neighborhood didn't hold many light poles, and Sam squinted his eyes to make sure he hit the right road. He didn't have to look for a house number as multiple news vehicles lined the street in front of a house on the right. Pulling behind a car, he noticed Adaline hunched on her porch, crowded by people.

Sam parked his car and jumped out, leaving the door open. He pushed his way through the people and moved to her side, bracing her back.

"You came?"

"I'm here. Hold onto my arm."

She nodded.

"Back up, people. Enough harassment for one night," Sam said. He laid her head on his shoulder and tried to shield her face. Getting to the car, he lightly pushed Adaline. "Get in."

Adaline lay down on the seat, still covering her face. "Get me out of here." She held herself in a ball like she did as a kid. Adaline hadn't changed at all. Even after running away, the past still caught up to her.

"What happened?" he asked

"I'm losing my mind. Cache was right. I do need help," she said, looking up at him. "If I tell you what I'm thinking, you'll think I'm crazy too."

"You used to say that to me, and I always believed you, Addi bear."

"My neighbors have my girls."

"What do you mean? Did you see them, your girls?"

"I told you you'd think I was crazy," she said.

Sam clenched the steering wheel. "I don't. I just need you to talk to me. Don't shut down."

"I made the girls peanut butter and jelly sandwiches, and I would take a bite, telling them that it was a kiss from me. It was my unique mommy thing just for them." Adaline paused and took a deep breath. "The neighbors don't have kids, and she made peanut butter and jelly sandwiches for dinner and . . . she kissed them."

"That's weird, I agree, but is there anything else that happened?"

Adaline whispered. "They have a room that's decorated in butterflies and it has two twin beds. Why would they have those?"

Sam cleared his throat. "We should report this to the police so they can look into it."

"No. We need to go back so I can prove it to you."

"We can't just go into their house."

She went back to holding herself in a ball and didn't respond.

"I promise I will help you. You just have to trust me," he said. "Ad, I need to ask you some questions from the past. I wouldn't bring them up unless it was important."

"What kind of questions? Why?" Adaline let go of her legs and stretched from her singular spot.

"They may help in finding your girls."

She put her hands over his. "You believe me?"

"I do."

"If it will help, then go for it, but I'm not sure what I can tell you that you don't already know."

Sam halted at a red light and squeezed her hand. He tilted his head and looked at her with concern. "Do you remember the night your parents died?"

She nodded.

"What do you remember?"

"I went to Aunt Arlene's for the night and came home to a burned house. Why are you asking me this?"

Sam held his mouth. "You didn't go anywhere else that night?"

Adaline raised her eyebrows. "Where else would I have gone?"

He shook his head. "Do you remember wearing an owl necklace that day?"

"You mean the one I have now?" She gripped its chain.

Where did she get that one?

Looking at the necklace she held in her hand, it rested right on her heart. Almost as if to block her from the truth.

"Yes. This is important. How did your parents die?"

She sat in silence and let go of his hand. "You're treating me like a nut case, doing therapy to fix an unresolved issue. I don't need that."

"I'm just trying to remember so I can help you," he said. The light turned green and he drove again.

"They died in a fire. An accidental fire. Dad left his grill on, and the propane tank was close by."

Sam tapped his fingers on the steering wheel and closed his eyes.

She doesn't remember. How does she not remember?

"What did your mother do to you?"

"Sam. Why would you ask that? You know what she did to me." Her lips quivered as she talked. "She beat me every day, multiple times. Stuck me in the closet and treated me like shit. Are you happy bringing up the past?" She sneered at him. "You came here to get back at me when I'm vulnerable for not marrying you, didn't you? That's low, for you." She looked out the window. "I need you to stop the car and let me out."

"I would never do that to you. Look at me."

She continued to stare out the window for a few minutes and eased up enough to look in his direction.

"I promised you I would protect you. I'm trying to keep that promise."

Her face softened. "Why would you want to do that, even after I left you?"

Sam winced at the image of how painful that day was. He laid out a blanket and had a picnic set up in a meadow Adaline favored, not too far from his home. The weather stayed clear and warm, and her long blonde curls radiated happiness when the sun's rays hit them. She gave him an inquisitive look and smirked. He never got tired of that expressive combo. Getting on one knee, he opened a black box. She just looked at him, tears in her eyes, and left. That's what she did when she got too close to showing her feelings. Adaline was incapable of letting anyone in, but he understood her in a way that no one else did, and she needed someone to understand her in that way, now more than ever.

"I know you, and I understand why you left. I just wish you had come back to me. I waited and hoped. But I'm glad you're happy."

Adaline released his hand. "Who says I'm happy?"

"What's going on between you and your husband, anyway? Why isn't he here with you?"

"Well, aren't you full of hard questions tonight," Adaline said. "I don't need anyone protecting me."

"Believe me, you've made that clear."

"Ouch. It's just . . . too hard to be with someone that doesn't believe you when you need their trust the most." She closed her eyes. "My girls are alive. I can feel it. If I have to look for them alone and be viewed as a crazy person, that's what it's going to be."

"You're not alone." He parked the car and got out. "Give me a minute, okay? I need to make a call."

Adaline nodded.

Sam stopped the car and got out. He chose number one on his speed dial. "Hey," said a voice on the other line.

"We have a problem."

"Meet tomorrow. Same place, same time. Don't be late."

"Got it," Sam said.

He placed his phone in his pocket and got back into the car.

Adaline smiled at him. "Everything okay?"

"Yeah. It was just work. I have a few things I need to tie up."

"Hope it's not too much work," Adaline said.

"Nothing that I can't handle. I'm good with loose ends." He turned his face to the side and frowned.

THIRTY

Officer Abbott
Thursday, November 11th
7:00 a.m.

HE TAPPED his pen on the counter a few times, then placed it on the top of his knuckle, letting it slide down his fist into a dish with stale jellybeans. Someone did not like orange. And they didn't want the dish bad enough to move it with their desk before Abbott came back to work. The small bowl was made of clay, and multiple colors splashed all over the side. A homemade gift from a child he would've never left behind. Adopting it was the only option.

Abbott smiled and held his head.

All the information Sam gave him about the owl necklace, and how secretive he seemed when talking about the Rushner woman, led him to believe Sam was hiding something to protect her. He knew that Sam was right in the middle of the whole case, whether he wanted to be or not.

"Good morning, Abbott," Lieutenant Stalk said. "Did you ever go home last night?"

Looking up, Abbott smirked.

"I told you to take it easy. You look like hell. You're still keeping your word, right?"

"Yeah, you bet."

Lieutenant Stalk tugged at his collar. "I need you focused on your duties. Let this go."

"I'm not done with this one."

"I think you are, Abbott. There's nothing to look into. Plus, I need my best officers ready to work. Okay?"

"You don't think we should look into Mrs. Rushner being attacked at her store?"

"It's being handled, but you won't be involved with it. Understood?"

Abbott cracked his knuckles. "Yes, sir."

"Good man."

He watched as the lieutenant walked toward his office and closed the door behind him. Abbott scoured the room and hunched over in his chair, bringing the phone to his ear.

"Abbott. It's seven a.m., man," Sam said on the other end.

"Some of us have jobs. How did you get time off, anyway? Never mind. The lieutenant doesn't want me looking into the Rushner case anymore. I need you to give me some answers so I can have closure."

"I don't know much."

"There's where you're wrong. I know you know things about the Rushner woman. Don't lie to me."

"This isn't the time. Can we talk somewhere else?" Sam asked.

"Where?"

"Jelly place, ten minutes?"

"Got it, brother," Abbott said.

———

Officer Abbott sat at a table in the bakery, tapping his fingers against the surface. The beat helped him relax while he counted how many times he would tap on each side of his hand. The bell rang as the door swung open, followed by loud footsteps. He turned around quickly and sprung out of his chair as he saw Sam coming toward him.

"Whoa. Have you been drinking? You look awful."

"No. It's been a reoccurring thought, though," Abbott said, licking his lips and pacing the floor. "I haven't slept in 24 hours."

"Stop thinking about it. That's going to take you down a road you don't want to travel again. Sit down."

Abbott didn't respond and continued to pace and fidget.

Sam stared at him. "How much coffee have you had this morning?" He waved his hand in front of him. "Hello?"

He glanced at Sam. "I'm on my fifth cup of coffee, trying to go over details in my head."

"Okay, dipshit. You're going to have a heart attack if you keep that up." He shook his head. "What details, and why are we here?" Sam asked, raising his eyebrows.

"You know things, and I want to know what they are," Abbott said, sitting down.

Sam gazed at him. "What are you talking about?"

"Don't fuck with me. You know something about the necklace I told you was at my home with my daughter's disappearance. I saw the look of fear in your eyes," Abbott whispered. "The necklace is related to the Rushner case, isn't it?"

"I don't know." Sam peered at the ground.

"How are you involved in all this? You and Mrs. Rushner know something, and I want you to tell me right now."

Sam put a finger to his lips and stared at Abbott. "Calm down, man. Let's not get all worked up. I do know things about Adaline, but it's not related to this."

"Then why did you look worried?" Abbott watched as Sam shifted his eyes. He appeared uncomfortable sitting with him, having this conversation.

He knows something, but what is it?

"You know Adaline and I go way back. I worry about her well-being. She's not in a good place right now, and bringing up more past issues about her daughters isn't going to help her," Sam said.

"So, you're worried about me asking her questions?"

"Yes. Clearly, there's a connection between the two cases, but all the girls are dead, and the man who took them is dead, as well. Why open this up again?"

Abbott clenched his fist. The pain of the words *dead* and *girl* suffocated his heart. The feeling would never go away, and the fact that even his friends were inconsiderate about that proved to him that he was on his own . . . alone. He sat and tapped his fingers against the table again, in a faster motion.

Sam hung his head. "I'm sorry. I didn't mean for it to come out like that."

"Sure, you didn't." He held his hand over the bracelet wrapped around his wrist.

"I just don't want you to torture yourself with something that's in the past. It's been a year."

"Don't be an asshole. Have you ever had a child?" Abbott asked.

Sam shook his head.

"You have no idea just how wrong you are. When your child is taken from you like that, you don't just move on. Every day, the world is moving. People carry on with their lives while you're still in the same dark shit hole you were in the day before, and the day before that one." He paused. "Thanks for nothing. I'll get my answers somewhere else." Abbott stood and grabbed his coat. Sam bumped into him on his way out.

A gold object fell on the floor.

Abbott looked at Sam, then back at the object on the floor. He froze and wiped at his forehead.

"You don't understand," Sam said. He leaned to grab the item, letting the gold chain dangle in his fingers.

Abbott's body tensed. "What the hell is that?"

Sam's hand opened, and an owl locket just like the one that was left after his daughter's disappearance lay in the palm of his hand.

Abbott rubbed his head and stepped backward. "You jackass. You're involved in this. Do you know where Aspen is?"

"Don't do this here. Let's go outside and we'll talk."

"I don't take orders from you, brother. Tell me what I need to know *right* now."

Placing the locket in his pocket, Sam put his hands out and stepped toward him. "I know things, okay? You need to be quiet before you get us killed."

He glanced around the café and noticed other people staring at them. A lady at the counter with a cup of coffee in hand seemed especially interested in what they were saying. She dressed professionally and had the glare of a lawyer accusing him of something he didn't do. Abbott sarcastically waved at her, and she turned back around to pay for her drink.

"Get in your car and meet me at my house. Make sure you're not followed," Abbott said. "Don't you take off on me. I *will* find you if you do."

Sam held his hand in his pocket and glanced back toward the café. "Will do."

THIRTY-ONE

Cache Rushner
Grand Capital Motel
7:30 a.m.

IT'D ONLY BEEN a day since he got kicked out of his house and sent away without a clue of when he could come back home. Staying at a trashy motel and waiting like a pathetic loser for Adaline to call was sheer torture. He wasn't about to let his marriage fall apart or sit around while she called the shots. He wanted to make things right with her.

A pizza box sat on the bed, and his suit smelled like pepperoni. He grabbed a new shirt and went to take a quick shower. The water was lukewarm, and the bathtub looked similar to his first place on Buckington Avenue when he was a dirt-broke college dropout. Mildew, rust, and mold clung to the shower.

Cache closed his eyes for the few minutes he was in the shower. He put his shirt on, brushed his teeth, and sprayed some cologne on his shirt. Adaline always complimented him on how good he smelled, and he hoped the cologne still had some of the same charm for her that it used to. On their first date, he had worn the same cologne, and she'd brush her nose against the side of his face, inhaled, and nuzzled into his neck.

He smiled at the thought.

Cache looked at himself in the mirror, pretending to be confident. He felt anything but that about this whole situation, but he loved her, and that's all that mattered to him. He peered at his watch. Just enough time to get flowers and drop by her store before he went to work. Getting into his car, he turned some jazz music on to soothe his nerves. This felt like their first date, and he would either score or flunk out.

Pulling up to Ivy Lane, he parked and got out of his car. He grinned, seeing Adaline's car in the parking lot.

Here we go.

A couple of stores down, a flower place called Magic Petals had an open sign in the window. Stepping inside, a wave of roses and tulips overwhelmed his senses.

"How can I help you, sir?"

"Yes, I would like a dozen roses and one Gerber daisy."

"Do you have a preference on colors?" the older lady asked with a smile.

"Six yellow roses and six red. The Gerber daisy needs to be white."

Adaline loved white Gerber daisies. She said they looked as though they still needed to be painted. When she was a kid, she'd imagine a color in her mind, touch her finger to the flower petal, and she'd pretend it would change into the shade she thought of.

"This woman must be a keeper with you buying love and friendship roses."

"She is. We've been through a lot, but I'm hoping we can get back to where we started." He paused. "How much do I owe you?"

"For you? I'll say twenty," she said. "Take it from me, no marriage is perfect, but if you give it water and sunlight continually and care for it often, it will flourish. Just like your bouquet there."

Cache grinned and took out twenty-five. "Keep the change. Thank you." He left, headed down to Adaline's store on the corner, and used his copy of the store key to get inside. Walking in, he heard laughing from the back of the store and moved through the aisle towards the noise.

Adaline's eyes opened wide. "Cache. What are you doing here?" She glanced toward a man that Cache didn't recognize.

He stared the man down. "I could ask you the same thing." Cache held the bouquet in her direction. "I came to see if we could talk and to bring you these."

"They're beautiful. Thank you," she said. "I'm sorry. Let me introduce you." Adaline pointed to the man with blond hair. He was tall, muscular, and around his age. "This is Sam. Sam Wendell." She paused. "I told you about him."

Cache scrunched his nose and chuckled. "You're the boy that proposed to my wife and then she ran off on you." He bunched his fist behind him. "Didn't you think trying to get with my wife once was enough?"

Sam looked away. He clearly hit a nerve.

Adaline gazed at him. "Stop it. That's enough."

"I'm just stating who he is."

She straightened her shoulders. "He's also the boy that helped me when I was younger with my mother when she did those horrible things to me."

"I remember." He looked toward Sam. "Why are you here?"

Adaline glared at him. "Cache, you're being rude."

"Am I? Because you're my wife, and you won't talk to me, but you'll talk to him."

She peered at the ground.

"I miss you. Can we talk without him?" Cache asked.

"It's not her fault," Sam said. "I thought you both could use my help."

"Or rather you thought *she* could use your help."

Sam nodded.

Adaline covered her face. "I miss you, too, but you don't want to be a part of my life."

"I do." Cache gazed at the flowers he held in his hands. "Remember our first date? I asked you what your favorite color of flower was, and you told me white."

"Yes. I remember," she said, tears welling in her eyes. "That was a long time ago, when we could trust each other. You don't believe me anymore, but Sam does, and I need someone that will help me find our girls."

"Sam believes you. How convenient. So, what does this mean for us?"

"I told you I needed time."

"Wait while someone else tries to come in and manipulate you? I don't think so."

Adaline sneered at him. "I gave you chances. Many. I know very well what manipulation looks like, and I can take care of myself."

He bit his lip, trying to hold his tongue. "You want time? You come get me when you're ready. I'm done playing games." Cache threw the flowers on the counter and stormed out of the store.

THIRTY-TWO

Adaline Rushner
Lost Treasures
8:00 a.m.

SITTING ON THE FLOOR, she hung her head and held her stomach, trying to contain her emotions. She hadn't expected Cache to come visit her at the store, but seeing him brought hope, until he threw flowers at her and left. The satin fabric from her skirt clung to her leg from the tears blending into the white material. Adaline could drown her sorrow in the cloth, and no one would even know about the tears she had shed.

"Adaline?"

A hand touched her back gently, but she didn't look up at him.

"Talk to me. Come here," Sam said.

She brought her head up off her skirt just enough to speak, but not enough for him to see her. "Please leave, Sam."

"You need a friend right now. Let me in."

"What I need is not a friend, okay?" Adaline wiped her face with the back of her hand.

"You do this when you're upset. Hide so no one can see your emotions." He paused. "I'm not just someone."

"Once I share my feelings, you might not like what I have to say."

His feet shuffled on the floor behind her.

"Maybe not, but you need to let things out sometimes. You can't keep holding all that built-up anger inside like this."

Adaline stood up and peered at his handsome face. She didn't see the face he wore now, but the face of the little boy who helped her as a child. He still was the same person, trying to save a damsel in distress. She was tired of being saved and having people view her that way.

"You want to know what I'm thinking?" The words came out so quickly that spit lingered on Sam's arm.

He wiped it off with his shirt and looked at her. "Yes."

Her body shook like a volcano ready to explode. "I'm tired of people thinking I'm crazy and delusional. I know that's what you, they, everyone thinks," she said. "I can see it in your eyes when you look at me. Poor little Adaline needs help once again." She paused. "Well, I don't. I don't need anyone's help."

"I heard you fell unconscious in the snow, and no one was there to help you."

"Dammit, Sam. People fall all the time." She put her hand on her hip and glared at him. "My girls are alive and I want them back. I want my marriage back, and I need things to be the way they used to, but we don't get what we want, now do we?"

"No, we sure don't."

She hesitated. "I'm not talking to you anymore, and I want you to stop thinking you need to save me. Go back home where you belong. I'm not yours to worry about."

He tightened his jaw and continued to stare at her.

She wanted to apologize, but she was tired of that, too.

It's not your fault.

"You know where to find me," he said, brushing past her toward the front door.

Adaline stared angrily at the antiques on the shelf closest to her and picked up an item. She squeezed a glass paperweight in her hand and threw it on the floor. Adaline screamed and grabbed objects, one by one, letting them shatter as they hit the ground.

Now you really are alone.

"Girls, don't leave me too. Mommy wants to play hide-and-seek still, and I'm getting warmer on finding you." Adaline closed her eyes and watched a slideshow of memories play in her mind of her girls. "There you are." She took a deep breath and sighed.

Melting to the ground, she held her legs and took in the damage she'd just created.

Maybe I am crazy.

A piece of glass clung to the wood floor near her foot, balancing itself up and down. Adaline picked it up and gently placed it in her palm, staring at the sharp edges on the corner. The glass was beautiful broken. Why did people always feel the need to fix things that were broken? She brought the glass to eye level. Taking her finger, she held it over the sharp edge and pressed down as the blood oozed off the tip.

This was real.

The prick of her finger.

The jagged glass piece in her hand.

Blood.

Pain.

Her reality.

Right here, in her store. The fire inside her that the girls were still alive continued to burn. Bristles brushing against the wood floor stole her attention.

"Step away from the glass, ma`am," Seth said, sweeping the floor.

"When did you get in? I didn't even hear you."

"I'm sorry. Is this a bad time?" He aimlessly looked around the store. "I thought you said to come back at eight today." Seth handed her a Kleenex.

Adaline wiped the small red clot on her finger on the napkin. "I did. I must've lost track of time." She pressed her hand to her face. "Why would you want to come back? To my store, I mean?"

"Ma'am?" he said, raising his eyebrows.

"You know, with all the rumors and news surrounding me. Why would you want to stick around? Most people would rather stay away."

Seth stopped sweeping. "Everyone deserves a second chance, right? You gave me one, and I'm very grateful." He let the broom lie against the wall and walked toward her. "You know, there's good in every one of us. Sometimes the bad outweighs the good, but it only takes one person to see it to make all the difference." He looked down at the ground and turned away from her.

"Thank you, Seth."

"For what?"

"For saying something that made a difference to me, and please, will you stop calling me ma'am? I'm too young for that." She smiled. "What was prison like? I mean, you don't need to answer that if you don't want to."

Seth didn't turn around. "Kind of what you might think it is. Hell. A deep, dark, and lonely place where you pay for what you rightfully deserve. I was in my own personal prison for a long time before I was locked away, but at least in that place, I felt like I was atoning for my sins. It gave me clarity on what I needed to do to make up for all the damage I caused."

"You really think people can change?"

"Yes. It's got to be up to them. You can't force someone to change or be something you would like them to be."

If only my mother could've been different and lived long enough for me to see a change in her.

"I sure hope you're right," she said, pulling back her hair.

Seth grabbed the broom and began sweeping the glass pieces into the dustpan. A sense of loss, watching him shovel it all in the plastic tray to throw away, pained her.

"Stop."

"Yes, ma'am? I mean, Adaline."

"That broken glass still has a purpose. We shouldn't throw it away just because it's severed. Everything can be fixed piece by piece, right?"

He smiled, placed the dustpan on the counter in front of her, and walked away.

THIRTY-THREE

Officer Abbott
Thursday, November 11th
Noon

HE OPENED the brown paper bag that sat on his passenger seat and took out a large bottle of Vodka. Staring at the glass jar, Abbott licked his lips with anticipation for the gulp he'd craved in the few months of being sober.

Since when did Sam become deceitful?

Sam never showed up at his house. He told Abbott he knew nothing that could help with his daughter's case, yet he had the same necklace left at the crime scene of Aspen's disappearance a year ago. That piece of worthless jewelry held the last sweet memory he had of her.

He came home early to take her on a daddy/daughter date. They'd talked about it for days. Walking into the house, he tiptoed and closed the door quietly, so she wouldn't realize he was home. Singing came from inside her room, and the smell of chocolate chip cookies from her

Easy Bake Oven filled the air. He tapped on the door, and she ran to it, squealing his name. Picking her up, he swung her in the air and they danced. She giggled for a while until she informed him he was dancing all wrong. After a few cookies and some karaoke, she smiled at him and sweetly asked for privacy to get dressed for their date.

Once she had finished getting ready, he could barely speak. Only seven then, but she looked at least four years older. A young lady, not a little girl. She had a green, sparkling dress on, with gold earrings, silver flats, and a frown. He lifted her chin and asked what troubled her. She sniffled and explained she'd made a bracelet for him, but she couldn't find it. He reassured her that it'd reappear. She nodded and put on her coat as they headed off on their adventure together. He'd never fully grasped why girls insisted on being put together from head to toe, but he understood some when they walked into the nail salon. Aspen's eyes grew wide, and the more sparkles the nail polish had, the further her mouth opened. She took her time gazing at each color, making sure she found "the perfect one." At last, her finger pointed to a silver and emerald mix. She grinned and exclaimed how perfect the color would blend with her green dress. On the way home, they got ice cream and talked about her day. He never knew that would be the last time they would share chocolate mint ice cream and talk about her friends.

She was so much like her mother. She enjoyed talking, ice cream, and the finer things in life. He missed both of his ladies every single day. One smile from Aspen made the world a better, happier place. She changed him. He felt like an honorable man and a good father being around her.

Abbott brought the bottle of vodka to his lips. He could smell the strength of the alcohol and smiled.

Only a sip. I can control myself this time.

He missed that feeling of doing something right by someone in the world. Being something other than a screw-up. She adored him, and he wanted to be the man she thought him to be. Aspen wouldn't have liked the drunken version of himself.

Fuck.

Abbott placed the lid back on the bottle and put it under his seat. He snapped the bracelet around his wrist. Aspen never had a chance to give it to him herself, but it did reappear, just like he'd told her. It kept him grounded. He watched people walk up and down the sidewalk, wondering how shitty their lives were through the forced smiles.

Someone knocked on his window.

"Are you all right?" Lieutenant Stalk yelled through the closed glass.

Abbott got out of his car and pulled up his belt buckle. "Fine."

Lieutenant Stalk narrowed his vision on him. "Have you slept at all?"

He scratched his cheek. "Some."

The lieutenant patted him on the back. "Good man. Let's get to it, then."

Walking into the police station, he halted after opening the door. "Do you remember what happened to the necklace at the crime scene with my daughter? I would really like to get that back."

"Again? You told me you were ready to come back to work. All I've seen so far is that my decision to bring you back wasn't a valid choice."

"It's my daughter's, that's all I'm asking. I'll get my shit together. Just...can I have it?"

"It's a piece of a crime scene. You know I can't do that."

"Not even for a long-time friend? It's important to me," Abbott said, bending down to tie his shoe.

The lieutenant didn't respond. He seemed calm but distracted. "Get to work, son."

Abbott bunched his fist and nodded.

What was that?

He brushed his bald head and walked to his desk. Punching in a number on his phone, he brought it to his ear and bent down. "Mrs. Rushner? Yes, it's Officer Abbott. I just have a few more routine questions I need to ask you. Could I swing by your home later this evening? No, tomorrow at 7:30 pm will work. Great. See you soon."

He was going to get answers, no matter what it cost. Nothing else mattered at this point. Finding out the truth about what happened to the Rushner girls could solve his daughter's case too.

THIRTY-FOUR

Seth Duncan
Thursday, November 11th
Noon

REPORTERS STOOD out front of the Grand Capital Motel, waiting for someone to come outside. Seth thought using his break from work to catch a small nap seemed like a good idea, but he grew suspicious as he got closer to his room. His next-door neighbor came out just as he'd stepped inside his room.

"Mr. Rushner, do you have any comments about the new information about your wife?"

Mr. Rushner, new information.

Seth poked his head through the blinds to watch the man that the reporters called Mr. Rushner get swarmed by a hive of bees, ready to make a sting. He had no idea the man next door was Adaline's husband.

They must be fighting with the media smothering them.

He heard the reporters yelling Mr. Rushner's name repeatedly, the voices growing further away.

New information. What new information?

Seth turned the TV on Channel 5 for the noon news to static. He hit the TV a few times and fixed the antennas to be positioned in just the right spot. Once he could hear talking, he turned to the screen to be face-to-face with Sienna Rhoades giving the update.

"Almost four weeks ago, Eliza and Leora Rushner were kidnapped from their home in Owling, Utah. That's caused many to wonder what could've possibly happened for those children to be the target of such a sinister act of violence against them. We've uncovered new information into the life of Adaline Rushner that may bring light to some very interesting questions."

Seth smacked his head and sneered at the screen.

"As a child, Adaline Rushner had been admitted to a psychiatric ward for schizophrenia and massive anxiety. This took place a week after her parents' tragic death when her aunt, who had graciously taken the young girl in, reported her being a danger to herself and others. Her aunt claimed Adaline made threats on her own life leading up to being admitted. Information about what hospital she was a patient at has been sealed at this time.

"We just got word from a source that two days ago there was a disturbance at the Rushner home, where Mrs. Rushner claimed that her dead girls were taken from the home. She's clearly unstable and unwell. We should be asking ourselves—would she be capable of harming her kids and have the memory of doing so? And was Braxton Wheeler the killer, or was he set up? Turning it over to weather, Charlie."

"Thank you, Sienna, for the update. And now…"

Seth sunk to the ground, glared at the ceiling, and

entwined his fingers to say a prayer. He never prayed until he got placed into the box someone hid him in and had time to ponder what path he needed to take to make his sorry life a better one. For once in his life, he realized someone was on his side. Seth stood and put his sneakers on. Any minute now, Adaline's store would be crawling with parasites trying to tear her down. Investigate her life so they wouldn't have to focus on the misfortune of their own. The lady couldn't get a break for the life of her. All this from her past on the news, the death of her girls, and her marriage seemed to be unraveling. He shook his head. Seth tied his long hair back with a rubber band and ran to her store as fast as his feet would allow.

He swung open the door. "Adaline."

She appeared cheerful, with a tint of color on her cheeks. After the morning she'd had, fighting with her husband and an old friend at the store, seeing her more relaxed made him smile. And now he had to drain the color and energy from her again. She looked up at him inquisitively and peered at her clock. "You never call me Adaline," she said. "Does that mean we're friends?"

He nodded.

"You still have a twenty-minute break. Go eat. I can handle things here."

Seth stepped toward her and opened his mouth to speak, but he couldn't bring himself to upset her. She had given him a chance, and she was his friend. The only one he had.

I can't do this to her.

"Seth. Are you well? Eating helps me when I don't have energy. Please go eat."

He smiled and walked toward the door.

Coward. You coward.

Before he got to the door, two news vans pulled up to the front of the store. He locked the door, turned the door sign to closed, and knelt on the ground.

"Adaline," he said, whispering. She turned to look at him and raised her eyebrows. He placed a finger on his mouth and pointed to the ground. He crawled toward her as she lowered her body to the floor, and before she could ask him anything, he placed his face against hers and whispered in her ear, "Do you trust me?"

She paused and gazed into his eyes. Adaline stared at him like she could see right through his soul and nodded. He gently grabbed her hand and they left through the back exit.

Outside, Adaline held his arm, forcing him to look at her. "What are we doing?"

"Your past is catching up to you, my friend."

THIRTY-FIVE

Cache Rushner
Thursday, November 11th
12:30 p.m.

AFTER REPORTERS HIJACKED him at his motel and arriving to work late, yet again, all eyes would be on him at his job. He needed his lunch break to clear his head. Grabbing a burger, he headed back to work. The parking garage filled quickly due to all the shopping malls sitting right next to Kirkmark Trading in downtown Salt Lake City. Cache could usually find a hidden spot on the first level, but not today.

Listening to the newest reports on the radio before he got into the parking garage confused him further about Adaline. They'd been married for eight years, and never once had she brought up spending time in a psychiatric ward, and she'd never shown signs of schizophrenia to him.

I don't believe this. It's not true. She would've told me.

On the fifth floor, one spot still sat open, so he swerved into it. He slammed on the brakes, stepped out of his car, and retrieved his briefcase. Cache walked into the elevator and pressed the main floor button. The doors began to shut when he heard someone yell, "Hold the door." He grabbed the small opening of the elevator door and let it open wide enough for the lady to get inside.

"Thank you, young man."

"Miss Tisher? Did we have an appointment today?"

"Well, hello, Mr. Rushner. No appointment today, just meeting an old friend. How are you? Wait, don't answer that. I watch the news," she said, folding her arms over her chest.

"We're fine. Just a bunch of lies." He cleared his throat. "I got your message about setting up an account. Let me know when you'd like to do that, and I'll be happy to help."

She smirked. "Understood. Will you kindly push the main floor button?"

Cache responded to her request and watched as she fixed her curly red hair. He wondered if she was wearing a wig, as it went awfully wrong with her oval-shaped head. It looked similar to a poodle getting groomed at a newbie salon by a woman named Diamond, who loves her Aqua Net.

"So, are you enjoying your new home? I mean the inside, anyway. Those reporters live on your front lawn, I see," she said.

"Yes. She loved it like you said she would. Thank you," Cache said, bowing his head.

"Well, that's what I do. I find perfect homes for perfect couples. So, do you know anyone else looking for a home?" She handed a small stack of business cards to him.

"I'm leaving town soon and would love to get a few more deals in before I jet."

He was shocked at her lack of professionalism. "Sorry. I don't know of anyone, but I'll be sure to put these cards out on my desk for you."

She smiled. "Well, this is my stop. Be a dear and help an old lady with her heel."

Cache glanced down at her shoe and bent over to place the blue heel back on her sweaty foot. Being around fifty hardly made her an old lady. She stepped out of the elevator and blew a kiss to him. "I truly do hope your wife isn't crazy. You seem like a nice young man, and it would be a pity for you to get burned."

He let her exit first, then followed behind her through the lobby. A man in a blue shirt looked up from the front desk. "Can I help you?"

"Yes. Has the UPS truck come yet today? I'm waiting for a package. The name is Cache Rushner."

"Sorry, sir. Nothing yet. Usually, they come around nine a.m. Try tomorrow."

"Thank you," Cache said, tilting his head. He went back to the elevator and hit the fourth-floor button. He bounced and stared at his watch.

If I have a job tomorrow, it will be miraculous

The elevator door opened. A strong scent of roses still lingered, even after Miss Tisher left. He held his nose. Cache watched the numbers go up, and a red light dinged as the elevator jolted to a stop. He stepped out, bumping into a lady. Her purse fell to the floor. Cache bent down to help pick up the contents spread across the carpet.

"Really, young man, it's okay."

He had just heard that same voice in the elevator. Cache gazed up at her. "Miss Tisher?" The lady looked like her, but she had long blonde hair rather than her red, short poodle do. Her eyes widened and she ran down the hall before she retrieved the rest of her purse contents.

Was that Miss Tisher? Why was she wearing a wig and running off so fast?

He proceeded to pick up the rest of the stuff off the floor. Letting curiosity get the best of him, Cache grabbed at a loose paper in the corner by a baseboard and read it.

Jaxon,
If you do this last job for me, I'll pay you well.

Cache wondered if that was why she hadn't called him back to set up an account. She was already doing that with his boss.

THIRTY-SIX

Adaline Rushner
1:00 p.m.

SHE SAT ON THE COUCH, feeling numb and confused by what Seth had just told her right before he dropped her off. Her feet curled beneath her.

It didn't make sense. Psychiatric ward. Schizophrenia. How would she forget that? *Or did it ever really happen?*

Counting to five in her head, she rubbed her fingers together. Adaline stared at the TV on her mantel. She couldn't bring herself to turn it on and watch what the media had to say, but the urge to see what repulsive lies they had up their sleeves stirred within her. She held her own hand and wished it was Cache's instead to comfort her frozen body. She wrapped a fleece blanket around her shoulders and turned the volume up as Sienna Rhoades received feedback from citizens in the area.

"What do you think about Mrs. Rushner and the case regarding her daughters?" asked the reporter.

"I think they should take a closer look at what really happened with those girls and keep digging into that woman," said a citizen.

"What about you?"

A short man in his fifties looked at the camera. "I feel she needs help. Get her the assistance she needs."

The citizens' comments went on and on.

"That woman's hiding something."

"Search her house."

"Someone who's crazy like her should've never had those kids to begin with."

Adaline turned the TV off. She kicked her couch, creating a loud crack and pain shooting through her toe.

Great.

Adaline took off her clothes, went to the bathroom, and turned on the faucet. The water filled up the bathtub and she shivered, dipping her feet into the tub. The warmth of the water didn't replace how cold she felt inside.

Icy.

Frozen.

She got in and scooted her body downward, letting her face submerge under the clear pool. Adaline watched it swirl above her for a minute and then closed her eyes. Her arms started to float, letting her mind relax.

"Drink this. You'll like it."

"What is it, Auntie?"

"It's lemonade. Your favorite."

Adaline brought the cup to her lips and took a sip. "This is horrible. I don't want this."

"It's good for you. I put some medicine in there to help you sleep."

"I don't want to go to sleep. Please don't make me drink this."

"It will help you feel better, I promise. You want to feel better, don't you?"

Adaline nodded her head and brought the cup back to her mouth, drinking until the last drop touched her tongue.

"Good job. Now come here and I'll hold you until you fall asleep."

Adaline smiled, lying on the couch next to her aunt. She brushed Adaline's hair back and kissed her on the forehead. "Everything will be okay. I'll be right back."

"No. Don't leave me," said Adaline, reaching for her arm.

Her aunt turned around and grinned. "Child, I'll be back."

Adaline held her own hand and looked at the ceiling. Everything seemed fuzzy now, and her eyes felt heavy.

"I can't do this anymore. Thank you for making the call," her aunt said. "I'll be ready when they come." The click of the phone being placed back in the cradle told Adaline she was done with her call. "I'm back." Her aunt came around the corner with a knife in her hand.

Adaline reached to hug her aunt, but she couldn't move.

Her aunt smirked and brought the knife to her own arm, making a deep cut.

"No. Stop. I need you." The words slurred off her tongue. Aunt Arlene wiped the blood on Adaline's shirt and gave her the knife. She opened a pill bottle and let the capsules scatter around her.

"It's too late for that, child. They're coming for you. You're someone else's problem now."

Her aunt began screaming for someone to help her. "Please don't do this to yourself, Adaline. Please."

A crash came through the house and two men grabbed her aunt and held her as she sobbed. "She's done this before. I know she's heartbroken over her parents, but I can't lose her. Can you please help her?"

"What happened?" said a man.

"I found her taking some sleeping pills, and I tried to stop her. That's when she came at me with the knife," said her aunt.

One of the suited men looked at her and ushered two others in his direction. "Take her away."

Adaline screamed in her mind as she felt herself being picked up.

Helpless.

Unmovable.

She stared at her aunt and saw her smile, lurking with deception. Hatred seeped into her eyes. Adaline held her gaze, making sure her aunt saw her in this form before the men carried her out of the house and took her away.

Adaline gasped and resurfaced from the tub, choking on water. She sat up, holding her shivering shoulders, and covered her mouth with her prune-wrinkled fingers.

My aunt framed me. Why? What else don't I remember?

Wrapping the towel around her body, she got into bed and clung to her pillow. The sheets glided against her skin, and her toes started to warm up. A woman's voice in her mind spoke to her in a calm tone, and then her face popped into Adaline's head. She remembered Dr. Vi Lynchester.

THIRTY-SEVEN

Owl Keeper
Thursday, November 11th
1:00 p.m.

BETRAYAL WAS a familiar look that Adaline plastered on her face. No matter where she went, that haunting glance followed her through the years, except there was a difference now.

Hatred.

To the blackest corner of her iris, he understood that look well. That used to be him, or maybe it still was. What other people saw in him.

Twenty-five years ago, he had that darkness inside him.

Sitting at the mall, watching families smile and laugh with not a care in the world, and he hated them for having something that he never had.

Love. Adoration. A place to call home.

He watched as they held hands and hugged each other,

another feeling he hadn't shared with anyone. No one hugged or thought of him. He had no family, no friends, just guilt that buried him alive every morning. Would anyone recognize if he was gone? No, no one. He hung his head and sat in silence, letting his thoughts tear him down until he felt ragged.

A woman's voice barked across the food court. He looked up to see where the commotion was coming from and saw her—a little girl with long blonde hair, no older than eight. Tears streamed down her face as the woman repeatedly took a tone with her in the middle of the store. Observers watched, but no one said a thing. They just pointed and stared, like the little girl was a part of a circus show, and then moved about their business. His fingers bunched together tightly listening to the distasteful words coming out her mouth.

Stupid girl.

No-good little snot.

Those words were familiar to him. His mother used the same on him while trying to drown him in the bathtub. He walked toward the girl and the woman, unsure of what he was about to do. As he got close to the girl, he dropped a necklace on the floor.

He watched as the little girl hunched over to pick it up. "Here you go, sir," she said, staring at him for a long moment. The girl had the most beautiful blue eyes, and the look of betrayal reflected there turned to warmth as she smiled, trying to hide it under her long hair. She reminded him so much of his sister—the sister who he couldn't save. Her hand touched his briefly.

"Thank you," he said, smiling back.

"Don't you talk to strangers. Do you even have a brain in there? Honestly, Adaline," said the lady who dressed as if she had won the lottery. She wore fancy jewelry, had perfectly manicured hair, and makeup that showed no flaws—but she was ugly, and he detested her.

"What are you staring at, you brute?"

He turned away and watched as the lady grabbed the little girl's arm with force.

"Stop it, Momma. You're hurting me."

He walked toward them again. "Let her go."

"Do you know who I am? You can't stop me. Look at you. You're a filthy mongrel." She stopped and glanced at him with pity and pulled out a twenty-dollar bill. "Go get some clothes and mind your own business." The woman threw the money at him. "Come along, Adaline."

The little girl didn't move. She peered at him with sadness in her eyes. "Can you help me, please," she said to him in a whisper.

He walked closer to her and bent down to place the necklace in her pocket. "Don't worry, you'll be okay," he said, in her ear. "I won't let her hurt you anymore."

The little girl nodded. "Who's protecting you?"

He stood. "I'm protecting myself."

"Me, too," the girl said. "It's a lot of work when you're alone, and no one believes you."

Barking sounded behind him. "I told you to mind your business. I will get the police if you don't step away from us, you dumb mutt."

The little girl put her hand in his.

"Adaline, what on earth are you doing? Come to me now, or you know where I'll put you," she said, hushed. Her eyes blazed as she moved closer to them, spitting in his face. She held her multiple shopping bags and laughed. "Security. My daughter's being taken."

The little girl let go of his hand and ran toward her mother. "I'm sorry," she mouthed to him as a drop fell from her eye.

He wiped the spit off his face with his hand and dried it on his pants, watching as Adaline left with the woman.

She protected and trusted him when no one else did. That started his mission to protect her, too.

Who did he need to save her from now?

THIRTY-EIGHT

Sam Wendell
Thursday, November 11th
2:00 p.m.

HE PULLED up to Abbott's driveway and glanced around at the surrounding neighbors' homes. No one was outside. Sam had every intention of leaving Abbott out of it, but now he'd seen too much. Fear that things were no longer in his control hung in his gut.

Why couldn't he have left it alone?

Walking toward the back door, he used the hidden key Abbott left for him under the dog bowl. The guy thought he was hilarious since he didn't even own a dog. Sam opened the door to a shrine of pictures and newspaper articles all over the floor in the living room. He stepped forward to see Abbott pointing a gun directly at his head.

"I could charge you for breaking into my home," Abbott said.

Sam took a deep breath. "We're supposed to meet, remember?"

"Really? Seven hours later. You asshole. Get out of my house."

"C'mon, man. Don't be like that."

"Like what?" Abbott asked. "You lied to my face about not knowing something about my daughter's case, and then you never show up. I thought you'd be long gone by now."

Sam stood in place and rolled up his sleeves. "I'm not leaving until we get something straight. Put the gun down."

"Get the hell out, unless you're going to tell me what you know about my baby."

I can't have him more involved.

"I want to talk to you. There's just a lot at play here."

"You don't think I see that?" He held his phone up to Sam's face. "Remember her?"

Sam cleared his throat. "Yeah, man. I do. She beat me at chess every time I came over."

"That's my girl."

The room fell silent.

"What's all this and why aren't you at work?" Sam asked.

"You don't get to ask questions. Shut the door and come inside," Abbott said. "You make a run for it, I'll shoot."

He nodded and did as he was instructed.

"Now, where did you get the owl necklace?"

"A friend."

"Mrs. Rushner, friend?"

Shit.

Sam pushed his hands in his pockets. "Please, drop it."

Abbott kept the gun on Sam. "You know I can't do that. You mentioned she got the necklace as a kid. If that's the case, why do you have the same one?"

He took the necklace out of his pocket and clung to it. "It's personal."

Abbott snorted. "Fuck. You bet it's personal. You're not done. You didn't answer my question."

"She lost this on the day she ran from my marriage proposal."

Pacing the floor, Abbott kept his eyes on him. "You never gave it to her?"

"No."

"Then where did she get the necklace she's wearing?" Abbott asked.

"I'm pretty sure it was left for her on the day her girls were taken."

Abbott lowered his gun and paused. "There was only one necklace reported that day as evidence. A second necklace was never mentioned."

Sam didn't say a word.

Getting too close.

"You know just as well as I do that there's a connection between the Rushner case and Aspen. Four of the same necklaces. Found at multiple crime scenes. And Adaline Rushner, the woman you're protecting and still in love with, is behind it all." Abbott peered at the papers on the floor again, examining them one by one. "Who's leaving her the necklaces?"

He loosened his collar. "Someone from the past."

"That's all you're going to give me? I'll ask again. How would my daughter receive the same necklace that those girls and Mrs. Rushner received?" Abbott asked.

"Let this go. It's nothing to worry about. It's got to be a coincidence."

"Shit, Sam. You don't actually believe that," Abbott said. "When people you think you know start acting guilty, or doing the reverse psychology on ya, they're hiding something."

Sam shuffled his feet. "Buddy, how about you have friends that care and worry about you with all you've been through. I think you need to sleep more than a few hours."

Abbott glanced at Sam sternly. "You're too close to this, and that's why you're not seeing straight. She's not well and wants people to believe her girls are alive. What better way to do that than leave an object that appears someone's following her?"

"She's not like that. You're reaching."

"Coming from the guy who's still holding on to something he can never have. I can't trust your instincts. I smell a coverup." Abbott raised the gun at Sam again. "You're protecting a girl who left you and who will burn you again once she's done with you."

Sam clenched his jaw. "Are we done talking about this?"

"You want to play games with me? Let's play. Remember who Aspen learned chess from?" Abbott asked. "Give me my key and get the hell out of my house."

"We're on the same side. That's what I came here to tell you." They stared at each other for a moment, then Sam placed the necklace in his pocket and shut the door behind him.

It's nice knowing you, Abbott.

THIRTY-NINE

Dr. Lynchester
3:00 p.m.

EVER SINCE SHE was ambushed by her client and left that note saying, "Protect Adaline," Dr. Lynchester tried calling Adaline only to be sent to voicemail each time. It was too risky leaving a message. Having her own people watch Adaline had to be good enough for now. She stretched and paced the room, wiping any sign of dust on her bookshelf with her finger.

"Dr. Lynchester?" asked her assistant on the intercom.

"Yes, Tayla. What is it?"

"There's someone on the phone for you. They say it's urgent."

She looked at her watch. Only five minutes until her next appointment. Most calls never took five minutes when it was urgent, but she had the occasional suicidal client that if you asked to call them back, it would be too late.

"Can you ask who it is, and if it's not Mr. Meyer, take down their number and tell them I'll get back to them as soon as I can."

The intercom clicked off. She fidgeted with her pencils, taking them all out of the cup holder and reorganizing them one by one so they didn't stand so close together.

"Dr. Lynchester?"

"Yes."

"It's not Mr. Meyer."

"Okay, then would you please take a message?" she asked, rolling her eyes.

"You might want to take this. It's . . . Adaline Rushner. The woman all over the news."

"Tayla?"

"Yes."

"Put her in as my 5:30 appointment today."

"Got it."

The intercom clicked off again.

Adaline called me. That could only mean one thing.

Smiling, she pulled her cell phone out to send a text.

"She's remembering."

———

The last time Dr. Lynchester had seen Adaline, she was twenty-five, right after she'd given birth to Leora. That visit, in her mind, should've been a great reunion since it'd been six years since she'd bid her farewell, but Adaline greeted her with much distaste. Time hadn't soothed the wound, and a lot had changed since then. A light knock on the door prompted her feet to move before she even knew what was happening.

"Hello. Come on in."

"Dr. Lynchester?" Adaline asked, throwing her arms around her neck.

"Dear. How are you?" she said, lightly holding her back. She wasn't sure what to think but hugged her back anyway.

Adaline stepped back to look at her. "You look the same as I remember."

"What do you mean?"

"That's why I'm here. I don't know what's happening to me. I need some help."

"Take a seat on the couch," Dr. Lynchester said, holding her hand out to direct her.

Adaline took off her shoes, sat in the middle of the couch, and crossed her legs. Dr. Lynchester watched her as she moved. She appeared exactly the same, just older and more tired, but beautiful. Her hair was just as blonde as she remembered, but instead of dangling ringlets down her back, a tightly-pulled-back bun clung to her head. Adaline's blue eyes struck her with a combo of being divine and haunting. Not a thing had changed in those lost years since she'd last seen her. She grabbed her notebook and a pen and sat in the chair opposite Adaline.

"I see you still like to be in the middle of couches...and you feel at home in my office," she said, pointing to her shoes.

Adaline shrugged. "I do, but I think I've always felt that way with you." She glanced around the room, wide-eyed. "This office clearly isn't the same one you had in Owling, but everything is placed in the same order."

"I'm surprised you remember that so well. I thought over the years you'd forget all about our sessions."

"I'm sorry I just barged in here without an appointment."

"I'm glad that you did." Dr. Lynchester heard that Adaline had lost some memories due to recent events, but she was acting as though nothing had ever happened negatively between them. Could it be a trick? That didn't seem like her, but Dr. Lynchester also knew what she was capable of when she got mad. Clearing her throat, she bounced her knee. "So...let's get started, shall we? What brought you here today?"

Adaline paused and stared at the ground. "Okay. I... um...didn't remember you."

"What do you mean?"

"Before this morning, I didn't know who you were, but earlier today I had a flash of a memory. One that I didn't remember. How is that possible?" Adaline scratched her head and played with her zipper on her jacket.

"Our mind is a curious thing. Some memories we hold in our subconscious and they come out at peak times kind of like a message."

"That sounds—"

"Crazy?" Dr. Lynchester asked.

Adaline chuckled and then got serious. "We're all crazy here, I guess."

Dr. Lynchester watched her face drop as she said the comment. "How does this make you feel, having this memory all of a sudden?"

"At first, confused and scared, but also betrayed."

"What did you see?"

Adaline pressed her thumbs together and put her head down. "My aunt Arlene. She accused me of being suicidal to get rid of me. She set me up."

"Do you know why she set you up?"

Adaline closed her eyes and clung to the couch. Her

reaction looked strained, but her mouth turned down as if she was in pain.

Dr. Lynchester gripped her pen, knowing the memory that was unfolding in her mind. All she wanted to do was take the pain away.

Adaline flinched.

Dr. Lynchester held the pen tighter.

"I can't."

"It's okay. Take a nice deep breath." Dr. Lynchester paused. "What's worrying you the most? Not remembering, or what you saw in your memory?"

She clasped her hands together like she did as a kid. "I don't know. Sometimes I wonder what's real, or what's a figment of my imagination, and that scares me. Maybe I *am* going crazy like everyone thinks. Do you think I'm crazy?"

"My dear. I don't think you're crazy, but you do have some missing pieces that we need to get back for you."

"Tell me, is this a memory that I lived, or am I making it up? Do I have schizophrenia like the news says? Is that why I saw you for years?"

"Take a moment to clear your head." Dr. Lynchester moved her chair closer and placed her hand on top of Adaline's. "What do you feel is real? Think."

"This is real. My being here."

"It's very real. Now close your eyes and think back to the last time we saw each other."

Adaline closed her eyes and placed her hands in her lap.

Dr. Lynchester let go of her hand and got up to pace the floor. Quietly, she walked around Adaline and leaned near her neck.

"What if I don't remember that moment?" Adaline asked.

Jumping backward, Dr. Lynchester held her hands behind her back and continued pacing again. "It's a part of the process, but you need to relax first. Let's take a few deep breaths."

Adaline closed her eyes again and her chest moved up and down a few times. Her hands fell to the couch, and her eyelashes started to flutter.

"I can see you're relaxing. Good. Keep breathing and think of something that makes you happy. Once you've got that in your mind, hold it there."

Adaline's mouth tilted upward and her dimples creased.

Dr. Lynchester stopped pacing and bent over the couch again, careful not to lean on Adaline. She hesitated and took a deep breath, but made sure to not make any noise. Inside, her breathing was loud as it thrashed against her chest to get out. Her hand shook, and before she gave herself time to steady it, Dr. Lynchester stuck a shot in Adaline's neck. She watched as her body went limp. "I told you. I'm here to help you."

Her eyes grew wide and she mouthed something, but sound didn't escape her lips.

Dr. Lynchester put a red, satin pillow down on the couch and laid Adaline's head on it. Placing a fleece blanket over her shoulders, she kissed her on the forehead and pulled her cell phone out of her dress pants. She held it in her hand, deciding what to do, when it vibrated with a call, signaling her to answer it.

"Is she there?"

"She's here, and I'm keeping her safe for now," Dr. Lynchester said.

"Make sure that you do."

FORTY

Cache Rushner
Kirkham Trading
5:00 p.m.

POUNDING outside his office door took him away from the account he was looking at. It didn't sound like a knock but like someone kicking it with their boot.

"Come in."

Naylor Todd, the guy who had the office next to his, came in with a smile that could've scared him as a child. It wasn't forced, but not genuine either. Something hid behind the crooked expression. All he needed was makeup, a wig, and a red nose. He brought in some cardboard boxes and handed Cache a message.

"What's this man?"

He shrugged his shoulders and walked out.

So much for small talk.

The message was addressed by his boss, Jaxon

Millstadt, to come visit him in his office. He threw his pen at the door and gripped his neck.

It had only been a week, and already the new beginning and possibilities he imagined for himself and Adaline were going down the drain, one by one. He straightened his tie, dusted off his suit, and walked toward his boss's office.

The receptionist stood and fixed her glasses. "Mr. Rushner. He's waiting for you." She glanced away for a minute and whispered lightly to him. "I'm sorry."

Cache paused before entering his office. The room was filled with full-length windows. Glass surrounded him.

"Good afternoon, Mr. Millstadt, sir," Cache said.

Jaxon Millstadt held up his hand to stop him from talking further. "I'm just going to cut right to it," his boss said. "Your wife is making quite an issue for this firm. Are you planning on divorcing her?"

He didn't answer.

"No, I didn't think so. Listen, we need to let you go."

"I need this job. I can work extra hours."

"It's really not that, son. You're a good worker, but you're always late, and the media is hounding this building. I can't have that for our firm. It's giving me a bad rep, keeping you around."

"My wife is just confused," Cache said.

"Maybe, boy, but I can't help you. Word of advice though. If you believe she's innocent, why aren't you with her when the media attacks her? She's always by herself."

"There's more going on here than just my wife. You hired me with a great position, my own office, and lots of opportunities right from the beginning," Cache said. "I appreciated it all, but that's not typically how someone starts a position they've never held before."

Jaxon grinned. "You've done your part and what you were hired to do."

"What exactly is that?"

"You know, you could give me a tip. You got game, I like that. How do I get away from my wife like you have? She's hounding me, and I'm seeing a tight, young thing on the side now. I need her out of the picture."

Cache sneered. "I care for my wife."

"Yes, you say that, which looks really good for you, but you're nowhere near her, like I said. See what I mean? That's pretty brilliant. Game." He pumped his fist in the air. "I've worked the business for a while, and I know when I see a con man."

He looked away. "Thanks for the boxes."

His boss saluted him as he shut his door.

Cache laughed and peered at the receptionist who poked her head out from the book she was reading. His laughter grew, and then he stopped and bunched his fists. He imagined throwing something at his boss's window and watching the glass fall with a domino effect. Maybe one would accidentally fall on him, getting Mr. Boss man out of the picture . . . for his wife, of course. Cache rolled up his sleeves and stomped to his office.

Some future he had.

It didn't settle well with him, what his boss said. He wasn't the kind to treat his wife well. She'd bring him lunch, and he would barely say two words to her.

Is that what our relationship has come to?

Cache began placing items from his office in the boxes when all he wanted to do was leave it all behind. He finished up the last of the objects and walked to the elevator. Too many things weren't adding up. He still didn't know what to make of Miss Tisher and that note he found. Was it for his boss? Cache worried that maybe she was a fraud. He had a hard time envisioning such a nice lady like her being a criminal. She didn't seem like someone who could even yell at a young child without crying herself. And now his boss, saying that Cache did his part for what he was hired for. What was that about?

Getting down to the parking garage, the elevator dinged and jarred open. The garage wasn't as congested as before, making it easier to get out of the area quicker to get home.

Home.

Cache missed it, and Adaline, and he could hardly call that little dump motel a house. He pressed his automatic car door button on his key ring, unlocking the car. He moved a few steps and halted. The hairs on his arm stood, and an unnerving feeling gripped him that someone followed close behind. He locked his car and glanced around the garage. Shuffling sounded from behind him. Cache started to turn and felt the hard crash of metal, smacking him upside his skull.

FORTY-ONE

Adaline Rushner
Thursday, November 11th
5:00 p.m.

THE LIGHT in Dr. Lynchester's office faded, and Adaline fought to keep her eyes open. Her arms didn't move on demand, and she willed herself to hold on, but unconsciousness infringed upon her.

A bed with a blue ruffled skirt and a tattered teddy bear invited her to sit down. She grabbed the brown bear and held him close.

"What's your name, funny bear? You look like you could use a bath." Adaline paused. "You must not have anyone that loves you, either." She held him tight and lay on the bed, snuggling her new friend. In the next room, she could hear someone chanting a song.

There was a little owl
High in a tree
She tried to fly away

But couldn't get free

Adaline sat up, kept holding the bear's hand, and walked to the next room, following the melody of the song. "Why couldn't the owl get free?"

"I see you found Mr. Speckles," he said.

"Mr. Speckles? This is a bear, not a frog. Can't you do any better than that on picking a name?"

He smiled at her. "Actually, it used to be my sister's."

"What happened to her?" Adaline blurted out. "I'm sorry."

"Why are you apologizing? It's okay. Sit down, and I'll tell you a story. You do like stories, don't you?"

She nodded and sat on the chair next to him. Adaline put her fist under her chin waiting for the story to begin.

"My sister, Emery, needed help just like you. You remind me of her, and you look very much alike.

"Like me?"

"Yes, like you. You both are smart and beautiful but trapped in a tree like the song says. People who should love you don't give you a chance, and that's not the way it should be."

"Did your sister fly away?"

"In a way. Yes."

He winced and gazed in the distance. Adaline hurt for him. She knew what not being loved felt like, and it made her feel horrible about herself. Something must be wrong with her if her own mother couldn't even see beauty or good within her. She grabbed his hand and held it.

"I'm sorry you're all alone."

He looked up at her and, in a whisper, said, "Thank you."

"Can I fly away? I would really like to. I've thought about all the places I would go if I could get away from my home."

"Where would you go?"

"To the stars, mostly. I just want someone to love me, and I don't want to leave my parents. They don't mean to hurt me."

He grabbed her chin and wiped a tear from her face. "You don't ever have to go back there again. This is a safe place, and you're not unlovable."

"How do you know that? I make a lot of mistakes and mess up. She punishes me because I'm a bad girl. If I was smarter, or prettier, she would love me. It's my fault, and I can't change who I am," she said, sobbing.

"Can I give you something?"

Adaline glanced up at him. He lifted her long blonde hair and placed a chain around her neck, latching it in place. She looked down at the gold chain into the eyes of a little owl. "Thank you."

He grabbed both of her hands and led her to another room. "Come with me. I have something I think you will like."

He opened the back door of the small yellow house and pointed his finger. "There."

Adaline peered in the direction of his finger and saw white Gerber daisies in a garden next to the house. Smiling, she ran to the flowers and brought her nose to the tip of the petal. She inhaled and closed her eyes. The broken yellow house with the perfectly groomed flowers radiated beauty. She had the urge to lay in the garden with the daisies surrounding her, something she would never be allowed to do with her mother.

"Can I lay in here?" she asked, looking at the ground.

His eyes lit up with excitement as he nodded and came toward her.

She moved the flowers making sure that she didn't flatten any of them, lay on her back in the dirt, and looked toward the sky. Clouds filled the vast blue space. Most of them appeared wispy, allowing the sky to say hello through the thin openings. The sun hid behind one of the few cumulus clouds she could see making the lining of the cloud glow. Adaline inhaled in and the fragrance of the daisies welcomed her senses, invigorating her, and she felt something new.

Something warm. Peaceful. Solitude at the greatest level.

Was it happiness? She did not know, but she didn't want the feeling to end. After a while she sat up and shook her head, watching small dirt pellets fling off her hair and across the garden.

She laughed.

What was that? She held her mouth, unsure of what just happened. Adaline looked toward him, and he laughed, too. This is a happy thing. Yes. It is. She gave herself permission to giggle until her stomach hurt.

He stood up and cut a stem of daisies from his garden, placing one bud in her hair, and the rest of the bouquet in her hand.

The man lifted her up on a bench that dangled by two loose ropes firmly knotted onto the large tree branch. He gave her a push, and she moved her feet back and forth, feeling the wind blow against her cheeks.

She was flying.

Adaline liked the force she felt when the breeze went against her skin moving in the opposite direction. This is what it must feel like to be free.

"Adaline? Adaline, wake up."

She opened her eyes and glanced around. The clouds had disappeared, and her legs shook uncontrollably. A piercing sensation made her shiver. She sat up and looked down at her soaked shirt.

The swing, daisies, and sun had vanished. Her happy place had been taken from her once again.

FORTY-TWO

Officer Abbott
Rushner Home
6:30 p.m.

SITTING IN HIS POLICE CAR, Abbott waited around the corner of Dreary Oak Drive for Adaline to get home, along with all the reporters. Except they stayed right outside her home. He'd already watched them ring her doorbell three different times in the ten minutes he'd waited.

Should've come up with a better meeting spot.

Abbott cracked his neck and sent a text to Adaline, *I'll meet you at your backdoor.* A white car drove past him and swerved up the Rushners' driveway. He squinted and held his door handle. Reporters jumped out of their cars and ran toward the vehicle.

Mrs. Rushner stepped out of her car and slammed the door. She wore sunglasses, which seemed strange to him since the sun had already gone down. He got out of his car and walked behind the homes down the street, toward the Rusher's place. Maneuvering his way around garbage cans and fences, he reached their backdoor and knocked.

The door opened just enough to see her ear. "Officer Abbott?" Her voice sounded hoarse. "I'm sorry. Have you been waiting long? I had an appointment and lost track of time."

"It's okay. Is now a good time to talk?" he asked.

She kept the door mostly closed, and he couldn't see her face. "You know, I'm not feeling good. I'd really appreciate it if we could do this another time."

"I understand. Let me leave you my card." Abbott pulled out a card with a photo attached to it.

Adaline reached for it. "I already have your number, but…" She paused. The door opened wide. "Come in, quickly." She took off her sunglasses and stared at the picture.

He wiped his shoes on the rug and glanced around her house. It had a cozy cottage feel, with a touch of elegance, but appeared as though no one lived in it. Whistling from a tea kettle rang from the kitchen. "Would you like me to take off my shoes?"

She paced with urgency. "It's okay. Come on in. I'll be right back."

Abbott placed his hands in his pockets and walked around the main level of her home. The last time he'd been to the Rushners' place, the inside looked thrashed, chaotic, and wildly uninviting. Now it represented a phantom model home.

"You obviously have something on your mind, Officer?" Adaline turned the corner and stared at him with red eyes. Her pale skin was blotchy, as if she'd been upset or crying. He could almost play connect-the-dots of where each tear fell, from the path of redness down her face. "Please take a seat."

He sat on the couch and bent forward. "I do have some questions for you, Mrs. Rushner, if that's okay."

"I thought I already gave you my statement."

"You did. But there are some things I would like to look further into," he said, scratching his neck.

Adaline sat on the edge of her chair and tapped her foot. "Who's the girl in the photo you gave me?"

"That's my daughter, Aspen."

"I bet you both have a great time together." Adaline looked away. "Would you like some tea?"

He bunched his fists. "Okay."

She shrugged her shoulders. "I was already making myself a cup. I'll make you one too."

"Glad to see you're feeling better," Abbott said.

She paused. "Do you have any leads on my girls?"

Abbott cleared his throat. "We're working on it." He snapped his bracelet, and the letters D A D spiraled around his wrist.

He turned around and noticed her staring at him from the kitchen before reaching for a towel tied around the fridge door handle. The rose tint in her cheeks vanished to pasty white like someone took an eraser and wiped off the tear-stained dots.

"Is something the matter, Mrs. Rushner?" he asked.

She shook her head and stared off for a minute. "Give me a moment, and your tea will be ready."

Adaline picked up the teacups and turned in his direction. She didn't smile or frown. It was a very honest and rare reaction. She set the cup down next to him and sat on the couch. "Now, tell me. What do you need to talk about if you have no new information to provide?"

He ground his teeth and stared at the gold chain wrapped around her neck.

She narrowed her gaze in on him. "You sure are very interested in my necklace. Why?"

"I told you. My wife likes antiques," Abbott said. "Has Sam been in your home with you?"

Her eyes widened. "You're diverting the question? You know Sam?"

Abbott brushed the bristle on his chin. "We go back."

"He hasn't been inside my home. Just dropped me off last night." She fidgeted with the buttons on her sweater. "Why are asking that?"

"Mrs. Rushner, I'm not accusing you of anything," he said. "You can trust me."

She laughed, almost a growl. "Trust. That's a good one. I don't trust anyone, Officer. Excuse me for saying so, but just because you have a badge doesn't mean you can protect me or make me open up to you."

He grimaced.

Get in line. I couldn't even save my daughter.

"Okay, then I'm going to trust you and let you in on a little secret." He clung to the bracelet again. "My daughter was taken from me, too."

Adaline picked the picture up from the coffee table and put her fingers on the photo, caressing it. Her mouth quivered and she sat in silence.

Abbott watched her. Watched every reaction, every twitch in her body—waiting for it to give her away. "It happened about a year ago...her kidnapping." He paused and pressed his hands together. "They've never found her body."

She stared at him and he could see sympathy in her eyes. "How old was she?"

"Eight."

Adaline covered her mouth and kept peering at the picture. "I'm sorry." She looked up at him. "This is why you gasped when you saw a picture of Leora the day I was attacked. They're the same age and look very similar, our girls.

Abbott bounced his legs. "Where is my daughter? I know you know where she is."

She glanced at him. "You...don't think..." Adaline held her head, and a tear dripped from her face. "I would never hurt my daughters or your girl. I know how much you want to blame someone. It feels better, doesn't it?" She wiped the tear away. "You need to hate someone, to be angry with them, because if you don't, it's like you're letting go of the pain and saying it's okay that this happened, and that's not an option. But I'm not who you're looking for."

She convinced him with her sincerity and openness. The fact that she understood his pain was refreshing. He felt he could connect with her, but he knew all about mind games. Adaline was playing a good one. He leaned in closer. "How do you have the same necklace that was left at my daughter's kidnapping?"

"What? That's why you inquired so much about my necklace, and why you think I'm involved somehow? You were left the exact same necklace as this?" She pulled the gold chain out from under her shirt and held the locket in her hand.

Abbott nodded and pulled out his phone. He tapped on a picture of the owl necklace left at his home, the day Aspen was taken, and gave it to her.

She tilted her head. "No. It can't be. Do you think there's a connection?"

He knew what he shouldn't say, but he didn't care. "I do, and it's you."

"But we've never met until a few days ago. How do I have anything to do with your daughter?"

"That's what I'm trying to find out," he said.

Adaline took her full cup of tea to the sink and stared at him. "I already told you. I didn't do anything. Does your boss know you're here, threatening me?"

Abbott glared at her.

"I didn't think so. Leave before I inform him of your misconduct."

He stood and held his hand out. "Okay, let's not be rash. He doesn't know I'm here, but we can help each other. I need some closure too, and you seem to be the person to provide that."

"You're not here to help me, are you? It's about what I can do for you."

"Put simply, yes." Abbott paused. "Why do you believe your daughters are alive? All evidence proves that they're dead."

She hesitated and held her heart. "I'm their mother. You know how you get that pit of your stomach sinking feeling when something is wrong with your kids?"

He nodded.

"I never got that, but I would on every broken arm, burn, cut, or illness they had. They are alive, and I'm going to find them. I just need to figure out who would do this, and why. And also, why I'm a target."

"You feel you're in danger?" Abbott asked.

"I wasn't making up that someone was in my house."

His hands got clammy and his fingers twitched. "Do you remember who gave you the necklace?"

Adaline shook her head. "I don't, but I'm going to

therapy to get assistance from someone who's helping me recover my past. That's why I was so late."

Abbott held his head. "Well, that's convenient."

"You think it's fun for me to not remember? My babies are still out there somewhere, and I have to sit and wait for my mind to decide to wake up. Or have people claiming to be helping me, only they think I'm a train wreck, and they tell me to be patient so they can do their job." She held her wrist. "I'm not sitting on this, and my girls will be found. I don't give a rat's ass if you believe me or not, just stay out of my way. You search for your girl, and I'll search for mine."

He could feel her rage and passion vibrate throughout the room. No one else backed him, either. Abbott sighed. "Tragedy is an odd thing. Either you remember too much and wish you didn't, or you make it go away and search for those details your whole life."

"It sounds like you know from experience." She walked toward the table.

"I remember too much, and that pain never goes away. The pictures in my head of her smiling, her laugh, even the way she smelled—of raspberries, from her shampoo— haunts me day in and day out."

Adaline placed her hand on his shoulder. "I'm so sorry for the pain you feel."

He glanced away and stepped backward. "I should probably get going."

"I don't get close to a lot of people. It's easier that way. You don't make friends, but you don't get enemies either. But then again, here I am, receiving threats."

Adaline seemed to know exactly what to say, like a mind reader, but she understood and took empathy on him in a very calming way, and she still held a sense of humor through her pain. That made him even that much more curious about the kind of person she was. He smiled.

"You and Sam are friends?" she asked. "You said you go back."

"Yeah, he helped me through a tough time when my daughter went missing."

"He has a knack for trying to save people that need saving." She reached to grab his cup of tea. "So, what do we do now?"

Abbott glanced at her. "You need to talk to Sam."

"What do you mean?" she asked, raising her eyebrows.

"I already talked to him about the owl necklace, and he said to leave you out of it. He wouldn't tell me much."

"Why wouldn't he tell you about the necklace?"

"I don't know. He's protecting you. Wait...Sam could've given it to you, right? You two do have a romantic tie, and a dark past, from what I gather."

Adaline put the teacup on the counter in the kitchen and walked back to the front room. "That's not up for conversation."

"Did you know Sam's dad well?"

"Well enough. I lived with Sam's family for years after my parents died in the fire. His father was a quiet individual, but he was a kind man when he was home."

"He wasn't around a lot?" Abbott asked.

"He was a truck driver and happened to be on the road often," she said. "He complimented me on my blonde hair and blue eyes. Do you like art?"

Abbott gazed at her. "Ummm..."

"I do, and the painting on the wall is a favorite. Do you recognize it?" Adaline pointed to the painting centered in her living room.

"I don't, but it's beautiful."

"Thank you. It's called Starry Night, by Van Gogh. It reminded me of something Sam's dad used to say to me. This painting gave me the same warmth that his words did." She smiled. "He said my eyes resembled the sun and moon blending together. Honestly, he was the closest thing I had to a father."

"Sam paints a different picture of him."

"Yes, he had issues with his father being gone all the time. I tried to talk to him many times, but he always worried about other people over himself."

"Sounds about right. His dad treated you like one of his own?"

"I thought so. He pushed me on the swings and would always bring me flowers, and he had the kindest eyes—" Adaline stopped. "I think I need to lie down."

She's hiding something

Abbott clenched his jaw. "If you remember anything, you have my number."

Adaline held her hands together and nodded.

"Make sure to lock up. You can never trust people these days," he said, letting himself out.

If no one would give him answers, he would dig until all their sins resurfaced.

FORTY-THREE

Adaline Rushner
Thursday, November 11th
7:30 p.m.

AFTER AN HOUR'S conversation with Officer Abbott, Adaline's head felt like it just got stuck in a hamster wheel. So many thoughts spiraled in a psychedelic blur that couldn't be understood. She turned off the lights in the living room, made her way upstairs, and lay fully clothed in her bed. The spinning subsided, but the confusion continued in her mind.

Her front door made a popping noise.

Someone's in the house.

Gliding off the bed quietly, she held her phone to her chest.

Maybe it's the girls.

Adaline's feet yelled at her to take them toward the front door—they needed to move, to respond to this thought. They ached, but she halted and remembered the message left at her store warning her that the girls were only the beginning of her pain.

She gripped a pillow and growled silently into it.

Footsteps danced around the entryway, and no attempt at coming her direction was made. Adaline peered around her room and noticed a hammer she had been using to hang up a picture of her girls. She grabbed it from the side table and crept near her door. Her fingers shook, and the harder she held the handle, the shaking turned to cramping. Breathing in deep, she concentrated on the pattern her breaths took.

I won't be put into a closet again.

The movement inched its way toward the stairs. She held the hammer against her leg, ready to strike before anyone had the chance to grab her.

"Adaline?"

She knew that voice anywhere, and her heart beat faster, making her forget about their fights.

Welcome home, Daddy. We missed you.

"Cache. I'm here." Adaline put the hammer back on the side table. Turning on the hall light, she ran to him. His curly hair, stubbled face, and side smile sent chills down her spine. She wrapped her arms around his neck. The warmth of his embrace—how tightly he squeezed her—was something she'd needed for days.

"Are you okay?" he asked.

She nodded and laid her face against his chest. "Just hold me for a minute, please."

He gripped her tighter and rested his head on hers.

Adaline glanced up at him and concern dwelled inside her. Blood was all over his forehead and above his eyebrow. She let go of his arms. "What happened to you?"

"I had a rough day at work," he said.

"Let me clean you up. Sit down."

He followed her into the bedroom, sat on a sofa in the corner of the room, and laid his head back.

Adaline got a washcloth from the bathroom closet and rinsed it under warm water. Wringing the rag out, she made her way to his side and placed the cloth on his head to clean off the excess blood. "How did this happen?"

"I saw our real estate agent today. That was rather interesting." He paused. "Then I got fired, and . . . when I walked to my car, someone smacked me in the head with something and slashed the hell out of my tires." He grabbed her hand. "I got worried that someone was going after you next."

Adaline didn't say anything as she sat next to him and worked on the dried blood stuck in his hair, but her insides turned to jelly.

"You heard I got fired, right?"

"I'm not worried about that. Someone hit you and slashed your tires?"

He nodded.

"Who would do that?" she asked.

"I don't know, but that's something I wanted to talk to you about."

"Me, too. I mean, I need to talk to you. How did you get home?"

"Sam came and got me," he said.

Adaline's face sunk. "How did he know to come get you?"

"I called you a few times, and when you didn't answer, I thought the worst. I figured if you trusted Sam, I needed to start trusting you more."

She leaned into him and planted a kiss on his cheek. Adaline appreciated the effort he was trying to make.

Every part inside of her yelled to kick Cache out and not to let him get close to her again, but she missed her husband. "Thank you."

"Why are you on edge? What happened with your day?"

Adaline scratched her head, debating how much she should tell him. Clearly, he was in danger, too. It was safer for him to not know about the details of her past that were coming into play. She hesitated. "Well . . . there's been some new evidence that links our daughters with my past and Officer Abbott's daughter's kidnapping." She grabbed her head confused about why she decided to tell him.

He already got hurt today for not knowing anything. What are you doing?

"How is he linked to our daughters?"

"He was left an owl necklace too, at the crime scene. He's never found his daughter."

"When did his daughter get taken?" Cache asked.

"A year ago."

Cache punched his leg. "I told you those necklaces were nothing but a token of death. Why do you keep holding on to it?"

"The person who gave it to me was kind. They were a friend," she said. "It's important to me."

"Honey, you have no idea who your friend is."

"I know." She took the cloth off Cache's forehead and set it on a side table. "His daughter, Aspen, looks exactly like Leora, and they both were eight when they were taken."

He grabbed her hand. "Leora looks like a copy of you, too. Does Sam know Officer Abbott?"

"Don't do that. I know where you're going with this."

"Does he?"

She sunk her head. "Yes, they're friends."

Letting go of her hand, Cache held the back of his neck and covered his mouth. "He's a part of your past, and now all of a sudden, he's back. He knows the officer, and he's obsessed with you. Always has been."

Adaline chewed her nail. "I want to share things with you. I need you to believe me, and I know how I might sound to you, but you know me."

He rubbed her shoulder. "Okay."

"I went to see a psychologist today. My childhood therapist."

"You found your doctor, and she's here in town?" he asked.

"I did, and she's not too far from us. A few streets away."

Cache fidgeted with his ring. "What made you decide to do that?"

"I watched all the horrible things the reporters said about me. Between being suicidal and locked up in a psychiatric ward, I remembered a memory that I'd forgotten."

"I heard it on the radio too." He held his chin. "How do you forget a memory? I mean, how is that possible?"

Adaline could feel herself pulling away from him again. The more questions he asked, the more she felt like she was on trial and had done something wrong. Peering at him, his brown eyes reminded her so much of Eliza. They were rich and golden, and she couldn't help but get lost in them. They used to joke about him having "Caramello" eyes. They're an addiction, like chocolate. "I have PTSD, or rather Post Traumatic Stress Disorder. Apparently, I have such horrible memories that I subconsciously hid them from myself."

"You can really do that?"

"I guess you can," she said. "After I watched the news, I took a bath, and I remembered something out of the blue about living with my aunt."

"Aunt Arlene. The aunt you liked?"

Adaline nodded. "There's more. My aunt's not who I thought she was. I somehow embellished a better story in my mind about our relationship."

Cache ran his fingers through his brown hair and held his hands at the base of his neck again. His eyes didn't leave hers, and she could see him pleading with her to tear down those closed walls. "Are you taking your meds?"

He won't believe me if he knew I wasn't.

She smiled at him sweetly and caressed his cheek. "Of course. Why do you ask?"

"No reason." He gripped her hand in his.

"I've . . . missed you, and I need you to be here with me." Adaline snuggled into his cheek. "I went to a psych ward, but not for what the news report says. I was framed by my aunt."

"Why?"

"I believe she only took me in for money, but I'm not positive. Sticking me into that place was a resolution to a problem."

"The reports that you're schizophrenic are clearly a lie."

"Yes. I believe so," she said.

"How did you get out of there?"

She frowned and lowered her eyes. "I don't know."

He rubbed her back. "It's okay."

"No. It's not okay that I can't remember everything from my past. It's like a jigsaw puzzle in there. Some pieces I remember, but they don't all connect. Like the owl necklace and Officer Abbott."

"Let me help you. It's Sam. Everything ties to him."

Adaline's hands shook. "No, Sam's in trouble."

Cache slammed his hands on the table and stood. "I knew it. He gave the necklace to you."

She didn't say anything and sat stationary.

"He couldn't have you, so he murdered our girls instead." He gripped the table and clenched his fists. "I'm going to kill him."

Adaline stood and grasped his arm. "Listen to me. I don't think it's Sam."

"Jealousy does some messed up things to people, especially when it comes to love. You don't know it wasn't him. You loved him too."

"I loved him a long time ago. I love you, not him." She held her mouth. "I know it looks bad, but we're talking about Sam. Besides you, he's the closest thing I have to family."

"No." Cache let go of Adaline's hand and opened his mouth to say something, but nothing came out. He paced the floor while he rubbed his forehead and breathed in deeply.

Adaline pressed her fingers together. "I think there's a lot more going on here than we realize. I don't know what people are capable of anymore. I just know that I can't trust anyone, and that scares me. Is there anyone you trust?"

"No. I don't think there is."

"What do we do now?" Adaline asked.

"We pretend as if we don't know what we know and see what other clues we can pick up from people that are supposed to be helping us."

She looked away. That was easy. She had done that for as long as she could remember. Adaline didn't have friends, family, or anyone she truly trusted. Three faces came to her mind of people she had let in.

Dr. Lynchester.

Sam.

Cache.

A voice sang in her head.

There was a little owl high in a tree.

She trusted the man with the swing. Who was he? Adaline couldn't help but wonder who was messing with her now.

They stared at each other for a minute before either one spoke. "What happened with the real estate agent?" she asked.

"Not tonight. We've had enough to think about for one night. I'll leave now."

"Cache? Will you please stay and hold me?"

"Of course, I'll stay with you." She lay down with him as he pressed his head against hers. The way he smelled of pine and a dash of nutmeg, and the way she found a home in his arms, made her heart warm. She loved being held, and it was the one thing that calmed her down whenever everything else in the world was black.

Please don't let him be the one that breaks my heart.

She curled closer into him, allowing herself to feel something other than pain. At least for a moment.

FORTY-FOUR

Cache Rushner
Thursday, November 11th
9:00 p.m.

THINGS DIDN'T ADD UP, and what did, felt wrong.

Was Adaline telling the truth, or was it a hallucination?

She seemed pretty conscious of what was going on around her rather than being in her head, and her spirits were heightened from the last time they talked.

Cache gently moved Adaline's head from his arm and maneuvered out of her grip. He sat up and watched her sleep, taking deep breaths in. She appeared as though she hadn't slept in days, and that she finally allowed herself to feel peace, even for a short time.

He tiptoed out of the bedroom, went down to the kitchen, and opened the cupboard where he knew Adaline had put her medication. The bottle stood right up front. He unsealed the cap, tipping the pills in the palm of his hand.

He counted each one, knowing it had a full month's worth in the bottle, one for each day.

Seven were missing.

Good sign.

Pouring the pills back in the bottle, he shut the lid, placed the container back on the shelf, and closed the cabinet lightly.

He smiled.

The pills must be working.

Cache wanted his wife back, and the new beginning he'd planned for them, which didn't include Officer Abbott, Dr. Lynchester, or Sam.

Sam.

He bunched his fists as rage built inside him. Adaline was his wife. She didn't need protection from anyone else —that was his job. He had the ring to prove it. His fingers became numb as he held his fists tighter. Cache wanted to believe Adaline more than anything, but she couldn't see her behavior as he saw it.

Protection from herself had to be the priority above everything else. He'd be the bad guy out of love. No one else understood that, but they didn't need to. Cache prayed Sam had a good excuse for how this looked, otherwise he feared for the safety of the man, and for the sanity, and control, of himself.

On the table, Cache saw the flowers that Adaline threw away at Lost Treasures, blossoming wildly and brightening up the whole room, including the warmth in his heart.

She'd kept them, and he was home.

Home.

Being away for a few days and living in a dumpy motel made him appreciate *now*.

Right here.

This very moment.

It wasn't the house that made the home, it was her.

He'd protect her at any cost. Cache went over all the details in his head, starting with someone attacking him. Could it be a coincidence? No one took anything from him, making it obvious that it wasn't someone needing money to grab a quick fix. He did just get fired. Did his boss have a problem with the way Cache handled things while working there?

He shook his head.

Don't let your mind go.

That brought him to the question of how he got his job to begin with. He knew he was massively underqualified for it. And who the hell was his real estate agent, who apparently had multiple identities? Both the agent and his job brought them to Salt Lake City, and all the strange incidents started happening once they arrived: Sam showing up after fourteen years of being a ghost, Adaline finding Dr. Lynchester out of the blue, who conveniently has an office a few blocks from their place.

Officer Abbott giving him the card for Dr. Lynchester?

Officer Abbott's case.

Adaline's clearly right in the middle of it, but what secrets could she be hiding?

Cache pulled out his business card case and removed more than thirty cards he'd gotten from clients, which he wouldn't need anymore. He flipped through the pile for Miss Tisher's card, throwing the others one by one into the trash. Near the back, he found her name and dialed the number on the back of the card.

The phone rang three times.

He glanced at his watch.

9:00 pm

"Hello. Who is this?"

"Miss Tisher? It's Cache Rushner.

"Who did you say you were again?"

"Cache Rushner. We bought a home from you."

"This is Miss Tisher," the woman on the phone said. "But your name doesn't sound familiar. Where exactly do you work?"

He scratched his head and wrinkled his nose.

How does she not know me?

"You know, we have some issues with our home too, and we need help."

"Can it wait until tomorrow?" she asked.

"I'm afraid not. Do you remember when we did a final walk-through on our house, a few months ago, and the top stair squeaked when the heater turned on?"

"Mr. Rushner, I can't say I remember that."

Cache shook his head.

What the hell is going on?

He rubbed his eyes. "Okay, we talked about the heater. You said getting a home warranty was a smart way to go to cover our asses if the heater ever died on us. Well, it's decided to do that."

She coughed and cleared her throat. "Young man, do you know what time it is? It's getting late."

Cache rolled his eyes and bunched his fist. She seemed off and unclear. Come to think of it, her voice sounded hoarse. Maybe she was coming down with something?

"I do. I'm sorry, and I'll make it fast. I just need to know if when we bought the house, did we purchase a home warranty?"

"What's your address, and I can see what I can find out," she said.

Cache hesitated. "256 Dreary Oak Drive."

"Yes, here in Salt Lake City. I remember this house. I met with the owner. She was quite a character."

"You don't remember meeting with me?"

"Like I said, I only worked with the seller, not the purchaser. Would you like me to email you a copy of the paperwork?"

"Yes, that would be great." Cache gave her his email address.

"I'll send that right over. Sorry I can't be of more help to you. Oh, and please don't call me again at this time of night. An old lady like myself needs her sleep."

The line went dead. Cache sat in silence, trying to figure out what just happened. Being in the elevator with Miss Tisher, or whoever she was, made him curious about her double identity and the secret under her belt. It seemed she had more secrets than he could've imagined even an hour ago. The first time he ran into her was in Owling, a few months before the girls' murder, also the same day that he suddenly received a promotion from Kirkham Trading located in Salt Lake City. She happened to be handing out business cards, trying to get some property to sell in that area, but she told him that she mainly worked in Salt Lake City. At the time, he couldn't believe how miraculous it was that everything seemed to be falling into place on its own. She asked about Adaline. He found that weird but didn't give much thought to it. Before Miss Tisher left, she gave him one of her cards and said if they needed a new start, Salt Lake's where to do it.

Salt Lake. What a joke.

His phone beeped, and the email she promised came through. Cache opened the attachment. Looking down, Miss Tisher didn't stare back at him.

Who is this? *I didn't make a purchase with her.*

A white-haired lady with a short bob and saggy eyelids peered at him. She appeared to be in her 70s, and the raspy voice he heard went well with the picture. This lady, the real Miss Tisher, was unwell.

Who the hell did I buy the house from?

Cache quickly glanced through the attachment until he spotted it. The seller was an Arlene Williams.

Arlene.

The only Arlene he knew of was Adaline's aunt, but he'd never met the lady before or seen a picture of her. Something to look into, leaving Adaline out of it for now.

One call down, two to go.

"Hello. Dr. Lynchester? I know it's late, but I'm Adaline's husband, Cache Rushner."

Rustling muffled on her end, and a light gasp escaped her lips. "Yes."

"I hear she's been seeing you, and that she's remembering things from the past. The thing is, my wife's really fragile right now, and I don't want anyone or anything giving her more ideas. She's been through enough. We both have."

"Mr. Rushner, I've been hoping you would call. I understand your hesitation, but did Adaline tell you what she has?"

"Yes. She said she has PTSD."

"That's right," Dr. Lynchester said.

"I'm going to be very forward with you here. I don't think you have her best interest at heart, and she won't be seeing you again unless I'm with her."

Silence lingered on the phone.

"Doctor?"

"Mr. Rushner, I honestly wouldn't have it any other way. Adaline needs your support."

"Why?"

"She hasn't handled the memories well. Every time is a first time for her."

"Are you saying you've tried to help her remember before?" Cache asked.

"Precisely, and it didn't take, to be honest. Each time she's rediscovering who she is and what has defined her. She's going to need someone there to support and believe in her. Someone she can open her heart to."

"You think that's me, yet you don't know me."

"I do know you," she said. "You have some secrets of your own. Secrets that can help Adaline unlock hers."

Cache shivered and debated throwing the phone on the ground. "How do you know anything about me?"

"You know what I'm talking about, don't you?"

"Are you blackmailing me? What do you want?" he asked.

"Nothing. Only to help."

The wind blew hard against the motorhome as he waited for his parents to get home. They should've been right behind him. There wasn't any food for him to eat, but he checked the fridge again for the fourth time.

Still empty.

He lay down and held his stomach, trying to ignore the pain and gurgling it made. Cache closed his eyes, but the hunger kept him from sleeping. He grabbed his coat and walked into the blistering cold, watching for any sign of his parents. A rich aroma of spices and meat filled the air. Cache licked his lips, his stomach gurgled again, and his feet carried him to the smell. He hesitated before knocking on a motorhome door. An elderly couple took one look at him and invited him inside for dinner.

Rushing in, he sat at their table.

Pot roast and rolls.

He tried to be patient while saying grace, and he carefully ate —until they glanced away, then he fed his mouth by the spoonful with haste. Halfway through his meal, a car horn honked. The older couple stood, and he wiped his hands on his pants, ready to flee. They opened the window a crack, looked outside, and exchanged glances.

"Stay here, son," the old lady said.

"I need to get home now," he said. "It's probably my parents."

"Son, you heard my old lady. Stay put. We'll take care of this," the man said.

Their faces were afraid, but the man looked at his wife, and she at him. They smiled lightly and nodded before they held hands and went outside. The front door shut, and a loud bang erupted in the air, almost like lightning striking the house itself. Cache ran to the window and pulled back the curtain. The older couple knelt in the snow with their hands behind their heads. Two men pointed guns to their faces.

He gasped and placed his hand over his mouth, bending down further toward the ground, but keeping his eyes glued on the elderly couple.

"Tell us where he is," a tall man said. "He took something from us, and we want it back. I'm not shooting at the air next time. Tell me where he is."

The couple stayed silent.

"My ass is on the line here. TELL ME."

The old man and his wife didn't say a word.

"All right then." The tall man signaled to the other man. Two shots, one after the other, rang through the night sky, and their stationary bodies tilted to the ground.

Dead.

"Mr. Rushner, are you there?"

Cache grasped the table and hunched over, holding his

stomach. Nausea hit him just like the day the couple was shot.

"I'm here," he said, hoarsely. "What do you need from me?"

"Come into my office tomorrow. Both of you." She paused. "Adaline doesn't know, does she?"

"No one does." Cache looked down. "I don't know if I'm ready to share this with anyone else."

"Not even your wife? You both have secrets. Believe me, you need each other, now more than ever," she said. "This isn't about you anymore. Every decision you make impacts Adaline, and every decision she makes impacts you. Do you want to put her in any more danger?"

"I never wanted to hurt Adaline."

"Tomorrow morning, 8:30. Come to my office together."

Cache closed his phone. He worried about how they would possibly protect each other after what he knew might ruin their marriage, or their trust in one another, for good.

FORTY-FIVE

Seth Duncan
Friday, November 12th
8:00 a.m.

LIFTING the white water pail behind Lost Treasures, Seth retrieved the store key underneath. He cracked the door open to let some of the cool breeze in and opened the blinds. Adaline had a true gift for making broken things into creations of wonder and beauty.

Building masterpieces with someone else's garbage.

Seth liked many things about her, that was only one. He grabbed the feather duster to remove lint clinging on some vases and restocked the shelves with new vintage items she'd been working on. Outside the store, sounds of happiness and laughter erupted. Stepping higher on the ladder, he peeked to see who the happy couple was. An attractive younger woman and that cop all over the news hugged each other. He tried not to stare, but she looked familiar. Uncanny, even. They stopped in front of Lost

Treasures and hid in the corner under the overhead. Both of them glanced around like spies before she waved goodbye, and the lieutenant grabbed the door handle to the store. Seth got off the ladder and jostled to the front door to unlock it.

"Lieutenant. Hello."

"Seth, is it?"

"You got me," Seth said, raising an eyebrow.

"You've been on the news, son. Working or being near Mrs. Rushner will draw attention."

"I suppose it would. Those reporters are on top of everything," he said, holding the door half shut. "You seem to be on the news often, too, these days."

The lieutenant smiled. "All a part of the job." He fidgeted and peered at the people passing on the street. "Listen, I need to get something before I jump into work this morning. Would you mind if I looked around before the store opens?"

Seth stared at the sign on the door and hesitated.

"I'll make it quick," the lieutenant said, with a wink.

I could get fired letting someone in.

Seth watched his face, staring at all the bedazzled items, and remembered the way the lieutenant stared at the woman outside…he'd buy something. Adaline would forgive him.

"Yes, please come in and take a look. Let me know if there's anything I can help you find."

Lieutenant Stalk nodded.

He pretended to dust and let his mind process the information in his head of how he knew that woman.

"Son. How much is this brooch here?"

Seth put the duster on the counter and moved toward him to view a blue and green crystal brooch lying in the palm of his hand. The sunlight hit the crystal in a way that made it sparkle and reflect a strand of glimmer on the glass shelf.

"I have a lady I'm fond of who has an eye for shiny items," the lieutenant said with a chuckle.

"She looked familiar," Seth said. "Do I know her?" His question was answered.

"Let it go, son," he said. "The price?"

"I'll run in the back and check in our books. One minute." Seth bowed his head and hurried toward the back room where the books were kept. His hands felt clammy, and he tried to wipe them off on his pants, only to have them perspire some more. He continued pacing the floor and smacked his head.

Glancing at the binders on the shelf, he found the one titled inventory. Seth opened the book and turned to the page with the prices for the brooches.

Bingo.

He kept the binder in his hand and walked toward the register. "It's $1,200, and a collector's item. Would you like it?" His voice trembled as he spoke.

The lieutenant peered at it. "Do you think I can get some ass from buying this for her?"

"Excuse me?"

Laughter barked from the lieutenant, a broken record of noise and odd beats between confidence and uncertainty. "I'm messing with you, son."

Seth scratched his face. "Is there anything else you need?"

"Can you box this up?"

"S...sure." He got a box and placed the brooch inside.

Lieutenant Stalk inched so close to Seth's ear that his

breath stung his cheek with germs. Seth wiped his face with his sleeve and moved two steps backward.

"You didn't see any of this today. I wasn't here, you got it?"

He nodded and moved behind the register to ring up the purchase. "The total with tax comes to $1,375.00."

The lieutenant pulled out a wad of hundreds. "Here's some for you. To keep you quiet. I believe five hundred is enough for a man that just got out of a cage." He held the money up in his hand and waved it around, mocking him.

Seth hesitated and grabbed for the money, only to have the grip tighten on the other end.

"Remember what I said. I know who let you out of your hole and I could end you. Keep that in mind."

Clenching his fists, Seth put the money in his pocket. "I understand you perfectly."

"Good." The lieutenant turned around and left the store without looking back.

FORTY-SIX

Sam Wendell
Friday, November 12th
8:00 a.m.

HE HADN'T REALIZED how tired he'd been until he woke the next morning, the steering wheel curled up against his face. Wiping away drool from his mouth, he glanced down Adaline's street. After picking up Cache last night and hearing about what happened to his car, the desire to keep an eye out for her safety amplified. Sam wished he was the one staying the night with her, and the "other guy" could be waking up at the wheel, right where he sat. Cache seemed like a good guy, but that should've been *his* girl. He should be inside that house holding her, not him. Sam patted his cheeks.

What am I missing here?

He knew everything from Adaline's past with her mom and her visit to the psych ward as a kid. Even her being taken by the strange young man known as Owl Keeper.

Sam gave him the name when he was nine, after the first time he'd seen the man, who was in his early twenties. A long burn mark crept behind his right ear, and he tried to hide it with his long, matted hair. He'd worn ragged clothing and smelled of sweat and gardenia. Rarely did the man smile, and he walked as if the world was on his shoulders, but Adaline changed him. She had a way of seeing the best in people, and she truly believed he was her friend—but Sam knew better.

His mind shifted to the night Adaline's parents died.

He waited in the cornfield for her like he did most nights, except that night felt different. She didn't meet at the usual time. Plucking the husk from the corn with nervous anticipation, he continued to wait. Minutes passed before the field swayed with movement, coming from the opposite direction of where he stood. Following the ripple of noise, he hid, making sure not to be seen in case it was her parents.

Blonde hair flowed behind a white nightgown.

Adaline.

She ran in bare feet away from something, or someone. He wanted to call out to her, but he watched as she dashed up the front steps to her home. Turning to leave, screaming echoed through the night sky. Adaline was in trouble. Running toward her took too long. Looking up, he lost his balance and hit his head on a large rock. When he came to, horror crept inside him. The Owl Keeper stood next to Adaline. Black residue stained her dress, and a box of matches was clutched in her hand.

What have you done?

Ashes and debris flew through the air, and bloodcurdling screams pierced the night sky. The smell of charcoal impaired his stomach, and he covered his nose and mouth, watching her home go up in flames.

Pulling his keys out of his pocket, he put one in the

ignition and hesitated. Leaving didn't feel right, but neither did sitting while she was in danger.

Dammit.

He started the engine and drove a few miles, until he came to an alley, and parked his car. Who would have a motive to take the Rushner girls and harass Adaline? All of the people that came to mind were dead or locked away.

Sam didn't have children but hated the thought that someone he loved had lost the most precious things in the world to her and knew they were tortured before they'd died. Sick and wrong.

He covered his mouth. The more he thought about Adaline, and the pain she must be feeling, a lump formed, like a piece of bubble wrap trapped in his throat. Plastic popping one by one, suffocating his air supply. He remembered reading that the bodies had fourth-degree burns, and facial recognition was completely obliterated.

Do we know that these bodies are the girls?

He felt a hunch rolling in.

Who signed off on the coroner's reports?

Sam took out his notepad and wrote the question in bold letters, determined to find the answer. He had to start piecing things together about Adaline again and uncover the truth of what really happened the night her parents died. If the wrong hands got a hold of that information, who knew what they'd do with it.

He started the engine again and turned to place his notepad on the passenger seat. A loud crash sprung him forward and glass exploded on his seat. A figure wearing all black and a ski mask jumped in his car and elbowed him in the bridge of the nose. Blood dripped down his shirt. He put his car in gear and pressed his foot on the pedal. The passenger seat door swung open, and the person shifted, holding on to the seat. Sam swerved the car into a trash can while the figure in the ski mask continued to take punches at his face. He pressed down harder on the gas. Grunting came from the other seat. Sam spun the steering wheel, and the car spiraled out of control. Sam socked the masked figure in the Adam's apple, and the man let go, free-falling out the door before the car crashed into a phone pole.

The windshield fell on top of Sam, and he tried to move his head from the steering wheel, but it felt heavy. His vision blurred, and his ears rang loudly. The man lay in the street. Sam scooted out of the car and limped toward him as headlights glared on his face, distorting his eyesight. He covered his eyes with his arm and continued to move in the same direction, until an engine purred nearby. Letting go of his face, Sam stared at the empty ground. The man was gone. He surveyed the area and caught the man's body being dragged by two masked figures, loading him into a minivan. They shut the door and revved away before Sam could even muster movement. He took a mental note of the license plate as it sped down the street.

FORTY-SEVEN

Cache Rushner
8:30 a.m.

DR. LYNCHESTER WELCOMED them both in with a smile and hugged Adaline tight, as you would a close friend. Cache stepped backward, hesitant to walk in, but he wanted and needed to help his wife. The office held a rustic, cozy feel, which seemed out of place for the woman standing in front of him. Her short blonde hair, slender body, and demeanor set a tone for an office with yellow curtains and lace blue walls—dainty and feminine, but sophisticated. She appeared to be in her late fifties.

Holding her hand out, she glanced at him with gentle eyes and held his gaze in a way that made him feel like they'd already met. Like she knew him.

He shook her hand and looked away quickly. "Hello, Cache. Thank you for coming. Can I take your coats for you?"

Adaline nodded and proceeded to hand her coat to the doctor.

"No. I'm fine," Cache said.

Dr. Lynchester nodded and moved to a closet near the back of the room, around a corner. She opened the door and closed it lightly. "Please have a seat next to your wife." She stepped in front of them and pulled out her thin glasses, placing them on her nose.

"Thank you." He sat down next to Adaline and held her hand.

Adaline peered at him, and then at Dr. Lynchester, then back at him again. Looking down, she squeezed his hand for a minute, let go, and spoke under her breath.

Cache put his arm around her shoulder and tried to hold her hand again, only to have her shrug and pick at her fingernails. "What's the matter? Do you want to go?" he asked in a whisper.

She didn't respond.

"It's good to see you, Adaline. How are you feeling after our last session?"

Adaline glanced up. "I want to know the truth, but I don't want to hurt anyone."

"That's a good start," Dr. Lynchester said.

Cache couldn't help but notice how calm the doctor seemed when she talked. Steady, mellow voice, but her shaky legs showed otherwise.

Was she nervous about what Adaline said, or something else?

"I guess so," Adaline said. "Bits and pieces are starting to come together, but not all at once. My memories come at random, unknown times. They just hit me."

"Those are your triggers."

"Right, my repressed memories." Adaline hesitated. "Cache was confused about how this happens."

Dr. Lynchester looked at him and pulled her glasses off her nose. "Your wife's been through a great deal. Triggers are things that link someone to their past. You lock memories deep in your mind that you don't want to remember, ones that are too painful to face. People do it without even realizing that they're doing this. Over time, an object, person, or place links to that memory and tries to connect it, like a puzzle piece, only you have fifteen puzzles that need to be connected. It's not sure which one it belongs to. Trying to find its place is when you begin to unleash those hidden, or rather suppressed, memories."

"Like when I saw the TV with reports of the psych ward. It brought something to the surface." Adaline squeezed her hands together.

"Right."

"So, this is a common thing that happens?" Cache asked.

"More common than I would like to admit. The things children and people are dealing with just keeps getting worse." Dr. Lynchester put her glasses back on. "One person can only handle so much violence and rage before their mind takes over. They either embrace the violence or fight back. Think of serial killers and abusers. They embrace the violence and continue expressing it in their own way. Some even believe it's a true art form because it's a form of expression."

"And what happens when you fight back?" Cache asked.

"If you conquer the problem head-on, it goes away."

"What if you couldn't solve the problem?"

"A lot of times, that's when PTSD comes into play.

You're trying to cope with a horrific problem without a solution," Dr. Lynchester said.

"Let me get this straight. You're saying that Adaline's problems would go away if she talked to her mother? That's not possible now. So, how can we find another solution?"

Dr. Lynchester squirmed in her chair. "The solution is inside her. It's an inner battle that she's fighting. One where she needs to see what really happened."

"But she knows what happened." Cache put his hand on Adaline's knee and glanced at her.

"No, she doesn't. This is where I've tried to help in the past, and it hasn't worked. Like we talked about."

Adaline grabbed her purse and stood up. "You've been working together against me. I knew it." She turned around. "Dr. Lynchester, you lied to me. I'm surrounded by a bunch of liars. No wonder I lash out and people get hurt." She glanced at both of them a few times and sneered. "Stay out of my way."

Dr. Lynchester leaped from the chair and gripped her shoulders. "Don't do this again." She held Adaline's face in her hands. "Look at me. Your husband and I just talked yesterday. We're trying to help you." She caressed her cheek. "I'm helping you both, Daisy."

Who's Daisy? Cache shook his head. He didn't know that name, but it was obvious both of the ladies did.

Adaline jolted backward. "How are you helping us?"

"Both of you need to see who you are inside—not how the world views you, but what defines your character—and love that person, not hide from it." Dr. Lynchester paused. "Please, come sit back down."

"Is it true? You just talked to her yesterday, Cache?"

He nodded his head. "I've never met this woman in my

life. I only called to make sure she had your best interest at heart. That's the only reason why we're here."

She stepped back to the couch and sat down. Placing her hand on her lap, Adaline gradually moved it into his.

"Let's move on, then." Dr. Lynchester sat in her chair across from them and pressed the bridge of her nose before she began. "How are things going with you as a couple?"

Cache cleared his throat and squeezed Adaline's hand. "I don't feel comfortable sharing that with you."

Adaline nudged him. "We've had a struggle with things. Trust issues mainly, but we're working on it."

Dr. Lynchester scribbled on her paper and crossed her legs.

"Cache, would you care to explain what kind of things you've been struggling with?"

He scratched his chin and sat up in his seat. "Honestly, I don't know if I want to answer. I don't know you, and it's feeling a tad warm in here," he said, undoing his top button on his collar.

"Fair enough." Dr. Lynchester put her pen down and stood up, walking behind her chair to retrieve something from her desk. She locked her drawer and sat back down in her seat, looking at both of them intensely. "I know you don't know me, but I know you and Adaline, and I need you to trust me."

"This is completely unprofessional. How can I trust you? I don't even know you." Cache stood. "Let's go, Addi."

"Please, sit down. She said she wants to help," Adaline said. "Don't take that from me. I need to figure out if she can."

Cache clung to his coat and strangled it in his hands.

"Of course, sweetheart." He grabbed her hand, sat down next to her, and put his arm around her shoulder.

"I understand that after what you went through as a kid, trust is still hard for you. I can appreciate that," Dr. Lynchester said in a steady tone.

His neck stiffened, and he sat on the edge of the couch. "We're not talking about this."

"I know a lot of things about you both."

Adaline turned toward him. "What do you mean as a kid? I thought you said you had a great childhood?"

Cache glared at the ground and hunched over. "I lied to you."

"What'd you say?"

"I...lied to you."

"Why?" Adaline asked.

"Because I didn't want you to know that part of me. I wanted you to see me for the man I'm trying to become."

After getting out of juvenile detention, he promised himself he would change his ways and make his life better. Stealing to get out of poverty became sport, but also his way to survive at any cost. Going from one foster home to another wasn't living for him, and he wanted more for his life. At eighteen, he thought he finally got out until he was approached to do one last job. He never prepared himself to fall in love instead.

Was the failed gig catching up to him? Was someone after him, and not Adaline?

"Tell me," Adaline said, pleading.

"I grew up poor, and my parents were con artists." He paused. "They had done it for a while, and then one day they got caught."

"I thought you told me they died in a car accident." Adaline's eyes were wide, and she sat away from him.

She's never going to see me as the same man.

"They were in a fire when I was nine."

"And they're alive?" Adaline asked.

"No. They died," he said, looking away. "They were good people, you know, they just chose to make the wrong decisions, and they paid for them."

Dr. Lynchester sat quietly, letting them talk things out while she seemed to be overly pleased with the conversation. "Keep going, Cache. You're doing well."

Adaline sat closer to him now and nodded her head in agreement, clinging to his arm.

"I got an older couple killed on the night my parents died."

"What happened that night?" Adaline asked.

"I went with my parents on their run. Our hit was this massive house in some town. I never paid attention to what cities or places we'd been to because I knew I wouldn't be there for long anyway. But my parents talked about how we'd score big, stepping inside this home. Anything in there would make us richer," he said. "They told me to stay in the car and wait. We parked two miles away so I wasn't in sight. My mom hugged me and let me know that they'd yell the word "Catchum" as a cue to start the car. Then they left." Cache cleared his throat. "That was their word for every run they did. I waited and did what I was told, until I heard screaming, a high pitch screech. I never heard the keyword, but I knew my mother was in trouble."

Adaline placed her hand tightly on his. "What did you do?"

Cache held his head. "I started the car but got out and ran toward the screaming. It was my mama. I knew it, but they weren't coming. Everything in me wanted to yell back to her to confirm she was there." He wiped at his face. "I heard a loud bang that sounded like an explosion or a gunshot. Someone grabbed me and yelled for me to go home. They said I wasn't safe where I was and told me to not look back, that my parents would be there soon."

He hesitated and glanced at Adaline, who seemed immersed in what he was saying.

She responded and brushed his cheek. "Who grabbed you?"

"A woman, but I couldn't see her face. It was dark," Cache said. "I ran as fast as I could and didn't look back."

Adaline covered her mouth and gasped. "Your parents?"

"They never came back."

"No." Adaline clasped her hands together and swayed back and forth.

"How did that make you feel?" Dr. Lynchester asked.

"Scared and worried, but I mostly felt guilt for leaving them. I should've stayed to help."

"Do you still feel guilty?"

"Every day," he said.

"Tell me about the old couple?" Dr. Lynchester asked.

Cache shook his head. "Isn't that enough for today?"

Adaline rubbed his back.

He envisioned this day a whole lot different in his head. She gave him a sense of wanting to open up and share the darkness he'd experienced, without concern that it would turn her away from him. Cache squeezed her hand and continued.

"I ran home to find that the fridge was empty, and I was scared and hungry. I went to a house nearby, and the older couple graciously took me in to have a nice meal and get changed into some old clothes that were too big on me." He grinned at the memory of drowning in a man's old clothing. It felt nice, warm, and smelled of soap, a scent that was foreign to him. He loved it. "A door shut outside, so they went to go look and see if it was my parents." Cache squinted, held his breath, and punched his leg a few times.

"Take a minute before you go on." Dr. Lynchester clasped her hands together and looked deep in thought.

"They died because of me. Someone was looking for me, and I killed them for being selfish. I should've stayed home like I was told."

"Did the men chase you?" Dr. Lynchester asked.

"Yes, but I lost them."

"How?"

"I went out the back door and ran for a while. I don't know how long," Cache said.

Dr. Lynchester gripped her hands together. "Where did you end up?"

Cache let go of Adaline's hand and clenched his fist. "I hid in a tractor, and the next day I was sent to foster care."

"That's it?"

He peered at Dr. Lynchester. "That's it."

Adaline held his leg. "You didn't kill those people. The last thing they did before they died was help someone in need. They invited you in, remember."

Cache tried to smile, but instead, he looked around the room. "Now tell me how this is supposed to help Adaline?"

Dr. Lynchester stared at Adaline like she was reading her soul. It was unsettling, and yet Cache was intrigued to figure out what she possibly could be thinking or doing.

"When he told his story, did you feel anything?"

Adaline's face dropped and she turned red. "Now, Dr.

Lynchester, that seems quite inappropriate to ask. Of course I felt something. My husband was hurting while telling us about his past, and I wanted to fix it. Make it go away."

"Dig deeper."

Cache raised his eyebrow and shook his head.

How did any of this connect? She lived in Owling. Her mother was abusive. Parents died at age eight. Went to live with aunt who didn't want her. What does this have to do with my past?

Ten years ago, when his last job was to kill a young lady who had plans to assassinate a young boy's family, he reacted instantly and accepted the assignment. No one should be left without parents like he was. Until he saw her—the girl, the vicious killer. He looked at her and saw himself. Someone bruised and alone, but not afraid to be so. Adaline.

She can never know.

FORTY-EIGHT

Officer Abbott
Friday, November 12th
9:00 a.m.

HE DIDN'T WANT to believe that Sam could be involved with his daughter's disappearance, but so many clues pointed in his direction. And what was with Sam's dad telling Mrs. Rushner that her hair and eyes were like the sun and the moon? She appreciated it enough to find a whole painting that held meaning to her based on that one sentiment. And why did she shut down after she talked about flowers and being on the swings? There was something she didn't want to talk about, and Sam and his family were right in the middle. Just looking at people made him feel like they should be wearing a guilty sign for all the mysterious secrets they hid. Trust wasn't a luxury that was welcomed anymore, even by the system. Everyone had their own agenda. It was a dog-eat-dog world.

His head pounded, and his whole body ached. He longed to find out what happened to his daughter and put the bastard in jail who ended her life. The doorbell rang as he stepped inside Lost Treasures Antique Store and saw a man at the counter. He appeared to be in deep thought while staring at a piece of paper. Abbott strolled around the store and glanced at his watch.

Maybe she's running late today.

"Excuse me. Is Mrs. Rushner coming in soon?"

The man didn't take his eyes off the paper. "What makes you think she's coming in?"

Abbott raised his eyebrows. The answer was rather odd, and he didn't know exactly how to take it. "Well, the store's open. I just assumed she'd be here. Do you know when she should be coming in, or not? I'd like to ask her some questions."

The man finally looked up. "Why? Is she in trouble?"

"No. Why would you say that?"

"Nothing. Forget about it. Is there something I can help you with?" He fidgeted with his hands and bounced his knees up and down like a small child on a sugar high.

"Could I leave a note with you to give to her—?" Abbott asked.

"Seth."

"Right. Seth, could you help me with that?"

Seth stopped bouncing his leg up and down and stared at him. "The police are still looking into her case? Why?"

"You sure seem interested in the case surrounding her. Would you like to tell me why?"

"Not really," he said, in an irritated voice. "She's a good person, and she could use a break."

His voice sounded sincere and devoted. Every picture Abbott ever saw of Mrs. Rushner in the news usually had this guy not too far away, which made him wonder why he wanted to be so close. Being a nice person was one thing, but there was more there. He either had a thing for her, or maybe he truly meant well and wanted to protect her, but no one was that nice without having a motive of some sort.

What was his motive?

"I only do trades," Seth said.

"Come again?" Abbott asked.

"I'll give the note to her, and in exchange, you give me one of your business cards." Seth smirked at him. "Just in case I think of anything that could help with Mrs. Rushner."

What a smart ass.

"Sure." Abbott opened his wallet to retrieve a card, and a picture of his wife and daughter fell onto the counter. The photo was two years old, but it was a perfect picture that captured their happiness exactly as it had been. They lived in an Abbott bubble where the world around them had its disasters and turmoil, but in their home, they had each other. Together, they could conquer the world.

"Officer? Your picture. Who's in it?"

Abbott glanced at the picture. "It was my daughter and wife."

"Your wife?" Seth asked.

"We're separated right now. Why? Do you know her?"

Seth looked away. "If I see Mrs. Rushner, I'll give her this note. Have a good day, officer." He raced through what he was saying and paced the floor.

He knows something about my wife.

"You know, I might just stay here and wait for her," Abbott said. "I don't have much to do this afternoon. Maybe we could catch up on who you are."

"S...sure. What bit of trivia can I enlighten you with about myself?" Seth asked, pulling back his hair.

His personality seemed to be morphing from calm and composed to extreme edginess.

"Why did you get so nervous once you saw my wife's picture?"

"No reason." He continued to pace and rub his fingers back and forth. "Mrs. Rushner's really not coming for a while, and I have a lot of work to do."

"So, you won't tell me?" Abbott asked.

"He made me promise not to say anything." Seth covered his mouth and peered at the ground.

"Who?"

His fingers moved back and forth again while he counted numbers out loud and scratched his head. "I've already said too much, officer. I'll let Mrs. Rushner know you stopped by."

Abbott watched him as he moved toward the back room and grabbed a box from the shelf. He must like her in some form. It showed by how gently he took care of her things and how protective he became when talking about her.

"I actually came here to warn Mrs. Rushner about people I believe are a danger to her."

Seth dropped the box on the floor. "Who?"

"At this point, anyone that comes in this store could be here to harm her, including my wife."

Picking up the box of items from the floor, Seth turned to look at him. "You think your wife could hurt her?"

Make something up.

Abbott cleared his throat. "Not my wife, but the people she's with. I'm afraid she's not in a good place."

Seth coughed. "She seemed in a good place to me."

He'd still hoped, even after their separation, that they'd get back together and rekindle things. Peyton said she needed time to recover from his alcohol addiction.

Abbott bunched his fist and clenched his jaw. "Tell me who she was with."

"Let's just say it's someone you know."

"Do you think Mrs. Rushner's safety is a laughing matter? Tell me."

"An older gentlemen," Seth said.

"Lieutenant Stalk?"

The room turned quiet. Seth didn't say anything, but that was an answer enough for him. Lieutenant Stalk had been there to help him through his daughter's disappearance. He had no idea how helpful he'd been to his wife, also.

Abbott dug his nails deeper into his hand.

Lieutenant Stalk was the one that put him on leave for his alcohol addiction, which led to their separation. Was that just a play at a dirty game to get him out of the way? Many times, the lieutenant had been there for them. Abbott thought of him as a friend.

"Tell Mrs. Rushner I need to talk to her," he said in a growl. He took his picture, tore it in half, and threw it in the garbage before he walked out the door.

FORTY-NINE

Owl Keeper
9:30 a.m.

THE MORBID BANNER down the street had a "two for the price of one" deal on headstones. Where the hell was that thirty years ago when his sister and birth deliverer turned to ash?

He hated that his sister, Emery, shared a gravesite, side by side, with the woman who gave him life. His sister still couldn't be free from the monster, and now she was trapped in the ground with her . . . forever. So many times, he wished he could start that day over again. He wanted to change her life and make it better, to get rid of the pain that devoured their inner happiness daily. Instead, he took their happiness and lit a match. Every day, he envisioned Emery's face, her cry for help, and his lousy attempt at saving the one person who truly loved him. The burn mark behind his right ear was proof of his failed pursuit to liberate her.

The day he met Adaline, a feeling of hope returned deep in his soul, in a place he thought wouldn't be opened again. They looked so much alike, his sister and Adaline, it was almost uncanny. It haunted him. Adaline saw something in him that he didn't deserve. He only hurt and betrayed those he loved. That was just who he was. Some people were meant to be good and to make a difference in the world, but that wasn't him. Only darkness lingered around him, and he welcomed it with open arms, embracing the dark core he was becoming.

Watching Adaline angered him—she lived her life in denial and pain. His sister would've lived hers differently. Adaline wasted it. She still was the same little girl from years ago, stuck in a past that wasn't going anywhere good. He lit a match and watched the flame bounce side to side. He knew what he needed to do. It was time to show Adaline his true identity. Either she would be the hero or the victim, and he couldn't help but wonder if the flame inside her would ignite or suffocate. He watched it flicker and create shadow images on the wall. The match danced to a wild beat, and it ended as a rush of air slashed its last breath.

FIFTY

Adaline Rushner
Friday, November 12th
9:30 a.m.

WALKING HOME, hand in hand with Cache after their therapy session, changed her perspective on her husband.

She wanted to let him in.

To try again.

Cache going to therapy with her and opening up enough to share his past secrets was new. A part of her stayed curious about what other things he hadn't told her, but she also felt closer to him, knowing he had his own deep, dark secrets she now knew. Something about making each other's secrets "theirs," rather than holding on to them alone, was invigorating. Therapy seemed to be the key in helping both of them to wash their hands of the past and move forward. To face all the pain and anger . . . together.

Adaline held her heart as hope hugged her and filled her with warmth.

Hope was all she needed to keep going.

To heal their marriage.

To find their girls.

"Thank you for going with me," she said, smiling.

He stepped in front of her and put his arms around her waist. "Please tell me this doesn't change anything."

"Not a thing. I admire you for your courage in there. It's not easy sharing secrets you think someone you love might not accept." Adaline brushed his face and looked into his concerned eyes. "I appreciate that you let me in."

He kissed her and held her tight for a few minutes. It had been a while since they stole a kiss in public after the craziness of the past few months, but this reminded her of the early years when they were first married. He'd kiss the back of her neck or dance with her in the middle of the grocery store.

"How do you think this all connects?" Cache asked.

She shrugged.

He rubbed her shoulders. "You're tougher than you think."

"Thank you." Adaline looked away from him and started walking again.

This is too good to be true. Something bad will happen.

"Are you okay?"

She nodded.

"You went somewhere. Where did you go?"

"Nowhere. Not a place worth visiting again." Adaline pulled a strand of hair behind her ear. "We should start looking for the girls."

Cache halted and stared at her, bewildered. "Have you been taking your pills?"

"My pills?" Adaline asked. "Oh, I see, you still think I'm off my fucking rocker. Nice, I thought we had something here for a minute."

"My timing was bad. I didn't mean that," he said. "I have a few calls to make, and then we can talk about what your thoughts are on the girls."

Clearly, he still didn't want to believe that they were alive, but she wouldn't give up.

"Okay."

They walked up the steps to their home, and Cache kissed her again before he went inside. Adaline sat on the porch and glanced up at the clouds, deciding how she would help him see where she was coming from. She desperately wanted them on the same brain wave, connecting on more than one level. Having his help to find the girls would change everything, but how could she show him a feeling in her gut? How could she explain this reason for betting everything on the girls still being alive?

"You're not alone, Mommy. You have us . . . always."

"I know, girls. You have me, too."

Adaline glanced at her front yard, realizing that for the first time in a week, she was able to sit outside without fear of reporters attacking her. Grabbing her prescription bottle out of her purse, she held it in her hand. The pills made her tired, depressed, and nauseated. She hadn't taken them for a while and had flushed her dose down the toilet each day.

Time to make choices for myself.

"I'm not crazy." She unsealed the cap and poured the pills out on the ground, watching them roll in different directions. A newspaper boy threw a paper, and it hit her front door. Adaline turned around to grab it and saw a yellow piece of paper with her name on it hiding underneath her welcome mat. Opening the letter, a picture fell onto her lap. The photo was of a young boy, no older than nine, sitting in a blue car next to a cornfield, dated twenty-five years ago.

She peered at it closer.

A gate near the car said Arlingston.

Adaline gasped.

The boy was on her childhood property at the Manor. His face held such resemblance to Eliza, her daughter—they even had the same dimples.

Cache.

No, it can't be.

Adaline shook as she read the bold words that screamed at her from a piece of floral stationery paper.

You're not going to like what you find in therapy. Who's going to die from their lies first? You or Cache?

FIFTY-ONE

Sam Wendell
10:00 a.m.

A CAR HORN HONKED. Standing up, he braced himself against a brick wall on the corner of the street. Sam called the only person he thought would help him, only to receive a threat instead. He glimpsed at the car, surprised to see Cache came after all. Sam limped two steps toward the car and grabbed the door handle with one hand, pulling as hard as his strength would allow. Nothing. Cache got out and opened the door for him.

Sam rolled his eyes.

Wonderful.

"Thank you, darling," he said, grimacing.

"Cut the crap." Cache grabbed him by the collar and shoved Sam against the car. "I'm not here to help you. You're going to help me. Got it?"

Sam put his hands in the air. "Cool down, man. I

thought I was having a bad day, but clearly, somehow yours is worse."

"Be straight with me. I'm not going anywhere until you tell me the truth," Cache said.

"Okay. Shoot."

"Did you give Adaline the owl necklace?" Cache peered at him before he continued.

"No."

"Then who was it?"

"Can't tell you."

Cache shoved him against the passenger door. "By the looks of it, you play dirty? What happened to your face?"

"Adaline has made enemies, it seems."

"Because of you. We were fine until you came along," he said, pointing at Sam.

Sam stared at him. "That's not true, and you know it."

Cache let go of his shirt. "Who then?"

Sam held his head. "I'm not sure, but Adaline's in trouble. Where's she now?"

"Gone." Cache grunted and pounded his fist on the hood of the car.

"What do you mean gone?"

"She just left, and I need your help finding her. One minute we had a therapy session, and things seemed like they were moving in a good direction for us. We shared some past secrets. I went inside to make some calls while she sat on the porch, and the next thing I know, she took off in her car."

"Why did you come to get me? You should be looking for your wife," Sam said.

"I did, and when I couldn't find her, I went to call you, but—"

"I was calling you."

"Right," Cache said. "Now, are you going to help me find my wife?"

Sam got in and buckled his seatbelt. "Drive. We need to find her quick, and I need to know what could've set her off."

"I don't know. Like I said, things seemed good." He hesitated and shook his head. "I asked if she was taking her pills."

Sam slapped his forehead. "How did she respond?"

"She was frustrated. Angry, maybe."

"And you didn't stay with her?"

Staring straight ahead of him, Cache appeared to be focused. "No. I figured she wanted space."

"That's the last thing she needs," Sam said. "Was there something that seemed out of place?"

Tapping his fingers on the steering wheel, Cache glanced at him. "Her pills were scattered all over the stairs."

"Dammit." Sam pulled out his phone and pressed a few buttons. "I got it. She's heading north."

"Wait a minute. You bugged my wife's car?"

"She's a runner, remember? I want her to be safe just like you do," Sam said. "What did you talk about in therapy?"

"First, you're a stalker, and second, are you for real? I'm not sharing anything with you."

"Not even if it helps us find her?"

Cache paused. "All I know is that our past is connected in some way."

"How?"

"Don't you know?" Cache asked.

"I've been working with Dr. Lynchester to help get the truth out of Adaline. I only know what she's been through." Sam said. "I'm only invested in you because she's your wife, other than that, you're meaningless to me."

Cache gasped and held his chest.

"Joke all you want, but your wife's losing it. You can see it. I can see it. If she doesn't get help and face her past, we're going to all lose her...for good, this time."

"You really do love her." Cache moved in his seat. "How exactly do you think we're going to lose her?"

Sam gripped the base of his neck. "Let's just say that she gets very angry, and it doesn't turn out well. We need to help her...gently."

"You're talking about someone else, not my wife."

"Really?" Sam asked. "Is that why you asked if she took her meds?"

Cache growled under his breath and pulled the car to the side of the road. "You remember what happened with her as a kid. I bet you could answer a question for me."

"Depends on what it is."

"She lived with your family after her parents died, right?"

Sam loved the day his best friend came to live with him, and he couldn't wait to be able to protect her in his very own home, rather than at the terrible place she'd been living. His two sisters squealed with delight at having another girl in the house to do girly things with. Sam's parents put together a brand-new room for her while the rest of them shared rooms, but they felt Adaline deserved something special of her own. That was the first night she'd run away from their home.

"Yes. She lived with her aunt first, then got sent to the psych ward for a few months. After her stay there, she came to live with us," Sam said.

"Her original house was small?"

"Why are we talking about houses?"

"Bear with me. This is important," Cache said. "Does Arlingston Manor ring a bell?"

Sam flinched and shook his head. "Nope. Never heard of it."

Cache's face grew pale. He jumped out of the car and hunched over the side of the curb.

Shit. He knows.

Peering at the overcast sky, Sam felt the wind whip his face as if to slap him silly. "Are you okay?" he yelled to Cache.

Cache stood in silence and straightened his posture out, turning to glance at Sam. "I think I just found our connection. The link between Adaline and myself."

Sam watched him and held his gun with one hand, his fist clenched on the opposite side.

"Care to share?" Thunder rumbled, and drops of rain drizzled, starting to tease and creep into his fears.

"The house my parents robbed was Adaline's home," Cache said.

Sam gripped the door handle. He placed the gun under his shirt, got out of the car, and walked toward where Cache stood.

Cache held his knees and his face turned pale. "No.

"This is crazy," he said, holding his mouth. "If this is right, then my parents and her parents were all killed that night in the same house. That's why—"

The rain fell harder, smacking Sam's face with as much force and anger as he was feeling. "You know, I always wondered how the hell you met Adaline." Sam put his hand behind his back, ready to grab the gun. "Who are you working for?"

Cache got close to his face. "I'm not working for anyone...*man.*"

"All right, if you say so." Sam gripped Cache's neck and hit him upside the head with his gun, knocking him unconscious. He inserted a needle into his arm, then took the keys and cell phone from Cache.

He pulled out his own phone and dialed a familiar number. "We have a problem. He's figuring it out, and I think he's playing her. What should I do?"

On the other line, a woman's voice replied, "It's all working as planned. Let it take its course."

"Okay, Dr. Lynchester. If you think it will work."

Sam hung up the phone. He carried Cache to the passenger seat and drove to the Rushers' home to place him somewhere out of the way. The injection would keep him down for a few hours.

It's my turn to save the day and help Adaline.

He got in the car and sped toward Owling.

FIFTY-TWO

Dr. Lynchester
Friday, November 12th
10:30 a.m.

THE SESSION with the Rushners went well, especially with Cache opening up as much as he did. It didn't trigger anything for Adaline, which was a setback, but in due time everything would click, and she would figure it out.

Staring at the fridge, a picture of Adaline looked back at her.

I never forgot about you. Don't forget about me.

Dr. Lynchester decided on the first day that eight-year-old Adaline came for a session, a few months before the death of her parents, this little girl would be one she'd save from the sins of her family. The anger and yet purity that came from that sweet child made her yearn to have a daughter of her own. Adaline was so real and full of love, but scared to share that very gift with others, afraid to not receive it in return. Dr. Lynchester wanted to take away the pain the child suffered and give her a life that every little girl should have. One full of playdates, dress up, baking cookies with her mother, and a million hugs mixed with *I love yous*.

Only, Adaline never experienced that. Her playdates were with imaginary friends in the closet, and she picked scraps of food off the floor like a ravenous animal. She received multiple beatings a day, alongside verbal abuse, that would break any child down. Over time, Adaline became filled with illusions of being happy and compelled herself into believing she was lucky enough to have what she did. All the bad things that happened to her were her fault for being a bad girl.

Dr. Lynchester shook her head at the thought. What she would've given to have a child when so many people didn't even care for the ones they had. She had a mission to mother these lost souls. Dr. Lynchester knew Adaline wasn't crazy when she got sent to the psych ward twenty-five years ago. Pulling her out of that horrific place and bringing Adaline home to live with her until they found a more permanent home was the only option to protect this child. She did it without regret or a second thought at the consequences that could be handed to her, because it didn't matter. Adaline became the daughter she never had. Playing with her hair, reading books, and making jewelry were fond memories of some of her favorite moments. Every Saturday was funny face pancake day.

She placed her dirty plate in the dishwasher and turned it on. Grabbing her silver heels, Dr. Lynchester put them back on her sore feet and sighed. The day still held a full schedule of appointments, and her energy level was already drained. Every client's life constantly weighed her down out of worry for the sadness and pain they went through. She tried for years to not bring it home but couldn't quite figure out how to do that. Dr. Lynchester grabbed her briefcase and espresso and headed back to the office.

———

Stepping out on the fourth floor to her office, there was a stillness that shouldn't be there. At this point in the day, her receptionist would be on the phone and a client would be waiting for her. She'd smile and tell the client to come back to her office, but no one was there. Even the lights were off. Dr. Lynchester sipped her espresso and pulled out her phone. Tayla didn't pick up.

Where is everybody?

Standing in place, she stared out the window at the view. The snow-capped mountains never failed to amaze her. Dr. Lynchester opened the balcony door and took in the cool November breeze on her cheeks. Her heart warmed knowing Adaline was getting closer to the truth, finding out who she was, and being rid of the demons that taunted her.

Please, God. Let it work this time.

A buzz took her mind back to reality as she retrieved her phone from her pocket.

"Sam. We're not supposed to be contacting each other."

"Are you okay?" Sam asked.

Dr. Lynchester lightly pulled back a strand of hair from her face. "It's feeling a tad like the Twilight Zone."

"What do you mean?"

"My receptionist isn't here. She's not answering her phone, and my client's late," she said. "This particular client is always on time. Actually, there's massive anxiety involved surrounding time with this person." Dr. Lynchester paused. "It's nothing, really."

"I'd be happy to help if you're worried about something," Sam said.

"I'm just happy to hear from you."

"Likewise," Sam said, huffing. "We're getting close."

"I couldn't agree more. The Rushners came in a few hours ago, and I think we're making a breakthrough," she said.

"No, I mean we're getting too close. Be careful."

"What do you mean? What's happened?" she asked.

"I was attacked this morning."

Dr. Lynchester moved the phone away from her face, took a deep breath, and returned to the phone. "By who?"

"I'm not sure. There were three of them, all wearing ski masks. There's more going on here than we know," Sam said. "We want to help her, but—"

"You're worried it will happen again?" Dr. Lynchester asked.

"What if it already has? You know Adaline. If she's figured things out, she might already be playing us and is the one behind these attacks."

"I can't believe that. It will be different this time."

"All I'm saying is, you don't know that, and opening up these old wounds could be putting us all in danger . . . again," Sam said. "Adaline's a danger to herself, too. She just doesn't know it."

Dr. Lynchester tapped her foot. "I'm not giving up on her. She's strong enough to handle the truth." She paused. "My concern now is that if Adaline didn't hire someone to attack you, then who did, and why? Do you have your eye on her?"

"I'm watching her now and…I'm not giving up either. Just being cautious."

There was a long pause on the phone.

"Doctor?" Sam asked.

"Hold on. Stay on the line, okay?"

Her hand shook as she bent down to take off her heels and put them gently on the patio. She tiptoed into the reception room, moving close to the wall. The sound of books smacking the floor and glass shattering made her flinch. Dr. Lynchester hesitated and held her body against the desk. The hairs on her arm stood straight up.

"Sam, listen to me," she said, in a whisper. "I trust you with her, that's why I asked for your help. Adaline needs you now."

"She needs you, too."

"There's no more time for talking. I left some of my belongings in locker 451 in Owling at the old gym I used to take her to. Do you remember it?"

"Yes," Sam said.

"Good. Take Cache with you, give everything in those files to Adaline, and…tell her I love her."

"What's going on? Are you in danger?"

"If you want to help, stay away from me. Don't call again and take care of my girl," she said. "She'll have wings. Believe in her."

"Who's with you?"

"Goodbye, Sam. Take care of yourself."

She hung up the phone and pressed her back up against the wall, slowly walking toward her office. Dr. Lynchester's heartbeat sped up as she fumbled through her purse to grab her taser. Bracing herself, she positioned near the door and tilted her head from side to side for a minute as she considered opening it.

Inside, the noise stopped.

Dr. Lynchester shifted her body and swallowed hard. Placing the taser in the waistband of her leggings, she tried to weigh her options on the best plan. She peeked inside again to view her files lying all over the floor and her desk with multiple pages torn to shreds.

Her nostrils flared, and she rolled up her sleeves. Rustling came from behind the door, and Dr. Lynchester waited for some movement. A gloved hand appeared around the frame. She dug her nails into their skin, smacking the door open. Someone moaned. Dr. Lynchester could see the muscles on her attacker's arms flex. She lunged at the culprit and flung her arms around his broad neck, knocking him to the ground. The culprit snarled at her, and she could feel his crooked smile burning a hole through the black mask. He kicked her leg and she fell to the ground, a piece of glass piercing the palm of her hand. Dr. Lynchester yelped and tried to stand up. He took his mask off and walked toward her, chuckling and cracking his knuckles.

"What are you doing here?" she asked, pulling the glass out of her hand. "Who are you? Speak." Dr. Lynchester held it tightly between her fingers.

The man laughed with amusement, and his eyes taunted her to take a stab at him as he bent down next to her face. He watched her hand holding the glass. She stared up at him for a long moment before he gripped her throat. She gasped for breath and smacked him with the shard of glass. He loosened his grip and stepped backward, clinging to the bridge of his nose. Dr. Lynchester rubbed at her neck and ran at him—full force. Her skirt tore, and she kicked him in the stomach. The man fell to the ground and glanced up at her with a dismayed face.

"I won't tell you a thing," he said.

She brought her taser to his neck. "Tell me, or I give you a jolt."

He laughed louder and gripped her arm. Dr. Lynchester pressed it to his neck and watched as his body went limp. From behind her, papers crinkled and boots shuffled toward her. She stayed in a crouch, gripping her taser as she turned toward the noise. A shiny metal object gleamed in one of the two masked figure's hands.

A wrench.

She looked at them and glanced at her surroundings around the room. There were two of them against one of her. Dr. Lynchester thought about running but doubted her speed against them.

"Back up, or you'll end up like this fellow," she said, stepping backward. She aimed her taser at them. "Put the wrench down. No one else needs to get hurt."

"You can't leave alive, lady, so give it your best shot," said one of the attackers.

The person who spoke was a man with a husky voice, but the other one was slender and had curves only a woman could have. She seemed to be hesitant, standing behind the masked man. They didn't touch like they were lovers or family, but he stood protective over her, and she seemed to wait for a command.

No running away. Give it your best shot.

Dr. Lynchester ran toward the man. From the corner of her eye, she could see the woman launching at her full speed to protect the man.

"No, Tayla. Don't," the man said. "Stick to the plan."

Tayla. My assistant?

Dr. Lynchester slapped her and grabbed at her mask, taking it off.

"Tayla. What are you doing?"

The brown-haired girl glared at her with distaste and pushed her backward. Dr. Lynchester fell, and the man punched Tayla, knocking her out.

"Well, that wasn't the plan. That girl has never followed commands." He walked toward her and took off his mask. "I guess the cat's out."

Dr. Lynchester gasped. "You?"

"That's right, kitten. Nighty night," he said.

Pain radiated through her head, and her vision blurred. The last thought she had was of Adaline playing Mozart on the piano in a blue lace dress. She hummed the song and closed her eyes.

Adaline.

FIFTY-THREE

Adaline Rushner
Owling, Utah
10:30 a.m.

GOING BACK to where it all began, to try and remember who was after her and why, seemed like the only thing that made sense. The sun felt warm for a November afternoon, and the snow agreed as water trickled off her car. Adaline loved the freedom she expressed when she drove. It was just her, the speed, and the wind all working together to make a powerful force. She relished the rush—revving up the engine, letting the car gear vibrate in her hand, and knowing she had full control and power of the car. Adaline would time it just right. Wait for the road to be vacant until she pressed her foot on the pedal and fly. She could drive all day like that.

Her speakers bounced with the heavy beat of the drums in the background. Blonde locks of hair swung in motion with the cold breeze as she raised her hand up and down outside her car window, drowning out the screams she heard inside her head.

Getting off the highway, she took a right-hand turn into Owling and stopped the car. It wasn't until a few miles into town, where their "home" sat, that people sprung about toward the one gas station they had and a few little mom and pop shops. Here, right where she stood, was a ghost town.

Old and rustic.

The railroad tracks ran on the right-hand side of the road throughout the city, while broken-down houses sat to rot on the opposite side. The few stores that they had in Owling, on the outskirts of town as a kid, were now boarded up with nails and plywood.

Vacant.

Adaline got back in the car. She knew where she needed to visit first.

Her *friend* had a place in this area. He always mentioned how he enjoyed the solitude of no neighbors and being off in the distance. She pulled up to his old home and closed her car door. It looked the way she pictured it from her session with Dr. Lynchester. The windows on the yellow home were shattered, and the house had taken a beating. She went to the backyard to find the swing he used to push her on and saw the garden only held weeds, though it used to hold white Gerber daisies. Adaline placed her purse on the ground and brushed her fingers through the dry bushels. Closing her eyes, she imagined the soft petals gliding against her fingertips, and she pressed her nose to the dead leaf, inhaling, revisiting how they used to smell.

Sitting on the bench swing, she pumped her feet back

and forth, allowing the cool breeze to get acquainted with her again.

I'm back.

"This is my friend's house, girls. Don't you like it?" Adaline dragged her feet to stop the swing and got off. She peered around and held her head. "Girls, why aren't you talking to me? Don't leave me."

Racing to the garden, she bent down to caress the weeds. "Come back, dammit. Come back to me." Adaline gripped a handful of dead plants, tugging from their roots, and threw them across the yard. "You're not gone."

She glanced around the yard. Her purse sat on a slushy pile of snow, next to a broken window. Adaline scurried over to it and knelt in the water, opening each zipper and looking through every pocket.

Please, let there be one of my pills.

Her hands shook, continuing to pry through every inch of her purse.

"*No.* I can't lose you. *No.* Mommy is here, girls. I'm here," she yelled, through tears streaming down her face.

Adaline tugged at her hair and stood. Kicking her purse, she screamed and let the rage in. Her mind remembered this very feeling as a kid. She continued to scream. Her tears drizzled along her face, forming a stream of sorrow.

Her mother spitting on her face and telling her to go away, to never come back, filled her mind. She screamed then, too. And…he was there—her friend. Why? What else happened?

Wiping her face dry, she sniffled and gazed at the home again. Adaline's feet crunched in the snow as she shuffled to the back door and turned the knob. It opened, and she coughed at the dust that blew in her face. Inside, an old furnace was placed in the corner, and a large cage hung next to it. Walking closer, Adaline peered into the cage at a stuffed owl. She froze and continued to stare, fascinated at the beauty it held. The owl had golden life-like eyes that made her feel as though this bird already knew her. Adaline spoke to the bird with her own eyes, hypnotized, waiting for it to converse, but it still sat…trapped. Its broad wings floated with stiffness in the confined prison, barely room to expand to their fullest extent.

She flinched and gasped. "I remember you. How did I forget that?" Adaline smiled, remembering the day she met the owl for the first time.

"You have an owl in that cage?"

"I do. Isn't she a beautiful creature?" he said.

"Why do you keep her caged?"

"She never had a chance to be free or to soar away from here. Something held her back."

Adaline held on to her necklace.

Something is holding me *back.*

The owl belonged to her friend, and he was the man who gave her the necklace. His eyes were the key to finding out who "he" was, and Sam's dad wasn't who they should be looking for. She'd seen these eyes…recently.

She covered her mouth and stepped backward.

He couldn't have been the one to kill her parents. But, if not him…who?

Adaline touched different kinds of jars filled with rocks, dirt, and other random contents that hung on the dusty shelves. She turned the corner to a little room. A bed with a blue ruffled skirt held cobwebs and a teddy bear.

"Mr. Speckles. Have you been here all alone?"

Sitting down on the bed, Adaline clung to the little bear that used to give her comfort. The last time she held the stuffed toy was twenty-five years ago, the same night she realized she was a ghost and no one wanted her.

Her friend came to take her away from her home. She went freely. He'd always been kind to her, but something changed that evening. He started panicking and calling her Emery multiple times. The care he usually showed her was replaced with anger when she told him she wasn't Emery. He didn't see her anymore...but wanted someone else. After being called a liar, and him throwing a chair at the ground near her feet, she fled, stopping only once to catch her breath, and didn't look back to see if he was chasing her. Corn husks hit her in the face as she ran through the cornfield and came to an opening toward her home. Her mother stood on the porch...waiting.

My mother does care about me.

She ran barefoot up the porch steps and flung toward her mother with open arms.

"I'm home, Mother."

No embrace. Her mother spat on her face and told Adaline to never come back. Adaline's feet gave out from under her, and she knelt on the ground.

"Mother, please. I can change."

"You'll never be the daughter I wanted," *she said, sneering.* "My daughter died a long time ago."

"Why? What have I done to you?"

"Goodbye, Adaline." *She smirked and went inside.*

Raging anger boiled inside her, and she screamed until her throat stung. What happened after was a daze. Flames engulfed the porch, like a snake slithering its way into the cave and swallowing it whole.

Her friend ran behind her. "What have you done?" *He caressed her face and held her hand.* "It's okay, Daisy. I'll take care of you." *She glanced into the smoke and stared at the place where her nightmares lived. It was over.*

Adaline dropped the bear and rocked back and forth.

There was a little owl
High in a tree
She tried to fly away
But couldn't get free

She jumped up from the bed, shaking.

She killed her parents. She killed Cache's parents. It had been her.

FIFTY-FOUR

Cache Rushner
Friday, November 12th
10:45 a.m.

GLANCING AROUND AT HIS SURROUNDINGS, bright lights made him squint with discomfort. Cache stood up and the room spun, but he knew he was home. The front room's décor was only an Adaline invention. She called it her Mosaic abyss, with blue and yellow printed pillows that meshed with the turquoise, tiled tables. In the center of the room, Van Gogh's Starry Night, a large mosaic mural made of tiles, enchanted the wall.

How did I get here? How long have I been out?

He vaguely remembered feeling drowsy and hearing Sam talk to someone on the phone once they were in the car. Cache gazed out the window again to see what he already knew. His car was gone. He reached into his pocket for his phone.

Empty.

Hunching over, Cache took a deep breath. The last thing he could recall was talking to Sam about his parents' death at Adaline's childhood home.

Who was Sam talking to on the phone?

Cache cracked his neck and walked around the room for a minute to gain composure.

Dr. Lynchester.

It had to have been her.

Sam said *doctor* on the phone, and they both were part of Adaline's past, but what did they have up their sleeves? Dr. Lynchester's cryptic questions didn't fool him. She clearly was involved somehow. All the info he needed to clear up the missing pieces, she'd have, and he knew she could contact Adaline for him.

He walked through the front door, trying to steady himself, one step at a time. What started as walking moved into running toward the direction of her office. Cache didn't have time to think about what he would do or say. He needed his wife, and fast.

The vacant parking lot held only one car, odd for a Friday afternoon. He took the elevator to the fourth floor and stepped out as the door opened. The receptionist wasn't at her desk, and no one sat waiting for their turn to express themselves to death.

Chuckling at his own joke, he gazed at the large, round clock on the wall.

11:00 am

Cache continued to move past the front desk toward Dr. Lynchester's office. The door was cracked open, but not enough to see inside. He knocked on it lightly.

"Dr. Lynchester. It's Cache Rushner. I found the connection between Adaline and myself. We need to talk."

He paused, waiting for a response. "Adaline's in trouble. I need your help."

He didn't receive a reply and opened the door anyway. File folders and documents were spread all over the floor. Broken table pieces and glass scattered around the room, and books hung off the bookshelves. A lump of soil sat in the center of the room, and a gold planter lay on the ground a few feet away. Multiple, lavish rugs had been nicely positioned in their proper spots this morning. Now, they were ransacked to one side of the room.

"Doctor? Are you in here?"

Oh good. She's gone. Maybe for good, along with Sam.

He'd thought about killing both of them off multiple times in his mind, and even went into detail about how he'd do it. If they were out of the picture, he could handle Adaline on his own terms without all the other roadblocks.

Moving inside, he peered from one corner of the room to the other and walked toward Dr. Lynchester's desk. A crinkle noise sounded. Glancing down, a photo clung to his boot. He tried to kick it off, but it held firm. Cache bent down to grab it and examined the picture of a woman holding a young girl with blonde hair. His fingers twitched and he gasped for breath. The lady, without a doubt, was a younger version of Dr. Lynchester . . . the woman who grabbed him in the cornfields and told him to go home.

He clenched the picture in his hand and punched the air. She lied to him. His parents never came home. Cache had a session with this woman, sat in this hideous room right across from her, and he could've easily strangled the life from her. Re-opening the piece of paper, he took a good look at this con artist and the young girl who stood near her, smiling with glee. His oldest daughter, Leora, resembled this girl that he knew had to be Adaline.

Cache gripped his chest.

He'd never seen this portrait before. Bracing his hand on her desk, a sharp pinch greeted him, and a piece of glass fell out from beneath his hand. Cache grabbed Kleenex from the tissue box on the table and pressed it on his cut. Bending down to retrieve the shard of glass that dropped, he stumbled backward and lost his balance, sending him sideways to the ground. Punching the floor for his carelessness, he halted to view a path of pearl beads, rolling back and forth on the hard surface. A thin thread held a few in place.

A necklace.

The strong metallic scent hit him, and his eyes followed the trail of beads that led to the decorated rugs in the middle of the room. A red liquid dripped in a puddle, and the beads were swimming to it.

Blood. Lots of it.

Cache put pressure on his shaking arm and slowly got up. Red stained fingernails creeped out from beneath the rug, and a muscular arm, bent backward, was yanked behind a man's back.

Covering his mouth, he retched and looked away. Two bodies. One woman and one man, but not Dr. Lynchester.

How was Dr. Lynchester involved? Why was she so invested in his life, as well as Adaline's?

I should leave and call the police.

He went to exit the room, and a loud thud halted him. Cache froze, listening to the direction of where it came from. The banging had a repetitive rhythm, much like a metronome. Cache remembered from their session about the closet around the corner when Dr. Lynchester took their coats. He carefully moved toward it and paused before turning the doorknob. Grabbing the handle, he twisted it quickly. A broom swung out at him, falling on the floor, and a coat swayed with the motion of the fall. Cache moved the coat with his hand to look behind it. Something flung out at him and hit the floor with a bang. He jumped to the side and peered down at bloodshot eyes staring up at him. Rope coiled her neck and legs. Cache turned around and bent down, hoping to not regurgitate his breakfast, but the smell was too pungent. Wiping at his face, he stayed stationary, praying the body would be gone once he got back up.

She's dead.

Dr. Lynchester is dead.

He clung to his knees, breathing in deep. His wife was in even more danger than he realized, because of him. Standing up, Cache ran out of her office and didn't look back.

FIFTY-FIVE

Officer Abbott
11:30 a.m.

AFTER HEARING about his wife's involvement with
Lieutenant Stalk, he couldn't even look at the picture of his
family on his desk without bitterness clenching his heart,
where love used to be. He felt sick to his stomach all
morning. He wanted to throw up all the memories he'd
had over the years with them. Be rid of all the toxins that
slowly infested inside him. In his mind, neither his wife
nor the lieutenant were the kind of people who would do
this. That hurt the worst. Who the hell did he know? They
were strangers now, which meant his life to a point was a
complete lie. He trusted them more than anything, and
they betrayed him. How long had he walked around
blind?

The lieutenant's office hadn't been occupied all
morning, and he didn't answer any of Abbott's ten calls.
He bunched his fist and hit the dashboard in his car.

Fuck.

His speaker suddenly crackled as the dispatcher's voice came through. "All officers near Main Street and Ivy Lane, 10-84 with possible survivors. Please respond."

"Affirmative. I'm arriving at the scene now," Abbott said.

"10-4. Sending back up."

Abbott pulled up to the building and got out of his car. He scanned the street for anything or anyone suspicious before grabbing his kit from the trunk. Another police vehicle drove into the parking lot, and Officer Keaton, his partner, tipped his head at him.

"I began thinking you fell off your rocker for good this time. Glad to see you're still kicking."

"Very funny, brother. We need to check the perimeter. Make sure the suspect's not on the premises."

Officer Keaton nodded. "I'll check down here. Go save the people upstairs."

Abbott maneuvered through the entrance and went up to the 4th floor. He laid his kit on the ground and pulled his gun from his holster. Stepping around the receptionist desk, he saw heels on the outside patio. Picking up his pace, he trudged into an office and held his back up against the door. "Salt Lake Police. Put your hands where I can see them."

Silence spoke back to him. Pearls rolled at his feet, and he stepped over them quietly to get inside. The room inside resembled an earthquake scenario. All the furniture and decorations, even the picture frames on the wall—tilted. Papers and file folders lay in every direction, and more pearls lingered in a pool of blood near two bodies. A male and a female.

Abbott put his fingers to their necks, checking for a pulse.

Dead.

Abbott halted.

Dr. Lynchester's body lay frozen near an open closet with a broom and coat flung next to her. Blood smears decorated the carpet where her body lay, and one noticeable impact splatter appeared on the right side of the wall. Gripping his neck, he trudged out to the reception desk.

The therapist is dead.

"Keaton. What's your twenty?"

"We're all clear here. You?"

"No survivors. No sign of the suspect," Abbott said.

"Affirmative. I'll tape the area and mark a path for responders coming in and out. Do you want me to stand guard outside to let them in?"

Abbott unlocked his kit. "Yes."

"Hallswell just got here. I'll have him call in other resources."

"Deal. I'm getting some pictures of the crime scene before the CSI get here."

"Okay," Officer Keaton said.

Pulling out his phone, he huffed.

Sam,

Thought you should know. The doctor's dead. This doesn't mean you're off the hook.

He pushed "send message" and placed latex gloves on his hands. Abbott took the camera out of the box and put a notebook and a few plastic bags in his pocket before heading back toward the office. Breathing in, he cleared his mind, ready to take in the scene fully.

Walking in, a musky scent lingered. Cologne. He

glanced at the clock and wrote down the time in his notebook, then checked the thermostat on the wall.

69 degrees.

He tugged at his collar and wiped his bald head. The room seemed warm to him, but his own anxious body heat was apparently the culprit, not the thermostat. Abbott pulled out a plastic bag, bent down, and retrieved some of the blood-stained pearls with tweezers.

Closing the bag, he set it on the desk. Dr. Lynchester's arms had been tied down, and only her left hand had remnants of blood, mostly in her fingernails. Wire wrapped around her neck and a puncture wound appeared on the right side of her collarbone.

Abbott assumed she'd been left in the closet, but who opened the door?

Her face was waxy, and streaks of black flowed from her eyes.

She'd been crying. The black spots are mascara.

The doctor's mouth gaped. From choking? No… something else.

Abbott snapped a picture of her face and paused. Her eyes had petechial hemorrhages—red dots in the sclera—from the pressure within the veins of her neck rising suddenly. They also captured panic and understanding. He looked back and forth at her mouth and eyes and hunched over. She knew the killer.

Surprise.

Shock.

Horror.

All said through her eyes. Could've been any one of her angry patients, but the other two dead bodies didn't add up quite yet. Abbott glanced at the file folders all over the office, tempted to see who had regular visits with the doctor. The other dead bodies took priority though.

Stepping over a broken planter, he squatted down to see how a man of this man's build and stature could possibly be tangled up like a pretzel. His arm bent back behind his back, and blood spilled from his head. A sharp object glinted from under the man. Abbott reached to grab the item—a wrench covered in the crimson liquid. If someone pushed his face to the ground suffocating him, while they hit his head multiple times with the wrench, that'd keep him down.

Abbott shook his head and placed the wrench in a bag. He could feel a headache coming on.

Moving toward the other woman, he could tell she was young, maybe early to mid-twenties. Blood drizzled from her wrists, appearing to be a suicide. He snapped a few more pictures and stood up.

"CSI and Homicide have arrived. They're coming in now."

"Copy," Abbott said.

Peering down at the bodies one last time, he saw a wallet under the man's arm, a picture of a child slightly exposed.

Poor kid lost their dad today.

He bent down to get a closer look at the photo, and a little girl stared at him.

Abbott's hand shook and his body convulsed. *His* little girl's picture was in this man's wallet. He grabbed the wallet and hid it in his coat before attempting to stand up.

Medical examiners came into the office and nodded at him as they made their way around the bodies and set up their equipment. Abbott picked up the bag of pearls he collected from the desk and placed them in his pocket before rushing out of the room. He moved down the hall past other badges, looking straight ahead. Getting into the elevator, Abbott waited until it began to move downward, and he pressed the "stop" button to hold it in place. Abbott pressed his face against the wall and bunched his fist together, punching the elevator. Fighting back tears, he punched two more times before his fist held blood. He fell to the ground and covered his face, cradling the wallet in his hand. His senses went from denial to rage, giving him clarity and impulsiveness as he re-opened it and searched through all the pockets. The man had been carrying only $20, a lottery ticket, and a few business cards. An auto body repair shop, a pizza delivery service, and a real estate agent's card stared at him. No identification to be seen, but two receipts had phone numbers scribbled on them. Abbott pulled out his phone and dialed the first number on the worn piece of paper. It rang three times and went straight to voicemail at Phil's Auto Body Shop.

He looked at the paper and dialed the pizza delivery number. A gruff voice answered on the second ring.

"I told you not to call me on this number." The man paused. "Is it done? Is she dead?"

Abbott listened to the voice. It sounded familiar, but he couldn't think why.

"Champ, are you there?"

He closed the phone and threw it on the floor. Lieutenant Stalk made the hit on Dr. Lynchester.

FIFTY-SIX

Sam Wendell
Friday, November 12th
11:30 a.m.

HE'D WATCHED Adaline's every move for the past two hours to make sure she was safe, just like he promised himself and Dr. Lynchester.

Dr. Lynchester.

Sam sunk his head on the steering wheel and closed his eyes. She'd become a mentor and a friend to him after Adaline left years ago. More than anything, she kept him from falling into complete destruction, and his life would be something else if it wasn't for her.

Would Adaline hire someone to kill Dr. Lynchester? He knew the rage that clung to Adaline and exposed itself when she felt threatened, but this...was too much. The doctor saved her. If she could do this to someone who had only the best intentions for her, they were all fucked, and they'd already lost her.

No.

His lip quivered, and he sat in his car, staring off into the distance. Without Dr. Lynchester the process of helping Adaline seemed like a lost cause. He thought about the last thing the doctor said to him on the phone before she told him not to contact her again. She still believed Adaline could pull through and that it wasn't too late.

Sam flexed his fingers and cracked his knuckles.

I'll find out who's behind this, and they'll pay.

Gazing at the home in front of him, he cringed. This place, where the Owl Keeper lived, held a lot of secrets that never sat well. So many times as a boy, he'd followed Adaline and secretly guarded her. Sam didn't trust the man, but she did.

He got out of his car and proceeded up the front steps toward the door. Sam wiped dirt off the windows with his sleeve to see if he could see inside. "Adaline?"

There wasn't a response.

Sam kicked the door open with his black boot, and it crashed to the ground with a loud bang. Someone screamed from the other side of the wall.

Adaline.

"It's Sam. No need to be afraid."

She turned the corner, peered up at him with swollen eyes, and fell to the ground.

Bending down, he put his hand out for support. "I'll help you up."

Adaline pushed his hand away. "Why didn't you tell me?"

"Tell you what?"

Glancing back up at him, she stared intensely and laughed. "The part where I killed my parents and you knew about it."

He straightened. She kept laughing. Dr. Lynchester was the one planning to help her with everything, not him. He never prepared himself to be the one taking the doctor's role, and it hurt like hell to see her this way. What if he made it worse?

Take care of my girl.

"We need to go, right now," Sam said.

"I'm not going anywhere with you until you tell me the truth."

Sam rubbed his hands together. "I'll tell you something real if you'll go with me after."

Adaline hesitated and nodded.

"I've loved you ever since I laid eyes on you as a little girl. I'm angry and upset that I will never have a chance at a life with you, but I've had a mission for a while to protect you. That's what I'm doing—what I'll always do. At least I can be a part of your life in that way, and I would rather that than never be close to you again." He brushed back his hair and turned away from her.

"You've been protecting me this whole time?" Adaline asked. "Why would you defend a murderer?"

Sam swallowed hard. "You're a…good person that got told you weren't your whole life. You've believed the lies people told you about yourself, but they're not true."

"Even you don't believe that," she said. "You hesitated. I'm dangerous, and you shouldn't get close to me."

She's taking responsibility. This is different than last time.

He smiled and peered into her eyes.

Adaline held his gaze. "Why are you looking at me like that?"

"I had to be sure, but now I am," he said. "Can we get in the car now?"

"No. You may be sure of things, but I'm not. Why would I go with you?"

Sam cracked his neck and opened the front door. "Because you want information about what took place that day, and I know where we need to go to get it."

She hesitated and stared down at the teddy bear in her arms. Adaline smiled at the stuffed animal, stood, and slowly glided out the door toward the car. She buckled the animal in the seatbelt with her.

He glanced at the bear, shook his head, and got into the driver's seat. "Who do you have there?"

"This is Mr. Speckles, and I'm introducing him to the girls when *we* find them," she said.

She's still not over their death. Maybe she's playing me, too.

Sam said a silent prayer that he could pull off what Dr. Lynchester needed him to do.

"I'm sure they'll be pleased to meet Mr. Speckles," he said. "That name makes zero sense, being a bear. He's going to have an identity crisis, if he hasn't already."

Adaline laughed with ease and joy. When she smiled at him, her deep blue eyes spoke to his soul, almost swallowing him into oblivion, and then she pushed her smile somewhere else, and her face held emptiness. "Even when we find the girls, our family will be broken. Cache will never look at me the same again. I killed his parents. I'm a monster."

"You're not," he said, starting the car. Sam wanted to tell her that he thought Cache had been playing her from the beginning, but if he opened that treasure of betrayal, there'd be no coming back.

"How the hell can you say that?"

"I was there that night."

"Where? In the cornfields?" Adaline asked.

"Yes. I knew you left with the Owl Keeper, and he made me nervous, so I followed you to his house. Once you were there, I watched to make sure he wouldn't hurt you."

"So, when I left his house, you followed me back to mine?"

Sam cracked his neck and gazed out the windshield with frustration. "Yes."

"Which means you saw my mother kick me out of the house, and you also watched the Owl Keeper, my friend, take the blame for the fire I set," she said. "You let me believe that someone else killed my parents, when I did it." Adaline smacked her hands against the dashboard. "I should be locked up."

"Stop it," he said.

"Let me out of the car right now."

Sam sped up. "I can't do that."

"Let me out now, dammit." She tried to unlock the door with no luck. "Get me off child lock."

Bunching his fingers around the steering wheel, he swerved the car to a halt. "Fuck, Adaline. Is that what you want?" he asked. "You want to roll your ass out of my car? Be reckless and get yourself hurt?"

"Go to hell. I never asked for you to protect me," she said. "You know, you came back into my life all the sudden after someone took my girls. Convenient. I'll bet you're enjoying how it's affected my relationship with Cache." Adaline glared at him. "What, did you think you could just all of a sudden move in?"

"You think I'd hurt you like that?"

Adaline glanced away. "I don't know." She stopped

hitting the dashboard and put her hand over her head, resting it on the window. "I need to get home and talk to Dr. Lynchester. I don't know if I can trust you, Cache...or anyone. Please take me back to my car."

Sam swallowed hard and shook his head.

"What's wrong?"

"You need to stay with me," he said. "You're in danger."

"I already know that. I've been in danger since my girls were taken." Adaline sat up. "Remember, I told you someone attacked me at the store and my neighbors have them . . . somewhere." She paused and peered up at him. "You never believed me, did you?"

He couldn't tell her what he felt to be true. Her girls were dead, and she needed to figure that out on her own. But someone *was* after her. Cache.

"I believe that you believe they're alive."

Adaline laughed and held her head. "You and Cache sound exactly the same. So, you're protecting me from... what, exactly? Because if no one took my girls, and no one attacked me, then what is this?"

"I think someone's out for revenge."

"On me?"

"It appears that way."

Adaline turned in her seat. "Let me understand this. Do you think that the same person who went after me went after my girls?"

He sighed. "At this point, it's a possibility."

"So, you're not trying to help me find my girls, but you're just making sure that I'm okay."

Starting the car, Sam huffed. "Still the same girl with a million questions. I've seen you when you're angry. You go to a place where you can't be reasoned with." He tapped his fingers on the dashboard. "Tragedy sets you off."

She shook her head. "Do you hear yourself? You wanted to help by directing me to remember that I killed my parents. That's enough to set anyone off the deep end. That makes no sense."

"Maybe you need to forgive yourself to move on. I don't know. We had a good reason for why we were doing this, and I trusted her."

"Trusted who?" she asked.

Sam got back on the road and ignored her question.

"Dammit, Sam. Answer the question."

"I can't."

"You said earlier that you had to be sure. You know I'm okay," she said. "Deep down, you're aware of that. I don't know how you saw me before when I had my...problems, but I can handle it."

She still thinks her girls are alive.

What if Cache found out somehow that Adaline *killed* his parents and wanted to get back at her? What if they were alive and Cache hid them to break her, to get her out of the picture. To make her look as though she'd had a mental breakdown from the loss of her girls.

Holy shit.

"Okay. What if I believe you? Then what?"

"Then we take a look at all the people I have wronged and find their motives to take my girls. Dr. Lynchester's help and the information you said you have will give clarity," she said.

She tilted her head as if someone might whisper in her ear, but her face reflected sadness.

"What's wrong?" he asked.

She shook her head and held her own hand. "Let's get that info."

"On our way."

"Dr. Lynchester was who you trusted. Something bad happened to her, didn't it?"

Sam gulped and stared out the window for a minute. "Yes. She's gone. It's just us now."

FIFTY-SEVEN

Seth Duncan
Lost Treasures
12:30 p.m.

SETH SHUT the blinds and turned the *closed* sign to face the outside window. He proceeded to count the money in the register, placed it in a bank bag, and dropped it into the safe. He wrote the last item on the inventory sheet and headed to the back to get his coat. Another evening at the motel with a TV dinner and some horrible reruns of *MASH* awaited him. Paying for a cheap place gave him exactly what he paid for. He took out his pocket sanitizer and sprayed some on his hands, inhaling the clean scent. Pulling back his long hair, Seth tied a rubber band in it and took a deep breath, ready to call it a day. Officer Abbott's visit earlier, and the lieutenant's threat, left some unresolved muscle spasms that pinched his nerves every time he thought about them. They were ticking time bombs. Parts of him didn't want to stick around to see what that meant for him, but intrigue kicked in. People amused and fascinated him with all their pride, entitlement, and sheer lack of taking responsibility for the revolting life they created. Who would win in the battle of Lieutenant Douchebag and Officer Egocentric?

He shook his head.

A cold breeze danced from the doorway, and the door slammed shut from the power of the wind. Seth jumped, looking toward the front door.

"We're closed. Come back tomorrow."

"Where is she? Tell me right now," a breathless voice yelled.

He walked toward the voice. "Mr. Rushner?" He squinted and moved forward. "You're bleeding. What happened to you?"

"I need to find her now. She's not safe," he said, bracing his hands on the counter to steady his shaking body.

Seth licked his lips. "I assure you she's safe."

Cache sneered at him. "How can you assure me of that, exactly?"

"Now, calm down." Seth placed his hand out. "She was with that old friend of hers. You should go to the hospital and get yourself checked."

"Sam? I assure you she's not safe with him," he said. "Wait, how do you know all this?"

"She called me."

Cache sat on the ground
and shook his head. "Why would she call you?"

"I had to do inventory. She's very exact on making sure things are in their proper place," Seth said.

He moaned. "That does sound like my wife. Now, tell me where she is."

"Let me take you to the hospital first."

"We can't do that, okay? I need to figure out what to do," Cache said. Blood stained his hands, and sweat dripped off his brow.

"Wait here. I'll grab you bottled water and the phone to call Mrs. Rushner." Picking up the phone in the back, he pulled out Officer Abbott's card and dialed the number.

"Officer Abbott, here."

"Yes, this is Seth from Lost Treasures."

"Listen, this isn't a good time."

"I'll jump right in, then. Mr. Rushner is here, and he's got blood all over himself. He walked into the shop saying his wife's in trouble."

Abbott grunted. "I'll be right there. Don't you let him leave your shop."

"Yes, sir, Officer, sir."

He put the phone down and scratched his cheek multiple times. Seth retrieved a bottle of water from the back room, then strolled to the front of the store. "Here you go. So, what happened?"

"I'm not talking unless you have a phone for me." Cache gazed up at him and clenched his fist.

He grinned. "You're no longer needed, and therefore, you don't receive phone time."

"What are you talking about?" Cache stood up, walked a few steps backward, keeping his eyes on Seth.

"You tried to kill Adaline. She's not safe with you," he said. "You're playing her, and I won't tell you where she is."

Cache's eyes widened, and he spat on Seth's sneakers. "I never had a good feeling about you."

Seth cracked his neck and peered at his shoe. "You're a disgusting man, spitting on my property." He grabbed the sanitizer bottle and a towel off the counter and threw them at Cache. "Wipe it off, now."

"You wipe it off yourself, you piece of shit. I'm not trying to hurt my wife."

A car door shut outside the store. Seth smiled. "I'm protecting her. Don't you see? Just like I'm protecting *them* from all of you liars that mean to hurt little girls."

"What girls are you talking about?" Cache asked.

Seth put his finger to his lips.

Cache growled at him. He resembled a donkey pretending to be a bull as he scuffed his feet on the ground and barreled in his direction. Seth fell to the ground and covered his face. Cache grabbed a chair to the right side of him and held it above Seth's head.

"Put the chair down, Mr. Rushner," said a voice coming through the front door.

Cache continued to hold the chair in place and didn't take his eyes off Seth. His glare ignited, like a lit fuse.

"Are you okay?" Officer Abbott asked, glancing at Seth.

Seth nodded.

"No one needs to get hurt." Officer Abbott took two steps forward.

"He's obsessed with my wife," Cache said. His hands shook, and he threw the wooden chair to the ground.

Officer Abbott clenched his jaw and spun a bracelet around his wrist. "Mr. Rushner, it's in your best interest if you take a ride with me." He leaped behind Cache and gripped his arms, placing cuffs on him.

"Am I under arrest?"

He shoved Cache's arms forward. "Get in the car."

"No!" Cache screamed. "You don't understand. It's not me, it's him."

"Keep moving." Officer Abbott tilted his head at Seth.

"Thanks for the tip. Once Mrs. Rushner's in, give me a call so we can keep an eye on her."

"Will do, sir."

They disappeared into the darkness, and Seth locked the door behind them.

Now, they were out the way. Exactly what he needed.

FIFTY-EIGHT

Sam Wendell
Friday, November 12th
12:30 p.m.

CALVIN'S GYM stood on the right-hand side of the road exactly as he'd remembered it. The place was no bigger than a department store that only five to ten people could work out of at a time. Taking a turn, Sam parked the car.

"Adaline, I need you to get out. I don't want to force you, but I will make you if you don't listen. You can trust me."

She didn't move. Her vulnerability was beautiful, yet her strength both in mind and spirit was more so. "I want to trust you." Sighing heavily, she dodged direct eye contact with him. "I'm just not sure I can. Why are we at a gym?"

He swallowed hard and glanced away. "Do you recognize this at all?"

"Sure. I came here a few times as a kid."

"With who? Do you remember?"

Adaline scrunched her nose and closed her eyes. "I have no idea who brought me here."

"Would you like to know?"

She nodded and peered at him, waiting for an answer.

He got out of the car and holstered a gun, keeping it near his body. "Come with me."

"Dr. Lynchester's death really has you on edge." Adaline followed closely behind him.

"Yes, it has." Sam placed his finger to his lip, directing her to silence. He moved toward the rear of the building and held his 9mm Glock as they turned a corner. Anything could happen once they got inside. He'd been attacked, and Dr. Lynchester was dead. Someone wanted to get to Adaline, and they were closing in fast. Sam pressed his back against the building and motioned for Adaline to duck down on the ground. He turned the doorknob, and to his surprise, it swung open. Waving his hand, he signaled for Adaline to follow him.

The gym smelled of sweat and plastic, and it hadn't changed a bit since the last time he saw it. Behind him, the door clicked shut loudly and he jumped, aiming his gun in the direction of the noise. He examined the room before he continued forward. "Stay back."

Lockers were on the right side, and a wood bench greeted him. Years ago, he had tied his shoes on that stool, many times after sweating off thoughts of Adaline.

"Sam?" Adaline asked.

He jolted out of his reminiscing and stared at her. "Sorry. We have to find a locker."

"Does it belong to you?"

"Sort of," Sam said, peering at the locker numbers. "There. That one. Would you open it?"

Adaline held her hands in her back pockets, glaring intently at it. "Why me? What are you playing?"

"I need to be on watch," he said. "Open it."

She hesitated. Her eyebrows twitched when she was unsure of something or someone. Just another thing he'd miss once she read the contents in the locker. Everything in there would change how Adaline looked at life.

Him.

Dr. Lynchester and her past.

His heart thudded, and his ears picked up the humming beat smacking through his chest. This could be it. He grabbed her soft hand and held it for a minute. She didn't let go and squeezed his.

"Remember that I've always wanted to protect you." He reluctantly gave her the four-digit code for the locker combination.

She spun the correct numbers and lifted the latch.

Click.

Adaline opened the locker to a big pile of papers.

"This is for you. All of it. The answers you've been searching for—they're all here."

Her eyebrows twitched again, and she gazed long and hard as she lightly brought her shaking hand to the papers and laid it on top of the pile. She closed her eyes and hummed a soothing melody to herself.

She's afraid.

Sam put his hand on her shoulder and she jerked with discomfort.

"My hidden secrets?" She gripped the stack and held them in her arms.

He nodded. His phone buzzed, saving him from answering her. "Abbott. We're talking now?" Sam paused. "Of course. I'll be there as soon as I can."

Adaline's nose wrinkled. "What's that all about?"

"It seems like the past is haunting all of us today. We need to go...now."

He slammed the locker shut and ran toward the back door.

FIFTY-NINE

Adaline Rushner
Friday, November 12th
1:00 p.m.

SHE PRESSED the edges of the file folder she'd received from the gym locker against her skin. It gave her a calming sensation as it pinched her nerves up and down her hand. Important information lived inside the folder she cradled —information she couldn't completely remember about herself.

Her past.

Periods of time kept static for her now.

She closed her eyes and pictured the life she'd wanted as a child. To have a family that loved her. To have a home, a place to feel safe and protected. A fancy dress or a diamond necklace, to let her inner child play and be a queen for the day. She'd had those with Cache and the girls, once upon a time.

Girls, talk to me. Don't leave me.

Adaline couldn't hear them anymore. She desperately wanted to talk to them and to listen to their voices, just once more. They had to be out there, waiting for her.

My pills. I need them.

Clinging to her shirt, she gripped and tugged it in multiple directions and clenched her jaw.

Fight, dammit. Face it.

She let go of her shirt and slid her finger across the side of the folder and opened it. A release form from the psych ward crossed her eyes. Adaline scrolled the page and read who gave permission to let her out of that prison. The signature belonged to Dr. Lynchester.

She gasped.

"Dr. Lynchester's the one who got me out of that place?"

Sam glanced out the window. "Keep looking."

Adaline turned the page to a picture with a black piano and a little girl sitting on a stool. The caption above it read, "You can do anything." She jolted as a song began playing in her mind. It was a pleasant melody, soft and light, like a linen sheet grazing her face. Touching her cheek, she closed her eyes and swayed her head, humming to the sweet tune, and connecting to a long-lost friend. One that had been forgotten for a time.

"I remember this piano. I loved playing."

"You always beamed when your fingers pressed the keys," Sam said.

Adaline placed the photograph back in the folder and picked up a new one. The picture appeared to be taken in a garden. The little girl wore a white satin gown, red high heels, and a long string of pearls. The beads of the necklace clung to the girl's long, blonde ringlets. Her smile captured beauty and happiness as she looked at a stunning, blonde woman sitting next to her on a picnic blanket.

Dr. Lynchester.

Her lip quivered and she hugged herself. "That little girl is me."

She caressed the photo as flashes of that day hit her. The clacking of the porcelain teacups, crashing into each other to do cheers for a day spent together, rang in her mind. She inhaled through her nose and revisited the muffins on the porcelain plates. Almond, vanilla, and berry greeted her vision.

Adaline exhaled and smirked.

Blueberry muffins.

Dr. Lynchester wore a blue summer dress, and her hair was pinned up in a yellow sunhat. Adaline pressed her lips together, remembering the crimson lipstick Dr. Lynchester placed on her to match her own. They had talked about the future, and Adaline heard two things that she hadn't been told in a long time: that she was loved, and she was special. She lay next to Dr. Lynchester and placed her head on her shoulder while they took turns reading *The Secret Garden* together. About mid-day, a flock of white butterflies flew around some of the bushes.

She smiled thinking about the grace and freedom the butterflies had. Adaline became a butterfly that day, throwing her arms in the air and flying right alongside them as they paraded around the garden with elegance. Holding her chest, she swayed back and forth.

"I remember her." She paused. "I did have a mother. It was her. She took me in."

He nodded.

"It wasn't your family?" She felt confused by the two memories.

"You stayed with her for a while, and then my family did take you in," Sam said.

An unexpected tear fell from her eye. "She was the closest thing I had to a mother, and I forgot about her. And now she's gone."

"She's never left you. She's always been protecting you, right from the start."

Adaline dipped her head. "You've tried to remind me."

"Dr. Lynchester wanted you to see this, to help you find yourself. That's all she's ever wanted," he said.

Staring down, she thumbed through more papers, stumbling across a newspaper article titled, "Orphan Boy Homeless after Thieving Parents Die in House Fire." The little boy in the picture had brown curly hair, brown eyes, and had to be no older than ten.

Adaline looked closer and pressed the picture to her face. She knew those beautiful eyes, like the treasures at the antique store she stared upon many times.

Cache. My Cache.

Did he know that I killed his parents?

The paper fell from her hand and she grabbed at her chest. Her chin quivered.

"I can't take it anymore," she said, gazing at the ground. The pain felt like fire, seeping through her body, one stab at a time, for everyone she had wronged. She clung to her arms tightly, and her eyes stung from the effort of holding in the tears that had to escape. The tears that should've been shed years ago. The tears that had clarity and understanding of what happened and wanted to wash all the afflictions away.

NO! NO! NO!

Screaming, Adaline opened her eyes for the first time,

letting all the pain and sorrow in. Her tears flowed to every memory, dripping off her chin onto her shirt.

I killed my parents.

I killed Cache's parents.

NO! she screamed.

I hurt the people I love the most.

I don't know how to let people in.

I was abused and thrown out.

I've never truly loved myself.

Adaline hit the door and continued to weep. Breathing in deeply, she held her own hand and peered out the window.

I'm not worthless.

I'm not a piece of shit.

I'm lovable.

She wiped tears from her face.

I'm a good mother and wife.

Cache, Leora, and Eliza brought joy and happiness into her life where a hole once had been. They helped her to find light and goodness in the world, and in people—to see the beauty within herself through them. Adaline would turn herself in for the things she'd done, but not until she found the girls and apologized to Cache for all the pain she caused him.

Sam placed his hand on hers and didn't say a word.

"You got to know Dr. Lynchester well, didn't you?"

"I did," he said, softly.

"I'm so sorry for causing you pain, Sam. I truly am. Now Dr. Lynchester is dead because she was helping me. I can't bear to keep putting those I care about in harm's way."

"We make our own choices, and helping you was what

we decided. You can't take responsibility for that. I would do it all over again."

"I know, and that's why I've never been good for you. Look at the mess you've tried to cover up because you love me," she said. "That's not okay. I want you to have a life full of joy. One where you're safe and happy." Adaline paused. "I wish I had allowed myself to remember earlier, but I can't fix the past. I can only change my future and try to make things right for the people I care for. Someone is after me, and you need to get out *now*."

He raised his fist and left it in the air while he growled. "But *we're* good together." Sam grabbed her hand and held it.

She shook her head. "I can't be yours in the way you want. I love Cache."

Sam stared at her with intensity, then let go of her hand. "I made a promise to my best friend that I'd always protect her. That's what I'm going to do. Nothing more," he said. "I'm not leaving until I avenge Dr. Lynchester's death and make sure you're safe."

"Okay, then." Adaline sniffled and reached into the folder again. She carried two photos in her hand—one of herself and one of Cache, as kids. Both pictures showed distance in their eyes.

Sadness.

An envelope addressed to both of them fell on her lap. She shook her head and paused before she opened the thin paper in her hands.

Adaline and Cache,
I wronged you both. My intention was to save Adaline from the life that was taking her nowhere and give her a happy life, full of things she deserved. Cache, I will forever be saddened by the

*death of your parents. They didn't deserve to die in that way. I
didn't know they were in the house. Please forgive me for all that
I've done, and know that I've loved you both as my own.*
Dr. Lynchester

Adaline clung to the letter and looked over at Sam.
"Why is she talking about not knowing Cache's parents
were in the house?"

"I have no idea. She never told me any of this." He
gulped. The silence was clear enough to Adaline that she
had to figure it out on her own if she wanted answers. She
glanced out the window. "When Cache and I met ten years
ago at the gas station, he didn't seem to remember me, and
I never mentioned growing up in Owling," she said,
frowning. Adaline bit the inside of her lip and her breath
quickened. "What if he knew all along who I was and
blames me for his parents' death? This is the revenge
you're talking about, isn't it?"

Sam nodded. "I've considered that many times. I don't
think he's the man you think you know."

*Play along. Sam may be playing you too. You can't trust
anyone.*

"He'd never hurt me or our girls. Cache is the kindest
man I know, but—" She tilted her head.

"But, what?"

"He's never believed me that the girls are alive. There's
no trust, which is why we've been so distant," she said. "It
would be easy for him to not trust me if he's
untrustworthy. He lost his family and hasn't allowed
himself to get close to anyone but me, yet he's still distant.
I suppose he's always been that way." Adaline fidgeted.
"No, he's not involved. He can't be."

Sam cleared his throat. "You have me."

That's what he wants. Me.

Adaline smiled and scratched her cheek. "I'm so grateful you are here, truly. You know, I need a drink. Could we stop at that gas station?"

"I could use some cigarettes," he said, pulling into the station.

"Since when do you smoke?" she asked.

"That's not important. Just calms my nerves." Sam pulled out a lighter and pressed the button on the side. "What do you want to drink?"

"Ginger ale. I'm feeling nauseous."

"You got it. I'll be back in a minute," he said, pressing the lighter again. A small flame lit and she stared at him through the glow. Adaline's chest tightened and she could see three lit flames now with the instant dizziness that hit her. She closed her eyes and nodded.

The door slammed shut. She slowly opened her eyes and held her stomach. Adaline glanced at the ignition. Sam took the keys. Of course, he did. The orange tint of the flame spiraled around like a wave of energy as she peered around the car. Pain surged in her skull, foggy with jumbled memories seeming to vote off the ones they didn't like—overriding her system. "Match. Fire."

Ravenous flames soared through the sky. Colors and faces flashed, but she couldn't make out any of the pictures or thoughts. She focused on the fire. The images formed, and she could see the brilliant blaze that swallowed her front door. Screams rattled the sky from within the rapid beast, and smoke clouded the air, carrying out whispered secrets. She hunched on the ground. The haze was thick, and her eyes stung. Adaline ran toward the home and halted as the temperature changed from warm to scalding.

Her skin hurt.

Adaline gasped for air and clung to her arms. Something happened before the fire. It was right there, creeping forward. The pain raged, and she fought it. Shaking her head, she went back to the memory.

She gripped a match in her hand and waved it like a flag— her own version of freedom. It lit, flying in the air toward the porch stairs—a torch of celebration. The flame sizzled rapidly across the wood planks and suddenly ceased in a thin smoke trail. An explosion erupted from the other side of the house, in the opposite direction of where she stood. Someone wearing a black jumpsuit and a mask glanced in her direction for a moment before they ran off through the cornfields.

Adaline clasped her mouth. The file folder on her lap fell to the ground. Her stomach gurgled, and she hung out the door just in time to save the car from her breakfast.

She fully wanted to harm her mother after everything she'd done to her.

The flames went out. I started the fire, but I didn't kill anyone.

Adaline slouched over and let out the breath she'd been holding their whole drive.

Dr. Lynchester caused the explosion in the house. That made sense why she apologized in the letter. The same people that she knew she wronged were the same ones Dr. Lynchester burned, and now she was dead.

She shivered.

The Owl Keeper took the fall for her, and she let him. Adaline's hand pressed her heart as she remembered the pain and guilt she felt watching him leave in the distance. Confined in a prison as she'd always been, only she caused his. He'd have every reason to hire someone to hurt her and Dr. Lynchester for being locked away like a mutt, something her mother used to call him.

Sam.

She broke his heart and never gave him a chance to be anything more than a friend. And the fact that she never remembered him or Dr. Lynchester for long had to have brought up some betrayal and anger. But the thought that maybe he set this whole thing up to come back into her life and try to be the hero unsettled her. To ruin her marriage and try to get a second chance. It sure appeared that way.

Cache.

My Cache.

She didn't even want to think about it. He had a strong motive to want to be rid of her for being a part of killing his parents. It didn't matter that she didn't mean to, because that wouldn't bring them back for him.

Her stomach gurgled again and she clung to it.

Adaline couldn't imagine any of them harming her, let alone hate her enough to kidnap the girls.

The car beeped, and the driver's door unlocked. Sam got in and put a ginger ale in the cupholder. "Long line. Sorry about that. What's wrong?"

"I'm getting a migraine. Can you take me home so I can lay down?"

"I can't do that, but we can stop by and pick up a few things before I take you somewhere safe."

She kept her eyes shut and shifted in her chair.

I need to get out.

Reaching for her ginger ale, she slowly opened the lid and pressed the drink to her lip. She intentionally coughed, dropping the bottle on her lap. "Shit. I need to get some more napkins. This is cold."

"That's okay. I can get them," Sam said.

Now what.

"Okay," she said, smiling.

Sam left and looked back at her before stepping into the gas station. She got out of the car and used her hand to glide the door shut quietly, then knelt on the ground. A click confirmed to her what she internally knew—Sam wanted to lock her in the car. Adaline shook out her hands and ran like she did when she was a kid through the cornfields. Never look back and keep moving.

SIXTY

Cache Rushner
Friday, November 12th
1:00 p.m.

OFFICER ABBOTT'S police car brought back memories of his thieving days as a kid and teenager. He'd stolen quite a few things being in and out of foster care, but the anxiety and thrill of it no longer held. This was the first time he'd sat in this spot since being with Adaline. She'd always built him up with her positivity and kindness. Adaline constantly saw the best in him, and that drove Cache to want to be a better man. Every day since he met her, he promised himself that he would do everything in his power to make a better life for both of them. His girls would not live off stolen goods to have the life they wanted. Not like he'd had to.

The handcuffs seemed awfully tight, and he wondered if Abbott had made it that way on purpose. Cache kicked the back of Abbott's chair repetitively.

"What?"

"I need you to call Sam and see where they are…now. Adaline's in danger," Cache said.

"I don't owe you anything, but you owe me everything," Abbott said. "I thought your wife was involved for a while there, but it's you."

"I can explain."

Officer Abbott swerved the police car to the side of the road and put it in park. He turned around with a cold expression on his face and rolled up his sleeves. "You son of a bitch. Where's her body?"

Cache shook his head. "Whose body?"

"No one knows you're with me. I could easily say we had an accident, and that lie would end with you."

"Except you won't."

"You don't know shit," Abbott said, glaring at him. "You know exactly who I'm talking about, you demented pervert. Do you have a thing for little girls?"

Cache stared at him wide-eyed. "Your daughter? You need to go back to the antique shop, now. He may have your daughter too."

Abbott clung to the bracelet on his wrist. "That's what I'd say if I was a child murderer too. It's clever. I'm not going anywhere until I get the answers I need from you."

"I'm not talking until I get a lawyer. So, take me in for questioning, or let me out."

Abbott punched the dashboard. "I can't take you in. You know exactly why since you're working with him."

"Working with who?"

"Stalk, you asswipe. He's dirty, and so are you," he said. "I want info, and I'm getting it out of you, even if that means tearing every last organ from your body."

Cache gulped.

Lieutenant Stalk is dirty. How's he connected?

He got a job position he was underqualified for and met the real estate agent on the same day, a few months before his girls were taken. Both brought them to Salt Lake City. Now, he'd been fired, attacked, and found out the agent who helped them buy a home wasn't who she claimed to be. Dr. Lynchester got murdered after their session.

Sam showing up.

Abbott's daughter being kidnapped.

Think.

Cache glanced out the window. A little girl with blonde hair and blue eyes stood on the sidewalk cradling a baby doll in her arms. She had a daisy in her hair.

Daisy.

Dr. Lynchester called Adaline that to bring her back to the conversation in their session. He couldn't figure out why she'd said that, but it felt familiar.

"Stalk is involved with your wife, isn't he?"

Abbott clenched the steering wheel. "Brother, that's none of your business."

"It is if it involves Adaline. Obsession over someone…" Cache said. "Seth and Sam have some obsessive connections to my wife."

"I'm not following."

"If you're obsessed with someone and can't have them, you'd want to find some other attachment to them," Cache said. "Maybe go as far as finding someone who looks how they used to be…as a young girl."

Abbott shook his head. "Sun and the moon."

"Where did you hear that?"

"When I went to your home to talk with your wife, she told me about your Van Gogh painting. She explained to me how Sam's dad used to say that her blonde hair and blue eyes reminded him of the sun and moon. And how she'd get daisies from their garden," Abbott said. "Wait, you think someone took my Aspen because they had an obsession with your wife?"

"Not just mine. Yours, too," Cache said.

Abbott scratched at the back of his neck. "Everything fell apart after Aspen was taken." He paused. "A setup?"

"It crossed my mind. To get us out of the way and make it appear to be a copycat murderer. My Leora resembles your oldest, Aspen. The kidnapper has a certain profile he likes. Eight-year-old blonde girls with long hair, exactly how Adaline used to look at that age. Do you know anything about Stalk? If he has children?"

Abbott growled and turned to look at him before speaking. "When I met him, he'd never been married or had children."

"Is it possible?" Cache glanced at Abbott.

"Will you listen to yourself? You think Stalk, Sam, and Seth are all involved with our girls' murders. Next thing I know, you're going to say we never had daughters to begin with."

"I've fucked up on many things, but I've done nothing to harm your family or mine," Cache said. "You can kill me, but we both know you want to figure this out just as much as I do."

Abbott continued to glare at him. "Did you visit Dr. Lynchester today?"

"You're wasting time on useless questions," he said.

"Our fingerprint specialist found a few newly latent

prints. When we scanned them, IAFIS pulled you up. Which places you right at a crime scene."

"IAFIS?" Cache asked.

"Automated Fingerprint Identification System. Your sweat marks were everywhere," Abbott said. "Why were you there?"

Cache sighed. "I went to get answers about my wife. Dr. Lynchester was dead when I got there."

"You didn't think to call the police when you saw her body?"

"No, I didn't think about it. I saw Dr. Lynchester lying there, and I got scared for Adaline's safety."

"Why?" Abbott asked.

Cache couldn't feel the circulation in his hands anymore. He shifted his body weight, hoping movement would resolve the problem. "Listen. You don't believe me. That's understandable. If the role was reversed, I'd want to fuck you up, too." He sighed. "Someone's coming after me for a job that I never finished, and Adaline's in the crossfire."

"Illegal job?"

"I was given a proposition to kill Adaline ten years ago, and I couldn't do it," he said.

Wait.

That day, he'd been given an anonymous note telling him to kill a woman who murdered a young boy's parents. By doing so, he'd be able to save a family in a way that he couldn't do for himself.

"Why would you be given that job?" Abbott asked.

Cache cleared his throat. "Because she killed my parents. I found out years after that."

Abbott cocked the gun. "You haven't told her that you know?"

"No. She'd know about my past con jobs. One being a hire on her."

Abbott moved in his seat. "I'm going to show you some business cards and you're going to tell me what you know, or I pull the trigger."

Keeping his sight on the gun, Cache could see that Abbott's hand held firm. He'd do it with no hesitation. "Okay."

"The man lying on the floor in Dr. Lynchester's office had a picture of my daughter in his wallet," he said. "Do you know who he is?"

"I've never seen him before. Did he have any ID?"

"No. But he had these." Abbott held out three cards in his left hand. "One is for an auto repair, another for a pizza delivery, and one had a real estate agent's name on it."

Cache tilted his head at the last. "Did you catch the real estate agent's name?"

"Why?" he asked, still holding the gun. "Tell me what's on your mind."

"Can you run a check on an Arlene Williams?"

Lowering his gun, Abbott stared at him. "That was the agent's card in the man's pocket. How did you know her?"

"It's the agent who sold us the home, and someone who may have a vendetta against my wife."

Abbott locked the doors and placed the gun on the dashboard. "No crazy moves, Rushner." He tapped something on his screen and waited for a few minutes before typing other things Cache couldn't make out.

"So?"

"Cool it," Abbott said.

Cache grunted and tried to find a place to lie his head down that would somehow be comfortable with his circulation cut off. He bent forward instead.

He thought back to the day they were told their girls' bodies had been recovered and there was nothing to see. Adaline didn't want to talk for days after that. She just gazed at the wall and began saying words to the air, claiming the girls sat right next to her. She'd changed, and so had he. Cache never felt satisfied with saying goodbye to urns. He couldn't see Leora's long blonde hair, blue ocean eyes, and a smile that lit up the room like the sun. Or Eliza's bouncy curly hair, dimples, and chubby cheeks.

No closure.

Who signed off on the coroner report?

"Got it," Abbott said. He tilted the computer some so Cache could see. "Do you recognize her?"

Cache laughed, but his grin faded quickly from the pit lingering in his stomach. "That's the agent we bought from, only she claimed to be someone else, a Miss Tisher. The real Miss Tisher is much older. But this Arlene Williams isn't an agent at all, just the seller of her home, looking for *very* specific buyers."

"How did you find her?"

"That's the interesting thing. She found me in Owling and gave me a card," Cache said.

"Another setup."

"That's what it's starting to seem like."

"I believe you," Abbott said. "We've both made shitty decisions, but we're trying to redeem ourselves to save the relationships that are most dear to us." He gazed down in deep thought. "I want to believe that my daughter's still alive. I found out some things today that have changed my view on everything. Stalk ordered the assassination on Lynchester."

"Are you sure it wasn't someone that sounded like him?" Cache asked.

"Apparently, he has a side job as a pizza delivery guy." He smirked. "I'm sure, brother. I know his voice. We have a long history. I'll call and get some men stationed at the antique shop for now."

"Thank you. I still don't see how this Arlene Williams and your Lieutenant Stalk connect?"

Abbott paused. "From my experience, Rushner, they're small fish in the big pond. I believe someone else is making them puppets to do the dirty work. Just a hunch." He got out of the car, opened the back door, and retrieved some small keys for the handcuffs. "Lean forward so I can undo these, would you?"

Cache maneuvered out of the cuffs and rubbed at his wrists. "Now what?"

"Now, we are partners until we solve this. We both have a part to play." He dialed a number and kept it on speaker.

Cache appreciated the respect the officer gave him. When he'd said he believed him, he clearly meant it, which showed by his generosity in providing information and wanting to help each other.

"Miles, I need this under the radar. Stalk can't know about it. I need some men stationed at Lost Treasures on Ivy Lane and some to watch over Peyton."

"On it," the man known as Miles said on the other end of the line. The phone clicked off.

"Peyton's your wife?"

"Yeah. She's living with the enemy, it seems," he said. "I pushed her away." Abbott shook his head. "I had my own addiction. The alcohol won."

"Let's go fix that."

Abbott grinned and jumped at the sound of his phone

ringing. He picked it up again. "I'll check it out. Thanks for the tip."

Cache sat forward in the back seat. "What's going on?"

"Got a tip that Stalk met with someone at your neighbor's house. I'm getting déjà vu," Abbott said. "It appears I'll be headed your way. Stay put and I'll drive you home."

Abbott started the car and did a U-turn. He peered at him through the rearview mirror. "What's on your mind?"

"It feels like a trap. Does Stalk have someone watching you?"

"Possibly. Why would you think it's a trap?"

"Adaline said something about the way the lady made peanut butter and jelly sandwiches," Cache said. "It's probably nothing."

"I remember her saying that when I first came out to your place. She takes a bite and calls it a kiss, right?"

"Yes."

"You didn't think that was odd then?" Abbott asked.

"Man, I didn't think my wife was with it. So, no. I thought she was being paranoid, and I wrote it off." His stomach ached, and he gripped his knees. He wrote Adaline off when she depended on him to listen and believe what she had to say. To believe in her.

Abbott parked his car on the corner of Dreary Oak Drive, four houses down from the Rushners' neighbor. He turned around in his seat to look at Cache.

"All I know is my wife hasn't been wrong about anything that has happened since we moved into this craziness," Cache rubbed his wrists.

"Will do," Abbott said. "You don't trust your wife?"

"Not sure where her head is."

"Noted. I'll cluck like a chicken if I'm in trouble," he said and left the car.

Cache bunched his hands together, suffocating the blood from his veins.

Where are you?

SIXTY-ONE

Officer Abbott
Friday, November 12th
2:00 p.m.

DOING a sweep around the house took on a whole new meaning compared to most calls he responded to. This was personal. Abbott tried looking inside to see if he could track down why Lieutenant Stalk would visit the Rushners' neighbor. The pieces in his life just kept growing more distant and unpredictable. The craving burned at his throat, taunting him to come back to his addiction where nothing needed to make sense. He could wash it away and forget all of it. He'd disappear into oblivion, at least for a night. He gripped his bracelet and closed his eyes.

Don't give in.

What's the point?

They're gone.

Peyton's not safe.

He opened his eyes. "I'll protect your mommy, Aspen."

Then I'm done.

The sound of a high-pitched scream rang from inside the home. Abbott ran to the front of the house and pounded on the door. "Police. Open up." There wasn't an answer. He knocked again harder and waited for a response. Another squeal resonated behind the walls. He kicked the door in and raised his gun.

"Police. Stay right where you are." The yelling got louder, and he moved in the direction of a bedroom where the noise came from. The pink walls had butterflies floating around the room on pieces of strings, drowning him again in his misery. He clung to his bracelet.

Mrs. Rushner was telling the truth.

Abbott gulped and peered around the room.

"Daddy?"

He stopped right in his tracks and blinked, frozen in his spot.

Daddy? Daddy, me?

Abbott's stomach dropped and his heartbeat sped up.

He turned toward the small voice coming from the hall. Abbott paced a few steps out of the bedroom. His lips quivered, and he halted.

"Aspen?"

The little girl smiled.

Bending down, he placed his gun on the floor and outstretched his arms. His daughter. After all this time, she was still alive and staring at him.

"Daddy, behind you."

Abbott spun around to catch a knee to his face. The person carried a tough build, knocking him down with force.

"You can't have them. They're my insurance," the husky voice yelled at him through a ski mask.

Grabbing the mask, Abbott attempted to yank it from the person's face. "Aspen. Run." Her pink light-up sneakers bounced with the motion of her feet.

The man put his arm out and caught her wrist for a moment...then let go, causing her to fall to the ground. "Daddy. Help me."

Abbott kicked the masked person in the leg. The man hunched over, and Abbott grasped the wool mask, revealing the face behind the disguise. "Stalk."

Clenching his fist, he punched Stalk in the face and raised his arm in the air, ready to strike him once more.

Aspen's eyes grew wide. "Don't, daddy. Stop, please."

Glancing at his daughter, he lowered his fist and spat on the man. "My wife and my daughter, Lieutenant? Let's go, Aspen."

Stalk kicked his shin and he fell backward. "I can't let you go. She's my leverage, don't you see?" He shook his head. "Peyton still has feelings for you," he said, brushing his mustache. "I've been patient with it as much as one man can, but I'm just done with waiting. Once I'm the hero that found Aspen, she'll have no doubts about being my side of sexy ass."

"She'll never be that with you."

Stalk chuckled. "Sure, she will, since you'll be dead and out of her life...forever. Come to think of it, I could have a two-for-one killing special," he said. "I could say I tried, desperately tried, but in the process, I got stabbed and almost died. The puncture wound nearly severed an artery in my heart."

Aspen scooted backward.

"She won't buy it. What happens when she finds out it was you that killed us? What then?" Abbott asked.

"I've covered up many things, son, and I have no guilt

about any of it, but...let's say she did suspect me, well, that would be a shame for her. You'd want to keep her safe, right?" he asked. Stalk stepped backward and stood on Aspen's fingers.

She screamed.

"You shouldn't try to get away from me. You know better, girl."

Abbott growled and attempted to move his legs but feared that any movement on his part would make Stalk hurt Aspen more. He couldn't harm his daughter. "She's just an innocent little girl. Your issue's with me."

Stalk grinned at him. "You're right. It's our issue." He took his foot off Aspen's hand and she held it in her lap. "But I have both distractions in the same place, and getting rid of you will be so easy. And quite sweet."

Abbott grimaced, breathed in heavily, and lunged for his gun on the floor. He grasped it and turned around, aiming it directly at Stalk, who had his arm coiled around Aspen's neck. She gasped for air. "Put her down."

Stalk tightened his arm around her neck.

Abbott's hand shook as he held the gun. "I've always admired your wit. You're always two steps ahead of everyone else, Lieutenant. It's a good quality to have."

He loosened his grip on Aspen's neck. "Got to get what you deserve, you know."

"I do. It's true, and that's why I've failed, and you've succeeded here. I let my emotions take over, and it's got me nowhere," Abbott said. "I lost everything all on my own because of my choices, but...you've been smart."

"Son, don't be so hard on yourself. Women are just vain creatures who want someone to provide for them. I have everything your wife needs—power and money," he said. "She sure does like high-end items."

Son of a bitch.

"I have money I can give you in return for letting Aspen and I go. We'll leave town and never come back. You'll be free and clear, living a luxurious life with Peyton."

Stalk barked with laughter and placed his hands on Aspen's shoulders. "I've already been taken care of for life, by a very wealthy provider, or maybe we can call her a sponsor since I'm doing all her dirty work."

Bigger fish in the sea.

Abbott kept his gaze on Stalk and examined his body language. He seemed pleased with himself and the situation. "Like I said, you're clever." Locking his gaze on Aspen's face, he lowered the gun. "Baby, I'm right here."

She pouted and nodded again.

"Let me help you get out of this, and you can walk away," Abbott said. "You're involved somehow with the Rushners. I can take the fall, just let her go."

"Wow. I've really done a number on you. Yes, the Rushners don't even have a clue what they're in for." Stalk pushed Aspen forward.

Abbott held her hand and brushed her cheek. "I love you so much. Can you hold something for me?"

"Of course, I can."

Taking off the bracelet that said *Daddy*, he placed it around her small wrist.

Aspen smiled. "You still have the bracelet I gave you."

"I wore it every day since you gave it to me. Now, it's your turn to wear it and keep it safe."

She clung to his leg. "No, it's yours. I'm not keeping this. You're staying with me." Aspen stared up at him with tears streaming down her face. "Daddy, please. Don't leave me again."

"Enough, already. This reunion has been rather joyous. To see you in pain, to lose everything, get some of it back again, only to lose it once more." Stalk aimed the gun at Aspen's head. "Time to die, little one."

"*No,*" Abbott screamed and shoved her backward.

"I don't think so," a voice said. Stalk spun around and hit the ground hard at the same time as a tire iron.

Abbott tipped his head back and closed his eyes. "Thank you." He stood and outstretched his arms. Aspen sprang into them, holding tight around his neck. He pressed his cheek against hers and breathed in.

Cache surveyed the bedroom. "Adaline wasn't hallucinating. This resembles our girls' bedroom back in Owling." He grabbed the tire iron and held it between his fingers.

"We're not golfing with the lieutenant's brain, put it down. He'll get what he deserves," Abbott said.

Letting go of the tire iron, Cache's hands shook. He stared at Aspen, then back at the room again. He put his hand on the doorframe and clutched his stomach. "That's your daughter?"

"This is *my* Aspen."

Cache glanced away. "She looks exactly like my daughter." He swallowed hard.

Grief tugged at Abbott. He could feel what Cache was going through— to see a man's daughter and wish for his instead. He tried to pretend that it didn't hurt, but every part in him ached, standing near them—with her. "I'm sorry."

Stalk began twitching his arms. "He's waking up. Please watch Aspen while I handcuff him."

Moving toward them, Cache smiled at Aspen and

stepped in front of her. "I'm here to help you take him down in any way that I can."

"I know, brother." He retrieved the handcuffs and put them on Lieutenant Stalk.

Stalk began squirming, peering around, and coughing.

Abbott kicked him hard in the side. "My wife is *not* an object or a piece of meat, and she's never needed a man to prove her worth, you jackass."

Stalk grunted and then chuckled. "You boys just made a big mistake. Now they're all dead."

Cache's eyes grew wide. "Who?"

"If I don't show up, you'll never see them again," Stalk said.

Abbott shook his head at Cache. "He's bluffing. He's looking for a way out, and you're who he's targeting. Don't."

"That's easy for you to say. You have your daughter."

The front door slammed, and a parade of officers came through, two men making their way toward Abbott.

"Sir. A call was placed by a Mr. Rushner requesting backup," Officer Keaton said.

Abbott glanced at Cache. "Take the lieutenant and find a nice lock up for this animal." He pushed Stalk toward the officers as they directed him outside.

"Wait." Cache tried maneuvering past the other officers. "Who's now dead?"

"It's too late, son. It seems everyone around you dies," Stalk said.

Cache grabbed at the officers to let him through, but they kept him inside. "Let me go."

"Daddy, look," Aspen said.

Abbott gazed down and brushed her cheek. "What is it, honey?"

She gave him a piece of construction paper with a drawing of three little girls, holding hands, and a woman with no face sitting on the grass not far away. The sky contained a blue sun, and colorful specks fell from the clouds, while a large house towered over them with owls perched on the roof. The saying "Remember the Owls" was off to the side, and a fire burned on the left side of the picture. The fire had a smile.

"Is this a happy emoji in the fire?"

"Yes."

"What're the colors raining from the clouds?" Abbott asked.

Aspen giggled. "They're sprinkles."

Cache halted and shook his arms from the officer's restraint, turning in their direction. "Did you make that picture?"

She shook her head. "My friends did before they never came back."

Abbott watched Cache's face drop. "What friends?" he asked.

"They lived here with me for a while, until their mommy was naughty and they had to leave."

Cache clenched his jaw and stared at Abbott. "My girl, Eliza, always drew pictures with a blue sun and sprinkles raining from the clouds. She was five."

Abbott stared at the picture where the blue sun smiled back at him. The paper shook in his hand.

Could it be?

"These are your friends?" Abbott asked, pointing to the picture of the three girls.

"My best friends."

"You should look at this," he said to Cache, presenting him a picture filled with utter horror and realization.

He grasped the picture and examined the portrait. Cache's eyes dropped, and a whimper escaped his lips. "Eliza." A tear dropped on the page, and he clung to it like it might blow away and never be seen again. Wiping his face with his hand, he paused and glared. "Who's this woman?" he asked.

Aspen shivered and pulled away. "She's a monster. The fire eats people that don't obey, and she creates the fire."

Abbott rubbed her back and held her hand. "If we can stop the monster, would you want to do that?"

"Yes, she killed them."

"Who is she?"

She gripped his hand tighter. "She pretends to sell houses, but she's really my friend's aunt. Aunt Arlene."

Abbott closed his eyes and bowed his head before he surveyed Cache's state.

"Adaline's aunt killed the girls. Arlene Williams." Cache's blood vessels popped in his forehead and he screamed.

Standing slowly, Abbott placed his hand on Cache's shoulders. He shrugged away from him, grabbing furniture, and throwing it across the room. "They were alive." He punched the wall multiple times. A few officers held guns at their side, and Abbott motioned to put them away. "My wife told me, and I didn't believe her. I could've had a raincheck, but I didn't listen." Cache combed through his hair as he marched around the room.

"She didn't kill your parents. It was Dr. Lynchester."

Cache turned around and gazed in the same direction as Abbott. Sam stood in the doorframe. His arms hung limply by his side, and his voice cracked as he spoke. He peered at Aspen and covered his mouth. Sam bent down and clung to his knees, staring at the ground for a moment.

"Bro, are you okay?" Abbott asked.

Sam slowly got up and looked at him with sincerity before pulling him in for a hug. "I'm so happy for you." He leaned down and lightly touched Aspen on the nose. She giggled.

"Dr. Lynchester killed my parents?" Cache asked. His shoulders tensed and he pressed his lips together.

"Yes," Sam said. "I didn't know until a few hours ago."

Cache's nostrils flared. He examined Sam and began to pace the floor. He laughed, and then his laughter turned deliciously joyful. "This is great."

Sam moved toward him. "Here's a letter from Lynchester that clarifies everything, but we need to go."

Cache grinned and continued laughing. "I thought my wife killed my parents." He bunched his fists.

"That doesn't matter," Sam said. "You have a chance to save her...now."

Abbott clung to Aspen's hand and noticed Sam nod to Cache. Sam's shoulders curled forward, and he avoided eye contact. "What's up?" Abbott asked.

Sam put something in his hand. "Partner, I have something I need to do," he said. "Stay here and spend time with your beautiful daughter." He whispered in his ear. "I guess you were right about the girl." Patting Abbott on the shoulder, he dragged his feet to the door.

Cache followed behind. "Take care of your girl, Abbott. You're okay."

He watched as the officers, Cache, and Sam all left, and a black mist of poison and clarity left with his friends.

"They're not coming back, are they, Daddy?" Aspen asked.

Abbott gulped and wrapped his arm around her shoulder.

SIXTY-TWO

Cache Rushner
Friday, November 12th
3:00 p.m.

FACES of people and objects faded quickly in the distance, but time stood still. A week ago, he would have been in the car with Adaline, driving on the same road. He'd watched all the shops gather together with uncertainty and promise, and now the stores brought feelings of pain, guilt, and regret. Cache attempted to text Adaline a few times, warning her about her aunt, but had no reply.

"How did Adaline get away from you? Weren't you with her?"

Sam smacked the dashboard. "She ran. Clearly, she doesn't trust anyone...including us."

"Have we really given her a reason to?" Cache asked.

"Listen, I was wrong about you. I thought you were trying to kill my best friend. I know different now," Sam said. Grabbing a file folder from the dashboard, he threw it in Cache's direction. "If Dr. Lynchester believed in you, then that's how I'll leave it."

Cache opened it and gripped each page before turning to the next. "You knew all of this?"

"No. I had no idea about Adaline's aunt being involved, but it makes sense."

"I never did the job she wanted on Adaline years ago, and now she's getting back at both of us," Cache said.

Sam nodded in agreement.

He returned to reading and paused. "Why are you showing me all this? You could've easily gotten rid of this and rode off with my wife."

"She's always seen me like family, a big brother, but never as anything more. I just kept hoping that would change." He paused. "Adaline loves you. I know what my role in her life is. Yours is to take care of her and to always respect and treat her with the love and appreciation she deserves."

"Or her big brother will kick my ass," Cache said.

"Damn straight, but there'll never be an *or* with Adaline. Got it, buddy?"

He glanced away. "I fucked up by not believing her. We could've figured this out days ago."

"Like I said, we're making things right, now," Sam said.

Cache closed the folder. "Did Adaline read this?"

"All of it, before she bolted," he said. "It's hard to have a different take on things when you've been focused for so long on one, and only one, perspective . . . your own."

Cache swallowed. "Yes, it is. For you, too?"

"I understood clearly a few hours ago that it's no longer about what I want, but what I can offer instead," Sam said. "You need to know that she went to Owling without you, not because she didn't believe you, but because she got a threat that you'd be in danger if she stuck around. Here we're thinking we're protecting her, when honestly, how many times has she watched out for the both of us." He started laughing. "When we were eleven, my older sister Jean kicked down the Lego tower Adaline and I made. I was devastated. I had perfected all the doors and windows, there was even a hatch to a secret entrance for the building. When she knocked it over, I just sat there in complete despair, and Adaline stood quickly and pulled on my sister's ear. She got in her face and had a lecture with Jean about being kind and not taking her anger out on my toys just because she had a rough day."

Cache laughed with him.

"Next thing I know, my sister is crying while picking up my Lego pieces. She apologized, and then she sat next to Adaline and they talked. Rather, my sister talked, and Adaline listened," Sam said. "Just another moment that made me fall in love with her even more. Fierce and gentle."

"That's her." Looking down, Cache gripped his elbows. Adaline always reminded him of the strength, will, and goodness that lived in him every time he forgot. She saved him from a life of self-destruction and brought him to a place of unconditional love, acceptance, appreciation, and sheer joy. With her, he was home.

Home.

They left Owling for all this. She never wanted to go. Cache clutched his elbow tighter and clenched his jaw.

Could the girls be alive?

The blue sun and sprinkles falling from the clouds infested his thoughts. He held his head and closed his eyes. "Where are you taking us?"

Sam rolled down the window. "We're making a trade," Sam said. "You for Adaline. I'm sorry, man."

"They have her." Cache gazed at his phone again, understanding why she never responded. He bunched his fist around the phone. "You think they're going to do a trade?"

Sam was silent.

"You don't, do you? We're going on a suicide mission." Cache covered his face.

"We're protecting Adaline at any cost. Yes."

He nodded. "How does Officer Abbott connect to all of this with his daughter Aspen?"

"No idea. We'll figure it out, only later—we're about there," Sam said.

Cache looked out the window. "I should go with you."

"Not yet. I need to be able to see Adaline before I send you to them." Sam pulled over to the side of the road, hiding his car in the fields from the view of passing traffic. A red Volkswagen bug parked further down. The location was secluded, out in the middle of nowhere, with vast meadows and a few horses in the distance. "Any wrong move and they could shoot Addi." He unbuckled his seatbelt. "Stay here, please."

Taking his gun out of his holster, Sam moved toward the Beetle. A thin-framed lady with curly red hair, standing about 5'4", got out of her vehicle and walked toward the back of it.

Their neighbor.

Sam followed her, and Cache watched as she opened her trunk and reached in to grab something. Cache quietly got out, closed the door lightly, and bent down before someone saw him.

"Where's Adaline?" Sam asked.

"I was instructed to give you this first," she said, planting a big manila envelope in his hands. He glared at her and ripped open the package, taking out what appeared to be pictures of some sort. Sam covered his mouth.

What did he see?

Cache knelt lower on the ground and moved through the field toward the red car. He peered toward Sam, who put something in his pocket, and noticed the red-headed woman wasn't with him any longer. A cold object pressed against the back of his neck.

The woman's voice yelled, "Kneel."

He got on his knees and gazed in Sam's direction.

Sam shook his head and swore under his breath. "I was told we're making a trade, so let's make a trade."

"Back up. I'm not going to jail. Can you promise me that won't happen?" she asked.

Sam stepped toward her slowly. "You don't have to do this. Think about what you're doing. You're Maggie, right? The Rushners' neighbor?"

"So?"

"Adaline just mentioned to me how lovely you are, and what great friends she thought you could become, after all this is sorted out, of course."

"She said that?" Maggie asked.

"You saved her from the media frenzy when she was trapped outside her house," Sam said. "You don't want to hurt anyone. Put the gun down."

Taking a deep breath, Cache thought about memories of his girls as Sam tried to get the women to take the cold barrel off his neck.

"That's it. Let him go," Sam said, signaling Cache to make a move.

Cache elbowed Maggie in the knee, and Sam leaped toward her, trying to grab the gun from her hands. Leaning over Maggie, Sam held his palm on her wrist and clenched it tight.

"Put it down," he shouted. "Now."

"You're not making a deal with me, are you?" she asked.

Cache saw him try to release her fingers from the trigger, as his eyes blazed with no reason to keep his promise. He moved toward Sam, and Maggie growled.

"Where is she? Tell me right now," Sam said.

"No," she said.

"Move back, Cache." Sam grasped Maggie's wrist tighter and she yelped. "Do you know what you've put people through?"

She attempted to lift her body off the dirt road. "I didn't know this was going to happen. I wanted the money. He told me the money would be delivered once I did the last job."

"Stalk?" Cache asked.

"Yes. Are you going to let me go?" Maggie asked, pleading.

"Give me the gun," Sam said.

"Not until you let me go."

Sam glared at her. "That's not how it works, lady."

Maggie kicked at Sam's legs, but he continued to hold her down. A shot fired, and Cache choked in a heavy breath. Sam's eyes widened. He placed his left hand on his chest before he collapsed on the ground. Blood dripped on the woman's shirt and she dropped the gun, frozen in place. Her hands shook, and Cache grabbed the gun, smacking her in the face, sending her to unconsciousness.

Cache bent down and grasped Sam's arm. "Stick with me." He pulled out his phone to call for help.

Sam held his arm up to stop him. "You need to listen to me before it's too late." He breathed in heavily and gasped for air. The shot in his chest seeped blood through his shirt. "Give this to Abbott. He needs to know this used to be Adaline's. He might understand." Sam laid an owl necklace into Cache's hands.

Cache nodded and placed the necklace in his pocket. "I need to take a look at that." He pulled up Sam's shirt and saw the wound, next to his heart. He rolled up his shirt sleeves.

"There's no time." Sam put a piece of paper in his hands. "I can't protect her anymore. That's your role now." He coughed, and blood squirted from his wound. "Tell her I always loved her. Save the girl."

"Hold on. You're coming with me," Cache said.

Sam shut his eyes and no longer gasped for breath. His body went limp.

"Man, come on. Keep it together." There was no movement. He felt for a pulse only to feel stillness.

His body shook. He unclenched his bloody hand, staring at a crumpled piece of paper with an address printed across it. Cache clung to the base of his neck and stared at Sam, saying goodbye for himself, but mostly for his wife.

Goodbye.

Thank you.

SIXTY-THREE

Adaline Rushner
Lost Treasures
3:00 p.m.

COMING BACK INTO SALT LAKE, fear gripped her already tense body. She had to get to her store and figure out the connection she felt to being locked in the closet on her first day of work. Heading toward Ivy Lane, a flash of red and blue followed behind her.

Adaline's heart leaped onto the passenger side, leaving her gasping for breath.

Shit.

After running from Sam, the only quick option she had for getting to Salt Lake City was to steal a helpless old lady's car. Her gut clenched, thinking about the stranded woman and that she was the one to put her in that situation. Adaline gazed back and forth between the side mirror and the rearview mirror.

Don't take me away. I still need to get my girls.

The cop car revved to the side of her and passed on the left. She pulled to the side of the road to get her bearings. Opening her eyes, Adaline peered down Main Street where multiple police vehicles planted themselves in front of Dr. Lynchester's office. She gulped, and a whimper escaped her lips. Covering her mouth, Adaline kicked the air and screamed. Clinging to her shoulders, she rubbed out the shivers that sprung through her body. Forcing herself to take a breath, Adaline grasped her cracked phone that the old lady had smacked from her hand.

Cache.

She wanted to apologize and hear his voice.

It was her turn to make it all right, for everyone. Adaline got out of the car and glanced at the two cop cars on the side of her shop.

Probably helping with Dr. Lynchester's crime scene.

She made her way to the front door, head down. Moving inside, the store felt good—warm, like an old friend catching up with her. The place was clean and organized, all the shelves stocked, and the objects placed with care. Spotless. Sanitizer bottles sat on the counter.

"Seth, are you here?"

Stillness welcomed her, and she hurried to the closet. Adaline hesitated, staring at the door that mocked her to come and play. Her hands shook as she walked slowly toward it and reached to grasp the handle. Turning the knob, Adaline jumped backward in fear that someone was already there waiting for her. She held her chest, taking a few steps forward, and tried to steady her breathing. Stepping inside, Adaline shut the door. Memories flashed back from her childhood.

You're no good.

You deserve to live in a dark hole by yourself with no one to love you.

You're a disappointment.

I never loved you.

I regret being your mother.

The voices in her head got louder, yelling, and she clung to her hair, pulling tightly on her scalp.

Stop it. Get out of my head. I am good. I regret that I let you take so much from me. She took a breath. *Not anymore.*

Adaline stood and let her eyes adjust to the darkness in the closet. No longer would she allow the destruction of her past to own her. She smiled as weight lifted off her shoulders, and a new release and realization awoke within her.

The door handle jolted and she glanced down at it. "I'm not afraid of you."

"Adaline? It's just me," Seth said. "It seems the door is jammed. Just a minute."

She heard rustling and the sound of boots clomping coming from the other side of the door, and for the first time, she didn't want to be rescued from the dark. Adaline found comfort in being one with it.

Light shone through the crack as the door opened, and Seth stared at her with excitement. Adaline examined his face, almost intrigued by his reaction. It felt like she was seeing him for the first time in a different light. The gray in his hair and the wrinkles on the side of his face were unfamiliar, but she knew his eyes. She knew them well.

Adaline gasped.

She didn't move and she couldn't speak. Even her thoughts were a tangled mess.

Owl Keeper.

Seth was the Owl Keeper.

He pulled back his hair behind his right ear, touched his mark, and smiled at her, the same smile she saw as a kid—kind and warm.

"My Little Owl. You remember me, don't you?" he asked, hope in his voice.

She nodded and tried to think of the right words to say, but nothing came.

"I'm glad you recognize me now." He reached his gloved hand to her. He had saved her by taking the fall and being locked away. *How was he out already?* Not that it mattered, especially since it had never been his doing to begin with.

"I'm so sorry that I forgot you," she said. "I forgot a lot of things, but I remember everything now. You took the fall for the fire." Adaline took his hand and stepped out of the closet. She embraced him. He kept his arms open in a way that made her think he was unhappy with her. But after a minute, he closed his arms around her and placed his head on hers. "Thank you."

"You're welcome," he said softly, almost in a whisper.

"Why did you do that for me?"

"I care for my girls, and always have." He let go and moved a few steps away from her. "I never had anyone be there for me. You deserved more, and truthfully, you reminded me so much of my little sister. I wanted you to have a better life, Adaline." He stared down at the ground. "But . . . you forgot me. I've tried to help you, help them, and you never really saw it." He bunched his fist and scrunched his nose. "You're all ungrateful."

Stepping toward him, Adaline pressed her hand on his arm. He pulled his arm away from her, and the excitement she saw earlier became bitterness and anger.

"I didn't mean to." She paused. "My mind tried to

forget the bad memories that I went through when I was younger."

He fidgeted and laughed. "I'm a bad memory from your past?"

Adaline covered her mouth, realizing how the words came out, but she couldn't take back what she said. "Of course not. The first memories that came back to me were the ones from being with you. I remember the swing, and the white daisies where I lay in the dirt with the flowers, and . . . Speckles the bear. Look, I still have the necklace you gave me," she said, pointing to the locket around her neck. "You brought me back."

He hesitated. "I hoped you'd remember with the locket. With all the lockets."

He didn't trust her, or did he?

"I'm still the same person you've always known." She extended her hand again and sang to him. *There was a little owl*

High in a tree
She tried to fly away
And couldn't get free
Until one day, he made her see
That she could be anything she wanted to be.

His face softened, and he hummed to the tune while she sang.

Adaline stood in front of him. "You left the lockets for me to find?"

He peered at her, grinning like a small child, and nodded his head.

"Do you know where my girls are?" She squeezed his hand and tried to hold her ground. "Where are they?"

Seth gazed at her and put his finger to his lips. "I knew

you weren't crazy when everyone thought you were. It was me who saved you. Saved them."

"Tell me what happened?" She tried to keep her voice low and calm while blood pumped through her veins.

Muffled voices echoed in the back room like wind carrying unclear sound. Adaline paused and listened for the noise again. "Seth?"

"They were going to ruin *everything*," he said.

She raised her eyebrows at him and moved quickly to the back room where two officers sat tied up to the chairs. Both had blood on their face and hands. "What the hell is this?" Adaline raced to the front of the store and grabbed a box cutter to cut the zip ties from their wrists.

He tapped his foot and licked his lips. "Let's play a game. If you let them go, you'll never find your girls. We don't have much time."

"Seth," she yelled.

He stopped tapping his foot and clenched his thin jaw. "You don't want to play a game with me?"

Adaline clung to the box cutter and placed it in her pocket. The tension in her arms wanted to choke the answers from him. She stared at the officers, then at Seth. "Please, help me get my girls. You saved them, right?" She glanced into his eyes that still held distaste. "How about you tell me where they are, and—"

"And you'll follow me like you used to." Seth clapped his hands. "That will be our game, and you'll find out everything soon." He left an item on the counter, grabbed the sanitizer bottle, and walked through the store toward the front door.

Adaline gripped her keys and moved to see the item he had placed on the counter.

A red glove.

She hurried to close her shop. Seth had already left and was waiting by her car. He liked games and a good chase. She didn't know if he actually saved her girls, or if he even knew where they were, but she wanted to be there to see for herself.

Could there be a possibility that this nightmare would end, or was this all a game to him? An illusion to suck her back into a friendship they once had.

She crossed the street and unlocked the car. Seth got in, and Adaline closed her eyes.

My girls.

Please let my heart be right.

Starting her car, she reversed out of the parking lot, ready to discover if Seth had them or if they were somewhere else entirely.

SIXTY-FOUR

Adaline Rushner
Friday, November 12th
3:30 p.m.

THEY'D BEEN DRIVING for fifteen minutes while she allowed herself to be directed on where to go with the address Seth had given her. Each turn brought a new sense of direction and closeness to revealing the truth, even with the road feeling like a maze of no return.

"Is your real name, Seth? Or what would you like me to call you?" she asked.

He stopped putting sanitizer on his hands and peered at her. "Thank you for asking. Seth is what I go by. Call me that," he said. "Owl Keeper was a name I was given by others, not one I care to have."

"Seth is nice." Adaline shifted in her seat. "Why didn't you tell me you had my girls?"

He scratched the side of his face with intensity and rubbed more sanitizer on his hands.

He's nervous. Why?

"Have you been to where we're going before?"

"Nope, but you'll be reunited with your girls soon. Maggie took really good care of them for you. I even told her to take a bite of the sandwich, like you do."

Adaline's body shook. "I was right the whole time. Why are you working with that monster?"

"She's a good person. Good, good person," he said. "I'm not working for her."

"Who's reuniting me with my girls, Seth?"

He grinned and pulled at strands of his hair. "It's part of the surprise. Your girls were in trouble, but now they're safe and can come out to play."

"Your destination is in one mile on the right," her phone commanded.

Seth put the sanitizer on the floor. He smiled and waved his hands with excitement. "All my little owls will be together. I love reunions, don't you?"

He's different now.

Changed.

She nodded.

Driving up the dirt road, rows of trees arched their limbs over her car like a cave of branches wrapping them into hibernation. She gazed at the home in front of her and stopped the car.

Adaline's face turned red and her throat burned.

The exact replica of her family manor in Owling teased her here in Salt Lake. The home where she was unlovable, unwanted.

Seth gaped wide-eyed at it and gasped. "No." He hit his head multiple times.

This place held nightmares for them both.

"Did you know?" Adaline asked.

He shook his head in disbelief. Seth held his knees and chanted a mantra out loud to himself as he moved in a circular motion. "I don't...I don't know why she brought your girls here, but there must be a reason for it."

"Who?"

A large gate opened, welcoming them into their past. Adaline entered and squinted, trying to see the woman coming into view.

No. It can't be.

Her chest tightened, and betrayal hit her once again as her aunt's smug face revealed itself through the tinted glass. The woman who had sent her to the psych ward stared at her. "You're working with her?"

"You lost it after you attempted to kill your parents. She just wants to help you."

"The story she told you is not what really happened," Adaline said. "She wanted my inheritance and tried to get rid of me. My girls aren't safe here."

Seth's head twitched. "No. She got me out of where I was trapped to save your girls, and you weren't well."

"You weren't in jail?" she asked.

He shook his head. "Someone hid me away. I don't know where, but your aunt got me out to save your girls."

Adaline's hand shook. "Who hid you away? Who were they in danger from?"

He hit his head. "I don't know. You're trying to confuse me."

Adaline glanced at him. "It's okay. You did well watching over us. Thank you." She gripped his shoulder lightly for a minute.

Get out of the car. Your girls need you. Be one with your fear.

She took a deep breath and let her body feel the freedom in her words.

Be one with your fear.

Adaline let go of Seth's shoulder and exited the car to come face to face with her aunt. "You." She spat at her feet.

"You still have the same disruptive behavior as before. No wonder your momma never wanted you," Arlene said.

Adaline bunched her fist together, breathing heavily. "Give me my girls, now."

Her aunt laughed and gazed off in the distance. Wrinkles creased around her eyes and mouth, and the platinum blonde wig she wore made her look older since the last time Adaline had seen her. Someone grabbed Adaline's hands from behind her back and tied them with a thin wire.

"Let me go."

Seth got out of the car and glared at them. "Stop. You told me she wouldn't get hurt."

"Yes, well, I lied, and you played right into it," Arlene said. "It's sad that you were so intent on saving yourself through Adaline that it had to come to this. Now, are you with me or against me?"

Seth glanced in Adaline's direction with forgiving eyes, and she remembered them always appearing that way. As a kid, she knew she could trust him by what she observed. Adaline saw herself in him. Lost, scared, and alone. He looked down at the ground, and when Seth peered back up at her, that person she knew so well disappeared and turned into someone unrecognizable. His eyes hardened, and he ground his teeth. The softness in his face had vanished, replaced with anger.

"I'm with you. She ruined my life," he said, pointing in Adaline's direction.

"No, Seth. Please. I care for you," she said. "Look at me. You know me."

Her aunt smirked and waved her arms in the air. "Wonderful. Then let's get started, shall we?"

Adaline pressed her heel in the dirt and kicked some up, trying to release herself. "No. This isn't you. I know you."

"You used to know me before you let me take the fall for you. You really are worthless."

A tear slid down her face as she fought the masked person to loosen their grip on her arms.

"Come along, son," Arlene said to Seth.

He halted, not looking back, and continued to follow her aunt.

Be one with your fear.

Adaline examined the massive house and the people surrounding her who walked away from her then and now. Family and friends. They got what they wanted and left her without a thought.

But that didn't matter anymore. She had changed. Adaline knew her great worth and value now. That all by itself gave her power.

The masked man put a bag over her head and pushed her forward. "Walk."

She smiled and allowed the dark to fold through her. The light within her would lead the way.

SIXTY-FIVE

Adaline Rushner
Arlingston Manor Replica
Salt Lake City
4:00 p.m.

SHE SHIVERED, hearing the wind howl, and cringed at the smell of citrus. Her home always reeked of the hideous scent when she was a kid, and to her, it resembled disgust, fear, and toxic perfectionism. Two strong hands forced her shoulders in a downward motion.

"Sit," a man's voice growled.

Adaline sat in a hard chair and listened to her surroundings as the man tightened the rope on her hands and bound her feet around what seemed to be chair legs. A ticking came from her right-hand side, the wind on the left, and footsteps hit the floor upstairs.

What have I done to make someone so angry with me? What is this about?

A sharp tapping came from behind her. Shoes, heels

maybe. Adaline felt dizzy and inhaled lightly, trying to save her air. Voices were talking behind her. Two voices, both women.

"Marcus, she wants you to station yourself outside the home. You know what to do if anyone tries to come in," her aunt's voice said.

"Yes."

"Now, be a darling and run along."

Adaline could hear a smile in her aunt's voice.

"Dear. Are you asleep in there?" she said, knocking on her head. "I hope you're feeling comfortable and right at home."

Adaline shook the chair.

"Oh, don't do that. You'll end up hurting yourself, and I might have to call a mental institution again." She pulled the bag off her head and tilted Adaline's chin so she could stare at her. "There you are." Her eyes held excitement, like someone watching the circus for the first time, and she clapped as a monkey would, waiting for a command. "Well, someone has been waiting a very long time to see you," she said. "Try to be on your best behavior, okay?"

Adaline glared at her. She glanced around, waiting for the mystery person to reveal themselves. The clicking sound came from around the corner, and bright yellow heels slapped the floor. Reddish blonde hair cascaded down the lady's back, and her face was polished to perfection with violet lipstick, powder, and Aqua Net hairspray to keep everything in place. Superiority. Nothing had changed.

"You're speechless," the woman said.

Her aunt clapped again and giggled.

"Y-you're…" Adaline, stuttered.

"Dead. Is that the word you're looking for? I'm

supposed to be. Sorry to disappoint you, but you couldn't get rid of your mother that easy."

Adaline's body shook as the memories all came to a front. All the abuse, hatred, and lies rushed over her, like she was taking a blow multiple times, hard. Just like she remembered.

"How?"

"How, what? Did I survive?" She laughed and sneered at her. "I observed you for a long time. I've always been ahead of you, even when you thought you had won the battle of moving forward." She pressed her face next to Adaline's. "You're not a winner and never have been. Just a disgrace and a disappointment to me."

"I'm not a disgrace. You are," Adaline said. "Don't you think for one minute that you're my mother. You died along with that fire, at least in spirit."

She chuckled. "I see you've grown some thick skin since I last saw you. That's new, but I made you. Every person in your lousy little life was placed there by me." She walked around the chair, leading her finger along the edge. "Oh, yeah. That's right. You still believe people love you." Her mother stopped to glance at Adaline and placed her hand on her lips. "No, little girl. I had to make them pretend to love you while their hearts deceived them and you."

"People do love me," Adaline said.

"There were people who loved you. But you went and pulled a classic case of Addi and ran away from all of them, which later turned them against you," she said. "Seth, can you be a dear and come here?"

Adaline gazed around to see which direction he was coming from. Clomping echoed down the stairs in slow motion. She moved side to side in her chair.

"You funny girl. Where do you think you're going? You're home now, and you're never leaving again," her mother said, spitting out her words like venom. "Ah, there you are." She grabbed his shoulders gently, and he waited for a command from the sinister woman she called mom. "Enlighten us. Do you love this girl?"

Adaline peered up at him, and he held softness in his face.

My friend, he's still in there.

He appeared beaten, like the world was weighing on his lanky shoulders, a man with nothing to hold on to. "Please, you're my friend."

Seth crossed his arms and clenched his jaw.

"Go on, tell her how you feel," her mother said.

"I did a long time ago. She reminded me of my sister, who I loved very much." He paused and bunched his hands together.

"Keep going."

"But you're not my sister, nor my friend," he said. "You forgot me." Glaring at her, he ripped the owl necklace from her neck, placing it in his pocket. "This belongs to me. You deserve what you get."

"I'm so sorry." She watched as he walked back up the stairs with his head down.

"Oh, no. There's the Adaline, I remember. The damaged victim. I told you that you'd make a mess of things," her mother said. "Did you do as I asked with the girls, Seth?"

He nodded.

Girls. They're upstairs. Here, in this house.

"Can I tell you a secret?" her mother asked.

"Knock yourself out."

"That brute did all this for you. He took your girls,

thinking he was protecting them, but really, he's been a pawn in my game the whole time. He had no idea I was alive until you did." She laughed. "All the misery and pain that I'm stirring in you both is simply beautiful."

Adaline stared at her intently. "His name is Seth."

"Only *Seth* to me when I want something from him. The man is nothing more than a waste of space, as far as human beings go. He'll always be The Owl Keeper, and people will run from him in fear—the savage man that collects owls and killed because no one would love him. Pathetic."

"He's not pathetic, nor a waste of space. Seth has worth. You treat him like he's nothing when he's kind and brilliant."

"Pigeon, you're weak. You try to save everyone and end up saving no one. When the cops find you dead, and the girls are gone again—this time somewhere where no one will find them—they'll chase after the Owl Keeper. His fingerprints are all over the crime scenes."

"You'll pay for this, and they'll figure it out," Adaline said.

"Who? It's just too bad no one believed you."

Cache.

"Oh, if you're thinking Cache will save you, little sweet cheeks, he's been playing you from the first time you met him."

She didn't look up at her mother and held her anxiety inside, not willing to show that a nerve had been hit.

"See, you killed his parents, or rather Dr. Lynchester did. You both tried, but only one succeeded." She tucked a piece of hair behind her ear. "You, of course, failed. Anyway, he wanted revenge, only he fell for you and didn't finish the job either. You're made for each other."

"What job?"

"To kill you, of course, puddin'. But he couldn't do it, and now he's a dead man, because of you," her mother said. "Everything you touch gets tarnished. No one believes you, they just view you as a pitiful, helpless girl, like I did. Why you even try and keep on going is beyond me. Just be done with it, already."

She gulped. "You're right. No one ever believed me. Did you have anything to do with Officer Abbott's daughter?"

"Well, that was a fun situation. The Owl Keeper has a particular interest in little girls with blonde hair and blue eyes. Reminds him of his dead sister, I guess. Morbid, if you ask me," her mother said. "Officer Abbott's daughter resembles Leora and you at age eight."

"You made him look like a copycat killer."

She grinned. "That's right, I did, and not only that, but your friendly Lieutenant Stalk wanted Officer Abbott and his daughter out of the way. He even planned a lot of it. He's been rather helpful—cleaning up some dirty work as we speak. I believe the names Sam and Cache come to mind."

"No. You can't do this. They haven't done anything to you," Adaline said. "Please, do what you need to do with me, but stay the hell away from my family." She shook her head like a bull ready to charge.

Her mother waved her finger and clicked her tongue. "Stop that, or I'll hurt your girls."

Adaline glanced up the stairs. "Don't *touch* them."

"Here we're having a nice conversation, and you ruin it with bad behavior. Do you remember what I did to you for bad behavior, child?"

The closet.

She felt herself relapsing into negativity.

Don't let her do this to you. You're not a child anymore.

"Yes. I remember what you did to me."

"Good. I hope it's fresh in your mind, because if you act that way again, your daughters will experience that same fate," her mother said.

Adaline breathed heavily and pounded her bound fists against the chair. *Don't let her have this. Calm down.* "Okay. I hear you. Let's talk."

Her mother smiled. "Whatever shall we talk about?"

"You held Seth captive somewhere for years?"

"There was substantial proof that our maid was indeed the person who blew us to pieces, making it possible for me to cage Seth like the dog he is. We let him out, right in time to bring your world crashing down."

"Just to set him up," Adaline said.

Her mother sneered and patted her face. "That's right. He ran right to saving you again, like we thought he would. The poor man actually cared deeply for you and has been protecting you this whole time, only to have to say goodbye once again. So, tell me, was it worth it?"

"What?"

"Your attempt to be rid of me. Was it worth dying for?" she asked. "Did you have a nice life? Because now I'm going to take it all away from you, one by one." Her mother turned around and walked toward the stairs.

Adaline fumbled with her pocket, trying to reach the box cutter that she took on her way out of the store. She held on to the base and pressed the blade against the rope, slowly easing it back and forth.

"Seth? Arlene? It's time."

Adaline picked up pace, gliding the knife against the grain of the rope and catching the flesh of her skin. She pushed down harder and felt circulation come back into her hands as the rope loosened. Sitting in silence, she gripped the blade between her hands and looked at the floor.

Here's your chance. Show her you're not the victim anymore.

SIXTY-SIX

Adaline Rushner
4:15 p.m.

FOOTSTEPS POUNDED DOWN THE STAIRS, and her mother turned the corner with a grin pasted on her face. "Bring them here," she said.

Adaline's body trembled, and her lip quivered, staring at the space behind her mother...waiting.

Please, God.

Arlene glowed with amusement. "Come, dear."

Soft shuffles moved forward, and a lock of blonde hair came into view.

Adaline gasped.

Little brown and blue eyes gazed up at her. They had puffy cheeks, dirty faces, and matted hair, but appeared to be unharmed.

Leora.

Eliza.

Their faces lit up and they ran toward her.

She blinked a few times and stared again at her girls, standing right in front of her, both clinging on to one another's arms.

"My sweet girls." Tears streamed down her face and she smiled at them. "Mommy's right here. I'm not leaving you." The urge to hug them and never let go gripped her until she was nauseous. She couldn't show her hands being free…not yet.

They leaned into her body and snuggled on her lap.

"Don't leave us again, mommy, please," Eliza said.

Her mother laughed. "Girls, your mommy doesn't want you anymore. That's why she was gone for so long. You can't believe her."

Adaline's face shook while anger embraced her. "I love you, my sunshine and my star."

In unison, the faint sound of their voices replied to her. "We love you, too, Mama."

Adaline saw a sadness creep over her mother's face, and for a moment, she felt bad for her.

How did you become like this?

She had to have been happy and not bitter at some point in her life, but what changed for her? Did she ever really, truly know what love was?

"Reunion is over. Time to go," her mother said. "You know. They were indeed at your house when you first moved in. Maggie kept them so close to you." She laughed. "Seth, come get the girls and place them in the car. Arlene, make sure that he does."

He hung his head and moved toward her girls, lightly picking up Eliza and Leora.

"We want our mommy," Eliza cried.

Adaline squirmed in her chair. "No. You don't have to do this."

Seth halted at the door as Eliza and Leora held out their arms, reaching toward her. "Mommy's coming to get you." She watched their little bodies disappear from her vision with Arlene following behind. "I forgive you, Mom."

"You forgive me, child? I don't forgive you," she said. Her mother hugged herself and swayed back and forth like she was rocking herself to sleep. She peered outside and dropped her arms to her side.

"You can change and make things right now. Please, come with me," Adaline said. "It doesn't need to be like this anymore."

Her mother looked at her with softness, which transitioned back into her hard exterior. She patted her cheeks. "It's too late. My mother told me I'd end up like her, and that having a child would destroy me. She was right. I don't want to be your mother."

"Don't worry. You never have been."

"But I am. Don't you see, silly? I've never been far away from you, have I? Even when you thought I was dead, I was right in there," she said, tapping on Adaline's head. "Just like my mother was."

"Get out of my head, dammit."

Adaline's mother grinned. "See? We've been together, you and I. Your mind tells you that you're not made to be a mother, that you're broken and will never be good enough for anyone." She walked around Adaline. "There I am. I'm right, and you know it. And that scares you, knowing you are just like me."

"*No.* I chose my own path. I'm *not* like you," Adaline screamed.

"You tried to kill your parents," she said. "That right there is my child, and I have never been more proud. I chose to embrace this side, just like you did. My mother would've killed me if I didn't do it first. See, pigeon? We're the same."

"You killed your mother?"

"Arlene poisoned her first, then I stabbed her twenty times, and we walked away clean. Only, now I'm stuck in the same fucking situation seventeen years later. You'd cry and cry, and I dropped you a few times, hoping you'd go away in peace, but you fought every time." She grabbed her head, hitting her temples. "The crying—it made me want to do things, and I couldn't control it."

"You can control now, though," Adaline said.

"Yes, I can. And the only solution is to have us both die. That way we'll never hurt anyone again. Come to think of it, your girls have our genes. What shall we do about that?"

Adaline gripped the box cutter in her hands. "Don't you touch them. They didn't do anything. I will end this with you. Just us."

"What a good girl you are. Such wonderful behavior." Her mother put her hand on her chin in deep thought. "Hmmm…very tempting, but I like my plans better." She opened the door, whistled, and waved her hand, directing someone to come inside.

Arlene came in and gripped the doorframe, gasping for breath.

"Put her where she belongs while I prepare for the ceremony." Her mother exchanged glances with Arlene, and she left the room.

Her aunt got close to her face and squeezed her chin. Pulling a vial out of her pocket, she opened it and poured the liquid in Adaline's mouth.

Adaline slashed at her with the box cutter.

Arlene smirked at her. "Aren't you clever? I always

wanted to be the first one to start the ceremony." She stepped forward and held Adaline's hand. "Thank you. I'm done being her puppet."

She stared wide-eyed at her aunt. "What ceremony? Tell me."

Arlene pushed the box cutter into her flesh and leaned into Adaline. The vial fell to the ground. "Thank you." Her eyes glazed over and blood trickled from her mouth. Crimson seeped through her shirt as her body went limp hitting the floor. Adaline's hands shook, and she looked at her palms. Wiping her bloody hands on her pants, her energy quickened, and she cut the ropes from around her ankles. She turned the corner with haste. Her mother smacked up against her, then looked where her aunt now lay.

"Selfish sister of mine. She started without me."

Adaline didn't move but looked directly at her. "Get out of my way."

"Okay. Go right ahead. Leave, see if I care."

She flinched, but she continued to keep her eyes locked on her mother. Walking around her, she paused. Mother never backed down; if anything, she was overly persistent and competitive—always proving her point about why she was better than someone else.

"Go on. You have a one-minute head start," her mother said. "I have to clean up the mess you made."

Adaline fidgeted with her shirt. She turned to run, but her legs wouldn't carry her forward. Her vision deceived her, and she collapsed, unable to move. Adaline's cheek felt cold against the hard surface. *No!* She tried to push herself up, but her head was heavy and pounded with pain.

"My sister wasn't capable of much, but she's good with

her poison," her mother said, peering down at her. "Scratch that. She did well as a real estate agent too. Don't you think?"

Looking at her, Adaline tried to push herself up to sit.

"I really do like these conversations we're having where you listen and I talk, so let me just say that you've been a fun challenge." She grasped Adaline's ankle and pulled her through the hall. "You really gave me a run for my money, and it's pleased me that my offspring has some fight in her."

Adaline's vision went in and out, but she knew where her mother was taking her. The basement. Her fingernails clawed at the floor and walls, chipping away from her cuticles. The intense pain made her aware. On edge, but clear-minded. She closed her eyes and let her senses soothe the discomfort she felt.

Leora.

Eliza.

Cache.

Keep going.

Her mother let go of her ankle, and the basement door creaked open. Adaline opened her eyes, only to see a heel coming at her stomach. Her mother's foot kicked her hard. She rolled down the stairs, hitting her back and head multiple times and landing at the bottom. Her mother raced down toward her with a sinister look. The same face she witnessed as a kid, with her mother's own version of hide-and-seek with a beating. "Count to twenty, then momma's comin' with a rolling pin."

When she reached the bottom, she pulled Adaline up. A group of five chairs formed a circle, and two were occupied.

Who's in the chairs?

Adaline's stomach hurt, burned, like her insides were eating away at her flesh. She bent over and threw up on the ground near her mother's heels.

"No wrong moves or someone dies." She tromped back up the stairs, taking her time with each step—showing her desire to continue teasing and playing with Adaline's emotions.

Controlling her vision to focus took effort, but she had more strength after getting rid of some of the poison in her system. Moving slowly toward the circle, a curly-haired man with tan skin held his head down, and his wrist dripped blood. A jar sat underneath him, catching every drop.

Adaline knelt and pulled his chin upward, exposing what she already knew. Cache.

Placing her hand on his cheek, she lightly slapped him a few times. "Babe, look at me. We've got to get out of here."

He hung his head still and didn't move or respond to her voice.

"Pigeon. Do you like what I've created for us?" her mother asked from upstairs.

Adaline clung to the chair and tried to maneuver herself to stand. She stood in front of Cache. The tapping against each step wrenched at her, preparing her to take action.

Her mother turned the corner and brushed back her hair. "Clean up your mess." She threw a towel at Adaline. "I can't decide if he's more handsome unconscious or when trying to save his lady. I quite enjoy both."

Sneering, Adaline didn't move. "You wanted us to both die. You're right. I can feel my urge and desire to kill creeping in. It's an addiction that needs to be fed," she said, licking her lips. "Stabbing Arlene was the fix I needed. We should end this, you and me. Let my husband go."

Pulling out a mirror, her mother spread deep red lipstick on her lips and puckered at her reflection. "I'm so delighted that you'll be joining me with this ceremony. I've waited a long time for this," She paced toward Adaline and reached for her hand. "Come, let me show you who will be taking part in this beautiful moment."

Holding her lower back, she limped with her mother. Adaline's eyes widened, and her legs started to give out, staring at what was presented in front of her. A photo of Dr. Lynchester stuck to the front of the chair, and a jar of crimson liquid sat under her picture.

"The coroner took the dear doctor's body too quickly, but we got the good stuff," she said. "I made sure we bled her out some so we could get this jar of redemption."

Adaline shook her head and closed her eyes.

"She's a killer, like we are. I was doing her a favor, keeping her from harming other people." She pulled her hair back and moved forward.

A chair of bones labeled "mother" was the next chair. Covering her mouth, Adaline glanced away. Her mother gripped her chin and pushed her face to the chair. "Don't turn away. This is our blood. Your grandma. The one who started the line of murdering savages," she said. "You'll look at it and show her respect."

"You hated her. Why am I showing her respect?"

"It's not her fault. She was born that way and couldn't get out of it."

Adaline glared at the bones and tilted her head to check on Cache. Still unconscious. "We all have a choice. It was her fault for treating you the way she did."

"So, you blame me for everything that happened to you. I was trying to save you from this curse. You'll always be an ungrateful shit."

Feed into it. Buy time.

"I'm grateful that we're stopping the curse. There are two more chairs," Adaline said. "Where did you want me to sit?"

Her mother sneered and examined her. "Pick whichever one you want."

Adaline let go of her back and walked to the chair next to Cache. She clung to his hand. "This next chair is for you?"

Grabbing a gas can from against the wall, her mother waltzed forward. "Yes."

"But Cache didn't do anything, so he shouldn't be here."

"Child, he failed me miserably by not killing you ten years ago." Puckering her lips, she paused. "I am a merciful mother. Someone will need to take your husband's place, and it can't be you."

"Who did you have in mind?"

"You have a choice. It can be your creepy friend Owl Keeper, or your daughter Leora," she said. "At least little Eliza will have one parent. It's a good trade, yes?"

Adaline peered at Cache and caressed his head. "My daughter's not a killer."

"Well, you'll be surprised to know she indeed is. Clearly, she's more like her mother than you thought." She paced. "You're taking too long to decide, so I'm choosing for you."

Staring at her mother, Adaline gripped the chair as a side door to the basement opened. A masked man carried Leora in his arms and brought her toward her mother.

"*No!* Let her go," Adaline screamed.

He placed Leora down and left. A soldier taking orders from the wrong leader, one who would only turn on him later.

Her mother glanced down at Leora and clicked her tongue. "Stay put. Don't think of coming over here, or little Eliza will have *no* parents."

Adaline clung to Cache's hand.

"When she dies, she'll stay this peaceful and still, like a porcelain doll. Perfection and beauty, frozen in time."

"She won't look like a doll, mother. Her skin will rot and fade away," Adaline said. "That's not your idea of perfection."

Tilting her head, her mother continued to stare at the still body. "In my mind, she will. Just like how I'm seeing her now." She strolled toward Cache and loosened one of his ropes. "Let's see if he wakes up to free himself."

Cache squeezed Adaline's hand and grasped the jar of blood from under him, smacking her mother over the head. Glass shattered, and she collapsed to the floor.

Adaline picked up a shard of glass and held it in between her fingers, staying stationary by the chairs.

"Get out of here. Grab Leora and run," Cache said, softly.

"Not without you."

He gazed up at her. "There's no time. I'll be right behind you."

She planted her lips on his, and he kissed back.

"Go."

Adaline limped toward Leora and held her in her arms. She nuzzled her cheek and looked back at Cache before she directed herself to the side door. Opening the door, a burst of fresh air greeted her, and the friendly face of Seth smiled back.

He put his hand in his pocket and brought out the Owl necklace that he gave her years ago. "This belongs to you." Seth planted it in her hand. "Eliza's in the cornfields where it all began. I'll get your husband."

She nodded.

Leora began opening her eyes. "Mommy?"

"Yes, Sunshine. I'm right here," she said. "Now let's go get your sister."

SIXTY-SEVEN

Adaline Rushner
Arlingston Manor Replica
Friday, November 12th

THE CORN HUSK embraced Adaline into the haven she remembered as a child wearing her white nightgown, the same kind her girls now wore. Brown curls blended into the yellow tones of the field. Adaline put Leora next to Eliza and bent down, reaching a hand into the cornhusks. "Eliza, it's Mommy. You're safe."

Her chubby cheeks and golden-brown eyes were soaked in tears. She reached and brought her little hand back to her chest.

"My star, it's okay."

Eliza jumped at her and squeezed Adaline tightly around her neck.

"My girls." She outstretched her arms, bringing Leora in, and held them tight, kissing their heads.

"You didn't give up on us," Leora said.

"Never," Adaline said, holding her heart. "Not for a minute."

Eliza snuggled underneath her chin, peered up at her with puppy dog eyes, and licked her hand. Adaline laughed. "Are you hurt?"

They shook their heads. "The man said you would come for us. That you're a fighter—even though others didn't see that in you, he did," Leora said.

Adaline wiped at her eyes and glanced down at the owl necklaces adorning their necks. "His name is Seth, and he's my friend. He saved you, just like he's saved me." She opened her hand, touched the emerald eyes of the owl, and clasped it around her neck. "I have one too."

Eliza laid her head on Adaline's shoulder and smiled. "I like him."

Screaming escaped from the side of the house, and they glanced at each other. Adaline brushed hair back from both of their faces and squeezed them again. "I need you to run and hide in the fields. Don't look back and hold on to each other. Can you do that?"

Leora gazed up at her and confirmed her understanding.

"Don't come out unless someone says the magic word," she said.

Eliza clung to her fingers. "You can't leave. You promised."

"I have to go get Daddy so we can be a family . . . together again." Adaline put her finger on their noses and Eliza giggled. "I love being your mom. Do you know that?"

They both smiled and nodded.

"Now go."

Leora put a hand out and Eliza took it. Their white gowns flowed as they ran through the cornfields for safety.

She couldn't breathe as anxiety tightened through her body the more screaming invaded the house. Her heart hurt, like it was beating it's last song and the stench of gasoline burned her nostrils as she got closer to the side door. Cache and Seth sat side by side, tied down in their chairs. They both looked at her and glared.

"Adaline, go."

"She can't." Her mother laughed. "She knows you are both here because of her."

"Mother, let them go. I'm here to end this with you." She moved inside slowly and tried to take a deep breath.

"The poison from the vial your aunt gave you is taking effect, I see." Her mother walked to her, giving her a package. "My child, I have a gift for you. Open it."

Adaline hesitated.

"Don't. We're ready to be the sacrifice," Cache said. "I don't blame you for anything. I love you. Please. Let us do this."

"You can't choose for me." She opened the package. A long, white gown beckoned to her. Adaline pulled it out and turned around long enough to undress, letting it glide down her body.

"Now, we're ready," her mother clapped. "Pick who will be sacrificed and who will live."

"You only need me. Let them both go, but first I need to say goodbye."

Her mother nodded and snagged a box of matches from the counter. "Any tricks and I light us all up."

Adaline's bare feet felt cold on the concrete floor, but her thoughts brought warmth inside her.

I'm no longer afraid of darkness. I'm one with it. I'll be the light.

She pressed her forehead against Cache's and let her hands slide through his curly brown hair. It bounced back in her hands and she smiled. So many things she loved about him—this was just one. Tears dripped from her face, and Adaline pressed her lips to his. He kissed her back, and the saltwater blended between their tongues. "I love you and always have." She leaned into his ear. "I have cards for you and the girls in the top drawer."

"We're going to get through this together," he said, weakly.

"Not this time. I can feel my body shutting down, Cache. You need to get out, okay?" Adaline stepped backward and grabbed the gas can, holding it in the air.

Seth moved his chair back and forth, and Cache tried to stand.

"What are you doing, pigeon? Put that down, before your hubby dies." Her mother looked at her wide-eyed, a match in her hands.

"I'm doing what needs to be done." She closed her eyes and tipped the can over her head. Gasoline poured down her face and body. Adaline screamed. The strength of the gasoline burnt the hairs in her nostrils, and the acid on her lips ripped the skin off. "Let them go, or I'll light a match without me being a part of your sacred circle."

"What have you done?" Seth yelled.

Her mother put the match down. "He's lost too much blood. Your hubby's going to die anyway. Release him for the brief moment he has left."

Adaline moved toward the circle, gasoline leaking on the ground in a path of her footsteps. Picking up a piece of glass from the floor, she cut into the rope around Cache. "I'll get you next," she said, glancing at Seth.

"I'll be right behind you," he said.

She untangled Cache from the rope and gave the piece of glass to Seth before wrapping Cache's arm around her neck and hobbling toward the door quickly. His face lacked color, and he dropped his head.

"Stay with me. The girls need you." Tingling surged through her face and arms and the room spun. Adaline's vision began to blur. The door sat right in front of her and she reached for the handle with shaking hands, pushing it open. "I'll always be with you, my love. Get the girls." A tug pulled at her feet, and she let go of Cache and dropped to the ground.

Adaline's fingernails clung to the cement. She peered back at her mother's bloodshot eyes, her hands gripping her leg. Adaline's fingers bled.

Seth sat in his chair. Frozen.

"No. No. What did you do to him?"

"Stabbed in the eyes with the blade he thought he could use to get free," she said. "He's never been free. He had to protect everyone. He can't do that now that he can't see, and he can join his dead sister."

Adaline pushed on her elbows to get up, but they shook and gave out. A match clung to the floor, and she covered her hand over it. She held her head on the cold surface for a moment, and then pushed on her elbows again, moving slowly toward the door.

"Now, it's your turn to bleed from the one thing that's been your weakness...your heart." She pulled Adaline back, rolled her over, and raised a shard of glass toward Adaline's stomach.

Adaline's heart burned, pumping way too fast. She

tried to take what she thought was a breath, but she couldn't swallow, and her mother stabbed her on the right side of her appendix with the shard of glass. Her body felt weak, zapped of life and energy. But she still held on to the match.

Her mother stepped on her chest with the point of her heel and chuckled. "You're dying. It won't be too long. First, I need to go back and grab Leora to see this." She smiled and removed her heel from Adaline's heart. "In the cornfields, I presume?"

No. This is the only way.

Adaline closed her eyes. "You'll never hurt anyone again." She sprung the match against the surface next to her face, and a flame sizzled.

There was a little owl
High in a tree
She tried to fly away
And a match set her free.

Adaline waved the flame like a sparkler and marveled in its glory—it would be the thing to end it all. Her girls were safe. Cache was safe. And she had been right all along. Her heart held strength, not weakness. She threw the match.

SIXTY-EIGHT

Cache Rushner
Saturday, November 20th

BOXES SAT near the front door, and trees arched over the house. Cache clung to his girls' hands and stared at the place that was meant to be their new home but only held nightmares and remorse. The place Adaline never wanted to come to but did to save their marriage, even though he never saw that until now. Stepping into the house only brought back memories of him not believing his wife and losing her for good.

A truck pulled up to the driveway, and Abbott got out and nodded at him.

"Aspen's here, girls. Why don't you go play for a bit?" he said.

The girls hesitated.

"It's okay to be with your friend."

"Mommy's sad though. We can't be happy," Eliza said.

Cache bent down and touched her nose. "I'm sad too,

monkey. It's okay to be happy. Mommy would want you to find joy in your life."

"Maybe she's flying with owls now. I bet she has giant wings," Eliza said. "I'm going to be an owl, too." She extended her arms and ran toward Aspen.

He smiled and continued to hold Leora's hand.

"Do you want to go play?"

She shook her head, clutching her journal and the note he promised his wife he'd give the girls. "I'm going to go take some pictures."

Cache peered at her face that held sorrow and long nights of no sleep. He hugged her. "I love you."

"I know, Dad." She let go of his hand and walked to the front door. A piece of paper fell from her journal.

Gripping the base of his neck, he grabbed the fallen paper from the ground and stood. Abbott walked toward him, holding a folder in his hand.

"Is your oldest struggling?" Abbott asked.

"She doesn't sleep. Lots of night terrors. I just gave them a letter from their mom," he said. "The girls have been through a lot, and losing Adaline—"

Abbott patted his back. "This might not be the best time, but here's the information you wanted."

Cache grabbed the folder from him. "Thanks, man."

"Where are you guys going to go?"

He shook his head. "I don't know yet. We can't stay here. You sticking around?"

"I need to stay and see that justice is served with Lieutenant Stalk," Abbott said. "Are you sure you want that? Digging for information only leads to more pain."

"We know Adaline's mother was behind all this. She tried to set up Seth as a copycat killer, and she had Arlene pretend to be a real estate agent to get us here so she could toy with us." Cache put his fingers through his hair. "Stalk confessed to killing Dr. Lynchester and kidnapping the girls."

"Isn't that good enough to close this case?"

"I need to know," Cache said.

He pulled out a death certificate from the folder and stared at the signature.

Edwin Stagg.

"Who is he?"

Abbott glanced at Eliza and Aspen chasing each other in the front yard. "No one knows who he is. He's a ghost."

"Yet, he signed the coroner's report and faked the girls' death," Cache said. "Which means our girls may still be in danger."

"I'll help you find him, and then we close this once and for all."

Cache nodded. "And the bodies. Who did they belong to?"

"Branxton Wheeler was John Doe. The girls' names were Ali and Devon," Abbott said, rubbing his head. "The parents are grateful to have some closure now. I'll catch you later."

Cache nodded. He stared at the paper in his hand and read the entry.

Dear diary,

Four funerals happened today.

One for a family friend. His name was Sam. I hear he was a good guy.

Another was for a man people called Seth, but Mommy called him her friend and the Owl Keeper. I think I like Owl Keeper best. I miss Mommy so much. I wore a daisy in my hair today. I think she would've liked it. She left and broke her promise, but Daddy says she's a hero and saved us all.

We got to see Aspen at Mommy's funeral, and we wore our owl necklaces.

I died today too, as they put Mommy in the ground. I can't sleep. I keep seeing blood. Lots of it, and it reminds me of what I did. A part of me left with Mommy. I feel empty.

I miss Mommy so much.

Leora V.R

Cache stared up at the house. Leora placed her hand on her bedroom window and peered out at the sky. Her blonde hair and distressed face gazed at him for a minute, but she didn't seem to see him—more like she saw something that wasn't even there, and in that moment, he saw Adaline. Someone who didn't want to leave her home and would wait for her mother forever to come back.

He held his hand up to wave, and Leora closed her blinds.

ACKNOWLEDGMENTS

Many people had a hand in supporting me through this ten-year journey, taking an ambitious idea about a woman's worst fears and turning it into a multiple-pov psychological thriller as my first attempt at novel writing.

A huge thank you to Michelle Jefferies, Jourdan Amerson, and Kathy Jenkins Oveson that saw magic in my words and stories from the very beginning and pushed me to continue to follow my dreams as a writer. Joani Lovell, your belief in me and my road trips to come to see you in Delta, Utah, inspired the whole setting of Owling.

To the Sweet Tooth Critique Group, the League of Utah Writers, and Night Owl Sprint Group, our gatherings motivated me to keep progressing and growing in my craft. Deepest gratitude goes to my lovely beta readers: Jenny Gamboa, Alice Beesley, Kimberly VanderHorst, Tara Mayoros, Eliza Crosby, Kate Palmer, Tiffani Clark, Maggie Fangmann, Jennifer Wolfe, and Jodi Milner. I appreciated the much-needed constructive criticism that prompted a new spin, which created the beef of this story. Much appreciation goes to my review readers who jumped in with excitement and waited with anticipation. Thank you, Cindy Hogan, Amber Schoenfeld, Karen Hoover, Cindy Christiansen, Susan Knight, Jen Wilks, Crystal Hopkins, Marlena Cahill, Anna Marasco, Judy Casper, Caylie Skeen, Tammy Theriault, Cary Kreitzer, and Cheryl Christensen.

I had powerhouse editors over the past few years, and each one of them pointed out the things that I couldn't see. You each taught me so much. Thank you, Michelle Jefferies, Cindy Bennett, Crystal Liechty, and Lindsay Flanagan.

Thank you goes out to many who helped in answering research questions. Alexandra Ringwood, I greatly appreciated your multiple voice clips and articles, answering all my questions as we neared the end of deadline time.

To Rebecca Lamoreaux, the best critique buddy ever, thank you for reading my chapters every single week and catching all my favorite words and adoring my characters almost as much as I do.

To my team of shining supporters who rallied around me and lifted me over the years, you're remarkable! Your texts, phone calls, treats at my door, funny writer or owl memes, constant love and belief in me, and LITTLE OWL made all the difference. It got me through some of the most challenging moments when the negative internal dialogue got way too loud. Thank you so much, Jenny Gamboa, Alice Beesley, Emily King, Jennifer Gordon, Allison Hubbard, Sammie Trinidad, Skylar J. Wynter, Brooke Heym, Robin Glassey, and Lacey Roberts.

So much love and appreciation go to Candace Thomas and the Shadesilk Team for all your hard work, seeing my vision, and putting together this beautiful book. I can't thank you enough!!! Candie, you've been a huge support for years. This was by far one of my best decisions. You're amazing.

And, to the biggest cheerleaders of all, thank you to my husband, Andy, and my three amazing kids, Belle, Lucy, and Peter, who've continually reminded me that the sky isn't the limit and to reach higher. I love you so much!

LAURI SCHOENFELD

Lauri Schoenfeld currently resides in Utah with her husband, three kids, and dog, Jack Wyatt Wolverine. She's a child abuse advocate, a Nancy Drew enthusiast, and is part cyborg. Teaching creative writing classes to her community is one of her favorite things to do when she's not having long conversations with her characters. Visit her at www.laurischoenfeld.com

Photo copyright 2018 Brooke Maneotis.

CPSIA information can be obtained
at www.ICGtesting.com
Printed in the USA
LVHW030013110821
695021LV00004B/80